DAMIEN KALAN AND SCARLET KING

Girl of Bone and Ivy

Book One of the Runebreaker Trilogy

Copyright © 2021 by Damien Kalan and Scarlet King

All rights reserved. No part of this publication may be reproduced, stored or transmitted in any form or by any means, electronic, mechanical, photocopying, recording, scanning, or otherwise without written permission from the publisher. It is illegal to copy this book, post it to a website, or distribute it by any other means without permission.

This novel is entirely a work of fiction. The names, characters and incidents portrayed in it are the work of the author's imagination. Any resemblance to actual persons, living or dead, events or localities is entirely coincidental.

Cover art by Chloe Kang

First edition

ISBN: 9781739938703

This book was professionally typeset on Reedsy.
Find out more at reedsy.com

*To everyone, like us, who has ever wanted to escape into a fantasy world.
This is for you.*

Contents

Preface		iv
Prologue		v
1	Elora	1
2	Elora	5
3	Elora	9
4	Elora	16
5	Elora	22
6	Elora	26
7	Elora	29
8	Elora	38
9	Elora	44
10	Elora	55
11	Elora	66
12	Elora	73
13	Aerin	86
14	Elora	93
15	Elora	97
16	Elora	102
17	Aerin	109
18	Elora	112
19	Fleur	115
20	Fleur	122
21	Aerin	129
22	Fleur	132

23	Aerin	139
24	Fleur	143
25	Aerin	150
26	Elora	154
27	Elora	162
28	Aerin	169
29	Aerin	172
30	Elora	179
31	Elora	185
32	Elora	194
33	Elora	201
34	Elora	207
35	Elora	214
36	Elora	220
37	Elora	227
38	Aerin	236
39	Elora	242
40	Elora	249
41	Elora	253
42	Elora	261
43	Elora	270
44	Elora	282
45	Aerin	290
46	Elora	292
47	Elora	299
48	Elora	303
49	Elora	307
50	Elora	314
51	Elora	321
52	Elora	334
53	Elora	338

54	Aerin	343
55	Elora	346
56	Aerin	357
57	Elora	362
58	Elora	368
59	Elora	372
60	Elora	381
61	Aerin	384
62	Elora	392
Epilogue		396
Acknowledgements		398
About the Authors		400
Also by Damien Kalan and Scarlet King		401

Preface

Please note that this book includes potentially triggering topics, as listed below. Please read with care.

Trigger Warnings:
   Abuse
   Anxiety and Panic Attacks
   Blood
   Death
   Drugging
   Graphic Sex
   Sexual Assault
   Violence

Prologue

Hiding the bodies was easier than they thought.

The night was thick and cool and there was very little blood to worry about cleaning. It was a good thing, she thought, that they hadn't had to resort to the daggers hidden beneath their coats. She didn't much like the idea of having to wash out the blood from her new coat. The man beside her huffed as they finished the job, wiping a bead of sweat from his brow with the back of his hand. Even in the dark, his green eyes gleamed with victory. He wasn't worried about the bodies being found. Nobody would bother looking for them anyway.

They left the scene hand in hand, a small smear of blood transferring from his palm to hers. She sneered and wrenched her hand away, wiping it on his black tunic. It wasn't as though she enjoyed killing, but it was a necessary chore. Really, she was just wishing for her bed and a cup of spiced wine. She could practically feel the soft mattress beneath her, the fire warming her aching feet.

"What now?" she turned to him to ask, ignoring his outstretched hand. He lunged for her and grabbed her by the waist, hoisting her up and spinning her round until she squealed and wriggled free.

He grinned, his teeth white and shining in the moonlight. "The last of our worries has been eliminated. Now, we celebrate."

They'd agreed not to burn the house down in case the light drew any suspicious eyes, but had trashed the scene well enough to cover their tracks.

Neither of them had looked in the linen cupboard though.

If they had, they might have noticed the still bloody towels stuffed into the bottom rack, or the damp nightgown still slick with sweat and water. Had they paid closer attention, they might have noticed the tiny half knitted hat, still hanging limply from the knitting needles, stuffed hastily into the bedside drawer.

But they didn't.

So, when he kissed her, she thought only of him and her bed and her wine. The faces of the dead had already left her mind, and she suspected that soon they would have forgotten them.

And, for a while, they did.

But that's the thing about messes:

You have to make sure to clean them up entirely.

Or else they stain.

1

Elora

New York was a beast and Elora Han was growing increasingly weary of its heaving rhythm.

It had been exciting for the first three years. The lights and dreams and giddy, naive excitement. But the few friends she'd had time for in college, between working and studying, had moved on with their lives. They had a clear plan, a career path to help them wade through the sea of student loans they'd all accrued. But keeping pace with the city that never slept was exhausting. She thought she knew what she wanted but getting a book deal seemed more and more like a fairy tale by each passing day. Without the guided structure of college, there was no path to follow anymore. She was lost. No, that wasn't quite right. She knew exactly where she was, she just didn't know how to get anywhere else.

"Elora? You're doing that thing again. Where you get your *starving artist having an existential crisis* look."

Startled out of her thoughts, Elora shifted beneath the covers and turned to face Alice.

"Sorry," she muttered. Letting the sheepish grin fall away with the blankets, Elora rolled out of bed and stretched. "I'm okay, just a little frustrated." She had a million ideas for a book, but none of them ever seemed right. She'd get halfway through writing one when another idea would hit her with the force of a hurricane and she'd abandon the first project to write the second. And on it went. Her mentor, Helen, encouraged every idea, but Elora knew she was running out of time. There was only so long she could accept her parent's offer of paying half the rent on her apartment, and working at the bookstore was lovely but it wouldn't work long term.

"You opening up shop today?" Alice asked while getting out of bed and idly scrolling through her phone.

"Yeah, I work the full eight hour shift today. I'm free on Thursday if you want to come over for dinner, though?"

"Sounds great. Should I bring take out or do you want to cook together?"

"I was thinking we could make pizza together? I promise I won't almost burn the house down like last time."

That earned a chuckle from Alice who was rummaging through her closet while simultaneously trying to reply to emails on her phone. She sighed. "The bank wants me to submit my reports a day earlier than scheduled, so work's going to be manic for the next few days. I still want to come over. I'll let you know tomorrow?"

"Yeah, of course. Don't worry about it."

Alice rushed into the shower while Elora packed up her things, and after hurried goodbyes, Elora was left alone in the high rise New York apartment to see herself out. The skyline that once brought awe and inspiration now left anger and despair, because who knew when Elora would be able to make enough money to live in a place like Alice did? Certainly not with the wage she made running the bookstore. Determined to not let her negative thoughts overrun her morning, she got ready quickly and headed out, crossing her fingers for a better day.

The sky was dark and thick with clouds, threatening to weep at any moment. Elora deflated at the sight, hoping the rain held off until she was inside. She'd lost her last three umbrellas and her coat was warm but not waterproof. Her feet found their rhythm, treading across sidewalks and roads she'd traveled a hundred times and she focused on the people around her to stop her thoughts from wandering. Across the street, an elderly couple walked hand in hand with slow, measured steps. Her heart clenched painfully in her chest and she bit the inside of her cheek as she watched the husband help his wife over an uneven crack in the sidewalk. She was only twenty two and yet she couldn't help but wonder if she'd ever have a partner to grow old with like the two strangers. She liked Alice, sure, but they had never had a connection beyond sex and friendship. They had fun, but something inside Elora begged for more, no matter how deep she tried to bury it. A young man ran past her, panting heavily, bumping her shoulder and yanking Elora from her thoughts.

New Yorkers always had a place to be. The hustle and bustle would normally give her a burst of energy, but today all Elora wanted to do was find the solace and comfort of the quiet bookshop. She immersed herself in the steady stream of morning joggers, cranky businessmen and street musicians as she hastened toward her workplace.

Nearly missing the pharmacy, Elora retraced her last few steps, pausing in front of the building. She pulled a black pen from the pocket of her jacket – a habit she'd acquired during college and had never quite abandoned – and scribbled a note on the back of her hand: *renew meds*. She'd been meaning to do it for the last few days and the little white pills were running low. If she wasn't running late this morning, she'd have done it there and then, even if the thought of the cost made her want to scream. She swallowed the urge and continued down the sidewalk, continuing to dodge people left and right as she reached the busier streets. A few hungover college students were dragging themselves along, clutching large cups of coffee, and she tore her gaze away before jealousy took root. Glancing down at her well worn boots, blue jeans and bobbled cropped sweater, memories flicked through her head. How eager she had been to carve out a place for herself among the collage of people living under the bright lights of the city. But, years later, her puzzle pieces were still out there floating, trying to find where they fit in.

Mythica came into view, a little shop with a chipped sign and an old-fashioned bell above the door. Elora smiled a little as she unlocked the door and stepped inside. The familiar scent of ink and paper flooded her senses as she set about opening and refilling the cat's bowls with food and water. Napoleon was technically the owner's cat, but Mr Bartlett had given up trying to make the animal come home and the cat now happily roamed the aisles like a prince in his castle.

After turning on the lights and setting the heater on the highest setting, Elora opened the mail that was waiting on the desk. There wasn't much, just a couple of invoices and an electricity bill she put safely in Mr. Bartlett's mailbox for him to find. She checked Mythica's email too but there wasn't much going on this week, which meant there was plenty of time to write. Done with the morning checklist, Elora eagerly pulled the notebook from her bag and set the torn out pages across the desk so she could take it all in. Half formed ideas scrawled in black ink, linked with arrows, some sentences scored out and rewritten again so many times they were practically illegible.

But at least she had another idea. Maybe this one would stick. It would be a nice change, she thought as she watched Napoleon stretch lazily and cross the red carpeted floor towards her, to be sure of something.

2

Elora

Napoleon leapt onto the table, scattering the various half finished manuscripts and notes that Elora had been in the process of organizing.

"Hey!" she complained, scooping him up and placing the cat back on the carpet, where he chased dancing sunspots across the room. The light made the white spots in his gray coat shimmer like snowflakes as he continued to prance about, not a care in the world. Sending a half hearted admonishing look his way, Elora bent over to pick up her papers. A familiar shadow fell across her desk, momentarily blocking out the tentative morning sun.

"You spoil him too much," a kind voice teased.

"You're early today! I have a few more ideas actually." Elora looked up to see Helen smiling down at her, her grin warm and soft like the cookies she always brought.

"You have more and more ideas every time I see you." Helen laughed, gesturing to the wild pile of papers that Elora was haphazardly clutching. "Last week, you had a half dozen or so stories you were working on, and you mean to tell me that you thought of even more, darling? You've got to be the most creative, albeit unpublished, author

I know."

Elora didn't say anything, but offered a wide smile as she helped Helen to the nearest table. She cherished their weekly meetings. She couldn't remember exactly when Helen had started coming by, but she'd been there since Elora's days at Columbia University, when she'd first started working part time in the little used bookstore that now felt like a second home. She didn't know how old Helen was, but she looked well on in her years, silver curls framing a face with deep set smile lines and brown eyes that constantly sparkled.

"I'll be right back with some tea," Elora said, heart warming when she noticed that Helen was wearing the lavender colored cardigan she had knitted for her last winter. "Try to make sense of those scribbled notes and ideas if you can."

Elora returned minutes later with two cups of Earl Gray to find Helen sorting the papers into neat stacks. *Leave it to Helen to actually make some sense of my madness*, she thought, amused.

"Your idea about alternate dimensions with Peter Pan being a famous kidnapper," Helen started as soon as Elora had settled down. "A dark twist, eh? I like it, especially with the twist that Peter thinks he's *saving* the children from our world. It would pair beautifully with one of your ideas from a few weeks ago…what was it…" Helen trailed off and Elora let her think. "Ah! The one where the princess wants to escape paradise to go out and save the rest of her kingdom."

"As always, Helen, you're brilliant." Elora grinned as she digested the woman's idea. "I need to drop my other works in progress and start this one, like immediately." She jotted some notes down on her phone while absentmindedly sipping her drink.

Helen stayed for another two hours. They talked about all the other books they had read, sharing ideas, tea and laughter. Elora helped Helen to the door, promising to share her banana bread recipe when she came back to visit next week.

"Maybe I'll actually stick to an idea this time and have more than a half baked idea with confused characters."

Helen stared back, her expression suddenly serious, before she burst out laughing. "My dear, I have faith that you will do all these stories justice someday, in your own time. The world will thank you for it."

With that, she was gone, ambling away across the old cracked sidewalks to the stop where the bus would come pick her up at precisely half past twelve.

Elora didn't mind that it had been a slow day at work so far, considering all the time Helen had spent with her. Making sure Napoleon hadn't gotten into more trouble than normal, she began tidying and organizing the shelves.

Sometimes, this entire place feels tailor made for me, she thought idly while rearranging a shelf of fantasy novels. Mythica felt more like home than her own apartment did at times. While she nearly always worked the shifts alone, Napoleon and an overactive imagination kept her fantastic company. The books they kept in stock ranged from non-fiction to romance to old texts on myth and lore. She'd read snippets of everything, hungry for the worlds the words offered. Her favorite, and the ones that often influenced her own half built stories, were the yellowed books with broken spines at the back of the store. She had no idea where Mr Bartlett had found them, but they'd remained a permanent fixture since she'd started working there three years ago. Their pages were filled with intricate illustrations and accompanying explanations of worldwide mythical creatures, long forgotten myths stored safely between the pages. Only in a bookstore like Mythica would Elora be able to find old texts and translations of all the world's mythologies and all things fantastical. Hefting a pile of books on Egyptian deities and Gaelic fae among other titles, she embarked upon the journey of returning the sizable stack she'd used for research to the *myth and lore* section.

Elora reached across the shelf, the book on top of her pile sliding off and threatening to fall. She grabbed at it, slicing the top of her finger across the paper.

"*Shit*," she muttered as the whole stack toppled, trying to grab the books with her other hand before the blood could leak onto them. It was too late. A few drops of blood rolled down her hand and splattered onto the pages of the fae compendium. Elora watched the whole thing unfold in slow motion.

Before she could so much as blink, her stomach plunged, and she looked down to see a swirling hole of red, orange and yellow swallow her whole.

3

Elora

She fell for what seemed like only a few seconds, eyes squeezed tight shut, terror racking her body. She screamed but the sound was ripped from her throat before it reached her ears. Her stomach rolled again and again, arms reaching desperately for something to hold on to.

And then it was over.

One moment she was falling and the next she was lying down on what felt like a bed of grass. Once her head stopped spinning, she patted herself down, making sure all her limbs were there and grimaced at the taste of sour bile in the back of her throat. When the air had returned to her lungs, Elora cautiously peered through her lashes. She saw nothing but faded sunlight. She grimaced and opened her eyes wide.

Elora gasped as she took in her immediate surroundings, shock coiling around her throat. She was lying on top of a small mound of grass ringed with flowers. A circle of stones with what appeared to be glyphs etched into them surrounded her, and beyond that was a forest that stretched as far as she could see. The sun was setting but there was something different about the sky she couldn't quite place her finger on. Evening colors painted the skyline with pale pinks and bloody oranges. But what shocked her the most was the sweeping state of autumn.

Gone was the chilly snow bitten scenery of New York. In its place, a balmy breeze lifted her hair off her neck and the sky above was clear of clouds. Elora scrambled to her feet, crunching burgundy and dirty yellow leaves beneath her boots as she tried to make sense of what she was seeing. The songs of birds she had never heard before trilled in harmony, and the air was crisp and sharp as she took a deep breath. Everything felt clean and fresh, a far cry from the city air of New York.

What the hell is going on?

Her curiosity and wonder could only hold back the confusion and fear for so long, and Elora could feel the panic bubbling up inside of her, threatening to spill over. *Calm down, Breathe. Figure out where you are.* But there was only forest, and Elora couldn't make out anything beyond the treetops, except for a hazy mountain range in the distance. She found her feet moving, searching for anything that felt familiar. She recognized nothing as she stepped over the stone ring, so she let her feet pick their path. *All I remember is cutting my finger...and a colorful hole opening up beneath me?*

None of it made sense, and the more Elora thought about it, the less sense it made. She wondered if she was hallucinating, but quickly ruled that out after she stubbed her toe on a tree root and pain shot through her foot. She briefly considered the possibility of having died, but the sweat that beaded on her forehead and the sheer tangibility of the world around her made that seem doubtful as well. Night was drawing near, and Elora admitted that she was hopelessly lost. *I don't even know how to start a fire,* she thought as she slumped against a tree trunk and looked up at the darkening canopy. The novelty of having somehow landed in such a place was wearing off, and faced with the grim reality of being stranded in a forest without a fire, Elora had no idea what to do.

"I am so royally screwed."

The sun dipped behind the distant mountains, coloring the sky a dusky purple. She tilted her head back to admire the fleeting beauty of it, allowing herself to revel in the last rays of light, even as she shivered in the evening breeze. Panic was building steadily inside her, and she was helpless to subdue it for much longer. It clawed at her throat and set her hairs on end, slicking her spine with sweat despite the dropping temperatures. The rough bark of the tree dug into her back through her knitted sweater, grounding her. She forced herself to breathe deeply, filling her lungs despite the lump stuck in her throat.

But the feeling only grew, until the panic blossomed fully inside her throat, choking her. Elora could hear her gasping, ragged breaths over the pounding of her heartbeat in her ears and the ground suddenly seemed much further away. She was shaking now, tears blurring her vision as her legs gave out. Her brain might not have caught up to the gravity of her situation, but her body certainly had. Elora found herself curled up in a ball in a futile attempt to stop the shaking, burying her face into her knees amid the crunching leaves.

The tingling in her hands and feet went away first, followed by the crushing feeling. Elora concentrated on her rapid, shallow breathing, slowing it until she could count her breaths again. Her surroundings snapped back into focus, and her gut told her only a few minutes had passed, despite the attack feeling like forever.

This is what happens when you don't pick up your goddamn meds, she cursed herself internally, getting back up to her feet.

She swallowed heavily and rubbed a hand over her face. *Now what?* She tried to think back to her childhood stint in Girl Scouts when they'd adventured outside the city to camp overnight. Elora had snapped one of the tent poles and lost the instructions. She'd had to spend the night in the half collapsed shelter and, shockingly, had quit a week later.

"Fucking shitting hell," she mumbled, kicking a tree root angrily. For the twentieth time in the hour or so she'd been there, she fumbled in her pocket for her phone, desperately trying to load Google Maps, only for the *no signal* message to pop up on the screen. No internet, no service, nothing but a useless brick in her hand. Her heart sank.

The waning sun had sunk even lower during her contemplation and Elora still needed to figure out where to spend the night, where she was, and how to get back home. She was about to change directions when the crunch of dead leaves underfoot and the snapping of twigs sounded behind her. Whirling around, she peered at the foliage but saw nothing. Her jaw ached, clenched tight for too long and she fought to keep her breathing even.

Dead leaves crunched again, but she still hadn't moved. Fear, greasy and sticky, slid through her veins. Trying to quieten the roaring of blood in her ears, Elora strained to hear the sound again. It was almost nightfall now and the happy song of birds that had filled the air earlier had died. The silence that followed was cold as it settled on her skin and Elora felt an all too familiar fear bubbling up in her stomach again. Was something out there? Was it going to kill her? Had she imagined -

"Who the hell are you?"

Cold steel pressed against her neck. A strong arm wound its way around her waist and tugged her back against a tall, warm body. Her breath hitched in her throat, both from shock and terror as the blade dug further into her skin. The man's breath was hot on her neck as he hissed the words, but his breathing was smooth and even, as though nothing about this situation phased him. Elora clenched her fists at her sides, anger flaring through her, mixing with the panic in her stomach.

"Where am I?" she croaked out, the movement of her neck as she spoke causing the blade to nick her skin. A warm bead of blood trickled down her chest.

"Answer my question." The man's voice was dark but bored. The sky was darkening rapidly now, and Elora couldn't see where he'd appeared from. She hadn't even glimpsed him among the trees before he was on her.

"Elora." She refused to give him her last name, figuring the less he knew the better. He scoffed but the pressure on her neck eased ever so slightly. She was still trapped against him though, and wishing that she'd taken up self defense like her father had suggested so she'd know what the hell to do. She had nothing to use as a weapon, even her boots were flat, and though she racked her brain for a way out, she could find none. Resorting to playing by this man's rules until he put the damned dagger away, she unclenched her fists.

"Where are you from? Who sent you?"

She frowned. "New York."

"What?"

Her brows drew together at the confusion in his deep voice. This man had clearly lived in the wilderness too long if he didn't know where New York was. And carried a knife instead of a gun, for that matter. Peering down, Elora could see the knife against her, and a glimpse of the intricately made handle - stark white like it was made of bleached bone. She shivered.

"New York," she repeated, trying to stop her voice shaking. "The city? Uh...the big apple?"

The man holding her said nothing, but his fingers flexed against her side.

"You'd do well not to lie to me," he nearly growled. Elora bit her lip to keep from whimpering at his tone. "Who sent you?"

She moved to shake her head before she thought better of it. His grip on her was painful, and another drop of blood joined the last. Tears of frustration spilled down her cheeks.

"I'm not lying. Please, I'm lost. I don't know how I got here. I'm from New York. No one sent me." Her voice wobbled, and she hated it. Her stomach rolled when the man said nothing, anticipation and fear curdling until she thought she might throw up.

Finally, the knife was withdrawn from her skin and she gulped in air. The open skin on her neck stung when tears met the wound, jolting her. Faster than she could process, he'd sheathed his weapon and pinned both her arms behind her back. Hair tickled the side of her neck as her captor leaned forward, his lips nearly meeting her shoulder.

He sniffed pointedly and Elora fought the hysterical laugh that bubbled inside her. *What the actual hell?* She tried to wrench herself away from him but he held fast.

"You smell...wrong."

"What the fuck is wrong with you?" she screamed, insulted, as she thrashed in his grasp.

A twig snapped to their left and Elora jumped, crying out when her captor twisted her arm painfully behind her. She could barely see her own feet in the cloying darkness now, and the loss of her vision only fueled her horror.

"Aerin?" a second voice called out, sending a cold bead of sweat down her spine. The second voice was deeper, more gravelly than her captor's.

The man holding her sighed before answering, "Here!"

Seconds later, Elora heard quick footsteps disturb the leaves on the forest floor. She fought the urge to sob.

"What are you doing? We have to get back. You-" The man cut himself off when he got closer to the pair, his steps halting as abruptly

ELORA

as his words.

"There was a complication," said the man holding her, through clenched teeth. Aerin, apparently. Elora took his distraction as an opportunity to kick backwards, nearly toppling herself over in the process. Her foot connected straight between his legs and his grip on her faltered. He groaned in pain, the sound making her grin as she took off running blindly.

She got five steps before a new set of arms caught her. She cursed loudly, flailing in his grip, desperation driving her every move.

"Now, now," the second voice said, amusement lacing his tone. "That's not a very nice way to greet a new friend." She could hear the smile in his words, the sickly sweet intonation he added to the word *friend*. His voice was darker than the previous man's, and the arms that held her were bigger.

"Go fuck yourself," she hissed back, still trying to fight despite the tiredness making her limbs ache.

"Feisty little thing, aren't you?" the new man chuckled, spinning her quickly so she was facing him, pressed tightly against his chest. He tipped her chin up to face him with one finger, his face inches from hers. She could just make out the shape of his nose, the strong curve of his jaw, the dark hair cut close to his scalp.

She spat in his face.

4

Elora

Laughter darkened the air, and Elora shook in the man's arms as he threw his head back with amusement. He wiped his hand across his face before returning his focus to her, teeth bared as he grinned.

"Ell-" the first man began.

"Quiet, Aerin," the man holding her immediately cut him off, stroking Elora's hair back from her face. It had come loose from its ponytail in the struggle and now fell in messy waves around her face. "As much as I'd love to spend more time with you, I'm afraid it's getting late. Let me see you home."

Elora gaped at him, shock rooting her to the spot. She shook it off quickly, latching on to his promise.

"Just tell me how to get back and I'll go myself," she answered, itching to be free of his grasp.

"Good luck with that," Aerin muttered from behind where they stood. Elora couldn't see him from where she stood, but his voice in the dark made her jaw clench. She knew the odds. She was alone, at night, in a strange forest with two men she'd never met before. Anxiety crawled up her spine, and she dug her nails into the palms of her hands, focusing on the pinpricks of pain.

"How do I get back to New York?"

"New York?"

Here we go again, she thought, despite herself. She nodded, though the man still held her chin and was staring at her with narrowed eyes.

"Ah," he said, tilting his head to the side to study her. She fought the urge to squirm in his grip, hating the way his eyes roamed over her. She had no idea how he could even see her in this darkness. "Well, that's unfortunate."

"What?" she asked, jumping as a bird screeched overhead. The man holding her tensed.

"I'm afraid you'll have to come with me, gorgeous," the man sighed, releasing her face and running a hand through his hair. She shook her head frantically, opening her mouth to object, but he cut her off. "I promise I'll keep you away from that stab happy idiot." He sneered at Aerin over his shoulder.

"I'm not going anywhere with you," Elora insisted, though her body began to shake in earnest as a whole flock of birds flew past above them, calling frantically to each other.

"We have to go now," the man repeated, trying to tug Elora after him. She shook her head, planting her feet in the soil.

"No-"

"It's us or the forest, beautiful," he interrupted, looking around them pointedly. "Hear that?" The sound of branches snapping echoed, then a low growl permeated the air. Elora tensed, bile stinging her throat. Reluctantly, she took a step toward the man, whose hand was outstretched for her.

"Elladan!" Aerin's tone was edged with warning, his voice oddly distant. Elora wondered how he'd managed to move so far away from them without her hearing his steps. Her head immediately emptied of thoughts when an ear splitting roar burst through the trees, shaking the ground beneath her feet. She pressed her free hand over her mouth to stifle her scream, terror fusing itself to her bones.

Elladan swore quietly and tugged Elora toward him, urging her to sprint beside him. She stumbled on unsure legs, tripping over the uneven ground and barely catching herself before she hit the earth. Before she could catch her breath, she was swung up into Elladan's arms as he ran, her head pressed against his chest. She would have protested the invasion of her space had she not been able to hear pounding footsteps behind them. The night rushed past them, wind buffeting through her ears, as she squeezed her eyes shut and clenched her teeth so tight they ground together.

She didn't know how much time passed before Elladan set her down again, her knees nearly buckling beneath her. She forced what she hoped was a strong expression onto her face, despite the fact she felt anything but.

"Where are we?" she asked through her teeth, studying Elladan's profile in the candle light.

Wait - light? She glanced around, noting that the trees had thinned and a few had lanterns hung from their branches that cast a pool of soft light over them both. As much as she wished she found him repulsive, she had to admit that he was handsome. The hood of his cloak was pulled up over his head, casting shadows across his cheekbones. His brown skin was annoyingly smooth, stubble dappling his jaw slightly. He was taller than her by at least a head and *strong.* She could make out the outline of muscles through his shirt, never mind the fact that she'd felt just how much he could overpower her when he tore through the woods as though she weighed nothing. She scowled at him.

"Don't like the view?" He smirked as he turned to her, dark eyes sparkling with amusement. Anger burned her throat.

"What was that thing?" Her voice came out annoyingly breathless and wobbly. She ignored his question, gesturing to the forest behind them. Elladan sighed.

"Nothing you need to worry about," he answered simply, eyeing her. She glared at him with more venom than she felt. Exhaustion weighed heavy on her bones, her body coming down from the high adrenaline had granted her. She tucked her arms behind her back and locked her knees, trying to hide her shaking from him. Given the way he stared at her, it wasn't working. "Come on. You need to rest."

"I want to go home."

"It's too late now." Elladan gestured dramatically at the night around them, rolling his eyes. She spotted the sharp gleam of steel in his belt and swallowed thickly. He was armed with the same intricate daggers that Aerin had held her with, not to mention a damn *sword* sheathed at his back. Her stomach flipped.

"Please." She wasn't in the habit of begging, but she was reaching the end of her tether. Her nerves were frayed so badly she feared she might unravel completely.

"I need to hide you."

She shook her head, peeling her sweaty hair off her forehead and tucking it behind her ear.

"Just for tonight." He held up his hands innocently. "We can't go back out there now. It's safer here, okay? I promise in the morning I'll try to help. But you look like you're about to collapse and I really don't need the headache."

If she'd had more energy, she'd have probably fired something scathing back at him for that remark, but instead she just nodded, defeat sinking into her skin

He's already saved you from the crazy guy with the knife, she reminded herself, putting a hand to the tiny nick on her throat. Dried blood crumbled onto her fingertips. She wiped it on her jeans. They were muddy already. She doubted a little blood would matter now.

"Okay," she eventually conceded. There were no other options, except braving the forest alone again, and she'd rather deal with this devil than whatever the hell roamed out there.

"Wear this," he told her, shucking off his dark coat and offering it to her. She frowned, but accepted it nonetheless. "To hide your... scent."

She narrowed her eyes with more indignation than she felt. "What the hell?"

"Look..." Elladan rubbed the back of his neck awkwardly, shrugging. "My father doesn't take kindly to...outsiders."

His father? She judged him to be a few years older than her - perhaps around thirty - so why the fuck did it matter what his father thought? *And what was with these two about smell? Was it some weird sort of fetish?*

Elora stared at the coat in her hands. The material was thick and soft, unlike anything she'd felt before. It was heavy in her arms and smelled like fog and crisp mornings when she wrapped herself in it.

"Happy now?" she mumbled, past caring. What harm could putting on his jacket do? And, she admitted, it was rather comfortable, if far too large for her.

He leaned down and buried his face in the crook of her neck, inhaling deeply. She pushed away from him, face flushed, anger and something she didn't want to analyze flaring in her chest.

"Get off me!" she protested, but there was no strength backing the words and they fell flat, unconvincing.

"Not great..." Elladan declared. Elora had no idea what this strange man was on about, but he'd agreed to help her, and she clung to that piece of information like a lifeline. "You're still obviously an intruder."

"I'm not an intruder!" Elora threw her hands up. "I'm just lost!"

"You're not from here," Elladan echoed, rolling his eyes. "I hate to break it to you, gorgeous, but that makes you an intruder."

"I have a name."

His eyebrows raised, and a smile curved his lips up. "Oh?"

She glared at him. "It's Elora."

"Elora," he repeated, savoring the word like it was chocolate melting on his tongue. "I'm Elladan."

She just nodded. "Ellada-"

He'd turned slightly and without the hood obscuring him, Elora froze.

"What…" The words dried out on her tongue, leaving her mouth tasting like ash. "You-"

Elladan frowned at her. "Something wrong?"

"You…your ears-" Elora stared at him, wide eyed, blinking repeatedly as if to clear her vision.

His ears were elongated, coming to a sharp point at the top.

He sighed heavily and crossed his arms over his chest.

"Yes, yes they're pointy," he drawled sarcastically. "And yours are short and round…fascinating." His tone indicated that he thought otherwise, but Elora barely noticed. She felt rooted to the spot.

"What's going on?" she whispered under her breath, digging her nails into her palms to remind herself that she was, in fact, not dreaming.

"I don't know about you, but I'm exhausted," Elladan continued as though he didn't hear her. "Aerin is fetching the horses. We'll sort out this … situation… in the morning." He gestured at her, and she grimaced. "You can even stay in my bed if you like."

She stuck her middle finger up at him, but her hands were still shaking. *Damn it.* He simply smirked at her and winked.

"Oh, and Elora?" he added casually. "I hope you're good at hiding."

5

Elora

The rest of the journey passed in a blur, with the trees melding into a single dark smear high across the night sky as the stars winked into existence. She spent the time on horseback too numb to think about anything except the two figures riding before her. The one who had held a knife to her throat - *the sheer audacity of the bastard* - Aerin, was farthest ahead of her. He had his hood pulled up so she couldn't get a proper look at him but the one who had sweet talked her, Elladan, struck an imposing figure on horseback, his broad shoulders framed by closely cropped dark hair. She remembered how intense his brown eyes were, felt them drill into her back as she tried not to fall.

She tucked his cloak around her a little tighter, and whiffs of charred bonfires and spiced apples tickled her nose. He smelled like...autumn. *Focus.* She shook her head, bewildered that out of all the things her useless brain could focus on, it had chosen his damn *scent.* Well, and his ears. She studied the sharp tips and how they curled slightly at the end. Subconsciously touching her own rounded ears, Elora racked her brain trying to think of who these people could be. If they even were people. In the dark, she couldn't tell if they were heroes or monsters.

The sudden clearing of the canopy above jolted Elora back into reality and her breath caught when she took in what lay before them.

They had exited the forest and now stood at the edge of a cliff with a dizzying drop. Above, the entire night sky was lit up with the brightest stars Elora had ever seen, as if this sky had never known pollution like the city sky did. Stars too numerous to count shone down on an enormous castle seated on a smaller cliff opposite the one they stood on. The castle that sat atop the opposite cliff was so big, it looked like the spires were brushing against the stars themselves. Between the two cliffs lay another thick, tangled forest, overrun with enormous pine trees.

"Elora, we're almost there. It would be wise to mask your scent before we enter the castle grounds," Aerin said, drawing his horse up close to hers.

"For once, you do have a point. We should cover Elora's scent up before we set foot on our dear father's domain." Elladan drew up his horse and stopped Elora's, before swinging himself off easily with the air of an experienced rider.

"Smell? Why do you two keep talking about how I smell? Do I stink that bad, also-" Elora's eyes widened as she processed what Elladan had just said. "Brothers? You two are brothers?"

Elladan smiled and yanked back Aerin's hood revealing a startled, pissed off expression. Aerin had green eyes and a sharp face, framed by shoulder length hair the same color as the night around them. His skin was lighter than Elladan's and Elora's, and if she was being honest, there was barely any resemblance between the two save for the strong jawlines and strong nose. Aerin's face quickly adopted a scowl as he tugged his hood back up, blocking her view.

"You have pointy ears too!" Elora blurted before she could stop herself. She immediately regretted saying it. Cringing internally,

Elora just nodded and stood there, wishing she had something to say that wouldn't make her look like an idiot.

"I'm exhausted, and I have a meeting with the duchess from Piertan in the morning. I have to look my best. Hurry it up." Elladan snapped his fingers at Aerin and shifted impatiently.

Aerin rolled his eyes and stepped up to Elora, pulling a notepad filled with strange colorful letters from beneath his cloak. *What is he doing?* Aerin held an oddly shaped pencil in his right hand, the lead an odd mix of colors, reminding Elora of the pencils she had as a child. He began scribbling indecipherable sentences onto the creamy paper, and Elora forced herself to swallow her questions. The shapes of the letters reminded her of the hieroglyphics she had seen at the Egyptian exhibit in the Smithsonian, but some of the markings also shared similarities to Chinese characters and old Germanic letters. He paused for a few moments, read over whatever he had written, and gave a self satisfied nod.

"This should do it. I've modified the rune for scent and written an Eolas script to find the human scent in her and added *another* runecast to cloak it by essentially holding the air in place-"

"Just shut up and get on with it," Elladan insisted, hands flexing at his side.

Aerin sniffed the air again, Elladan following suit.

"Smells just like a regular fae now," Aerin confirmed.

"Eolas? Runecasts? What the fuck are you talking about? And why the hell do you keep talking about scents?" Elora couldn't help the panic that crept into her voice, her eyes widening as she scrambled away from the two...beings. She wasn't sure she could call them people anymore.

"Relax gorgeous, it's just a little runecast that my dear brother whipped up so nobody will freak out over your human smell."

"...Then what am I supposed to smell like? I'm obviously not you, whatever you are."

"Elora," Aerin butted in. "I don't know how else to tell you, but I covered up your human side. Your other side *is* us."

There was a heavy pause in which Elora's heart decided to try to make a break from her ribcage. She stared at him, open mouthed, confusion written across her face.

Aerin looked vaguely sympathetic before he continued.

"You're half fae."

6

Elora

"Half *what?*" Elora's voice rose, jittery with disbelief, fists clenching at her sides with the uncontrollable urge to fight that ridiculous statement.

"At least she isn't shrieking. Or freaking out about faeries. Seems like we're in the presence of an educated woman, eh brother?" Elladan chuckled, his tone slightly sarcastic and disinterested

Elora felt the weight of Aerin's words sink into her bones and she paused. So far, she had fallen into a weird and colorful hole, landed in a place that was most definitely not New York and met these two strangers in the woods with pointy ears. Granted, they had saved her from freezing to death or being devoured, but still.

"You said I'm part fae, but where are my pointy ears?" A ridiculous argument. The best she could muster. Her brain felt like a swamp, her thoughts slow moving and murky.

"Do I look like a scientist to you? I don't know why your ears are rounded." Elladan answered, voice clipped.

"That's why you were smelling me earlier," Elora realized, glaring accusingly at Aerin. "What does that even mean? I've read the folklore, but you two really look like elves from *Lord of The Rings*."

Perhaps she'd lost her mind in the forest. That was really the only explanation for all of this.

"Where do you think Tolkein got his inspiration from?" Aerin asked, far too serious for her liking. "Most fae look like us, or the elves you're used to reading about ."

"What about that magic you just did? Can you all do that?"

Elora's question was cut by the steady beating of wings. Above them, two eagles cut across the sky, blocking out the stars, the steady flapping of their wings filling the air. *Big* was an understatement. Elora stared at two huge eagles, larger than she had ever seen, circling above her. Their wingspan had to easily be thirty feet, and they descended lazily until they were adjacent to Elora near the cliff's edge. Up close the birds were even larger than she had originally thought. Elora could only stare, frozen in awe.

"Guess you don't have eagles this size back in the mortal realm," Elladan said, a smirk tugging at the corners of his mouth. "Don't worry, I promise I won't let you fall." He hooked an arm around her, pulling her close to him and abruptly stepped off the cliff onto the back of the waiting eagle.

Elora clamped a hand to her mouth to stifle her scream. *I'm going to kill this bastard.* Before she could say anything, she felt Elladan shift and murmur something into the thick feathers. The eagle shot straight up until they were among the clouds, looking down at the tiny cliff below them. For the second time in the day, Elora felt like her heart had been left behind, but the view took her breath, and her anger away. The warmth of the beast beneath her grounded her, the feel of the silky feathers clenched in her hands. She worried she might hurt it, but it didn't seem to even register her grasp. The entirety of this new realm stretched out before her. The trees that had towered over her now seemed like little play things, the colors muted by the night. The moon hung low and yellow, and Elora felt as if she could touch if she just stretched out her hand. The clouds floated by them, little fluffs shaped like cotton candy. Elladan muttered more commands and the eagle gracefully soared back down, in the direction of the castle.

"You shouldn't have been so reckless," chided Aerin, jumping down from his own eagle. They landed on what Elladan proclaimed was his private terrace.

Large enough to host an entire party, Elora thought. Trepidation replaced the delirious adrenaline of the flight.

"Lay off," Elladan replied, walking up to the balcony doors and throwing them wide open. "After you."

Elora stiffened, but seeing no other option, obeyed and walked in. She still felt like she was in a dream. Or a nightmare.

A large bed came into view, and once her gaze fixated on that, it was hard to think or notice anything else. Despite the events of the day, and the sheer impossibility of everything, exhaustion crashed down on her, its incessant waves threatening to drown her.

Elladan watched her carefully. "Sleep," he instructed, pulling back the thick blankets for her. "You have my word that you'll be safe tonight."

Her mind warred with itself, uneasy at the thought of sleeping in this place. But he'd promised to help her, and she was so tired she could barely stand. In the end, her body made the choice for her.

She barely had enough energy to flop onto the bed.

She fell asleep with Aerin's words ringing in her ears.

You're half fae, Elora.

7

Elora

Warm sunlight tickled the tip of Elora's nose, and she turned over, trying to preemptively find her alarm to snooze it before it went off. Her outstretched hand found nothing but empty air.

Where is the damn thing? I had the funniest dream...

Elora bolted upright, blinking at the unfamiliar picture coming into view. Her sheets were...satin? She didn't remember ever buying satin sheets and the soft, luxurious feel of them on her skin made her wince. The room she was in was massive, nearly the size of her entire apartment, with rough stone walls and a plush red rug sprawling over the floor. Streams of sunlight spilled in through windows taller than her, encasing the room in a golden glow. The bed she sat in was the biggest she'd seen and across from her was a fireplace and red velvet sofa. A man sat sprawled across it, a sheet of paper in one hand and a teacup in the other. Elora stifled a scream and scrambled out of the bed. In her haste, her legs tangled in the sheets and she stumbled, sending herself clattering onto the polished wooden floor. She grunted, her mind still sleep fogged, and ignored the outstretched hand that came into view seconds later.

"Good to see you're still alive," a vaguely familiar voice joked as she pulled herself back to her feet. Her clothes were crumpled and sticking to her skin uncomfortably, and she pulled at them self consciously.

"I want to go home." She looked up at the man, recognizing him as Elladan. She blinked a few times, fighting the urge to gape at him. In the daylight, she could see that he wasn't just good looking, he was beautiful. He looked like the work of an artist - all chiseled cheekbones and jawline, with a smirk that she hated to admit made her heart flutter. *Traitorous thing.* His dark eyes met hers, mischief sparking in them.

"Such impatience." He waved a hand dismissively and took her by the elbow, leading her over to the sofa. The fireplace was empty, the room warmed instead by the morning sun, and Elora reluctantly sat across from him, frowning as she did so. He thrust a teacup into her hand, light pink liquid nearly splashing over the sides. Elora winced.

"What is this?" She sniffed it suspiciously and was pleasantly surprised when it smelled sweet. Her mouth watered. Elladan watched her unabashedly and she fought the urge to hide her face as her cheeks heated.

"Tea."

"What kind of tea?"

Elladan grinned, and Elora tried to ignore the stupid little flip her stomach did at the sight. God, this would have been so much easier if she hadn't found him attractive. It was entirely inappropriate.

"It's made from a rare flower found in Summer."

Elora scrunched her nose, confused. "What? I have no idea what that means."

She set the cup down on the small table, remembering the lore she'd read about consuming fae food. That it would trap you there forever, never allowing you to leave. And while the logical side of her brain argued that there was no way the claim the brothers had made about being fae had been true, she didn't feel like risking it.

"Please just take me home."

Elladan sighed and reclined in his seat, arm sprawling over the back of the couch so his fingers nearly grazed her shoulder. She shuffled further away from him, skin buzzing with unease.

"I have urgent matters to attend to today," he said, sounding unenthusiastic. "Boring court nonsense but necessary nonetheless. I won't be able to help you until tonight."

Elora bristled and pushed to her feet.

"Can't your brother help me?"

Elladan's jaw clenched. "He's useless. Don't waste your time with him. Just stay here, out of the way, until I get back. I'll have a servant bring in some food for you later."

"I'm not staying here!" Elora threw her hands up, frustrated.

Elladan's eyes darkened and she found herself fighting the urge to back away further. She didn't want to show any weakness, especially after the night before. None of this felt real and she shook her head to clear the fog of confusion.

"Yes, you are," Elladan insisted, standing and straightening his jacket. He was dressed as though he was going to a formal event and she looked out of place beside him in her dirty sweater and jeans. "Look, I'm sorry, but there isn't another option. You can't be caught."

"Why?"

"Because bad things would happen to you." Elladan met her eyes and shook his head.

She bit her lip, focusing on the tiny prick of pain rather than the panic gathering inside her like a storm cloud. "Where am I?"

"The castle. My home."

She clenched her fists. "In what state?" Her mind was swimming with incredulity.

"State?" Elladan's brow furrowed as he tilted his head. "In Autumn...the Dioltas Kingdom."

Elora shook her head and ran a hand down her face. Her head pounded insistently. She needed to get out of there. Needed it more than she needed air. A sense of urgency washed over her, followed closely by burning panic, and when Elladan finally left for his *important duties*, she could no longer stand it.

She rushed to the door and rattled the golden handle. Locked.

"Fuck!" Her heart was beating so loudly she could barely hear her own thoughts. She looked around with wide eyes, desperate for a way out. There was no way she was waiting in this man's supposed home for an entire day with no information. The whole situation confused her, made her feel like she was losing her mind, and she needed to get out. Now.

She ran to the window and wrenched it open. Below was a steep drop with vines of ivy climbing the side of the stone wall, supported by a large wooden trellis to encourage its growth. She sucked in her breath and braced herself, seeing no other option. Slowly, she eased herself out of the window, gripping the ledge with white knuckles while her feet searched desperately for grip on the trellis. She gripped the old stone beneath the wood with snapping fingernails, the pain barely registering now over the panic spurring her on. She scurried down the side of the wall, nearly falling in her haste. Her fingers were scratched and near bleeding from gripping so hard by the time her feet touched the grass beneath her. She paused to catch her breath, staring up at the imposing castle before her. She thanked whatever gods she could name that Elladan's room hadn't been in one of the tall towers at either side, that seemed to stretch so high they met the sun in the morning sky.

She broke free of her reverie and looked around. The forest she'd come from the day before was out of the question. Not only did she not want to find out whatever the hell had been chasing them, but she also had no way of getting there. Even if she still wasn't convinced she wasn't hallucinating this whole thing, she had to admit she was kind of jealous of the giant eagles that seemed to respond to the brothers like pets. One of those birds would've been damn convenient right about now. She shuddered a sigh and fished her phone out of her back pocket, cringing when she saw the battery flashing red at the top of the screen. Still no reception. *Shit shit shit.*

There was nothing else for it. She set off in a random direction, hoping that she'd find someone without pointy ears and delusional ramblings about *faeries* to help her get home.

No more than half an hour into her departure, she was cursing herself for not eating something before she left. Her throat ached with thirst and her stomach kept growling so loudly she'd scared herself twice now. Her nerves were still on edge, and every whistle of the wind through branches or chirp of a bird made her jump. The sun was still bright overhead but the air was crisp and every tree and plant she passed seemed pulled straight from a storybook illustration. Burnt oranges and deep browns colored the landscape and as much as she wanted to hate everything about this place, she couldn't help her fascination.

There were no obvious landmarks or even signs of a road or town. She hadn't passed any other person, pointy eared or not, since she left and she was beginning to doubt her confidence in escaping at all. She was almost at breaking point and panting with thirst when she heard the trickle of a stream. Hope sparked through her as she took off in the direction of the water, nearly tripping and falling face first into the little stream when she found it. Eagerly, she knelt at the edge and cupped her hands, splashing sweat off her face and scooping water into her mouth, soothing her raw throat.

She didn't notice that the birds had stopped chirping until she was done.

Slowly she sat back on her heels, the hair on her arms standing on end. It was eerily silent, save for her breathing and the babble of the stream and the air seemed to have thickened. She was having trouble getting it into her lungs. Teeth clenched to mask the ragged sound of her shuddering breaths, she stood and spun on her heel, facing the clearing.

The scream slipped out of her mouth before she could stop it.

The *thing* in front of her grinned at the sound, exposing a row of deadly sharp teeth. It stood on all fours but seemed vaguely humanoid, with long straggly hair and scraps of cloth covering its thin body. It moved with quick, jittery movement as it crawled along the grass towards her, a long strand of saliva dripping out its grinning mouth.

Instinctively, Elora scrambled backwards. Her foot slipped on the muddy bank of the stream. She was falling, slipping into the icy water. Her head was submerged and she fought the urge to gasp with shock, fighting to get upright again. The stream was shallow, barely deep enough to cover her, but by the time her head broke the surface the thing was at the bank, its black soulless eyes meeting hers unblinkingly.

A tortured sob broke free from her throat as she met its gaze, her skin chilling under its inspection.

Out of nowhere a cloud of buzzing insects flew past her head, confusing her senses. She sputtered and blinked, managing to find enough grip with her sodden shoes to drag herself back onto the banks again. She watched in awe as the swarm surrounded the creature, halting its advance. One of the insects flitted back towards her, hovering in front of her face. Elora rubbed her eyes to clear her vision, water dripping from her drenched hair into her eyelashes.

"Come with me."

Elora trembled with the cold and panic but felt the horrible urge to burst into laughter wash over her. It wasn't an insect at all. No, it was a tiny fae-like creature with the same pointy ears and otherworldly beauty as Elladan, only this one had wings and was small enough that she would have fit in Elora's palm. Her shock of red hair streamed behind her as she urged Elora to follow her, her tiny iridescent orange wings glittering in the sun.

This is it, Elora thought as she followed the little fae, *I've finally lost my fucking mind.*

"Here." The girl stopped behind a thick tree, and Elora sunk onto the mossy floor, pulling her hair out of her face and begging her body to stop trembling.

"What the fuck is happening to me?" She stared at her shaking hands, tears stinging her eyes as she blinked.

"It's okay," the faerie said, landing on Elora's knee as she hugged them to her chest. "Elladan's coming to stop that bauchan. You're safe now."

Elora shook her head, wide eyed. She opened her mouth to answer the winged faerie but an ear piercing shriek echoed through the clearing. She pressed her hands over her ears, squeezing her eyes shut against the awful cry.

She only opened them again when the noise faded, leaving her ears ringing. She found the girl still perched on her knee, looking at her with wide blue eyes filled with pity. Elora's stomach rolled.

She forced a deep breath into her lungs, ignoring how it burned, and peered round the edge of the trunk.

Elladan stood in a shaft of bright sunlight, poised over the creature that had run at her, a sword hanging casually from his hand like an extension of his arm. It was coated in thick black liquid that dripped onto the moss beneath his feet. The creature's head was severed from its body and had rolled into the stream, turning the water dark and cloudy with its blood.

"Elladan!" a familiar male voice shouted from above. Elora watched in horror as Aerin leapt from the back of a giant eagle and landed smoothly beside his brother. "What have you done?" His voice was thick with anger and a hint of pain.

Elora frowned, pushing to her feet to get a better view. As horrible as the sight of the headless creature was, relief flooded her. It couldn't hurt her now.

"Saving our favorite half fae with a damn death wish," Elladan answered smoothly, cutting a look to Elora that made her cringe.

God, this had backfired.

"You didn't need to kill it!" Aerin threw his arms in the air, his shoulder length hair ruffled with the wind. "It was only a damn bauchan, Elladan!"

"A hungry bauchan," Elladan corrected as he wiped his blade on the ragged clothes of the dead creature.

"They don't eat fae!" Aerin's voice was dark now and Elora wrapped her arms around her waist as though she could shield herself from his anger.

"Did you want to test that theory?" Elladan sheathed his weapon and turned on his brother. "Forgive me for not stopping to have a friendly conversation with the beast about to take Elora's head off!"

Aerin's fists clenched at his side but he made no move to hit his brother. Anger bubbled in Elora's veins. Was he seriously suggesting that creature hadn't meant her any harm? Had he not seen the damn thing?

"And now you've contaminated the fucking water supply for all the other creatures." Disappointment was thick in Aerin's tone as he reached into the stream and plucked the severed head from it. He threw it unceremoniously beside the body, staring into the now gray water with a frown on his face. A strand of dark hair fell over his forehead and he looked so upset that Elora found herself feeling a pang of sadness for him. It was quickly extinguished when she met Elladan's gaze, however.

"I told you to stay."

"I'm sorry," she breathed, watching in awe as the group of winged fae came to flutter beside their redheaded friend. They were all beautiful, ethereal and apparently utterly fearless. The sight of them twisted Elora's stomach. "Thank you for killing it." She gestured to the body, still on the opposite side of the stream from her.

Aerin looked up from the water and glared at her.

The sight of them, the dead *thing* - a bauchan apparently - Elladan's casual mention of her supposed half fae heritage and the group of tiny winged fae surrounding her all became too much. Her head swam and the world became fuzzy as her vision blacked out.

At least the mossy forest floor would break her fall, she thought, as she hit it and blacked out completely.

8

Elora

Colors swirled before her, dizzying and entrancing and horrifying. The sensation of falling swept her stomach away and the wind ripped away the sound of her scream. This time when she landed, the grassy hill was nowhere to be seen and instead the forest was dark around her. Growls and screams and wild laughter broke out from all around her, white flashes of teeth and claws shining in the moonlight as the monsters approached with their mouths open -

She was trapped.

She wrestled in the moment between sleep and waking, a gasp surging from her throat as she fought to sit upright, skin damp with tears and sweat. Her stomach clenched and bile stung her throat as she kicked out at whatever was holding her down. She snapped her eyes open and -

She was tangled in the damn satin sheets again.

Elora forced her body to calm and pried herself from the prison of a bed, barely making it two steps before her stomach had enough. The meager contents of her stomach splashed across the floor as she coughed, eyes stinging.

Shit.

The room was the same as before. Her hair stank of damp and there was a smear of black across the front of her jeans. The thought of that creature's blood on her made her skin itch and she clawed at her clothes helplessly, tears streaming down her face.

"This isn't real, it isn't real it isn't-"

Her voice gave way to sobs as she choked on tears, heartbeat ringing through her head. She couldn't stop shaking. The world was suffocating her, gripping her by the throat. Elora could only let out a strangled sob as her vision swam, black spots dancing across her eyes. She was numb, floating, slowly fading away.

Suddenly her shirt was being lifted over her head and she raised her arms, not caring who saw her without it as long as she could get it off. Her clothes were suffocating her, she was sure of it. If she could just get them off if she could if she could just -

A comforting female voice cooed in her ear, humming a soft tune that Elora had never heard before. Elora's breaths came in ragged gasps as she tried to peel her jeans off, tripping on her feet in her hurry and falling back onto the bed.

"It's okay, it's okay," the voice said again and Elora saw a burst of red hair through her blurry eyes. The winged faeries were back, two helping her undress while a few more cleaned the mess she made.

"This isn't real," Elora repeated to herself, even as she watched them work.

"It's okay."

"No, no -"

"Would you like to bathe?" the redhead asked, her pretty face coming into focus as Elora brushed the tears from her lashes. Tiny freckles dotted her rosy cheeks, and the dress she had on appeared to be made of dried leaves. She placed her hand on Elora's cheek, her fingers cool against her flushed skin.

The faerie motioned for her to follow her to a bathing chamber attached to the bedroom. The bathroom was nearly the same size as the bedroom, with a giant claw foot tub placed near the window so the user could look outside while they washed. Elora frowned at it and shook her head, scratching absently at her arm.

The faerie giggled a little and began running the water, pouring in what looked like lavender and salt. "It's one way, don't worry. Nobody will see you."

Elora nodded again, looking down at herself, not quite sure whether she was still dreaming or not.

"My name's Raewyn," the faerie told her as she prepared the bath, smiling. "I work here along with the other pixies. It's Elora, right?"

"Yes." Her voice cracked when she answered.

"It's nice to meet you," Raewyn said, her voice calm and soothing. "Elladan told us he had a guest. Don't worry, we won't tell anyone." Raewyn winked at her, Elora didn't have the energy to answer.

She padded over to the mirror above the sink and looked into her reflection. Her dark hair was still damp and hung in dirty strands around her face. Dark bags weighed her eyes down and her skin looked near gray from exhaustion and mud.

She wrenched her gaze away. Normally she liked how she looked, was confident in her skin. But the girl in the mirror looked like a ghost.

"It's ready," Raewyn chirped as the sound of running water stopped. Elora tried to smile at her but her lips refused to move. She realized with a start that she was still wearing her underwear and shed it before sinking beneath the hot water with a sigh.

She didn't care if Raewyn saw her naked. After everything that had happened, it was the least of her worries.

"Elladan has found some outfits for you," Raewyn said as she helped Elora wash the forest from her hair. "I'm afraid we don't have anything in the style you were wearing, though. Where did you get those clothes from?"

"Target, probably." Elora's voice sounded distant as it rang through her head.

A frown crossed Raewyn's face. "Oh…" She looked thoughtful for a minute. "I thought Elladan was joking when he said you were from the mortal realm."

Elora snorted. "Do you know how I can get back?"

Raewyn bit her lip and began combing a sweet smelling shampoo through Elora's hair. "You'll need to ask Elladan that."

Anger heated Elora's cheeks but she said nothing. She scrubbed the salt tracks from her face and let her aching muscles soak in the hot water. If she closed her eyes she could almost pretend she was back home in her little flat, where her main worries had been dealing with her asshole neighbor and overdue prescriptions.

Not in some fucked up world having an identity crisis in a hot guy's bathtub.

Eventually the water lost its heat and her hair was shining, her skin scrubbed clean and no longer sticky. Raewyn brought Elora a fluffy black towel and brushed her hair, styling it in an intricate plait that kept it out of her face.

"Thank you for helping her, Raewyn," Elladan's voice came from the doorway when Raewyn had finished helping Elora into a long deep orange dress. Though the outfit was gorgeous, Elora shifted uncomfortably in it, not used to the odd undergarments Raewyn had provided. "I'll take it from here."

Raewyn nodded and patted Elora's shoulder before flitting out of the room, pulling the door closed behind her.

"Take me home," Elora said immediately, her voice hollow and heavy.

"I can't, beautiful."

"Why?"

"That dress looks lovely on you," Elladan deflected as he took up his seat on the sofa. She stood at the side of it, staring out the window, willing herself to feel something, anything. But she had become so overwhelmed, she was numb.

"Please, Elladan." She hated begging.

He sighed heavily, the sound of ice against glass jolting her. She turned to face him and found him sipping amber liquid out of a short tumbler.

"You've seen too much, Elora," he said, surprisingly softly. His kindness set her nerves on edge. "And we need to figure out how you even got here in the first place. It shouldn't be possible. Plus, there's the issue of how a half fae ended up in the mortal realm at all."

"I'm human," she insisted, clenching her jaw. "And I won't say anything to anyone, I promise. I'll pretend this was all just a dream."

After all, she still wasn't sure that it was real.

Elladan shook his head and placed his glass down, coming to stand beside her.

"You must be hungry," he said, stroking a stray hair away from her face with gentle fingers. "Have lunch with me."

Lunch? How long had she been out for? She sighed, feeling heavy all over. She had to admit she was starving, but hungrier still for answers.

"Just let me leave -"

"Do you want a drink? I imagine you could use one."

Elora stared at him, swallowing her retort. He *had* saved her from the bauchan without a second thought and now he was trying to take care of her. A pang of guilt shot through her and she nodded, allowing him to pour her a glass like his.

"This won't do anything to me, will it?"

"Like what?" Elladan smirked, the light dancing in his dark eyes.

She blushed. "Well I read that if a human drinks faerie wine-"

"Ah," Elladan nodded knowingly, the smirk never leaving his lips. "But you're not human, beautiful."

"Still, I can't drink. Your drinks or the ones at home. Can't mix my medication with alcohol."

"Medication?" The word was coated thick with unfamiliarity as Elladan tried it out. "Like herbal remedies and such?"

"Sort of, sure. Back home, we have various different types." She watched Elladan's brows pinch together and shrugged. "I suppose it's different here."

"Every season has a cadre of dedicated healers that can runecast away just about any sickness, though Spring's are the most talented. They can't heal everything, but they come quite close. As for regular aches and pains, most of us can do it ourselves. Part of the general set of runecasting abilities."

"Right." She still wasn't sure what he was talking about, but remembered the spell thing Aerin had done the night the two brothers had found her. Elora hoped Elladan would sense her confusion and elaborate, but instead he grinned and asked if she was hungry.

As if on cue, a line of pixies arrived with trays of food and set them out in front of them. Raewyn wasn't there but Elora recognized a few of the others from the forest.

"After we eat, I'll make sure you get a tour of the grounds," Elladan was saying as he served her a plate.

She nodded and ate robotically, barely tasting the bursts of flavor on her tongue. She craved the bitter coffee and fresh muffins of the cafe below her flat.

When Elladan suggested he show her the castle, she took his outstretched hand and savored the feeling of his fingers twined with hers.

9

Elora

"You've only seen my personal chambers so far," Elladan said as he led her away. "I'm sure you must be curious about the rest of the castle."

They walked through the grand doors of Elladan's chambers and out into the hallway beyond. For what seemed like the hundredth time in the day, Elora gaped at the architecture before her. The hallway was made of what looked to be white alabaster and the walls were painted with beautiful murals of all things autumn related. Shades of red, orange, brown, and yellow all danced around her, framed by the sparkling white of the walls.

When she tilted her head back she was met with a clear blue sky, a few picture perfect clouds floating lazily by.

"Where's the roof?"

"Ah, yes. My favorite part of the entire residence. My personal chambers are actually towards the bottom of the castle, near the base of the cliff. It's a security thing, as most nobility and the royal family tend to have their chambers towards the top. You know, to make it harder for assassins. Anyway, the castle does have a roof, despite what you see. The roof in each ceiling is magically tempered to reflect what the royal in residence wishes. I'm in a good mood today."

Nobles? royals? Who does he think he is, the bloody prince of Wales? Elora huffed, brows furrowed.

"Royal? So you're what...some sort of King?"

Elladan's gaze darkened momentarily, before he lightened again and smiled easily at her. The sudden change gave her whiplash. "You'll see soon enough. I have some more errands to attend to, but I'll see you later tonight."

Before she could form a protest, Elladan walked down the hall and turned right, disappearing from view.

Elora blinked after him for a few seconds, dazed.

"Elora?" a lilting female voice startled Elora from her confusion. "Prince Elladan can be a bit... difficult sometimes, especially when he is challenged." Raewyn paused, noticing Elora's surprise. "Sorry to startle you!"

Elora turned away from the faint sound of Elladan's footsteps. "No, it's fine."

"Prince Elladan instructed me to show you around the castle today." Raewyn looked Elora up and down, a little line appearing between her red brows. "Only if you want, though."

Elora pasted a smile on her face. "I would love that. Thank you, Raewyn."

She relaxed a little in Raewyn's presence, the tension that had been knotting at the top of her spine unraveling a little. They walked down the hallway in the same direction Elladan had gone which opened up to a wide hexagonal hall with five other hallways leading out at each point. What captured her imagination the most, though, was the giant red oak tree that took up most of the main building. The oak spanned what had to be at least a hundred feet in circumference and at the base of the tree, sat a throne made of burnished wood inlaid with dozens of bright gemstones that shone in the sunlight. The roots of the enormous oak tree sunk into the white floor, and the branches stretched wide on either side, connecting like bridges to passageways higher in the wall. Court attendants milled around, several clutching papers in their hands shouting orders and instructions to each other.

"King Harkan isn't here at the moment which is why Elladan is allowing you to explore at all, but it's always busy in Dioltas," Raewyn said. "Would you like to see anything in particular?"

"Hmm?" Elora's eyes followed the fae in front of her, studying the grace with which they moved, trying desperately not to stare at their ears. "No... I'll follow your lead."

Raewyn nodded and smiled.

"The branches are for the convenience of the Royal family and their most trusted advisors only. The rest of us need to take the stairs," she explained, zipping through the air and tugging at Elora's hand. Her auburn dress complimented her red hair and on the underside of her left wrist, Elora noticed a pair of interlocked circles tattooed over her pulse point.

"What does your tattoo mean?"

"Oh this?" Raewyn glanced down at the tattoo on her wrist, eyes shining with love. "This is my soulmark to my wife Lydia. It's to signify marriage," she added, noticing the confusion on Elora's face. "Hopefully you'll be able to see her later!"

"I hope I can meet her too," Elora stammered. Before she could ask more questions, a flood of pixies passed by, many of whom joined them.

Elora soon got lost, climbing through dozens of stairways, being shown ballrooms and heavily decorated but unoccupied sitting rooms and gardens that sent shivers down her spine. Though they were beautiful, the flowers were half withered, the trees in a perpetual state of loss, everything touched by the threat of death. Half of her wanted to revel in the colors - bright oranges and crisp, deep browns

- but the other half of her was cold and open mouthed in shock. She wondered if anything ever moved past the in between of autumn - whether anything ever wilted fully, or if it all just clung with snapping fingernails to the last breaths of life indefinitely. She was exhausted just looking at the unsettling beauty of it all.

As the pixie led her back into the castle again, Elora plucked up the courage to ask about the residents.

"Elladan mentioned the King..." she began, clearing her throat to shake the lingering chill in her lungs. "Is there a Queen, too?"

Raewyn stopped sharply and the air turned thick and cloying.

"The queen passed away years ago." Raewyn said with a finality that Elora knew meant they wouldn't be discussing the topic any further.

The tour continued, and Raewyn quickly regained her jovial attitude, flitting this way and that way, chatting animatedly. The castle truly was busy, with dozens of fae running around each floor.

The first two floors were where all the behind the scenes action took place, with kitchens, washing rooms and servant's quarters. The third floor was just a giant ballroom, easily the size of two football fields. Elora felt tiny standing in it, the size of the space oppressive in its grandeur. She was relieved when they left for the fourth floor - where all the king's scholars resided.

"Raewyn!" Elora squealed a little breathlessly, heart lifting. She could barely contain her excitement as she took the space in. "Is this entire floor a library?"

"Yes, most of the fourth floor is a library, with many individual study rooms, but the fifth floor and up is where most of all the castle's fun rooms and attractions are-"

"I want to be here." Seeing the library with its wide open floor plan settled Elora's heart in a way few other things could. The giant oak's branches were interwoven among the white alabaster floor but there were many plush rugs in warm colors holding up thousands of bookshelves. The fourth floor was circular and the bookshelves stretched almost all the way around as Elora slowly twirled around. In between the shelves, various rooms sectioned off at regular intervals. Inside, fae in fancy scholarly robes were huddled around tables, holding manuscripts and pointing at each other. Their mouths moved as they gestured animatedly but she couldn't make out what they were saying.

"Raewyn, is there any reason as to why I can't spend the rest of the day here?" The thought of leaving this place made Elora's skin crawl. She'd already seen enough. This tiny slice of normality was all that was holding her together.

"No...I guess not." Raewyn bit her lip as she thought. "But wouldn't you rather see what the fifth floor has to offer?"

Elora shook her head, feeling the tension that had buried its way into her muscles slowly release as she breathed in the familiar scent of old books.

"I suppose you could just stay here until Prince Elladan is done with his duties," Raewyn continued a little stiffly. "The pixies and I will be here to provide you with food, drink and anything else you may need, as per Elladan's instructions. Just call for me if you need anything." Raewyn gave Elora a bubbly smile that didn't quite reach her eyes, and disappeared between the stacks.

Elora closed her half open mouth, having missed her chance to ask where Aerin was or press Raewyn for any other information. She let herself get lost among an endless sea of books and was soon tottering around, trying to carry a stack of books nearly as tall as her. She found a welcoming cushioned couch by a window and settled, ready for an entire day's worth of research.

She spent the next days curled up in the same sport devouring books, scripts rather, about the new land she found herself in.

She caught glimpses of Aerin between the rows of shelves, but the second she got enough courage to stand and talk to him, he would disappear, leaving nothing but growing resentment and a sour taste in her mouth. It was fine, she told herself. She had better things to do anyway.

Better things like learning as much as she could about these people, their world, storing tidbits of information away to use in the future. She hated being in the dark. The more she knew, the more leverage she had, she figured, and the faster she could get home.

Occasionally, the clawing urge to leave would quieten, her mind going fuzzy around the edges as she sipped the sweet water left for her. Then she would snap back, the beast hungry again and devour more information, skin itching with the need to corner and question Elladan. But she didn't see him and he didn't come for her.

Save for eating, bathing and sleeping, Elora would come to the library, read until she got hungry and then read until Raewyn came to escort her back to Elladan's chambers to sleep. She didn't see Elladan at all for the next two days but there was plenty of material in the library to keep her occupied.

Raewyn wouldn't answer any of her more serious questions; either evading them or telling her she didn't know while refusing to meet her eyes. Aerin was purposely avoiding her and Elladan was nowhere to be found. For the most part, though, the gnawing anxiety had eased slightly and the food was delicious once she got past the lingering fear of being bound by consuming it. As desperate as her predicament was, the inner author in Elora marveled at the knowledge around her.

The reading was confusing at first. She knew she couldn't simply go about asking for books all about the fae or the magic they cast and they world they lived in, so most of the first day was filled pulling random titles off the shelves, trying to find what she needed. Eventually, she found what she was looking for.

The first title she found was a thick leather bound tome, pages worn with age and years of reading. *Original People*, the front cover proclaimed.

It told her of Áine and Nox, two siblings born from chaos and emptiness, godlike beings who became the embodiment of order and sentience. Nox created the world while Áine crafted the seasons. Áine birthed the first fae, four sisters, and Nox followed suit by creating humanity. The four sisters then created their own children, molded after themselves with Eolas. Needing further explanation, Elora searched for tomes explaining what *Eolas* was, or what the term 'runecasting' meant, but found nothing that offered any sort of proper explanation. Frustrated, she reminded herself to ask Raewyn the first chance she got. Elora wondered if the legends of Áine and Nox were something the fae truly believed in, or if it was similar to the Greek and Norse myths she loved reading about. She skimmed the rest of the book, unable to focus on the tales of magical creatures and the fae. Normally, she would have been thrilled with the prospect of reading about new worlds and people, but what she needed was concrete facts, not bedtime stories and retellings. Annoyed, she went in search of something else to read.

The afternoon sun hung heavy in the cloudless sky, a stark difference from the white, snow kissed clouds that she would be seeing this time of the year back home. Walking past several elderly fae in deep reading or animated discussion in closed rooms, Elora tried to remember where the bathroom was. *Did Raewyn say it was a left from this hallway, or a right?*

Spying a rather large fae outfitted in full armor idling nearby, she thought to ask him for directions. She started towards him, but the second they made eye contact, he turned, quickly walking away. She frowned after him, confused and mildly hurt by the dismissal.

She wandered a little longer, eventually locating the bathroom and hurried back, hating to linger anywhere outside of the comfort of the library.

She ambled over to the history section again, admiring the beautiful tapestries that graced the space between bookshelves. The walls themselves told a story, with portraits and pictures of strange creatures and epic battles, interspersed with the most gorgeous paintings of forests and falling leaves. What intrigued her most though, was the strange glyphs she found all over the walls of the castle. At first Elora thought they had been signs - after all, why wouldn't the fae have their own language? But she'd seen similar glyphs in the books she'd read and again on the paintings and tapestries on the walls. *What am I missing here?*

A tome with 'Royal Histories' written on the spine caught her eye, and Elora wondered if information on Elladan or his family would be in here. He was a prince here right? Grabbing the book, she found her seat and settled in comfortably, sipping water from the glass next to her.

Genealogies were almost always boring. Elora didn't know why she expected a genealogy and history of the fae would be any different. She struggled to focus on the words and ancestries before her. There were so many terms she didn't understand, Eolas being the chief of them. She had seen 'runecasting' several times already, but this particular book mentioned 'runecarving,' too. Words like 'Athnachuan' and the consistent references to places she could hardly read, much less pronounce, made the entire process difficult and frustrating. The book was a couple thousand pages to boot, containing information about every known royal member of Autumn, including illegitimate children and affairs.

Elora vaguely remembered Elladan speaking about the seasons as if they were somehow countries and as she read, it began to make more sense.. Bored with the long list naming every city in each Season, Elora skipped to the end of the book where the most recent entries would be. *House Veryadrin*, the last chapter read. House Veryadrin was the most recent dynasty, stretching back around seven hundred years, one of the longer and more prominent Autumn dynasties. The most recent king was Harkan Veryadrin, father to Elladan...and Aerin? Her interest now fully piqued, Elora dove into the pages.

Harkan Veryadrin: Chancellor of the Unseelie Court, King of Autumn, Lord of Dioltas, Duke of Erebaeus. Father to Elladan Veryadrin and Aerin Aurataeas. Former husband of Falina Edelvane. Current ruler.

She stared at the surnames with wide eyes. If they were brothers who shared the same father, why were their names different? Why had Aerin taken a different name than Elladan? Confusion settled in the furrow between her brows. Elora searched for entries on Elladan and Aerin but she was disappointed at the brevity of their profiles. Elladan was the first born son, and his mother had died shortly after giving birth. There was no mention of Aerin's mother, only the last name Aurataeas.

Confusion clouded her brain, and the swarm of information she'd just ingested was cloying.

Taking another break to stretch, Elora asked Elise, the pixie assigned to her for the day, to take her back to Elladan's chambers. She was tired and hungry and he'd yet to provide her with anywhere else to sleep. She had no idea where *he* was sleeping but as long as it wasn't in the same room as her, she supposed it didn't matter.

She entered, fully prepared to flop down on the bed and pretend she was back in New York, not trying to keep her balance in a world that confused her more every time she tried to understand it.

Except, naturally, the bed was taken. Elladan sat against the headboard, long legs stretched in front of him, his dark eyes watching her nearly trip over her own feet in surprise as she entered.

"Where have you been for the past few days?" Elora blurted, face heating. He'd ignored her for two days and then suddenly appeared like that was *normal?*

"I actually have some good news. It's almost time for -"

"Take me home right now!" Elora snapped, the anger that had been simmering beneath her skin overflowing as tears stung the back of her eyes. God, her family would be beside themselves by now. And she normally texted Alice at least three times a week - what would she think? That Elora had just abandoned her? It struck her as absurd that she only now realized how long she had been here. Guilt threatened to swallow the anger. "I need to go home. Right now. I was supposed to meet friends for lunch two days ago and my parents were supposed to visit last night." It was ridiculous, really, that the *lunch* was what she was upset about. But the world felt like it was slipping around her, her throat tightening with tears. She couldn't even imagine how she had let this situation fester for as long as it did. Shouldn't she have felt more concerned? Why was she just confronting him about this now? Nauseating terror sprouted up from her stomach, locking her body up. Elora hated crying in front of people, never mind *him*, and she wanted to demand the tears stay put. But they didn't listen - sliding down her cheeks and soaking the collar of her dress.

"Everything is going to be fine. I promise. We'll get you home."

Elladan's arms wrapped around her tightly, until his shirt was damp beneath her cheek. She could feel the muscles in his arms straining to relax as he held her. She wanted to hate him, to fight him, but *dammit* it was nice to be held. There was something soothing about him, something intangible, much like the water she drank here. Letting herself fall into his broad chest, Elora exhaled deeply. Once, twice, three times until her heart rate settled. She let herself take comfort from him, just for a little while.

"I've spent the past two days trying to figure out a way to get you home without anybody noticing," he said quietly as her sobs died down. "If people found out you came through the portal and that you're half fae, it would cause way too many complications."

"How long do I have to wait to go home?"

"Maybe just a day or two longer. Once we go back to New York, I can write something in Eolas to help explain your absence," Elladan assured her, running his hand through Elora's hair. "I'm not really sure how to explain it, but that thing Aerin did to mask your smell. Do you remember?"

Elora nodded against his shoulder.

"Well, I can do something very similar so that the people you know won't have noticed the time that you were missing. It's a rather simple runecast really, so please believe me when I tell you that there is nothing to worry about. Nothing at all."

He still held her close, and she inhaled the soft scent of fresh nutmeg and spiced cherry wine. Abruptly, she untangled herself from his arms, hoping to whatever the hell the fae prayed to that he hadn't noticed her blushing furiously. She sank into the couch where he met her eyes, gaze cool and confident.

"I don't smell that bad, do I?" Elladan winked at her. "You'll be home soon, beautiful."

The moment of tension was unraveling and as Elora looked into Elladan's eyes, she found herself believing him.

10

Elora

"Good morning," Elladan's voice drawled. "You really do sleep in late."

Elora rapidly blinked the sleep away, scrambling upright in bed. Elladan was never here when she woke up and she didn't particularly want to look like a mess in front of him. As if sensing her embarrassment, he smiled widely and laughed, the sound taking up all the air in the room. "It's okay, you do this really cute thing where you mutter in your sleep."

Heat crept across her cheeks, worsening when Elladan stood up from the couch he was lounging on. The late morning sunlight streaked across his face and Elora clenched her jaw to stop her mouth hanging open. His jawline looked as though it was etched from marble, like one of those old statues she'd studied in the single art class she'd taken with a friend. His short, dark hair was impeccably styled, as always, and his brown eyes were bright with amusement as he looked at her. She looked down at the bed sheets crumpled beneath her, desperate to focus on anything other than how annoyingly handsome he was.

"You can turn away from me all you want, but I can see you peeking."

Dodging the pillow Elora threw at him, Elladan laughed again. "I'm going to go pick up breakfast for us, so bathe and get changed. We have a big day ahead of us."

Before Elora could even answer, Elladan swept out of his room, leaving echoes of his amusement in his wake.

"Cheeky bastard," Elora muttered as she shoved the duvet back and got out of bed. "Didn't even ask me what I wanted."

"That's Prince Elladan for you," Raewyn said, and Elora could have sworn she heard a hint of something darker behind the honey coated words. "I saw some of the titles you were reading so I assume you know most of the information about the royal family now. He wasn't happy that you were in the library but he said it was better to be there than anywhere else in the castle."

Elora blinked at the pixie.

Why wouldn't Elladan want me in the library? It was too early for this, and his appearance and cryptic words hadn't made her head any clearer. She furrowed her brows and pushed the questions to the side, focusing on going through the steps of getting ready. It was easier, she found, to focus on concrete things like the warmth of the water when she washed, or the silky feel of today's deep red dress on her skin. It clung to her curves and the matching ribbon Raewyn tied into her hair kept catching her vision whenever she turned.

When she was done, her head was clearer and the buzz of confusion and anxiety she was getting all too used to had quietened a little. She found Elladan waiting by the couch with a huge platter of food sitting atop a small cart.

"You brought enough food to feed a small family," she told him with a smile that was only slightly forced, plucking a fresh strawberry from the tray and biting into it.

"I didn't know what you liked, so I asked for a bit of everything." Elladan flashed an easygoing smile and Elora firmly told her heart to stop fluttering.

The sweet smell of syrup washed over her as she filled her plate with pancakes topped with jams of every color, scrambled eggs, and fresh fruit, something of everything now that she wasn't worried about the food casting some sort of curse on her. The only food she left untouched was the little platter of various cut meats.

"You don't eat meat then?" Elladan asked, spearing a few more rashers of bacon with his fork.

"No, not since I was fourteen."

"You'd get along with my brother, he hasn't eaten meat in years either." Elladan's tone turned brittle at the mention of his brother, as though one wrong step now would have Elora falling through the cracks in their hastily built companionship.

"Where is Aerin? I saw him a few times at the library, but he didn't seem very…uh…sociable."

"Who knows? I've known my brother twenty five leaf fallings, and I still don't understand him," Elladan said, waving around an apple slice to emphasize his point. "What I do know is that the glamour he wrote for me better work or I'll tear his damn head off."

"Glamour?" Elora asked, trying to ignore Elladan's threat. "Like the lore where you turn something into something else? Or make it invisible?"

"Yes, basically," Elladan replied coolly. "I wasn't aware that humans were so… knowledgeable about the fae."

"It's not really knowledge as much as myth and legend," Elora said with a small smile. "We study such tales and accrue knowledge as historical mythology and as a part of cultural studies."

Elladan's eyes narrowed as he regarded Elora with his head cocked to one side, face serious. "Anyway, as I was saying, this glamour is similar to the scent masking Eolas script Aerin performed on you. It will change your appearance and sharpen your features a bit, especially around the ears. Afterwards, we'll go through your alibi."

"Why is it so rare to have a human here though? I arrived here by accident and I don't pose a threat." Elora choked back a laugh at the idea that she could threaten any of these people. "Why can't you just tell your father the truth and have him help me get back home?" Desperation bled into her voice, but Elladan remained unflinchingly resolute.

"It's a lot more complicated than that. Did you know that humans and fae used to live together? In peace? There are plenty of books in the library that mention it," Elladan said. Elora shook her head, trying to convince herself she was imagining the mocking tone in his voice.

"What happened?"

"Nobody really knows or remembers the exact cause. Some historians believe that the fae were the cause, others believe humanity was at fault," Elladan sighed, setting his fork down. "You ready for a history lesson?"

"Sure." Elora was actually excited at the prospect.

Clearing his throat, Elladan began. "The fae and humans lived in prosperity for the first few thousand years. The fae had access to runecasting, runecarving, Eolas and such while the humans did not. We helped humanity build empires and civilizations, but the descendants of Nox turned out to be much more creative than we initially thought. They didn't have access to Eolas but they filled the gap with innovation." Elladan took a drink from his chalice. "Is this all making sense so far?"

"Yes. Áine and Nox are the two creators that the fae worship, right?"

"Looks like someone has been doing their reading. Yes. Áine and Nox created our world and its first inhabitants."

Not wanting to get into an argument about science or what she had learned in school, Elora merely nodded, reaching out and biting into another pastry. "Áine divided your realm world into four Seasons right?" Despite Raewyn having told her that Elladan had not been happy to hear about her escapades in the library, he seemed more than willing to answer her questions now.

"Yes - Summer, Autumn, Winter and Spring. Think of them as countries. Within each Season there are several provinces, overseen by dukes and duchesses, with each city or town overseen by a mayor. Each Season has a King or Queen, a ruler who oversees every province and has final say in decisions."

"What about the Seelie and Unseelie Courts?" Elora had seen them mentioned in the books, and knew the human legends, but she wanted to understand.

"Traditionally, Summer and Spring have aligned as the Seelie Court while Autumn and Winter allied under the Unseelie banner, even when we lived among humans and warred with them and ourselves. The fae separated entirely from the human realm around seven hundred years ago. We had been slowly cutting ourselves off from humans for several centuries prior, but the final great human-fae conflict ended in the late thirteen hundreds with the complete withdrawal of the fae."

"But why?"

"Why?" Elladan's voice was suddenly laced with venom. "Because the humans wanted more. They always wanted more." The rage in Elladan's voice sounded intensely personal, which was odd considering that the genealogy she had read reported his age to only be a handful of years older than her. "The fae helped the human race grow from its infancy, providing for them, nurturing them, holding their hands. But it was never enough for them. They wanted our lands, our resources, our Eolas."

"What exactly is Eolas?" Elora finally bit out, trying to steer the conversation away from the topic that had incited such anger in Elladan. "I keep reading it everywhere and I know it has something to do with the magic you have but none of the books have explained it in detail." Clearly, the authors of the tomes had assumed everyone would know what it meant. The hadn't accounted for a girl from the mortal realm desperately wanting to know more.

"You should have asked ages ago," Elladan said smoothly, anger gone from his tone. "Eolas is a language. Áine gifted it to her daughters so that they could also speak the language of creation, of will, of life. They, in turn, passed it onto their creations. The fae."

"So you can write something and it just happens?"

"Not exactly. It's more complicated than that."

"Well how did I end up here then? I don't know the slightest about runecasting or Eolas." Worry, fear, stress, and anxiety rose up from nowhere, threatening to swarm her. "I literally cut myself on a page from a book about the fae and then I found myself here." Angrily, she swiped the tears from her lashes, near sick with the warring emotions inside her. "The more I learn, the more confused I get. I just want to go home."

Elladan set his plate down and sighed heavily. "I believe the story you told me about cutting your finger on a book about fae and activating a portal, but nobody else is going to. I can't activate the portal to take you home from this end without getting caught." Elladan must have noticed the anguish on Elora's face and said preemptively, "You just have to trust me. Here, drink some water and calm down a little so we can figure out how to get you home together."

Elora deflated. Logically, she knew that Elladan had done nothing but take care of and look out for her, as busy as he'd been. If he promised that they would find a way home together and that he could make everything alright once she was there, what reason did she really have not to trust that he meant it? Debating it was pointless. There were no other options.

At least he's gorgeous. An old hag could have found you instead.

"Fine. It's hard saying no to you." She hadn't meant to say that. *Dammit, Elora*, she cursed herself. Maybe he'd suddenly lost his hearing.

He smirked at her, one brow raised in amusement. No such luck then.

"Thank you," Elladan said after a weighted pause, resting against the back of the couch contentedly. "We need to cast a glamour on you and make sure you memorize your alibi so you don't have to hide in the library anymore. Aerin put up a small runecast the first morning while you were asleep so that everyone would see a normal fae girl, but we need a more permanent one so you can walk about freely around the castle. I've already been getting questions, you know."

"Is that so?"

"Yes, everyone thinks you're the mystery girl I've been seeing."

"Am I?"

"Are you?" Elladan winked at her and stood up, stretching, the movement causing his shirt to ride up slightly. "We don't have much time. I'll be quick and it won't hurt."

She nodded cautiously as he unrolled a large piece of parchment paper and took out a brush. Unclipping a small bottle hanging from his belt, Elladan set everything on the table next to them and went to work. He dipped the brush in the small rounded bottle and painted intricate brush strokes across the paper. He crafted glyphs similar to those that she'd seen Aerin draw, but poured a small bowl of water over the paper after he was done. Elora looked between him and the smudged ink, but Elladan merely smiled.

After a few more heartbeats, Elladan turned an appraising eye on her and looked her up and down. "Now you look like a proper fae lady. Have a look."

Elora walked over to the mirror and found an elven girl staring back. Her eyes were still large, but the her lashes were longer and hair was a few shades lighter than the deep, rich brown she remembered. Her rounded ears were gone, in their place the sharp tips she had become so accustomed to seeing on others. Her skin had smoothed out slightly, and her lips were fuller and pink like she'd been biting them for too long. The girl in the mirror was pretty, sure. But she wasn't Elora.

"I look…"

"Beautiful," Elladan interjected, finishing the sentence for her. "This is what you would have most likely looked like had you been born full fae. Even though you're half fae, not much of it shows." He said it kindly enough - like he was stating a fact - and yet the implications stung.

"Why is that?" She tried to keep the bite out of her words, but failed.

"How would I know? I've never even heard of someone being half fae. You somehow are, and you got into this world. It's dangerous for you, it's complicated, and we don't have a lot of time because of the Athnuachan ceremony. So let's get your alibi memorized, then you can be out and about, which means it will be easier for me to function and for you to find a way home. Okay?"

Elora sighed. "Do we have to go to this…ceremony thing?"

Elladan's expression softened slightly and he laid his hand over hers on her thigh. She refused to acknowledge the warmth that spread from his touch.

"I know it's overwhelming. I'm only trying to protect you, gorgeous." He released her hand to tuck her hair behind her newly pointed ear, tracing a finger over her skin. "Let me do that."

Elora bit her tongue and simply nodded, not trusting herself to speak. She knew he was putting himself on the line for her, even if he wouldn't tell her the extent of it all. She'd be lying if she said she fully understood him, or his motivations, or what the damn ceremony he was talking about was. But the more he looked at her like she was the most precious thing he'd ever had, the more those things didn't matter. She realized with sharp clarity that she trusted him. Maybe not fully, but enough. It had to be enough.

Eventually, Elladan's hand fell from the side of her face and he sat back. Elora picked up her cup of lukewarm floral tea just to have something to do with her hands. She didn't even realize Elladan was talking again until she glanced up from the purplish liquid and found his mouth moving.

"When were you going to tell me you were a prince?" Elora teased.

"Ah, that. It's a bit pretentious to just come out and introduce myself as one, isn't it?"

Laughing, Elora stood up and tried curtsying the way she thought proper, failing miserably.

She was joking, but Elladan just blinked at her, brows furrowed.

"We haven't done any of that nonsense for years, except in formal ceremonies and rituals. If anything, that would make you stand out even more."

"Well, how should I act around you then?" She fought the urge to roll her eyes, a small smile pulling at her lips.

"Now, that depends on who you are, doesn't it? I told Aerin to make the alibi as airtight as possible and it seems he actually listened to me for once. So you're a noble from Spring, specifically the Zahra kingdom. You're to be the second youngest daughter of an old, yet relatively obscure family there, the Atwater family. You'll be going by Fleur Atwater when we're in public. You can decide how old you are, what your favorite food, colors and hobbies are to make the facade more believable." Elladan waved a hand as if the details weren't important. Elora swallowed heavily. "As for our relationship, we've recently met so just seeing each other and having a good time, you know?"

Elora stared at him wide eyed, hands clenched tight around the fabric of her skirt.

"Are the people here - I mean fae - used to just seeing you around with girls from random kingdoms? Is that a familiar sight?" The words surprised her as they flew from her mouth. *Ridiculous,* she chastised herself, smoothing her dress out and trying to do the same with her expression, *I shouldn't give a shit who Elladan sees. I don't. It's fine.*

Elladan cocked his head at her, mouth opened slightly in what appeared to be surprise. "I - no Elora, it's not like that. If it makes you feel better, I'll just say you're a dear friend I've met from a trip recently and-"

"A friend all the way from Spring?" Elora laughed but it was flat and humorless. Something ugly was curled in her chest, born from confusion and panic and another emotion she refused to put a name to but that felt suspiciously like envy. She didn't like the idea of being seen as nothing but a prince's plaything. "I've seen the maps Elladan. I know how far Spring is from Autumn. Everyone must be *really* used to seeing Prince Elladan having his way with whomever he pleases."

Elladan's jaw dropped for a second before he composed himself and his face returned to its usual cool uncaring facade. Elora shook her head slightly, her mind buzzing with information and feelings and the sight of him and God it was too much it was all just -

Too much.

Elora didn't know what to do or where to go, only that she couldn't sit there any longer.

She stood abruptly, ignoring the hand he reached out to her and hurried to the bathroom, shoving the door closed behind her so fast that it shook on its hinges. She expected him to follow her but there was only silence and the cool press of tiles against her legs as she slumped against the wall. She knew she was being unfair. She knew he was helping her, when he easily could have thrown her back into the forest with all its horrors and saved himself the hassle. She knew that without him she couldn't get home and the ache that came with missing her family grew by the hour.

She also knew that the colors were brighter here. That everything was utterly terrifying but also horribly beautiful. She knew that when she returned home, she would never be able to look at the gray skyline of the city the same way again.

She knew that, buried beneath the suspicion, she'd miss him, too.

By the time she crept back out, the moon was hanging high in the sky and Elladan was long gone.

11

Elora

Word around the Dioltas Castle was that Elladan and Aerin had recently run into a friend they grew up with and that she was one of the representatives from Spring. Elora was satisfied enough with the explanation and the hours blurred together as she met dozens, if not hundreds of attendants and nobility that wanted to meet the *lady* Elladan had personally brought for the Athnuachan celebrations.

She stuck close by Elladan's side or, if he was busy, with Raewyn. Her palms were constantly clammy and her stomach was so tied up she could barely eat, instead sipping the sweet water Elladan brought her when he proclaimed she was looking *too pale*. She allowed Elladan to speak for her, not wanting to say the wrong thing and ruin the whole charade. Every night, she asked him when this would all be over and he could take her home and every night he told her the same thing.

Soon, gorgeous.

She might not have spoken, but she listened. She watched and learned and by the third day was beginning to grasp exactly why there were so many fae in the castle. The Courts stayed separated for the most part - Unseelie and Seelie mingling only when necessary, but nobody dared fight or threaten. No, they all seemed to agree, despite their clear differences, that this was sacred. The Unseelie respected that boundary, if little others.

Athnauchan itself appeared to be a series of games - though she'd yet to glean *what* these games consisted of - that both nobles and representatives competed in. Rafters and makeshift buildings were being constructed through the castle grounds in preparation. It had been a week since she'd arrived in Fior Domhan and though she ached for the cozy mess of her apartment or the smell of her mother's perfume, she drank in every sight and sound from Dioltas. The mixture of fear and excitement in her stomach was heady and she found herself starry eyed and sweaty palmed more often than she cared to admit.

Until Aerin burst her bubble. She rounded the corner in the direction of the library, her sanctuary, and smacked straight into his chest, barely avoiding falling flat on her face when he pushed her away. The pixie escorting her - Lianna - had paused a few steps behind to talk to another worker about preparations and Elora wished she'd insisted on having her stay with her. She didn't want to face him alone, especially with the glare he was shooting her way.

She adjusted her stance, smoothing her skirt, dark purple today, and straightening her spine.

"Guess you're not avoiding me anymore?"

"Sorry," Aerin muttered, his cheeks turning scarlet. His hair was tied back in a ponytail and he was dressed in simple clothes, just a loose white shirt and dark trousers. "I shouldn't be talking to you. Don't want anyone getting suspicious." There was a ridiculing hint to his tone that made Elora bristle. Hostility radiated off him as he crossed his arms over his chest.

"I saw you in the library quite often," Elora tried again, trying to keep her voice even and unaffected even as anger rose in her gut. "Do you like to read?"

"I have to question why you were there at all. Brother dearest not entertaining enough?"

Elora's jaw tensed and her fists clenched. This man was determined to blow her cover, she swore. At least he didn't have that bloody knife this time. Well, not that she could see.

"What is it with you and Elladan? Sibling rivalry?" She put on an exaggerated pout that matched the sarcasm in her voice. He didn't answer, merely stared down at her, a bored expression on his face. She sighed and ran a hand over her face, suddenly exhausted. "Fine. Will you at least tell me what exactly this Athnuachan ceremony festival thing is for? And then you can go about your day pretending I don't exist until I get back home, okay?" She feared she'd butchered the ceremony pronunciation but tried not to act like it bothered her. She conveniently refused to mention that she'd barely spoken to Elladan since their falling out and that the mention of him had started all sorts of nervous-slash-anticipatory butterflies in her stomach.

Aerin narrowed his eyes. "If only I had such luck. I'm the one making sure your scent doesn't get you strung up on the castle walls." Elora's eyes widened and a choked sound scrambled from her lips before she could stop it. His unfazed, borderline bored tone about the matter only poured salt into the wound. "But sure, Athnauchan. Renewal ceremony. War games, drunk fae, debauchery. Ah, where to begin." Sarcastic enthusiasm dripped from the last words. "I have to get going to a council meeting to get to so let's make this quick. I'm only telling you this since my brother is clearly incompetent and as much of an inconvenience as you are, I'd rather you didn't get yourself killed for your ignorance." She was about to take that as a compliment when he added, "Really don't feel like cleaning that up."

"Maybe I'll just read about it -" She tried to push past him, sick of

ELORA

him, the conversation, the way he looked down at her.

He blocked her path, apparently unfazed, and continued as though she hadn't spoken. "Fae have to purify and renew themselves once a year in order for our Eolas to work properly. The nuances are too complicated for you to grasp. Emissaries from many other kingdoms take this opportunity to renew diplomatic ties and lay the foundation for trade deals and any other sort of joint endeavor for the following year. The entire ceremony is two days. The first day is when the games happen - competitions between representatives from every Season. The winner receives a substantial amount of gold and, more importantly, bragging rights. It's a way to show off more than anything. The second, final day is when the actual renewal ritual happens. Got it?"

Before she could answer, Aerin nodded at her once and then left, long legs carrying him off faster than she could try to catch him. Elora stared after him, watching the way he moved so fluidly it was as though he too had wings. *What the fuck is wrong with him?* She forced her body to relax a little now that he'd left, but annoyance still simmered under her skin. *He was easier to deal with when he had a dagger to my throat.*

She inhaled deeply and smoothed her hair back from her face, forcing her expression into one of a mild mannered Spring lady. Around her, pixies flitted about hanging up little lanterns with string so thin and spindly she could have sworn it was spider silk. The scent of spices and vanilla warmed her, and she smiled as she noticed Raewyn flutter over to her, a little iced cake in her hands.

If anything was going to fix the mood Aerin had put her in, it was cake.

It shocked Elora how used she'd become to the pixie's presence, how little it surprised her now when she saw her wings, though she hadn't quite managed to fully suppress the urge to reach out and touch them. Mouth watering, she gave her attention back to cake, inhaling the sugary sweet scent, reaching out eagerly as Raewyn handed her it.

"I stole it for you." The pixie winked, flying alongside Elora as she continued to her usual spot in the library.

"Thanks," Elora mumbled, already stuffing her face with the dessert. If she had to be stuck in this strange world, she may as well enjoy the food while she could. She had to admit that the cooks here were excellent. The cake tasted like heaven.

"So…" Raewyn was eyeing her, an all too innocent expression on her freckled face. Elora's stomach clenched as she tried to anticipate the pixie's next words. "I know you're not staying, but if you're attending the celebrations, you need appropriate outfits."

Elora frowned down at herself, thumbing the material of her dress. "What's wrong with this? I liked it." She wasn't used to wearing dresses, though she loved them - she'd never had much occasion to wear anything more than jeans and a nice top in New York.

Raewyn scrunched her nose. "You look different than when you arrived."

Elora bit her lip, suppressing a sigh. "Do I?" She didn't know how much Elladan had disclosed to the pixies, and she didn't want to land herself in any more shit by telling her about the glamour. She'd almost entirely forgotten it was there, if she was honest.

Raewyn studied her closely, reaching out and pushing back a lock of her hair to expose her ears. Her sigh landed heavy in the air.

"Oh," the redhead said softly. "It's a shame. I liked your hair the color it was. Although you do kind of suit the fae ears."

Elora smiled, but her heart missed a beat when she remembered Elladan's praise over her new appearance. She was confident in the way she looked despite that, aside from their shared heritage, she barely looked like her parents, though she often found herself curious about her family history. Her parents had adopted her in South Korea before they immigrated but had no information about her birth family. It was clear from Elora's looks that at least one of her parents had also been Korean, but when her mom had bought her a DNA test kit for Christmas, the results had come back as UNTRACEABLE. They'd even called the damn company, and been told that there was nothing they could do. The sample must have been contaminated, the woman on the phone had said. But the same thing had happened the next three times she tried to send in a sample, all to different companies. Fifty percent Korean and fifty percent untraceable. She'd searched every forum on the internet for someone else who'd experienced the same issue and come up blank.

Except, now, Elora was wondering whether it wasn't the sample that was the problem, but her. Maybe, if she allowed herself to believe Elladan, it wasn't that her ancestors were untraceable, just that they had been looking in the wrong place.

The wrong *realm*.

She shook her head, expelling the ridiculous notion. The more she thought about all this, the more confused she got. The next breath she took was so shaky she was surprised she even managed to take in any oxygen at all.

"I don't have any money for a fancy dress," she said to Raewyn, steering the conversation and her thoughts back to the original path.

Raewyn waved her hand in the air, dismissing Elora's concerns.

"Elladan is the *prince*," she reminded Elora, placing a warm hand on her elbow and redirecting her course. "What he wants, he gets. And, right now, what he wants is for his guest to be properly prepared and looked after."

Elora supposed she couldn't argue with that. And, secretly, the thought of getting a dress tailored just for her sent a spark of excitement through her veins.

"Follow me, Fleur," Raewyn said smoothly as a noblewoman passed them, her eyes a shocking shade of green as she studied Elora with blatant curiosity. Elora nodded, swallowing the knot in her throat and trying to quelch the fear snaking through her stomach. She'd nearly forgotten about the persona she was supposed to be playing, or about the stakes in this game she'd got herself tangled up in. Still, she steeled herself and walked the halls like she'd been rubbing elbows with royalty her whole life.

Like she was royalty herself.

12

Elora

"What the hell is happening?" Elora hissed out the corner of her mouth to Raewyn.

The night was closing in around them now and they were perched on the edge of a bench, at the edges of what Raewyn had explained was the arena. After her session with the prince's favored tailor that afternoon, during which he had grumbled about not having enough time to create a true masterpiece for the renewal ceremony, the pixies had pinned Elora's hair into an elaborate crown atop her head, and forced her into a plain but flattering deep red dress. While Elora liked the garment, she was fascinated by the sheer capelike attachment that trailed from the back of it, fluttering like wings in the slight evening breeze.

"The games are starting," Raewyn whispered back. Her own dress was a gorgeous orange that complimented her hair, long enough to cover her feet when she flew. Currently, she was sitting on Elora's shoulder, after complaining that her wings hurt and she was too short to see over people's heads if she sat on the padded bench beside Elora.

"Why don't you go sit with the rest of the pixies?" Elora asked, nodding towards the other side of the circle, where the crowd of castle helpers were seated in an elevated section so they could see down into the arena in the middle of the circle of seats. The set up was reminiscent of a sporting stadium, Elora thought, but the seats were undoubtedly more comfortable, padded with thick velvet cushions, and the air didn't smell of stale peanuts and hotdogs.

"I'm not leaving you alone."

"I'd be fine," Elora argued, though she knew it was a lie.

"Don't be ridiculous," Raewyn pushed back, yanking on a piece of Elora's hair to drive her point home. "Even with your alibi and glamour, you need to stay with one of us at all times. It's dangerous here, Elora. You don't know the games the fae play, yet. Maybe one day -"

"I'll never learn," Elora countered, more sternly than she'd meant to. "I'll be gone before I can."

Raewyn snapped her mouth shut and nodded, and Elora fought to ignore the sinking feeling that came with the words she'd spoken. Yes, she missed her parents terribly, but she'd barely kept in contact with most of her friends since college ended and they'd all ended up in different places, trying to find a job with the degree they'd earned. Elora, stuck in the solid but uneventful bookstore position she'd had since freshman year, had taken on more shifts, and lost touch with her classmates and starry eyed dreams. She needed a stable income more than she needed adventure or dreams.

Until here, until now. This enthralling, terrifying place with its gorgeous, horrifying people enchanted her. The itch to explore every corner of the library, the forests, the kingdom, was almost unbearable.

Fanciful, stupid wishes. Elora bit her lip to ground herself. She wanted to go home. She wanted to go home.

Why did the words sound so hollow?

"Sssh," Raewyn nudged her, bringing her attention back to the present. "The King is about to talk."

Elora watched as a tall man dressed in deep red stepped into the center of the ring, an elaborate gold crown atop his clean cut dark hair. He raised his head and met the eyes of the audience. Even from her distance, Elora could see he was handsome, but there was a cruelty to the square of his jaw and the steel of his eyes that set her on edge.

"Citizens of Fior Domhan," he began, his voice deep, sure and steady. "Tonight marks the first night of our Athnuachan ceremonies. This ceremony unites the Seelie and Unseelie courts alike, representatives from all four Seasons coming together to replenish and renew our magic. As is tradition, the Athnauchan games will be held on the first night, a test of bravery and strength to see who, of all our kingdoms, is truly worthy of the title warrior and the duty of protecting our lands."

A heavy pause settled over the crowd, and Elora shivered. She couldn't take her eyes off the King, despite the icy chill that scuttled down her spine as his cool gaze met hers.

"The standard rules apply," the High King continued. "In the combat rounds, participants must only aim to incapacitate, not kill. Healers are available to participants when they are eliminated, but not a second before. To see a healer is to forfeit your place. Any use of Eolas or runecarving is forbidden during the combat rounds, and any use of either will result in disqualification and be treated as an act of treason."

Another weighted pause as his words sank into the skin of the audience. Elora stared, wide eyed, her heart thumping so loud she wondered if Raewyn could hear it. She might have, as she began stroking comforting circles on Elora's shoulder.

"Don't worry," she whispered, her voice barely audible. "It's not as scary as it might sound. It's fun, really."

Elora wasn't sure if Raewyn was trying to convince her or herself.

She couldn't find it in herself to answer.

The King broke the silence with a few words in a language Elora couldn't understand, but that sounded ancient and melodic. Then, he raised his hand in some sort of signal and a steady stream of fae entered the arena from doors tucked under the seating area that Elora could barely make out in the dim light. Lanterns and floating balls of what appeared to be sunlight lit the area, but Elora's eyes still strained to see.

Her breath caught in her throat as her eyes settled on a familiar figure. She opened her mouth to say something to Raewyn, but the King cut her off.

"Let the games begin."

Elora sucked in a breath as all the contestants paraded onto the field amidst the fanfare of beating drums and trumpets. Fireworks and flames burst apart in the sky, lighting up the clouds for miles around, a stunning array of colors washing over the arena. The roar of the crowd drowned out even the music and there was a rhythm, a beat that pulsed through the stadium, washing over her, filling her. There was a feeling of collectiveness in the air, and Elora wasn't sure if she was imagining it or if it really was the result of this Athnuachan ceremony. The moment was broken when a herald stepped forward, raising his hands to silence the crowd.

The first round was starting.

Raewyn leaned across to whisper that there would be three rounds, two combat rounds, and one round filled with Eolas. She wanted to ask Raewyn exactly what they entailed but her thoughts were interrupted by the four hooded fae that stepped into the field, one from each direction, each holding a large piece of paper in their hands. One began burying the paper under the hard dirt of the field while the other poured water from a small bottle over their sheet. Another dropped the paper and it somehow caught on fire, and the fourth fae simply held theirs. A few moments later something erupted up from the ground, to the great pleasure of the crowd. Elora's eyes widened and her mouth hung open in shock. The four fae had created an entire castle from nothing. The castle was an open structure, with various levels built into it, ensuring all the spectators could see exactly what was happening. At the very top of the castle's parapet was a brilliant diamond, larger than any she had seen before. The diamond was easily the size of a soccer ball and it lay suspended in mid air, hovering.

From what she'd gleaned so far, over the excited roar of the crowd, participants from each Season were to pit themselves against each other, race to the castle and be the first to reach and claim the gemstone.

A trumpet sounded, loud and piercing, and the contest began.

As one, the contestants surged forward, battle cries echoing through the stadium. The fighting began almost instantly and Elora's stomach flipped with the first spatter of blood that coated the ground.

Nearly half the fae were on the ground wounded before they even made it to the castle, Elladan leading the pack racing for the entrance. Fae armed to the teeth were cutting and hacking at each other with weapons Elora had never even seen before, all cruel, sharp and efficient. Before she could even blink, the mound leading up to the castle entrance simply collapsed, taking most of the remaining fae with it.

A handful of fae barely managed to leap clear and land inside the open entrance to the castle and Elora breathed out a sigh of relief to see Elladan among them. Before they could resume fighting, animated warriors made from dirt, rocks and clay rose up to attack the contestants. The earthen warriors were not formidable fighters, but what they lacked in skill they made up for in numbers. Soon the fae inside the castle were forced apart, each a lone island among a sea of enemies. Many of them ducked and escaped into other hallways of the castle, where a plethora of traps awaited them. Spiked pits, arrows shot from holes in the wall, poisonous fumes and a multitude of other traps that had Elora gripping the railing of the stands with bated breath. She watched Elladan fight his way up the castle levels, nearing the top. He was a force of nature, dodging this way and that, his twin swords a constant whirlwind.

But he was the second fighter to reach the top of the castle onto the parapet where the diamond was. Realizing he would be too late, he hurled one of his swords at the other fae warrior about to grab the gem. The sword lodged neatly into the back of his upper thigh and the warrior went down with a cry. She could make out Elladan's grin even from up high in the stands as he stalked over, stepping over the fallen fae.

Elora sucked in a quick breath as a woman with hair woven in tight braids across her head approached Elladan from behind, grabbing him in a sort of choke hold that had Elora clutching her own neck in sympathy. Faster than she could track, Elladan had the woman on her back, his own dagger pressed to his neck. Elora gripped the edge of a cushion to steady herself, fighting to stop bile rising in her throat. He wouldn't kill her, would he? He couldn't -

Elladan pressed the blade until a thin line of blood dripped onto the dust beneath them. The woman beneath him just stared, stony faced, at the Autumn prince. Judging by the deep green armor she wore, Elora guessed the woman was Spring fae. Elladan grinned, exposing his teeth, before releasing the woman and settling for slashing a line across her stomach, tearing her tunic and earning a hiss of pain. He walked back over to the floating diamond and slowly took it in his hands, raising it over his head.

He was spattered with blood but his usual smirk had returned to his mouth, and Elora couldn't decide whether she was repulsed or attracted to him. She refused to analyze her feelings further, unsure whether she wanted to know the answer. The crowd went wild, screaming and chanting Elladan's name as he basked in the glow of thunderous praise.

A man in fine clothes sauntered over the people on the floor, his dark skin unmarred with blood. He gripped Elladan's hand in his own and raised it above his head, announcing him the winner of the round.

This time, when the crowd cheered for him, Elora joined in.

After rounds of applause for the victorious Elladan, King Harkan stepped up from the dias to address the crowd once more, wearing a smug grin.

"Prince Elladan of Autumn is this year's victor of the jeontu round! Continue defending all of Fior Domhan with this courage and bravery. You have brought great honor to Autumn!" He sat back on his throne with a flourish, and Elora thought she could see a grin beneath his beard.

Three other fae were seated on elaborate chairs next to him, watching the games with interest. King Harkan sat on a gnarled chair shaped from a tree trunk with falling leaves held up by nothing frozen in place around him. To his right sat a fae lady with snow white hair and piercing blue eyes atop a chair that looked like it was carved from an icicle. On her right sat another lady, with dark brown skin and beautiful braids adorning her head. She sat in a chair sculpted from vines and flowers, a sparrow perched on her right shoulder. On King Harkan's left sat a man that looked a lot like Elora's adopted father, albeit with less wrinkles. He was dressed in resplendent gold and red, and seemed to shine. Even his chair was bright to look at, with countless shimmering sparkles that glinted like miniature suns.

King Harkan's voice rang out once more. "It is time for the second competition. Let the Althimachi round commence!"

More cheers rang out as the four hooded figures from before stepped out once more, and performed what Elora assumed was runecasting. It was the same process as before, but this time the stadium took on a whole different transformation. The castle simple disappeared and the now empty sand packed floor of the massive arena was suddenly divided into four quadrants, with a circle in the middle where each section met. A grassy hill with geysers spewing fire every few seconds took over one section, next to a quadrant covered with snow with a frozen lake in its center. Below that was a section filled with a wild jungle, covered with trees vines, and dense forestry, impossible to peer inside. The final quadrant held a cliff that soared above even the tallest stands, so tall it looked like it touched the sky. A single oak tree with deep orange and read leaves perched at the precipice.

"Is that each of the Seasons?" Elora's voice was soft and awestruck.

"Yes," Raewyn answered. "One quadrant for each Season."

"Why does Autumn have a giant cliff?"

"Well, each Season is aligned with an element-"

Before she could continue, the second round of games began with the crash of a gong. Eight figures stepped forth and met in the middle of the four quadrants at the small circle made from gleaming black stone. She recognized Elladan, of course, and... *was that the guard from the library?*

Elora craned her neck and upon further inspection, confirmed her earlier guess. The figure standing next to Elladan was indeed the guard that had aggressively walked away from her in the library. He was the most massive warrior on the field, with only one fair skinned fae in brilliant gold armor coming anywhere close to his size. Deep red shining armor covered the Autumn contestant's skin, though Elladan stood out thanks to the golden crown above his heart..

Elladan immediately leapt into the fray at the center, clashing swords with a fae in gold armor. The guard, on the other hand, nimbly leapt back into Autumn territory and began rapidly scaling the cliff. Arrows bounced off the cliff face mere inches away from him, forcing him to drop back down. Elora could see a slender fae with features similar to her own hidden behind geysers of flame firing red hot arrows at him. Elladan was still in the middle, locked in a battle with two opponents. Two other contestants were dueling amidst the frozen tundra, and Elora gasped as a female fae warrior in black armor nimbly dodge a spear thrust as she shouted, slashing her hands in a furious arc. The ice underneath them exploded and a blast of water sent the attacking fae warrior spinning away. Waving her hands again, he was encased in a solid block of ice, crashing into the ground. The golden armored fae from earlier now attacked the warrior who had so blatantly manipulated water, trading her flaming arrows in favor of a flaming battle ax. It was obvious that the fae in golden armor was far stronger and quicker and each time the warrior in black tried to counter with a spear thrust or send shards of ice hurtling towards him, they would melt and dissipate before they got close enough to do damage. He soon had her backed up inside of her own territory, and a few more ax combinations later, the fae in black armor was kneeling in defeat. She tapped her breastplate three times over her heart with her right fist, the apparent symbol of submission.

Elora swiveled her head to the other side to see Elladan still dancing around two fae warriors in the small circle. His armor was battered in places and the two fae he was facing off against now were offering a far stiffer challenge than the fae he had fought in the earlier round. One was a female warrior, her hair elegantly tied atop her head. She wore emerald armor and fought with two long swords. The other warrior in violet armor, twirled a giant spiked mace in the air with a speed that belied his smaller stature. Elora looking around for the guard to see how he was faring but he was nowhere to be found.

GIRL OF BONE AND IVY

Until the Spring quadrant erupted in a mass of vines and the mystery guard went flying. Flying wasn't quite the right word, as it looked like he was falling through the sky, his fall broken by regular intervals of abrupt stops. Landing unsteadily on his feet, the guard put his back to a tree and sliced incoming vines that snaked out at him from all angles. The tree behind him began moving, its branches reaching for him. Yelling something unintelligible, he sprang away and thrust at it with his free hand. What Elora could only describe as a blade of air arced through, neatly severing several branches. His other arm still hastily slashing away at the vines, the guard backed up until his feet were at the edge of the platform. As if sensing the end was near, his opponent stalked forward, a young woman dressed in white and pale green armor, she wore a smug smile on her face. Suddenly both her hands snapped to her neck, clawing, her smile fading into open mouthed gasps. She was choking, but Elora couldn't see what on. Until she looked at the guard. His legs and left hand was firmly encircled by vines, pulling him out of bounds. He had dropped the sword in his right hand and was stretching his arm out, clenching his fist. Flexing his fingers, he squeezed hard, leaving his opponent tearing at the skin of her neck, her face turning an ugly purple. With a heave, she kicked her foot out, sending the guard tumbling out of bounds. Disqualified. The fae in white and green collapsed to her hands and knees, heaving for breath.

A victorious shout cut through the air and Elora looked back at the black circle to see Elladan disarm and send the fae warrior holding the spiked mace tumbling out of the center, landing limply in the Autumn quadrant.

"Is he dead?" Elora whispered, a chill sweeping over her.

"No, just knocked out. Killing is not allowed in the games," Raewyn answered.

Elladan was now circling the female warrior in emerald armor, who had an ugly gash running down the side of her left arm. It hung limp, and she now only had a single sword. Elladan's armor was battered - a chunk torn out of his breastplate - and dark blood dripped steadily from a gash in his upper thigh. He was quick and nimble even while limping, and Elora watched with her heart in her mouth as the final two battled it out. The fae warrior who had taken out the guard was still on the grassy forest floor panting, and didn't look like she'd offer much of a threat, if any.

Then it was over. Elladan lunged and as his opponent moved to counter he threw his sword directly at her. Using her own momentum against her, Elladan pivoted on his good leg and tackled her. This carried them straight out of the black circle firmly into Autumn territory, where Elora expected Elladan must have a significant advantage. But instead of using any magical powers, he grappled with her, putting her in a choke hold. After a few agonizing seconds, she tapped and the crowd roared their approval as one.

Noticing that everyone else was standing, Elora hastily got up and began clapping, though the overwhelming violence of the day had her feeling slightly nauseous. The adrenaline from watching the contest wore off, and Elora shakily found her voice, needing to understand what she'd just witnessed.

"Raeywn?"

"Yes?"

"How is it that the warriors in the second round were able to use magic without writing it on a piece of paper? Is that the runecarving I saw mentioned at the library?"

Raewyn immediately shushed her, clamping her hand over Elora's mouth.

"You mustn't say stuff like that out loud, even if the crowd is being raucous. You have to maintain your cover. I'll answer your questions later."

Elladan was still parading around, as much as one could while limping. As much as the violence unsettled Elora, Elladan's easygoing smile and clear confidence was attractive. His dark eyes caught the sunlight, a small spatter of blood on his upper lip glinting as he grinned. No being who fought the way he did had any business being that handsome.

"This year's Althimachi champion is Elladan Veyadrin!" King Harkan's voice echoed throughout the entire stadium, no doubt amplified by Eolas. "You've demonstrated great bravery in all circumstances. While our borders have been peaceful for centuries, I hope that you will rise to the occasion and defend Fior Domhan when necessary."

Elladan merely put his right hand to his battered breastplate over his heart and bowed his head in acquiescence. The crowd screamed their approval once more, a multitude even stamping their feet. *Guess, the fae and humans aren't that different after all. Except sporting events here were far more dangerous.*

"Are you thirsty darling?"

Raewyn was holding a clear glass filled with a deep violet liquid that sparkled, and Elora could smell the hibiscus and elderflower wafting from the glass.

"Is it alcoholic?"

"By Aureole's locks, no! I remembered that you can't have alcohol." Raewyn blushed. "I might have overheard you talking to Elladan a few days ago about it. Everyone else has been drinking and feasting, and I had this made just for you!"

Elora thanked her and accepted the glass, taking a long sip. While the drink didn't soothe her the way the water here did, it was far better than anything she had drank back home. The natural flavors of hibiscus and elderflower were powerful, but not overpowering.

The sun in Fior Domhan was merciless, and sweat trickled down her temple, pooling at the base of her neck despite the tarp she was under. She briefly wished Aerin was here to write in his little notepad and possibly conjure up something to stave off the heat, but given his cold and distant manner yesterday, she dismissed him from her mind, trying to focus on what King Harkan was saying.

"...A contest of creativity and Eolas, to remind ourselves of why we've gathered here and to practice the very skills gifted to us by Áine. Remember, no runecarving is allowed, runecasting only. We will be watching and I'm sure you all remember the consequences of not obeying the rules. The third round, sehrli, begins now. May the most talented runecaster win."

The cheering was a bit more subdued this time, Elora noticed as she surveyed the figures making their way to the stadium. She didn't recognize any of the fae on the field when their names were called, except Aerin. He was one of the few representing Autumn, and she didn't miss the faint scowl that crossed Elladan's face when his younger brother's name was called. Elladan had stepped off the field and watched from the side with a curl of his upper lip. Elora turned her attention back to the stadium when the trumpet sounded, and an elderly fae man stepped forth.

She held her breath as the final round began.

13

Aerin

Aerin squinted against the bright glare of the sun, eyes burning as he stepped into the arena. Anticipation curled around his bones.

The carefully carved runes in the woodwork around the stadium ensured that the contestant's natural defenses, glamours and all other personal runecasts were stripped away. Here, they were even. Trying to remain discreet, he looked at the competition for this year's sehrli round. Alathea, of course. She'd been competing against him for as long as he could remember. He missed the days when they had trained together, before everything with his father went south. This year, she was dressed in no nonsense black, her wavy black hair tied back in an elegant ponytail. She held her brush in one hand, rolled up papers in the other. A water skin hung in her belt and she caught his glance and gave him a stern nod. *All business then*. He could work with that.

Next to her stood Ramir from Summer. His tight curls were swept back from his face in a leather band, his brown eyes staring intently at his charcoal pencil. The paper he held in his other hand was thick and light brown, as though he'd stripped slices of bark straight from the tree. He, too, had been competing in Sehrli almost as long as Aerin had and was a formidable opponent.

A cursory glance of the rest of the opposition confirmed that Aerin did not recognize anyone else. While the first two rounds might see many of the same warriors year after year during their prime, sehrli was different. The difference in runecasting ability could be a split second, the line between right and wrong as thin as a single letter or punctuation mark. Competitors became easily frustrated by the specifics, of the time it took studying and training until they were able to produce the correct script quickly. Because of this, the eight contestants every year were nearly always different, save Alathea, Ramir and himself. Aerin was the reigning champion, three times in fact, and currently tied for the record of most consecutive wins. A fourth win today would make him the longest reigning sehrli champion in modern fae history, not to mention the youngest champion consecutive champion as well. Except the prospect of winning did not excite him at all. Not in the slightest.

His father's voice began echoing around his head again and Aerin silenced the threats, sneers, and strikes. He could win today, if he wanted to.

Already knowing the rules intimately by heart, Aerin ignored the judges' droning and studied his opponents to see if he could glean anything. While sehrli's rules didn't specify or limit the sex of the participants, this year each Season had sent a single man and woman. He didn't know the girl from Autumn standing next to him, no doubt one of his father's cronies, and had no intention of working with her. He knew that the other Seasons would try to cooperate and have both contestants team up at first, but Aerin didn't care. He just wanted the contest to be over with already. He hated using runecasts to fight. While they were excellent for combat, Aerin knew that they could be better used for so much more. It felt archaic to reduce them to violence.

The judges yelled "commence!" as the sound of gongs indicated the contest had begun.

Immediately springing backwards in a somersault, Aerin landed lightly on his toes, his back at the edge of the arena's borders. He was already gripping his notebook in his left hand and his right hand found his favorite pencil in the second satchel on his belt. Quickly, he scribbled the runes for 'air' and 'current', finishing off the runecast with directions and movements that would allow him greater control: 'mind', 'desire' and 'will'. His breath dusted the paper and he waited, counting his heartbeats until the Eolas took effect.

One, two -

Heat singed his hair as he threw himself sideways, barely avoiding the flames as they shot through the air. He cursed under his breath, eyeing Ramir's shadow, hidden by twin columns of bright flames. He cursed under his breath, righting himself, immediately ensuring the pseudo tornado he'd cast was now acting as a shield. The cold air whipped the hair off his face and he pinned the page down with his free hand to stop it being torn out, scribbling two more of the same runecasts, modifying their language slightly to include a perpetual circular direction.

Two more tornadoes sprang up around him, spinning rapidly around his body, deflecting several more blasts of flame. He barely felt the heat now, but the wind rushing off his make shift shield turned bone achingly cold as sharp icicles hit them. Predictably, monstrous vines came next, spindly deep green whips that made to reach for him before the force of the wind snapped them in half. His opponents were testing him, seeing which form of attack was likely to break through.

Through his defense, he could make out three fae converging on his location and willed his tornado to move away, leaving him exposed.

In his haste, he missed a vine that had snaked around the edge of the arena and rose up behind him. He threw himself to the right, his tornadoes following like dutiful dogs. But the target hadn't been him. The vine curled around his wrist, pinning his hand and forcing his fingers to open, the notepad dropping from his grip. It was snatched away before he could fight back, leaving him with no way to runecast.

Fuck.

Aerin steered his defense away as best he could. Thankfully, they were still in tact but Aerin knew he was going to lose unless he could get his notebook back. He sprinted, making for the edge of the arena with the least competitors. He knew the others would view his running as retreat, as weakness, would drop their guard as smug glee blinded their sight. He knew how to play their egos against them, unworried about damaging his own pride in the process. Aerin had learned years ago that this, as with everything else in his life, was as much about mind games as it was about casting and skill.

He paused near the edge, scanning the arena. Both representatives from Winter were out, one excluded for being out of bounds, the other unconscious. Ramir was busy engaging the other Autumn contestant, lobbing balls of fire at her while she dodged them with glowing wings. It seemed that both Spring representatives and the other Summer competitor had an unspoken agreement to take him out first, as they had originally all teamed up together to target Aerin. Apparently now considering him taken care of for the moment, they had turned on each other, their alliance dissolving quickly.

But targeting Aerin's notepad wouldn't nearly be enough. Not even close. He hated his father but the agility, strength and conditioning he put Aerin and his brother through had paid off. He darted back towards the three fighting fae, smirking when he saw that both Spring fae had turned on the one from Summer. It was a quick, dirty battle that ended with animated rock golems swiftly taking out the Summer contestant, despite her smashing the first few into dust. Dodging debris and his competitors, Aerin slid across the dirt, kicking up dust in his wake, snatching his notebook from where it had been discarded as the Spring fae turned towards him once more.

He still had seven pages out of the ten allotted to them for this contest. As long as he could still write, there was hope. Aerin barely had time to cast a solid wall of air in a shield around him before attacks started slamming into it. He braced, reinforcing the wall, summoning another in anticipation of the first falling and steady gust of air to elevate him, in case the Spring fae tried underground attacks like he'd seen them do in the past.

Four pages left.

The Spring fae were constantly shifting, one was popping in and out of the ground where they'd retreated, making it nearly impossible for Aerin to target them. It would have been comical if it was less frustrating. In the distance, he watched his Autumn counterpart sink to her knees in surrender. Satisfaction flooded him, warm and heady.

He shook his head, focusing once more on the competitors before him. He had to take one out, and fast, before they organized enough to team up on him again. He let the tornadoes deflect the animated trees and stone golems that ran towards him as he scribbled a runecast that would suck the air out of the ground just an inch in front of them. Wisely, the Spring fae already guarded against air manipulation by summoning olaga leaves that would give them a steady air supply as long as they bit down on them. So Aerin choked the earth itself, taking away the source of their power.

When both of them ducked down behind an earthen wall they'd created earlier, Aerin tore out the two pages in his notepad containing the runecasts for the walls made of air and crumpled them, deactivating the Eolas. With the walls out of his way, he lurched forward and spun his tornadoes towards them, rapidly bearing down. Both competitors sprang back up, consternation on their faces as they realized the runecasts they had buried weren't taking effect.

Satisfied, Aerin wrote one last runecast, a smirk twisting his lips. Blowing over the page, he tucked his notepad back in his belt and thrust both his hands out towards his opponents as the customary three heartbeats passed. A gust of air hit them in the chest, causing them to scramble for something to hold on to as they were pushed out of bounds.

Giving them a nod, Aerin turned to face his last opponent.

Ramir stood about a hundred paces away, waiting. Aerin smiled at him, recognizing the man's talent, before quickly glancing down at the single page left in the notepad. He didn't know how many Ramir had, so he waited for him to make the first move. Ramir didn't make him wait long. He wrote something short in charcoal before burning it, the flame swallowing the paper quickly.

Aerin winced as the air beneath him grew uncomfortably hot, Ramir's runecast heating the air he was standing on. Crumpling yet another page from his notepad, Aerin dismissed the Eolas, ending the runecast and sending him back down to the ground. Ramir simply stood there, waiting.

So that was your last runecast too, he thought, cocking his head to the side to analyze the man. Depending on the defenses that Ramir still had in place, this was Aerin's chance to win. The throne box was elevated just behind where Ramir was standing, and Aerin saw the sly grin on his father's face. His father almost never smiled at him and it made Aerin nauseous that he would do so now. Though he wasn't surprised. The way to his father's heart had always been brutality.

Breathing in the dirt, sweat, and dust of the arena floor, Aerin relaxed his shoulders as the crowd fell silent, waiting.

"Hey, Ramir."

"How's it going Aerin?" Ramir's easy going nature was constant even in battle, making it obvious why he was so well liked.

"Correct me if I'm wrong. If you win, you receive more than enough money to get your city back in order, no?" Ramir's hometown had been damaged a month prior, thanks to a rogue citizen and the wrong runecasts.

Ramir's smile briefly faltered, a serious expression sliding onto his face. "Yeah, I do."

Aerin met his father's eyes above Ramir's head.

"Well. it's settled then."

His father bared his teeth, a warning bright in his dark eyes, filling Aerin with revulsion. His father wanted him to win so he could parade around his two boys, one a champion warrior and the other a master runecaster. Both unparalleled at creating violence and destruction. It was the only time he called Aerin his son. He used to crave it, the validation and attention it brought him. Now, the disgust and anger that rose inside of him was a swift and unrelenting river, driving his feet away from Ramir.

And then it was over.

Aerin stood on the dirt floor, just out of bounds from the sand packed floor of the arena as Ramir stared at him with the same stunned silence everyone else in the arena did. Savoring the look on his father's face, Aerin turned his back and walked through the chambers underneath the stands to find a cool drink. Perhaps that hibiscus and elderflower tea they were serving.

14

Elora

Elora was frozen, heart loud in her ears as she watched him walk away.

She couldn't believe that Aerin had just given up. He had been on the brink of victory. The entire runecasting business still confused her, but if Aerin could still cast once more and his opponent couldn't, why had he just walked out of bounds? She hadn't been able to hear what Aerin had said to his competitor, she was too far away and he'd not raised his voice, but the subsequent expression on the King's face made it clear he was displeased with whatever had happened.

The tangy scent of blood hung heavy in the air, making Elora scrunch her nose as Raewyn urged her to her feet. The other fae had begun moving, some crowding into the arena, eyes wild and excitement practically dripping from them. Some had snuck off into the darkness, wrapped in a whole other type of excitement, and Elora winced at the apparent blood lust evident in the Unseelie fae. Raewyn was stuck to Elora's side as they drifted out through the ornate doors with the crowd into the night of the courtyard behind the castle.

She and Raewyn began making their way back to the castle, Elora shaken enough for one night and wincing every time she caught a glimpse of the color of her damn dress. It's not as if she'd never seen blood or violence before, but never like this. Never for sport.

A hand latched onto Elora's elbow and she froze, eyes wide as she looked to Raewyn frantically. The pixie smoothed her face into one of careful happiness before urging Elora to turn and greet whoever had grabbed her.

"Hello, Balor," Raewyn chirped, bobbing her head in greeting. She flitted a little closer to Elora, her wings so close to her ear she could hear the soft beat of them.

"I believe I haven't been lucky enough to make your acquaintance yet." The man, Balor, released her elbow only to hold out a hand expectantly. Elora took a steadying breath and forced a calm, pleasant mask into place.

Fleur, she reminded herself, *a fae girl from Spring. You can do this.*

"Pleasure to meet you," she replied, her voice sickly sweet to her own ears. She placed her hand in his and he brought it to his lips, pressing a wet kiss to her fingers. She fought the urge to shudder.

He was tall, but shorter than both Elladan and Aerin, with light blond hair and eyes so pale blue they were nearly white. His cheekbones were sharp and his jawline severe. He was handsome in an alarming way, but Elora found herself desperate to put distance between them.

"I find it odd that I've never seen you around here before," Balor pressed, still gripping her hand in his.

"And I, you," she returned, panic and anger flaring inside her, along with steely determination. Sure, she was lying, but who was he to question her so soon?

He huffed a short laugh, but his condescending expression didn't shift.

"I hear you're Prince Elladan's newest play thing." His eyes slid down her body slowly, stopping at her chest though it was covered by the high neck of the dress. Elora forced her arms to her sides, refusing to give him the satisfaction of covering herself. "He has always had good taste."

"We are simply friends."

"Tell me, what's your name, pretty thing?"

"Fleur."

"That's far too innocent a name for a girl like you." Balor cocked his head to the side, gaze turning predatory.

Panic fluttered in Elora's chest. What the fuck was she supposed to do now? Run?

She was saved from answering by a welcome presence at her side. Elladan's strong arm wrapped around her shoulder and Balor dropped her hand like it stung. Elora sank into Elladan's side gratefully, not caring how it looked. She would have kissed him if it got this creep away from her.

"Balor."

"Elladan."

The former nodded once, winking at Elora, before he turned on his heel and sauntered off. Elora felt her mask slipping, dangerously close to undoing this carefully crafted persona. Elladan brushed a strand of hair behind her ear and bent down to whisper,

"I need to get cleaned up before I return to celebrate my win. Do you want to retire?"

Elora nodded gratefully and took his outstretched arm, fitting her hand into the crook of his elbow. He had wiped the blood from himself, but the coppery scent of it still clung to his skin and a patch of his hair was damp with it. His clothes were new, though, and the distinct scent of autumn comforted her.

He led her back through the halls of the castle, away from the mingling voices and laughter, and sat her on the edge of the bed.

"I'm going to wash off," he told her, holding her eyes. "You can get changed if you like, while you wait for me. Although I do love that color on you."

He didn't wait for her to answer, turning and heading into the bathroom. He didn't even close the door properly behind him, leaving it ajar, and Elora watched the steam curling through the gap as the bath ran with wide eyes.

The urge to follow him into the room ran hot in her veins, surprising her with its fervor. She was just grateful, she told herself as she smoothed the silk of her skirt. He was simply, objectively, attractive. It made sense that her body was reacting to him. That was it. That was all.

Still, she didn't hate the color red on herself anymore.

15

Elora

"Elora, it's time. We need to get you ready for the ceremony." Elora blearily opened her eyes to Raewyn and her band of pixies floating by her side, all tugging at various parts of her body. Raewyn was shaking her right shoulder, while another pixie with black hair, Lydia if memory served her correctly, was tugging at her hair. More pixies flew about, smoothing out several dresses and arranging makeup products on the vanity

"What?"

"Did Elladan or Aerin tell you nothing? Today is the day of the renewal ceremony," Raewyn said, still rapidly tugging at Elora to get up. "We need to hurry so you won't be late!"

"Okay, okay. I'm up."

Elora stretched and rubbed the sleep from her eyes as she was hustled into the bath. The events of the day before had plagued her dreams and though she marveled at the display of dexterity, speed, and strength the fae had shown, her stomach still turned a little if she thought about the games too closely. Still, she had to admit that even the most graceful dancers and athletes from back home paled in comparison to the beauty the fae seemed to possess while moving.

She'd fallen asleep almost as soon as she'd changed last night, after Elladan had changed into another suit and returned to *be diplomatic* with the other fae. She'd tried not to think about his powerful arms enveloping her as he hugged her goodnight or his calm voice steadfast against her nervous fear when he'd saved her from that creep Balor. No, she hadn't once thought about the curve of his jawline and the unrelenting strength in his eyes. She certainly hadn't replayed the way his eyes raked over her red dress, or the way he said her name in that teasing tone of his.

Ice cold water pelted her skin and she yelped.

"*What the hell Raewyn?*" So far, every bath had been steaming hot and Elora couldn't see why that needed to change now.

"Sorry dear. It's Athnuachan custom. Everybody shows up without the comforts of a hot bath or tea."

"What kind of stupid rule is that?"

Raewyn immediately clapped a hand over Elora's mouth, filling it with soapy bubbles. She spluttered, the bitter taste coating her tongue.

"You mustn't talk like that," she chided, blue eyes wide. "It will get you in deep trouble."

Not wanting to agitate the sweet pixie, Elora shut her mouth for the rest of the miserable bath and let the pixies dry and arrange her hair. They pinned it back from her face, but left it unadorned and loose and swiped pink blush across her cheekbones. She was at least allowed to drink some of the water in the pitcher by the table, sweet and cool. Three dresses they'd deemed suitable were laid out on the bed, and Lydia instructed her to choose. She pointed, the angle allowing Elora to catch a glimpse of a tattoo on the underside of her wrist, black against her brown skin. *Raewyn's wife.* She smiled at the sight. They made a perfect match.

She chose the red dress. Purely because it was form fitting and she liked the way it highlighted her waist and splayed out slightly at the hips. Not because Elladan had said he liked red. It hadn't crossed her mind.

Get a hold of yourself, Elora, she chastised herself, exhaling harshly. *It's a means to an end. Play by the rules so you can go home. That's it. That's all.*

Then again, she'd never been very good at lying.

"You look great. Amazing actually."

Elora jumped and whirled around, staring at Elladan who was suddenly standing right next to her. "Holy hell Elladan, why are you sneaking up on me like that?"

Elladan, in his classic fashion, ignored her. "Did you wear red again for me?" His voice was low and laced with a teasing tone that sent butterflies fluttering through her stomach.

"Keep dreaming, red just happens to look stunning on me." It did, she knew. It wasn't a lie. Just…an omission.

"Is that why your face is starting to match the color of your new dress?"

Elora was about to smack his arm when she realized that Elladan wasn't alone. In fact, it seemed like he had brought his entire retinue with him. She saw several guards, albeit without armor, and a group of what looked to be attendants as well. Awkwardly stepping back, she cleared her throat and attempted to be normal. She recognized one of the guards - a tall, very muscular man with deep brown skin and dark eyes that seemed to be trained on her. The one from the fight yesterday, and the library before then.

"Will Aerin be joining us?" Not that she particularly wanted to spend more time with the grumpy asshole who clearly hated her, but Fleur Atwater was supposed to be his friend.

"I don't know. I haven't spent a renewal ceremony with him since we were children," Elladan replied, his mood abruptly darkening, voice harsher. His eyes flickered over the tall guard Elora had noticed and his fists curled at his sides. Elora fought the instinct to back away. Neither of them mentioned the fact that his brother had abruptly forfeited the sehrli round for no apparent reason. "The ceremony is starting soon. I'll escort you. If you please." Elladan stuck his arm out, and not knowing what else to do or why his mood had shifted so suddenly at the mention of Aerin, Elora took it, tucking her hand into the crook of his elbow.

Over her shoulder, she spotted Raewyn and Lydia holding hands tightly, the former's brows furrowed as she watched the pair. Elora offered her a smile and the redhead abruptly smoothed her features out, offering one back. Lydia bit her glossy bottom lip, opening her mouth as though to call after Elora as she began walking away. But she didn't speak and so Elora turned and let herself fall into step beside Elladan. She didn't have time to analyze their strange behavior. She knew precious little about today as it was and she didn't have the energy to add more to the pile of stuff she had to figure out. Still, the thought that her newfound friends - if she could call them that (and she could admit to herself that she desperately wanted to call them that) - were … well… upset? Worried? Just generally *off*, sat heavy in her stomach.

Elladan led Elora out of the castle and atop the hill, where a grand tent had been erected, it's auburn and hickory colored pennants flapping lazily in the wind. The hill overlooked a valley that left Elora at a loss for words. It stretched for miles, with tents of every color dotting the hillside and valley below - a palette of vibrant greens, pastel pinks, bright yellows, icy blues. Flags and family crests filled the space as far as the eye could see and everywhere Elora looked were fae. Not just fae, but partying fae. Every single person she could make out had some sort of drink in their hand, wearing wide grins and laughter spilling from their bellies.

"Welcome to the renewal ceremony."

"I..uh…what do you-"

"We spend most of the day drinking and doing whatever we fancy until night falls upon us, and then we offer our lifeblood to mother nature in return for the power we're granted." Elladan stated the facts simply, as though they were obvious. Seconds later, he burst out laughing at Elora's incredulous expression. "It will make sense later. Now come, let's have some fun."

Realizing that some of the fae from Elladan's retinue were already glancing at her with strange expressions, Elora cursed herself for letting her ignorance slip. She was supposed to be Fleur Atwater, youngest daughter of an obscure lord from the Zahra Kingdom. Not a clueless human girl. Hurrying down the hill behind an exuberant Elladan, she hoped nobody would think too deeply about her mistake.

16

Elora

Elora lost count of how many times a passing fae had shoved a drink into her hands. She was getting good at pretending to drink them, though the grass behind her was far soggier than it had been when she'd joined the party. She stood on the edge of the celebrations, watching fae spin wildly to the music, apprehension crawling over her skin. She knew the legends, the risks of dancing to faerie music. How once you started, you couldn't stop. How you'd dance until your feet bled and your bones ache. How you'd dance yourself to death as long as the music kept playing.

It didn't seem like the time to test the myth.

Her throat was dry and scratchy, her cheeks a little sore from the fake smile she refused to let slip, but the night was warm and the people were beautiful. It wasn't all bad, watching them twirl and letting their wine sweetened laughter settle over her skin.

Elladan had left about an hour ago to do whatever the hell it was princes did at such a celebration. Mingle, she supposed. More *diplomacy*. So far, nobody had questioned her when she insisted she was happy to observe, but she wasn't sure how long she could keep pushing the same excuses for.

"Not in the mood for dancing?"

Elora spun, hearing the familiar voice. "Elladan!"

"Fleur," Elladan greeted, moving to stand at her side and sliding an arm around her waist, drawing her close. He smelled of spiced wine intertwined with the autumn air he always carried with him. She tilted her head back to offer him a smile, savoring the closeness.

"I haven't seen you in ages," she said, trying to keep her tone light. Elladan sighed a little, hand flexing on her waist.

"I'm sorry, beautiful," he answered, accepting the flute of fizzing golden liquid as it was handed to him by a passing server. "I tried to keep it quick."

"It's okay," she told him, resting her head on his chest in an attempt to calm her frayed nerves with his familiarity. It only set her skin aflame with acute awareness. She hoped he couldn't see her blushing from his angle.

"I should have taken you with me," he mused, looking down at her through his lashes.

She couldn't think of anything worse. She shook her head quickly. "No." He raised a brow at her, amused and she added, "I liked watching the dances. Their happiness is…" she trailed off, unsure how to finish.

"It's contagious," Elladan finished for her. She nodded. He wasn't wrong. If it wasn't the truth, she'd have been in a state of panic since she'd arrived. Instead, she was only on edge. Barely anxious at all, in comparison. "It's the one time of the year when we all get together like this. When the inhibitions and worries and hold ups fall away and leave us stripped bare. Add alcohol and, well, *celebration* is an understatement." He nodded to a corner where two fae were tangled in each other, lipstick stains on their necks and hands half disappeared beneath the skirts of each other's dresses.

Elora looked away quickly, face on fire. Elladan laughed lowly, taking a sip from his glass.

"Does everyone participate in such…celebrations?" She wasn't sure why she asked it, but she didn't entirely regret it given the slow shock that spread through Elladan's features as he released her slightly to look at her.

"No," he said slowly, setting his half empty glass down on a passing tray. "Not everybody."

"Do you?" It was like her damn tongue was moving without her permission. She couldn't help but chase the dark spark in Elladan's eyes at her line of questioning.

"Occasionally." He frowned at her a little. "It's not *mandatory*, Fleur. We are simple creatures, beneath the gifts bestowed on us. Why deny ourselves such indulgences on nights like this?"

Yes, Elora thought, heart hammering as she watched the way the light played over his features, casting him half in shadow, *why indeed?*

She inhaled deeply before rising on her tiptoes to brush a soft kiss to his cheek. "Thank you for looking after me this week. I appreciate it. And you."

Elladan froze.

"Elora…" he trailed off, sounding almost unsure for the first time since she'd met him.

"It's Fleur," Elora laughed. "Don't worry. I don't think anyone heard you."

Something like regret flashed over his face, gone before she could analyze it. He smirked and raised a brow at her. "I lost my retinue a while ago. Besides, everyone's too drunk to pay attention."

His hands captured her waist, and she sucked in an involuntary breath at the contact. Warmth spread from his touch, anticipation near searing in her veins. She was past the point of denying the attraction, especially tonight, surrounded by revelry. Besides, she would be going home soon. She didn't have time to wait.

He smiled at her, and the fading sunlight caught the edges of brown eyes, turning them a burnt umber. Her breath caught as he angled his face slightly and began leaning in. *Is this really happening?* Her heart picked up pace as she closed her eyes and met Elladan's lips.

His lips are normal. Elladan's lips didn't feel any different from the human ones she had kissed, and the thought was as hilarious as it was absurd. She managed not to laugh against his mouth, pressing closer to him instead to hide her ridiculous train of thought. He tasted just as he smelled, sweet and rich, and Elora gave herself fully, wrapping her arms around his neck as he drew her in. Elladan slid his hands a little lower and Elora kissed back harder, their tongues meeting. He ran one hand up her hip, tracing its curve up across her back and gripped the back of her neck, tangling his fingers through her hair. He was gentle at first, but as the kiss deepened, his grip strengthened and Elladan tugged her head back, giving her neck a slight squeeze. Elora couldn't help but moan into his mouth.

The tingling low in her stomach spread as she melted into Elladan. His hands were torches, lighting her aflame everywhere roamed.

"Come on, let's find some cover." Elladan's voice was husky with need, an almost feral look in his eyes. He led her through the dancing crowd, out of the tent and into the night. The sun had set almost entirely now but the area was lit with lanterns and little specks of light that blurred when Elora tried to focus on them. Fireflies, she suspected, reaching out her fingers to grab one. It shot away too fast to register, and she laughed, head tilted back, tangled hair spilling over her shoulder. Everything was so *pretty*. So *sweet*. Like magic laced the very air here, made it easier to breathe. Well, in the few minutes when she wasn't terrified out of her damn mind. She liked being Fleur. Carefree, kissing princes, trying to catch fireflies.

Elladan led her to the nearby forest, dark and out of view, and pinned her against a thick tree trunk, the bark digging into her back through the low cut of her dress. The slight pain only heightened the sensations of Elladan pressing into her again, kissing her like he needed her more than air. He wrapped his arms around her waist and lifted her up, stepping between her thighs so Elora was straddling him. Elladan yanked her head back with a tug on her hair and trailed his lips over the sensitive skin on her neck, nipping slightly at her pulse point with his teeth. His nips grew into soft bites as Elora ran her hands through his short hair, breaths short and quick.

She pulled him closer, the solid length of him pressing against her. Her dress had ridden up around her thighs, leaving her perilously close to exposed, but she didn't care. She ground against him, needing the friction to ease the sudden ache between her legs, feeling the proof of how affected he was against her. The knowledge sent a rush of power through her. She whimpered slightly at the sensation of him rocking against her and it sounded dangerously like his name.

"Fuck," Elladan groaned against her skin. Elora half moaned in reply, sliding her hands down his toned chest to fumble with the fastening of his pants. She didn't care if the whole world saw them at this point, she wanted him so badly. No, she *needed* him -

Drum beats filled the air, steadily increasing in volume, startling them both from their lust filled daze. All around, fae took up a chant in a language Elora didn't know, but vaguely recognized from the games.

"Fuck!" Elladan's curse was very different from the same word he had used just moments before. Frustration straightened his spine and forced his body away from hers, slowly setting Elora down. Past his shoulder, she could see crowds from the valley moving towards something. Elora took a moment to readjust her dress and hoped to God her clothes hadn't stained with the moss from the bark. She took a few deep breaths to collect herself, starting when she noticed Elladan gazing down at her, lips parted as if he wanted to say something. Evidently, he decided against it as he shook his head and merely said, "The ceremony is starting soon, let's go."

The silence was as heavy as it was awkward, wrapping them together but keeping them impossibly separated while they walked in the direction of the other fae, farther into the dip of the valley. A cool breeze filtered through the drum beats and the fresh, clean air cleared Elora's head.

"Where are we going?" She asked, hoping to clear some of the tension that had risen between them.

"To the altar in the middle of the valley, where the ceremony takes place." Elladan didn't offer any further explanation and quickened his stride.

Elora shoved the pang of hurt that shot through her into a box at the back of her mind as the huge altar came into view.

The structure was shaped like a giant bowl, with knives placed carefully in equal intervals along the lip at the edge. Fae were gathered around it in a wide circle, but Elora couldn't find whoever was playing the drums even though the beats still filled the air with anticipation.

She watched in shock and awe as, one by one, the fae walked up to the altar. Without hesitation, they used the ceremonial knives to cut a clean wound across their palm or forearm and let a few heavy drops of blood fall into the bowl.

"Elladan," she hissed, heart racing She couldn't make herself look away, though the fine hairs on her arms stood on end, and her mouth was suddenly dry. "I don't have magic. What do I do?"

"Nothing should happen, you'll be fine. Just participate. It'll hardly hurt, and unless you want all the fae here finding out you're from the mortal realm and risk tearing yourself apart, you'll go to the altar and give a few drops of blood."

Elora gaped at him, throat tight, tongue refusing to argue back. What was she supposed to say to that?

Elladan took advantage of an opening at the bowl and quickly sliced his skin open, held his bleeding arm over the altar and walked away, swallowed by the crowd.

Elora was cautious of how unsanitary this entire process was, but her fear of being discovered won out in the end. Shoving Elladan's shitty and confusing treatment momentarily out of her mind, Elora promised that she would get his over with and somehow make it back to the castle to sleep this entire nightmare off.

The drum beats reverberated through her body as she arrived at the altar, and took the same knife Elladan had used not a minute before. It was heavy and warm in her palm, the blade sharp and clean. Her brow furrowed, but she could find no hint of blood, no matter how hard she studied it. Fae were closing in around her, others wanting to perform the renewal ritual for themselves, and the longer she stood there, panic eating up her determination, the more she risked being found out. The knife shook in her hand, but she took a deep breath and placed the cool blade against her left forearm. She closed her eyes, counted back from three and pressed down, slicing a shallow cut along her arm and watched hazily as a few drops of blood warmed her skin and took their time dripping into the giant bowl, leaving scarlet trails down her arm that cooled in the night air.

Someone approached from behind and she blinked, clutching the wound as she hurried away from the altar. She stopped at the edge of the crowd, unsure of where to go. She could see spires of Dioltas Castle in the distance, but hadn't the faintest idea of how to walk back in the dark.

She was contemplating looking for Elladan, as awful as he'd been, when the first cramp hit. A sharp, lancing pain pierced her stomach and Elora bent over gasping. Bullets of pain shot through her torso, chased by overwhelming dizziness and nausea. She dropped to her knees, contents of her stomach spilling onto the dew damp grass until everything went dark.

17

Aerin

"Áine above," Aerin rolled his eyes, sighing. "This is fucking ridiculous." He crumpled yet another sheet of paper scrawled with runes in his fist.

"Any more and it's going to be taller than you," Tarhael joked, looking at the pile of ruined paper with raised brows and idly spinning the shaft of his rhomphaia.

"Do you have to spin that in here? You're going to take my head off, or cut one of my books."

"You're in a touchy mood. I literally *have* to be here to guard you," Tarhael narrowed his eyes at him. "But I'm bored and you never go anywhere dangerous. I miss the days where we would sneak around the forbidden quarters."

"As soon as I hear any rumors of more lost tomes being hidden in the castle, you'll be the first to know. I just can't figure out this stupid runecast."

Pushing back his chair, Aerin stood up and stretched, the scowl on his face deepening.

"You scowl any more and you're gonna split that pretty face apart."

Letting out a short laugh, Aerin turned to face Tarhael. "Let's go outside. I need some fresh air."

The difference of air quality in the dingy basement and the castle grounds was remarkable. Aerin breathed in deeply as they stepped outside, inhaling the perpetual autumnal scents he'd grown up with. Today, the air carried the flavors of pomegranate, backed by the subtle yet strong scent of sandalwood. Hate his father as he may, Aerin had to admit that King Harkan had excellent taste.

"I just can't figure out the right wording," Aerin sighed, breaking the peace. "Without having Elora actually here, I can't test out the various runecasts, and the one I showed Elladan was only a temporary relaxant. She shouldn't be experiencing anything like Elladan claims she is."

"Do you think he's lying?" Tarhael asked, voice tense.

"Well, he won't let us see her. It's suspicious. I just don't get it. Elora said something about not having her medication, and the pixies said she's panicked before, but she's never just *collapsed*. The runecast I gave Elladan should have only really worked for two or three days at best, and wouldn't cause her to faint."

Tarhael fell into step besides Aerin and merely nodded, letting his friend express his frustrations.

"Athnuachan was the best time to get her home before anyone notices, and I'm getting absolutely nowhere with the Dohari Gates. We can still get her home but Elladan is making this impossible."

Tarhael's steps faltered and Aerin watched indecision play across his face as he opened his mouth to speak. "Truthfully, Aerin, I don't know why you're taking Elladan's word on anything here. I know you have the pixies reporting back but," he broke off, shaking his head. "I don't trust him not to hurt her, especially if she is who you think she is."

Aerin clenched his jaw. He didn't like the idea of Elladan having her in his grasp either, but what else could he do? He couldn't risk exposing her. If anyone else realized who she was and connected the dots with the prophecy, she'd be in much more danger than she was now. His stomach soured as he tried and failed to figure out how to help her.

They needed to get her home, out of Dioltas, and then balance would return. She could go back and forget this ever happened. And he…well…

He'd figure something out.

A pixie flitted by his head, startling him from his thoughts. She furtively dropped a small scroll in front of Tarhael, who reached out with lightning fast reflexes and caught it midair. The pixie was gone as fast as she came, and Aerin and Tarhael checked nobody was watching them before slowly unfurling the scroll. His eyes widened as he read the message, and Tarhael sucked in a deep breath.

Aerin stared hard at the small, loopy letters, heartbeat picking up. He looked at his friend, finding a similar state of distress on his face.

"Raewyn says there's a problem."

18

Elora

It wasn't the pain that woke Elora. No, it was the hurried footsteps, a male voice muttering unintelligible words, her closed eyelids turning red under a bright flash of light. The pain was secondary, slowly seeping into her bones until it rendered her breathless. Her head, she was sure, had been split open down the middle, a pulsing drum beat of agony pressing on her brain.

"Don't fucking question me."

The voice sounded familiar. Why did it sound familiar?

Someone whimpered.

Was it her? She couldn't tell. Her body was disconnected, a series of sharp pains and aches, her limbs leaden and lathered with pins and needles.

Something shifted beneath her and she tried to open her eyes to see, but her lids felt as though they were glued shut. It felt like a mattress, she thought. But why the hell would she be in bed? She was supposed to be going home -

Home. Maybe she'd been transported back? Maybe the journey had scrambled her memories. Maybe she had finally woken up from whatever fever dream caused her to believe in faeries -

But, no. She remembered the feel of the silk on her skin, the scent of blood in the air at the games, the soft, then urgent, crush of Elladan's lips, his body against hers. It all flashed behind her eyes, making her heart clench painfully.

She was shaken from her thoughts by the sound of flesh hitting flesh, the soft grunt of someone trying to catch their breath, the hissed inhale as a fist connected.

Fighting.

"Stay the fuck away, Aerin."

The name itched something in Elora's head, but she couldn't figure out why. Had she met him before?

"What are you *doing?*" another male voice, not as deep or harsh as the first, asked a little breathlessly.

"None of your concern." A strangled sort of noise was wrenched from what Elora assumed was the second man, and she fought with her useless body to sit up, scream, do something, *anything* as slick fear slid over her skin. "Stay in your lane, little brother. Remember your place. My actions are not for you to question."

Every word was short and lethal, like the letters had been sliced raw with his teeth. A shudder tore through Elora, her spine lifting off the bed as she shook.

"Leave." The creaking of hinges sliced through the air. "Now. Be glad I'm letting you walk away at all. Keep your fucking mouth shut, or I swear on the crown, I'll rip out your tongue."

Shit shit shit. Nausea twisted Elora's stomach and she choked on the bile building in her throat. The combination of pain, fear and dread was heady, and the fog in her brain thickened.

She couldn't move. Barely managed to twitch a damn finger. The need to get up, to run, to fight coursed through her, but she was helpless. Couldn't obey every instinct, despite how badly she wanted to.

"It's alright, beautiful."

A warm hand stroked her sweat damp hair away from her face. A finger traced the curve at the tip of her ear, then down the side of her throat, pausing over her collarbone.

"I'll take the pain away."

Terror had Elora's back rising from the bed again, her body fighting against the assault of pain and numbness, desperate to do whatever it took to not find out whatever the hell that meant.

"It's okay, gorgeous." The pad of his thumb pulled her bottom lip open, and she gritted her teeth despite the agony it sent along her jaw. He *tsked* quietly, his warm breath tickling her skin as he lent over her. Her damn eyes still wouldn't open. "Don't fight. It's okay. I'll make the pain go away."

She didn't care if he promised her the world, no part of her trusted what he was saying. A pathetic protest slipped past her lips, tongue refusing to move to form any words.

"Open up."

She clenched her jaw harder, but it was useless against him. Glass clinked against her teeth, and cold thick liquid spilled down her throat. She choked, coughing and sputtering, until the man propped her up, her limp body resting against him.

"Back to sleep, beautiful." His voice was so calm, too calm, why was he so calm? "I'll see you when you wake up. You'll be so happy to see me."

What the fuck is happening? Don't sleep don't sleep don't sleep. Elora recited the thought in her head over and over but darkness encroached, urging her to give in, to let it carry away the pain and worry.

She drowned in a sea of fear and darkness.

19

Fleur

"Fleur?"

Fleur blinked, watery early morning sunlight streaming in through the gap in the curtains. Áine above, her head hurt. What had she drunk last night?

"Fleur?"

Her hair was knotted and caught in her fingers when she tried to brush it out of her face. Who the hell was saying her name?

"Yes?" she called back, voice thick and sticky with sleep. She could taste stale wine on her tongue.

"Oh, good, you're awake." Elladan appeared in front of her, a tall glass of water in hand. Back lit by the sun, dressed as impeccably as ever, he looked every inch the hero prince he was. Something fluttered in her chest at the side of him. He handed her the glass and she gulped the contents down in one, the cool water soothing her raw throat.

"Thanks."

Elladan nodded and perched on the edge of the bed, the mattress dipping beneath his weight. He reached over to pluck the glass from her hand, balancing it on the side table before resting his hand on her knee. She tried to ignore the heat radiating from his palm, the way his thumb absently stroked lazy circles over the silk of her dress.

Wait. Her dress?

She flushed, looking down at the rumbled outfit, a dark stain on the edge of the skirt.

"How are you feeling?"

She frowned, hating how her skin felt sticky with sweat and spilt wine, all too aware of the messy mane of her hair.

"Umm," she mumbled as she fought for words. "I'm alright, thank you." She looked around the room, a frown forming a line between her brows. "Why am I in your room?"

Elladan smirked, and rubbed the back of his neck sheepishly. "Uh, well, you kind of passed out and this seemed like the safest place for you. So I could make sure you were alright. You're free to go back to your guest room, of course."

Fleur nodded and smiled a little. It was nice that he was taking care of her. He surprised her, this prince. She'd heard rumors of him in Zahra, of course: that he went through women like he went through wine, that he was stuck up, that he was devastatingly good looking. Well, the last one, Fleur confirmed, was true. She shook her head a little to clear her thoughts.

"Thank you for looking after me. Can you show me back to my room? I'd like to get cleaned up."

He nodded and extended his hand, helping her off the bed and giving her a pointed look over.

"How you look so beautiful in last night's clothes is a mystery to me."

A blush crept up her neck and she couldn't hide her smile. She accepted the arm he offered her and followed dutifully through the long castle halls to her guest room. She was sure she should remember the way, but she couldn't. In fact, it was as though she'd never seen this part of the castle before at all. Ridiculous. She shook her head again.

"Here we are, gorgeous."

He opened the heavy door for her, gesturing for her to enter. The room was open and spacious, with deep red accents, and a giant four poster bed. She tried to mask her surprise and act like she'd seen it before, not wanting to make a fool of herself. Her bags were waiting by the wardrobe for her to unpack fully, a few dresses hung over the back of the sofa from where she was picking out what to wear the night before.

"I really must have had too much to drink," she muttered, her head and memories fuzzy.

"Fleur?" Elladan called from the doorway, the sound of her name on his lips causing a riot of butterflies in her stomach. "When you're ready, it would be my honor if you'd come with me for a formal meeting with my father." He raised an eyebrow expectantly.

"Oh," she blinked, registering his words. "Right. Because we..." she trailed off, embarrassed. Because they were together. Because she was stupidly in love with him. She took the invite as a good sign. Maybe Elladan really did feel the same about her.

He was polite enough to hide his smirk by glancing at the floor, bowing a little at her before he left, leaving her to clean up.

She'd tried on five of her dresses before she settled on the first. Her nerves were driving her crazy and she forced herself to stop chewing on her lip before it bled. She was used to royalty, used to court politics, so why was this sending her heart racing? Maybe it was because of the King of Autumn's reputation, but maybe, more likely, it was because this was Elladan's *father*.

"Get it together," she chastised herself, readjusting her hair so the silver cuffs at the pointed tip of her ears poked through the loose waves.

"Are you ready, Fleur?" Elladan appeared at the door behind her and she spun so fast she nearly lost her balance. She cursed herself internally. For as long as she could remember, she'd lacked the natural grace of the other fae.

He walked her through the castle with an ease and elegance she was fascinated by. Everything about him was cool and calculated, from the clean shave of his jaw, to the suit without a single wrinkle in it. She wondered if he was tired. It must be exhausting, she thought, to be so perfect all the time.

She wondered if she could make him come undone.

She was snapped back to the present by a guard in royal uniform opening the grand double doors of the throne room and announcing their presence. Elladan had to lean over and tell the guard her name, *Fleur Atwater of the Zahra Kingdom.* Why did her title sound so hollow?

"Son."

The King's voice rang loud and strong through the air, taking up every inch of the room. A shiver ran down Fleur's spine. The man sat on a raised ornate, golden throne crusted with jewels, the crown on his head so bright it hurt to look at. He looked nothing like his son, Fleur thought. His hair was dark, yes, but his eyes were a pale green, and his skin was paler than Elladan's. No queen sat beside him. Fleur wondered if she had looked more like her son than her husband did.

"Father." Elladan sketched a quick bow and Fleur followed with a curtsy, begging herself not to stumble this time.

"What's the occasion? You don't normally bring your girls to meet me."

Fleur bristled at that, tightening her grip on Elladan's arm. He ignored it, his cool, unruffled expression still firmly in place.

"We're courting, father."

The King's laugh was so loud Fleur wanted to cover. She made herself stand tall, forced a pleasant smile onto her pink lips and refused to let her hurt show. Sure, she hadn't been seeing Elladan for long, it'd only been...

Fuck. How long *had* it been?

"Elladan," the King continued, leaning forward to rest his elbows on his knees as he surveyed her. "I've never even heard of this *Fleur Atwater* before you started dragging her around a few days ago. I have to question your story, son."

Elladan stiffened, his jaw clenching visibly. Defensively, he put his arm around Fleur's waist and tugged her to his side. She softened slightly, but still planted her feet firmly on the ground, determined not to show weakness. How dare this man question who she was? Just because she'd never been to his kingdom before. She'd never seen him in Zahra, and yet she wasn't insulting him because of it. Anger flared in her stomach, and she met his eyes unflinchingly.

"Pretty," the King acknowledged, talking to Elladan as though she wasn't there. "Although normally you go for blondes." Fleur clenched her fist at her side, hating being compared to anyone else. "What about the suitors I had lined up for you? Those girls are much more suitable-"

"I don't want those girls," Elladan argued back, his voice never changing from the bored tone he'd taken up when they entered. "I want Fleur."

"This is not about what you *want*." The King pushed to his feet and Fleur fought the urge to move away. He pointed a thick finger at Elladan, eyes hard and mouth set in an unforgiving line. "This is about the kingdom, Elladan. You are selfish, foolish-"

"I have made my choice." Elladan stared down his father, grip tightening painfully around Fleur's waist. "Come on, beautiful. We've said what we needed to say."

The King blustered at their backs as Elladan led Fleur out of the throne room, arm around her all the while, and she only took a deep breath when the doors slammed closed behind them.

Neither of them spoke as they walked back to her room. Elladan, out of anger and Fleur out of confusion and annoyance.

She was so caught up in her thoughts that she walked straight into a solid body, only saved from falling by Elladan's grasp.

"Shit," she cursed, trying to gather her composure. "Sorry."

She did a double take when she saw who it was she'd bumped into. The man was tall, with shoulder length black hair that Fleur had the absurd urge to run her fingers through. His eyes were the same striking green as the King's, only darker.

Fleur had no idea who he was.

"Aerin," Elladan said, the name sounding like a curse in his mouth.

Oh, Fleur thought a little sadly. Clearly the two didn't get along.

"Elladan," Aerin returned through gritted teeth. "Elora."

Who the hell is Elora? Fleur's eyebrows drew together as she racked her brain for any memory of meeting someone with that name. Maybe Aerin had got her mixed up with a girl from the night before. Aerin turned to meet her eyes and she inhaled sharply. The skin around the man's right eye was a deep purple, bruising spreading down onto his cheekbone. That had to have *hurt*.

Elladan grabbed Fleur's wrist and began walking away without another glance at Aerin and she rushed to keep up.

"What you're doing is beyond fucked up, Elladan." Aerin's voice echoed after them, chilling Fleur to the bone. "Even for you."

Elladan paid the remark no heed, loosening his grip on Fleur's wrist and shooting an apologetic glance down at her.

"Sorry," he sighed as they closed the bedroom door behind them, out of earshot of the rest of the castle. "Pay him no mind."

Fleur's brow furrowed. "Who is he?"

"Nobody important, beautiful," Elladan assured her, pulling her close and wrapping his strong arms around her. Despite her confusion and residual anger, Fleur sank into him, relishing the closeness.

"Okay."

He dropped a kiss onto her head, and she breathed in the warm spice scent of his clothes.

"I have to go," he told her reluctantly. "Princely duties call."

She nodded and forced herself to step away from his grip. She was already mourning the loss of his arms as he turned and left her alone.

20

Fleur

leur remembered Raewyn. Who could forget the lovely pixie and her overprotective motherly qualities? Raewyn fussed over her as usual, closely helped by her small army of pixies. They flew around, gorgeous wings dappled in the sunlight. Each pixie had a different colored set of wings: Raewyn's an orange that reminded her of vibrant sunsets, Lydia's a stunning deep purple, Elise's a pale pink that she'd matched with her dress. Working as quickly as they did, they looked like a rainbow tornado buzzing around her as they did her makeup and fixed her hair.

"What do you want for breakfast dear?"

"Hmm... I'd like some oatmeal - I mean porridge." *What the hell was oatmeal, and why had she said it?* "And some eggs, softly scrambled and strawberries too. And that purple tea that tastes like violets!" She offered a sunny smile, despite Raewyn's alarmed expression.

Raewyn stared at her for a moment before disappearing with a few others to grab the food. She came back much quicker than Fleur had anticipated, the pixies all holding the tray between them and a tall, muscular man in guard uniform in tow. He stood at the door, even as Raewyn pushed it shut in his face, trapping him in the hallway.

FLEUR

They chatted politely about the weather and upcoming parties while she ate, the conversation pleasant but stilted.

Raewyn didn't take her eyes off her the whole time, watching every bite she took with unnerving interest, mouth pursed and a tiny line between her furrowed brows. Fleur tried to ignore the scrutiny, but the pixie's bright blue eyes bore into her. She bit her lip and sipped her tea, a strange sensation of loss building in her chest.

She tried to ignore that, too.

"May we go to the library?"

"Not right now. Prince Elladan wanted me to show you the royal gardens, but maybe after that okay? There's a big meeting there today, and visitors aren't allowed."

Fleur frowned. The library hadn't seemed busy at all when they'd passed earlier. There was only the usual amount of scholars she remembered reading and studying, but Raewyn would never lie to her, right?

"Excuse me. You are needed at once." A brusque voice interrupted their brisk walk, startling Fleur and the pixies. "There has been an accident in the lower levels and several of the machines for laundry and the kitchen have been broken. We need all the Tinker Fae to help immediately. Ambassadors from Winter are due tomorrow and we can't afford to lose time."

Raewyn sighed and flitted up to the lanky and out of breath messenger that fought to keep his composure as he tried to calm his wheezing. "Fleur, stay here honey. I'm going to go meet with some of my Tinker Fae and get this mess sorted out. Don't go anywhere, okay? Stay right here."

Fleur watched Raewyn and her pixies follow the messenger fae away, unsure of what to do. Was she really supposed to just stand there in the hall? She looked around, the bright autumn colors splashed against white walls looking much more familiar then they had earlier. It brought a strange sense of calm to her - at least her stupid brain was rebooting itself after the drinks on Athnauchan. She still felt hazy, like she was trying to catch up with everyone else, but the fog was clearing ever so slightly.

Fleur was wondering if there was at least a chair she could wait in when a small blue bird flew in through an open window and landed near her. It's bright blue feathers were shot through with streaks of ashy gray and its plumage was far different from any other Fleur had ever seen. It's stunning blue eyes bore into her as it turned its head in her direction. The bird cocked its head and gazed at her inquisitively, as if challenging her. The soft flutter of features filled the air as the bird moved to settled down behind her, prompting Fleur to turn around. She held its gaze, confused but pleased for the distraction, until her patience ran out.

"Well, what do you want with me?"

The blue bird stared at her without blinking for a few more seconds and then flew a few feet away to the edge of the windowsill and turned to look at her again. Fleur bit her bottom lip, blinking at the creature as it flapped its wings.

"Do you want me to follow you?"

The bird chirped, the sound sweet and light. Fleur laughed and followed a few steps, obliging it. They repeated this process until Fleur was on the verge of exiting the castle through one of the smaller side entrances. She hesitated, remembering Raewyn's orders. A quick foray outside wouldn't hurt would it? She promised herself that she would be back in a minute, long before Raewyn returned.

She followed the little bird out of the castle and into the courtyard garden where golden sunlight was streaming through over the high brick walls. The garden had all manners of flowers and plants blooming, all trapped in a perpetual state of autumn - leaves half wilted, some petals soft beneath her feet.

Elladan said I've been here numerous times, but his father doesn't recognize me and I don't remember these gardens at all. In fact, the courtyard unsettled her slightly, an uneasy sense of foreboding chilling her skin. It was as though the plants couldn't decide whether they were dying or thriving and the perpetual reminder of their fragility sent a chill down Fleur's spine. The bird was flying again, hopping from tree to tree and Fleur hurried after it, pushing the unpleasant thoughts from her mind. The bird continued the merry little chase until Fleur was at the heart of the garden. She stopped short, shock rooting her to the spot. The stranger Elladan had been so cross with stood before her, shirtless and dripping with sweat. Aerin, Fleur recalled. His muscles rippled beneath his tanned, tattooed skin as he moved through various martial arts sequences, his face tight with concentration. He wasn't as bulky as Elladan, but was clearly fit - all lean muscle and smooth movements. He moved with a certain feline grace that both fascinated and scared her. She could sense the danger he posed, the fluid deadliness of his routine, even from her distance. Fleur managed to shift her gaze up away from his abs and found herself equally as fascinated by his green eyes that sparkled in the sunlight, emerald one moment and turquoise the next. She observed him for a few more moments before deciding that the official color was shamrock green.

"Hey!" Aerin's sharp voice startled her and she jumped back, falling on her ass and she hastily scrambled back up, brushing away the dirt and leaves. "What are you doing here?"

"I...um..the bird. The blue bird!" Fleur frantically cast her gaze around for the little blue bird that had led her here, but it was nowhere to be found.

"You mean this one?" Aerin lifted his hand and the bird flew down, perching on his outstretched fingertips. "Well, *Fleur* -" he said her name with near sarcastic emphasis that had set on edge - "this is Blueberry, my pet bird. I don't know why he brought you here, but I think you should get back before anyone notices that you're missing."

"Oh uh right…" Fleur trailed off, biting her bottom lip, feeling suddenly very exposed as Aerin stared her down. Even standing with a damned bluebird perched on his hand, he cast an imposing (albeit annoyingly attractive) figure. "Yes." She swallowed thickly, darting her gaze around. Despite the unsettling state of the flowers, the air was crisp and clean and the sky was so clear there was barely a wisp of cloud. She didn't want to leave, to return to the oppressive brick walls of the castle, the stifling sense of uncertainty the rooms infested her with. "It's just so…lovely…out here and Elladan said I'd been here before but I don't remember it at all and I'd like to take it in some more." She was scrambling and they both knew it. Fleur slowly spun in place, taking in the flowers nearly as tall as her and the nearby chirping of birds.

Aerin dropped the hand that he'd been idly running through his long hair and closed his eyes, taking a deep breath. He didn't say anything while he tied up his hair into a sort of bun and he breathed in deeply again before looking directly at Fleur, as if steeling himself.

"We need to get you back. I don't know how you managed to get here without anyone noticing, but-"

"Wait - are those bruises on your arm?" Fleur interjected, concern flaring in her voice. "What happened?" Upon closer inspection, she could see the purple and blue bruises that mottled his upper stomach, chest and arms. She didn't know how she'd missed them before. "These bruises are fresh."

"It's just training exercises. You know, sparring and such. Not a big deal."

Aerin tried to play it off, but Fleur had noticed the slight hesitation as he had answered, and she pressed him again.

"No, I don't think you told me everything. What's going-"

"I said I'm fine. I just had a hard spar, that's all." Aerin's voice noticeably dropped lower and harsher as he spoke. "I see," was all Fleur replied, pressing her lips together into a flat line as though fighting back emotion. "I best get going then."

"Hey beautiful, miss me?" Elladan's voice brought Fleur back to the present, away from the conversation with Aerin she'd been replaying in her head.

"Yes, hi. How was your day?"

"Just the usual, boring princely stuff."

"Do you want to talk about it while we wait for dinner?" Fleur glanced up at him, a small smile on her lips. "How come we always dine here, together, instead of in the dining hall?"

"You have so many questions today, gorgeous. I just adore spending time with you, that's all. Now, where did we leave off this morning?"

Elladan stepped forward and swept her up in his arms, leaning in to kiss her. Fleur returned the kiss happily, but while she wanted to do nothing but melt in his arms, she couldn't get the nagging questions to leave her mind and his change of subject hadn't gone unnoticed.

"Hold on, Elladan. I mean it. You've told me that I've been here, but your father doesn't remember me and I don't even remember the gardens or anything. I keep feeling this sense of deja vu and-"

Fleur was abruptly cut off, Elladan's lips crashing into hers. She was so surprised she couldn't react for a moment as Elladan wrapped his arms around her hips and hoisted her back onto the bed she had been relaxing on. He pressed into her, hand sliding up her shirt.

"Elladan, stop! I mean it, I'm not in the mood. Get off!" Fleur pushed him and his confused look hardened into anger.

"What did you just say to me?" His voice was a whisper, but she could feel the steel edge in his voice.

"I-I'm just tired and confused today Elladan, it's-"

"Nobody tells me no. Nobody."

Elladan stepped back into Fleur's space, his huge frame looming over her, blotting out the sun that had streamed in through the window. He wore a smile, but it was feral - all teeth and intent. Slowly raising his hands, he stroked Fleur's hair and wiped the single tear sliding down her cheek.

A knock at the door gave Elladan pause.

"Who is it?" he barked.

"It's me, Raewyn, sir. There's been an incident with one of the visiting dukes from Winter, not sure which kingdom yet. He got into an argument with one of our barons and things turned violent."

"Just get the guards to deal with it."

"It would be a tad awkward to have our guards manhandle nobility of a higher rank, from either Season sir."

Elladan swallowed an audible snarl and stalked away, slamming the door open and shoving past Raewyn as he left. The pixies rushed in, trying to comfort her, but Fleur too, brushed past them and ran in search of some fresh air, heart pounding so hard she could hear it, the walls closing in on her as she sprinted.

Out. She needed out. *Now.*

21

Aerin

Aerin hadn't meant to yell at her. She'd interrupted him, all innocent doe eyes and concern, and frustration had taken him over. It was a novel concept - concern, especially from a relative stranger, and it had sent something sharp through his chest. He glanced down now, half expecting to find a bleeding wound. Actually, that might have been more comfortable.

He didn't know how to help her, and it hurt that *she* wanted to help *him*. She shouldn't have been concerned about anything except herself, but there she'd been, questioning his bruises and casually mentioning that she couldn't remember the bloody gardens.

His body ached, a combination of exhaustion and the beating Elladan had given him when he'd interrupted the ritual he'd performed on the half fae girl. He should have known better than to think force would work with his brother. Elladan had always been physically stronger - more muscle than brain, Aerin sometimes thought - but he hadn't paused to think it through before he burst into his bedchambers, intent on stopping him. Instead, all he'd got was a bruised body. Elora was no better off than if he'd not bothered at all. Anger and guilt swept through him in an agonizing torrent.

He hadn't trusted his brother for years, but he never believed he'd go *this* far. And, perhaps the worst part was, he couldn't figure out why he'd done it at all. Aerin had sent Tarhael after her when he could - instructed him to watch from a distance and report back - and the pixies were with her constantly, but nobody had told him of Elladan's plans. Surely, they couldn't *all* have missed it?

He stood sharply, scattering the paper on his desk. He couldn't afford to delay it much longer. Áine only knew how Elladan had hurt her now that she didn't remember herself. The thought made him sick. His messy, quickly made plan would have to be enough.

Someone knocked at the door, the distinct pattern and forceful pounding telling him it was Tarhael.

Aerin yanked the door open with more force than was strictly necessary. Tarhael stormed in, locking the door behind him and stopping in the middle of the room, throwing his hands in the air.

"What is it?" Aerin's whole body felt tense and on edge.

"You better have a fucking plan, Aerin," Tarhael warned, voice laced with frustration. His jaw was clenched so tight it looked painful. Aerin waited for an explanation, pacing in front of his friend. "Raewyn just had to intercept them in his bedchamber. He was...Áine above, she won't survive him. Not after what he's done to her mind and what he'll put her through. We need to get her out."

Aerin forced himself to breathe past his anger.

"You know what it means for us if we get her out," Aerin told him, running a hand through his hair.

"I know."

"We may never be able to come back."

"I know."

"Tarhael I'm serious-"

"Aerin." Tarhael interrupted, grabbing him by the shoulders and pausing his pacing. Aerin glared at him, muscles tense. "I know. This

AERIN

place is only home if you're here. There's no question that I'm coming with you."

Aerin relaxed slightly, Tarhael's words softening his guilt. He nodded sharply and moved back to the desk, grabbing his leather notebook and turning to his friend.

"This is what I need you to do."

22

Fleur

Fleur was basking in the evening breeze, watching the sun bid the world farewell for the night when she heard a rustling from above. The same little blue bird that had led her to Aerin perched atop one of the pillars of the balcony, staring directly at her.

"You again?" Fleur asked, happy to see the bird once more. "Aerin called you Blueberry, so good evening to you Blueberry. Maybe you can calm me down."

Her pulse had calmed now, but the clawing urge to wash every part of her Elladan had touched remained. But the thought of returning to her room to do so made a swell of panic build in her chest, so for now she just lay on the grass, taking stock of her body, reassuring herself that she was still here. She was still here and she was okay. She was okay, right?

Blueberry cocked his head to the side again and flew closer to Fleur, landing next to her feet. She rose up on her knees to get closer and Blueberry trilled, a melodic voice that surprised Fleur with how it made her heart clench. Blueberry sang, the notes vibrating, hanging until she could almost *see* the music dissolve into the air.

"That's very pretty Blueberry," she cooed. "You're just full of surprises, aren't you?" Her voice sounded distant, like she couldn't quite bring herself to speak properly just yet.

Blueberry's response was to trill his music even louder, providing an outlet for everything Fleur had felt during the day. His music matched her mood, bouncing around from confusion to sadness to exhaustion. She felt like she was missing something she couldn't even remember and was frustrated beyond belief with the entire mess of the day. She didn't know what was going on with Elladan, or why her memories were so hazy, or why she felt so lost, but Blueberry's music melted the cage around her heart and tears began to flow freely. She was Fleur Atwater of the Zahra kingdom. She had seven siblings, but why did she feel like she didn't know any of them? She had magic of nature and life. Why did she not remember how to perform any of it? Why couldn't she remember so much as her bedroom at home?

I'm be losing my mind. Fleur put her face in her hands and let go, sobbing. She let it all go while Blueberry showered her in his mournful music.

"Fleur Atwater?"

"You're back rather quickly, Raewy-" Fleur cut herself off as she noticed the imposing figure taking up the balcony door. "You're not Raewyn," was all she managed to say. *Of course that's not Raewyn, you idiot.*

"Sorry to disappoint ma'am. My name is Tarhael, guard to - I mean, one of the royal guards."

She turned to face him fully, frantically wiping at her cheeks, her body heavy and rusty. Tarhael was so tall she had to tilt her head back to take him in. He was dressed in the same uniform all the guards wore, but he made it look impressive. He was obviously strong, the muscles in his arms visible through his jacket, and his dark eyes were narrowed in question at her. His black, tight curls were cut close to his scalp, his dark skin smooth and annoyingly perfect. He was handsome - full lips, strong jaw, dark brows raised at her. *Dammit* did everyone in this bloody castle have to look like a fucking god?

"Oh, um, well how may I help you?" Fleur replied, hastily rising from her knees.

"I'm glad to see you've met Blueberry. The sly bastard feeds off your emotions and amplifies them with his song. Part of his enchantment long ago, I think." Tarhael shrugged, smiling wide. "I need to pay better attention to when Prince Aerin goes off on his tangents about Eolas."

"Did you say Prince Aerin?"

"Yes ma'am, Prince Aerin. He is Prince Elladan's younger brother."

"Oh... I don't think he's ever told me that. I was with Elladan this morning when we ran into him, and there was so much animosity..." Fleur shifted on her feet, remembering the thick tension between the brothers.

"That's an understatement," Tarhael said, his laugh not sounding amused at all. "Anyway, don't worry too much about your tears. Like I said, Blueberry feeds off your emotions. Happens to the best of us." She'd known him for all of two seconds, but Tarhael radiated a calm, comforting energy that had her relaxing. His smile was so friendly it was impossible not to return, though hers felt tight and awkward. She hid her shock as she realized she recognized him from the crowd of guards earlier. He'd been staring at her. The calmness she'd felt in his presence dissipated quickly.

Blueberry abandoned his post beside her to perch on Tarhael's shoulder. She was sure her face was splotchy and knew her makeup was ruined but she didn't care. She ached with the weight of the day and she was beyond caring whether a stranger was judging her for it or not. Besides, Tarhael didn't seem to mind. Now that she was closer, she could see drops of sweat glistened on the skin that wasn't covered by his heavy leather clothes and armor, and he gazed at Fleur with an intensity that sent slight shivers down her spine.

"Um, so why are you here?" Fleur didn't know how else to ask it. She worried it sounded blunt but…well…

"Yes, right. Prince Aerin was wondering if you would be able to help him with a certain script that he's been working on. I'm not too sure about the specifics of the entire project, but as you may know, Spring and Autumn generally haven't gotten along very well in recent times, so Prince Aerin isn't very picky about how he gets his help. Discreetly of course."

"I'm sorry, this is all a little much to take in." *Spring and Autumn don't get along?* She supposed it made sense - with the whole Seelie, Unseelie divide, but still it seemed odd that she and Elladan were seeing each other if there was such tension between their kingdoms. Why didn't she know about this? *Prince Aerin wants help with what?* "What, ah, does he actually want?"

"Well, you know how Blueberry is directly linked to his soul marks instead of normal castings?"

"Can you pretend that you're explaining all of this to someone with no knowledge?" Seeing the incredulous look on Tarhael's face, Fleur quickly clarified. "I've struggled with Eolas a lot since I was little, and I actually haven't used it much in recent years, so it might be better for all of us if you can give me a little refresher." *Gods, I hope that's believable. But what else can I say? I have no idea what the bloody hell he's talking about.* She was spiraling. She dug her nails into the palms of her hands, grounding herself.

"…Sure," Tarhael replied slowly, voice full of skepticism. "Runecasting is the informal all purpose name for writing in Eolas." He pulled something out of his belt - a small multicolored pencil and a roll of paper. He walked over to the rail and began writing. Tarhael mouthed the runes as he wrote, left hand tapping the railing as he did so. He breathed over what he wrote and looked at her, brows raised as if to say *any moment now.* A cool breeze washed over the both of them, gentle in its caress and careful in its hug. The air swirled around them for a moment before dying down and Fleur's eyes widened in surprise.

"Just the simple runecast for air," Tarhael said. "Don't look so impressed. Anyway, runecasting is something that all fae can do. Depending on what season you're born into, each fae is gifted with a certain set of powers, almost always two. Each Season is associated with an element. I'm from an Autumn kingdom not far from here, and Autumn has affinities to air. I possess the power to move things with my mind, known as telekinesis. I can also summon and shape the wind. But nobility, particularly royalty, are also gifted with another set of powers. They get two runes carved on their body, allowing them to have several more types of magic under their belt. As the royal guards are required to be of nobility, I also possess two additional powers from the carvings on my back. I can ease stress on the mind, basically calm people down, essentially accelerating and delaying growth. That is usually primarily used for healing, but as Autumn doesn't get along well with Spring, it's kind of a useless ability at the moment. My second ability is manipulating the air, summoning and shaping the air to my liking. Are you with me so far?"

Fleur nodded, and it was only half a lie. She was doing her best to take it all in.

"Alright, when you want to do some basic magic, you need to create runes. Runes are written manifestation of Eolas, otherwise known as the *language of all living things*, which sounds a little pretentious if you ask me." Tarhael chuckled. "I'm honestly the worst person to tell you the intricacies, and I know nobody better than Aerin to explain fully. But all you really need to know is that we fae have the ability to convert runes into specific magical activities. Like I was saying, for an Autumn fae like me, I write something, in my case with this pencil-"

"Why does the lead have so many colors?" Fleur cut him off.

"Well, each of the four seasons is tied to various powers and an element, as Áine decreed it," Tarhael replied, the look on his face narrowed in concentration as if he was trying to remember a lecture. "Autumn fae write runes in colored ink to represent the invisibility and indifference of air. We write it down like this, and the Eolas takes hold." Tarhael scribbled more runes on his paper, breathed out over them, and the leaves lying scattered around on the balcony all came to life, levitating in the air. Fleur couldn't keep her gasp in as she watched the leaves float through the air, moving in all directions. They began to converge on Fleur, slowly but surely picking up speed, each leaf performing a complex dance in the air around her. Blueberry began his song, and the leaves danced in the wind to the tune, forming shapes: a flower, a lion, and *was that a dragon?*

She didn't know how long the show lasted for, only that she was sad when it ended, each leaf lazily floating back to the floor.

"Pretty neat huh?" Tarhael asked. "It's my favorite party trick whenever anyone asks. Oh, please, you don't have to look so stunned," he drawled, noticing Fleur's open mouthed stare. "Plenty of people can do much better than me. Anyway, like I was saying, we're usually given two sets of powers we're able to manipulate, but how creatively we can apply them depends on the runes we can come up with." Tarhael tapped the side of his temple for emphasis.

"Y-yeah," Fleur stammered out, still amazed at what she had seen. There was a slow, sinking feeling in her gut, though, that warned her something was wrong. Why didn't she know *any* of this? Where the hell were her memories? "Why did you breathe over them?" She hoped that the question wouldn't give her away.

"Well, just like how Spring fae bury their runecasts to activate them, the Autumn fae breathe over them. The Winter fae activate their runecasts by pouring water over them, and the Summer burn theirs. Different activation methods for different seasons. That's the gist of everything though, I think. Ah, before I forget, yes. Aerin and Blueberry actually share a bond. He's tattooed on Aerin's back. A little different from the other runes that Aerin has, but a magical bird nonetheless."

"I see, yes, I do remember some of this stuff now." Fleur tried to sound convincing but saw the doubtful look in Tarhael's eyes and didn't know what else she could do. An empty sort of feeling hollowed her out.

"I hope that answered some of your questions. Like I said, Prince Aerin does want to discuss some aspects of a runecast he has been working on, and apparently needs Spring fae expertise. Blueberry will be in contact whenever Prince Aerin asks for your help." It was obvious in the way he looked at her that Tarhael didn't believe she could be of help to Prince Aerin for even one second, but he was ever the professional soldier dutifully relaying his orders. "I hope you'll be discreet about the meeting tomorrow night. I'm afraid Prince Elladan wouldn't be too happy if he found out."

All Fleur could do was nod. Tarhael gave her a graceful bow and disappeared through the balcony doors, Blueberry perched on his shoulder.

Fleur stayed long after the stars had come out to play, wondering why all of this seemed so new to her. She could almost feel the gaps in her memory, but pressing them felt like prodding a bruise - tender and aching. It made her flinch. The awkward, clumsy, lingering feeling of unfamiliarity haunted her. The word *home* felt like a punch to the gut. Home was supposed to be here. Fior Domhan. But this strange place didn't feel like home at all.

23

Aerin

The stacks of books and piles of scrolls weren't making it any easier for Aerin to find what he needed. Soft chimes rang out and he counted them under his breath. Eight. It wouldn't be long before Elladan arrived. He wasn't ready to see him. Then again, he was never really ready for a confrontation with his brother.

Gazing down at the cryptic prophecies arrayed before him, Aerin read the words over and over again. The answers seemed just out of reach, and his head pounded as he went over the facts for the hundredth time. It was obvious Elora wasn't from here. But no mortal had set foot in the fae realm since the assassination of Queen Endra's husband over twenty years ago. But before that…no mortal had ever been welcomed inside Fior Domhan in hundreds of years.

Regardless of the intricacies, Aerin had a more pressing problem, one that made nausea roll his stomach and guilt sweep over his skin. He didn't know how but Elladan had twisted the calming runecast he had devised for him, turning it into something far more sinister. Something that Aerin didn't even fully understand yet.

A brief knock at his chamber door shook Aerin from his thoughts, and from the pattern Aerin could tell it was Tarhael, not Elladan. *Thank Áine.*

"Come in."

Tarhael's massive frame took up most of the doorway, momentarily blotting out the light from the hall beyond.

"Do you have to cramped up in this hall? This is the basement for Aine's sake Aerin. I'm too tall for this shit," he frowned, indicating to the ceiling bare inches from his head.

"This room being in the basement is exactly why I need to be here. Why would father ever come down here? Besides, Lydia sneaks me as many snacks as I want." He tried to sound lighthearted and failed miserably, anger clipping his words. Tarhael noticed, Aerin knew, but played along anyway, making small talk in an attempt to diffuse the tension in the air.

Tarhael cast a critical eye over the tiny room." This room is smaller than my bathroom, and that's saying something. But I do suppose it has a certain 'Aerin-ness'. How do you know where anything ever is?"

"Shouldn't you be doing your job? Guarding?" a deep voice cut through the conversation, laden with disdain. Elladan stood in the doorway, staring at Tarhael with amusement in his eyes. "Tarhael right? Son of Maximus and Priscilla? I would say you slept your way to the top, but you certainly do have a guard's build." Elladan chuckled, his grin never quite reaching his dark eyes. Shifting his feet, he lazily flicked one finger in the air, the dismissal apparent.

"Prince," Tarhael bowed his head and marched back out of Aerin's little study. Elladan watched him until he turned the corner and was gone from sight.

"I cannot believe father assigned him to your retinue, but then again, he probably had no idea you were fucking him. The funny things is-"

AERIN

"Never bring up his parents again," Aerin cut in, voice low. "What's wrong with you? Why can't you ever-"

A burst of pain bloomed on Aerin's right cheek. The slap had him seeing stars as he blinked against the shot. His ears rang and his eyes blurred. Elladan stood close to him, fury written across his face.

"Don't interrupt me."

Aerin nodded mutely, pressing his hand to his cheek and glaring at his brother. It wasn't worth the argument, not when he needed Elladan to listen to him. The last time Elladan had properly struck him was years ago. Before his carvings. Well, besides when he had confronted him about Elora a few nights ago. It shouldn't surprise him, the casual violence, but it still sent a spiral of grief through his chest.

Elladan leaned against the wall, arms crossed over his chest. "I saw Tarhael lurking around Elora earlier. I don't know what you've told him, nor do I care. It's not like that orphan has any power, but I want him to stay away from her. If I see him near her again..." he trailed off, as if considering his options. "Just know that there won't be a second warning." Elladan gave a contemptuous glance around at Aerin's study before turning around to leave. Aerin gritted his teeth. He knew fine well that Elladan could lobby their father into getting rid of Tarhael. Aerin was prince in title only, as far as his father and Elladan were convinced. His standing never gave him any sway with the king.

"Elladan," Aerin called after him, moving to follow his brother. Elladan paused at the entrance, back still turned to him. "What are your plans for her?"

"Whatever do you mean, brother?"

I have to play this carefully. I can't blow Raewyn's cover. "I haven't seen her for days. Where is she?"

"Since when did you care for her?"

Since I discovered her in the forest. Since I've been trying to help find a way to replicate the medication she needs. Since I began to fear what you're going to do to her. "She's the child of the prophecy. We both suspect it. It puts her in danger, so I'm going to ask you one more time. What are you doing to her?"

Elladan turned slowly. "Do you think I've hurt her?"

Aerin was silent as Elladan laughed, the sound devoid of warmth.

"What kind of monster do you take me for Aerin? Áine above, I would never dream of injuring a prophesied one."

But you would do it to my best friend. Aerin sighed, clearly getting nowhere with this line of questioning. He didn't trust his brother for a second. His words were too carefully planned, too cold. "We need to figure out what her arrival means, and I have a few other runecasts-"

Aerin dodged the next blow, ducking and moving quickly, putting the chair between them to stop Elladan advancing again. His brother seethed, but uncurled his fist and remained where he was.

"I'll take care of Elora," Elladan said. "I suggest you stay out of it and away from her, unless you'd like me to tell father who she really is?"

The threat hung between them, heavy and cloying. Aerin stared, open mouthed at his brother. He hadn't thought he'd want to reveal her identity, least of all to their father, considering what the backlash would be. Apparently, he'd underestimated him.

Elladan grinned, his laugh echoing off the stone walls as he sauntered out.

Aerin forced air into his lungs, dizzy with the blow of Elladan's words. There was no way he would leave Elora in Elladan's grasp, but he had to be careful not to hurt her even more.

And he was running out of time.

24

Fleur

"What's all this for?" A line of confusion appeared between Fleur's brows as she studied the intricate silver bracelet wrapped around her wrist. Raewyn sighed, the sound seeming far too loud to come from such a small woman, and crossed her arms over her chest.

"The Solstice Ball," Raewyn repeated, padding a fluffy brush into the tin of pale pink blush. "It marks the end of Athnuachan. It's basically just yet another excuse to drink and socialize, although much less feral than the renewal ceremony." She raised a red eyebrow pointedly and Fleur turned her head to allow her to brush blush across her cheekbones.

"I don't remember Elladan saying anything about a ball," she mused, watching the other pixies lay out a stunning lavender colored gown. She'd returned late the night before, somehow both hollow and heavy, and slept until she was woken with the order to get ready. She'd missed breakfast and the sun was high enough that she knew it was past noon, but she couldn't find it in herself to care. The mention of Elladan had her hiding a wince. The thought of seeing him again sent nausea through her.

Raewyn's frown only lasted a second but Fleur swore she saw a spark of worry in her pale blue eyes. "You must have forgotten," she insisted, though she sounded like she wanted to say more. Fleur only shrugged a little, the bubble of worry that had been slowly growing all morning rising in her throat. Maybe she needed a healer, someone to tell her what was wrong with her mind. It surely wasn't normal to forget this much. Maybe it was just an aftereffect of the renewal ceremony or...

"Will the king be there?" she asked, changing the subject as Raewyn plucked a pink rose from the bunch of dried flowers she'd brought and began to weave it into Fleur's hair, securing it in place with a shiny clip in the shape of a leaf.

"Oh, yes. All the royals will."

"So...my parents, too?"

Raewyn didn't answer, quick fingers making fast work of her hair. Fleur didn't press her question, scared that she'd made a fool of herself. After last night, she vowed she'd get Elladan to bring her to the castle healer. Her stomach clenched. The little hairs on the back of her neck stood on end, her nerves on high alert. He'd scared her yesterday, in a way she'd never been scared before. His words had played on loop in her head all day, a sorry, repetitive track of *nobody ever tells me no* that made her fight the urge to cry.

But..he loved her, right? She loved him, she reassured herself as she worried at her bottom lip. She loved him. She loved him...so why did she dread seeing him again? She couldn't very well avoid him all night - she was in *his* kingdom, in *his* castle, courting *him*. Maybe she could dance with him, then claim a headache and slip off to her bedchambers, alone.

She was wrenched from her thoughts by Raewyn tugging on the end of her hair.

"What's wrong, E-" she cut herself off, freckled cheeks suddenly paling. "Fleur."

"Did you call me Elora?" Fleur's eyes widened, the name familiar even as Raewyn denied it. "Aerin called me that earlier, too. I really must look like her. Maybe I'll meet her tonight!"

"Maybe so, Fleur." Raewyn smiled, but it didn't meet her eyes. "Maybe so."

The dress required every hand in the room to do up. Lydia told Fleur to *stand still dammit* as she tugged on the corset strings until Fleur worried she wouldn't be able to take a deep breath without bursting free. As it was, the neckline plunged dangerously low, showing altogether far more cleavage than she was used to, and the thin straps fashioned to look like sparkling vines did little to help support her chest. Though, Fleur had to admit, the effect was gorgeous. The pale purple gown flowed effortlessly to the floor, just covering her high heel clad feet, decorated with glittering fabric flowers that shone in the light.

It was almost worth not being able to breathe.

Fleur felt like a damn princess.

"You look stunning," Raewyn said, jaw slack as she stared at Fleur. Fleur grinned, her happiness uncontainable.

"I feel it."

"Come, Elladan will be waiting for you," Lydia cut in, tugging Fleur's hand.

The dress felt like armor, and she held her head high as she followed the pixie down the halls. Elladan was usually sweet and thoughtful, she reasoned as her heels *clicked* on the polished floors. He'd just been stressed last night. He'd welcome her with open arms and she'd melt into his chest and it would be like it always was.

So when she saw him, dressed in deep red, arms crossed over his broad chest, she smiled. She felt his eyes rake every inch of her, lingering on her chest, and shivered under the weight of his gaze, sparks skittering over her skin.

When she raised her eyes to meet his, he was frowning.

"What the hell is in your hair?" He reached for her, plucking a dried rose and crushing it in his fist. She watched, lips parted in shock, as the petals crumbled to the floor. A lock of her hair sprang free and dangled in front of her face.

"I liked them."

"And the dress…" He trailed a hand over her waist, thumbing a fabric flower. "You can't be so on display like this, Fleur. You look like some sort of Spring hussy."

She balked, stumbling a few steps away, horror sliding through her - oily and thick. She felt her face heat and her heart pick up as she fought for control of her words.

He beat her to it.

"Here," he said, removing the rest of the flowers from her hair and letting them drop unceremoniously to the floor. He crushed one under foot as he lent over her, tucking some sort of wreath into her hair in their place. "Rowan berries. Much more appropriate, don't you think?"

She couldn't fathom why. "What was wrong with the flowers?" She liked them, liked the dress, had loved how she looked in it. She didn't want him to ruin it for her.

"You're Autumn fae, now," he answered, as though it was obvious. "You need to start dressing like it. Never mind, we're late. Come on."

She let him slip her hand into the crook of his elbow, too stunned by whatever had just happened to so much as complain as he strode towards the grand double doors, the scent of sticky sweet wine and the lilting tune of fiddles leaking under the door.

The guard from yesterday stood outside, talking in hushed tones to Aerin, their heads tucked close together. She perked up at the side, making to go and talk to them, to thank Tarhael for their talk. She'd liked him, wondered if maybe they could be friends, even if she was still a little wary.

Elladan tucked her closer to his side.

"Come on," he insisted, nodding to the second guard to open the door for them. The music swelled as the door opened, revealing a packed room, lit with the little lanterns Fleur was growing used to, fae in outfits of every color under the sun spinning on the dance floor. A band played enthusiastically at the front, a quick, lively song that instantly lightened Fleur's mood.

When Elladan asked her to dance, she said yes. She said yes and she spun and she lost herself in the music and the wine and the swelling, floating feeling of being part of something bigger than the confusing mess she'd found herself in lately.

The song broke and Elladan kept her close, but she didn't mind. His hands were gentler now, his smiles soft and heart wrenching, the kisses he placed on her lips teasing and sweet. She didn't forgive him, but she wanted to.

"Can we talk to some of the others?" she asked giddily as he plucked another glass of ruby wine from a passing tray.

"I want you to myself tonight, beautiful," he grinned, hand flexing around her waist. She frowned.

"But-"

"There'll be time for mingling later," he insisted, leaning down so he spoke his words onto her neck. She shivered at the contact, breath hitching. "I missed you. Is it so bad that I want some time with the woman I'm courting?"

Well, when he put it like that...

They danced again and Fleur drank and Elladan tasted sweet when she kissed him so she kept kissing him and spinning and everything felt *light* and distant and so unbearably close.

She didn't know how long passed before Elladan suggested they return to his room. She was dizzy with energy and drunk on the way Elladan looked at her through thick, dark lashes, and how his thumb skimmed over her collarbone as though he couldn't resist touching her.

"I'll go to my chambers," she told him, smiling. She was tired now, after all, even if the party showed no signs of slowing down.

"No," he shook his head, eyes narrowed. "I'm not finished with you."

She shivered, blinking at him. "Oh."

Before she could say anything else, he'd grabbed a guard by the arm and told him to escort her to his room. The guard was young and scruffy and clearly a few drinks deep, but nodded dumbly at Elladan's request.

Fleur glanced back over her shoulder, but Elladan had already turned away, engrossed in conversation with a man in bright blue - Winter fae, if she had to guess.

She missed the heat and laughter of the ballroom as soon as they left, the cold chill of the open hallway bringing her arms out in gooseflesh.

"I'll take her." A warm voice said from the shadows. Fleur's guard froze, a frown on his thin face.

"Who are you?"

The man stepped out, and Fleur instantly softened. "Hi, Tarhael." She waved, stumbling a little as she broke free from the guard and moved towards him.

He hid a smile behind a cough and raised a brow at her guard. "I'll ensure she gets back safely. I'm sure you want to get back to the ball. I heard they were bringing out the spirits soon."

At the mention of alcohol the guard relented, nodding before turning away and slipping back into the ballroom.

"Come on, Fleur." He extended his arm to her and she took it happily. He wore a deep green suit, the color complimenting him wonderfully, Fleur thought.

"You look nice," she told him, voice slurring a little.

"Thank you." He grinned back at her. "You look stunning."

She blushed. "Really?"

He nodded, frowning. "Why would you ever think otherwise?"

She shrugged, biting her lip, and played with the straps at her shoulders. "I love this dress," she said softly, and when Tarhael didn't answer, she wasn't sure he'd heard her.

"We're here."

She looked up and frowned.

"This isn't Elladan's room."

"No," he confirmed, opening the door and pulling her inside with pitying eyes. "It's Aerin's."

25

Aerin

Aerin stepped out of the shadows, dark hair tied out of his face with a thin leather band, bright eyes narrowed as he looked her over. He couldn't see any bruises or marks, but that didn't mean his brother hadn't simply hurt her somewhere he wouldn't see. He wouldn't put it past him. Aerin watched Elora's dark brows furrow in confusion, one hand bunched in the skirt of her gown to hold it off the floor as she walked. Áine above, that dress. The color against her smooth brown skin, the way the glitter caught the light...she was radiant. Although-

"Why the fuck do you have rowan berries in your hair, Elora?" It came out shorter, harsher than he intended and he cursed himself internally when her eyes widened in fear.

"Oh...uh..." She chewed her bottom lip, eyes darting around the room. "Elladan gave me it. He said the flowers were too spring-y so...and my name's not Elora. It's Fleur."

Anger flared white hot in Aerin's stomach. He'd been the one to spin this fake identity, convinced it would help her, keep her safe until they could send her home. Now, he felt guilt slide down his spine. He might be the bastard, but Elladan was *cruel*. Sly and slick and cunning and far too confident.

Tarhael dipped his chin at Aerin before untangling the damned wreath from her wavy hair. He threw it unceremoniously into the fire and Aerin watched it burn with grim satisfaction.

"What the hell?" Elora squeaked, long lashes fluttering as she stared into the bright flames as they devoured her hair piece.

"Rowan berries," Aerin continued in a low voice, heat turning his cheeks pink as he stoked the flames. "Are said to protect humans against faerie enchantments. They don't obviously, it's an old folk tale humans like to tell themselves. Elladan was *mocking you*, Elora."

Hurt and confusion flashed over her face. He hated that he'd put it there. *No*, he reminded himself. His brother had put it there.

"But I'm not human."

Aerin's face softened. To his credit, Elladan's work was very convincing. The delicate points of her ears, the expertly masked scent, the subtle emphasis of some features. But Aerin was better. This, Eolas, was the one area he had the advantage against Elladan in. When his brother was sparring, Aerin was in the library, studying lore and runecasts and old magic.

So he saw the gaps in the seams of Elladan's glamour. The clumsy stumbles Elora still took, the split ends of her hair where she needed it cut, the tiny pale white scar on one knuckle.

"Drink this."

He offered a glass of pale liquid, thin and as close to water as he'd been able to get it. It still smelled vaguely of the herbs he'd used though and Elora's nose scrunched as she sniffed it.

"What is this?" she snapped, the words coming out as an accusation. "I'm not drinking some random *stuff* from you. Elladan made it quite clear you weren't someone to trust."

He raised a single brow, unfazed. He'd expected as much. Ever since he'd first seen her, he'd known she wasn't one to be easily swayed.

Well, without the use of illegal magic, that is. Elladan obviously hadn't been impressed that she wouldn't bend to his will. His moral compass had never really pointed north, though this was the first time he'd thrown the whole damn thing into the sea.

Aerin pinched the bridge of his nose, the stress headache that had squatted behind his eyes for days rearing its ugly head.

"If you can answer my questions, I won't make you drink it. I'll let you go back to Elladan's bed if that's what you want."

Elora's frown lifted a little, spine straightening with misplaced drunken confidence.

"What's the rune for water?"

Silence. Aerin's jaw tightened and he continued.

"The names of the other Spring kingdoms?"

Nothing. He watched the panic bubble inside her, shaking his head.

"Your parents' full names?"

A tear fell down her cheek, smearing wet black kohl with it. Her hands shook at her sides, the bottom lip she was chewing now wobbling.

"Your name's not Fleur. You're not from Spring. You're not even from this *realm*." Her mouth dropped open a little, but he saw the soft spark of recognition in her deep brown eyes and latched onto it. "I'm trying to help you. Elladan will ruin you, hurt you. He's already tried, hasn't he?" It was an educated guess, and her wince confirmed it. He would kill him. "Drink."

The look in her eyes was enough to rip the air from his lungs. He refused to let the torment show, steady hand holding out the cup again, coaxing her to take it. She did, gaze darting between him and Tarhael, looking utterly lost.

Her gaze lingered on his guard, as though waiting for him to tell her it was okay. For whatever reason, she seemed to trust him at least a little. Aerin was grateful when Tarhael nodded, placing a comforting hand on her shoulder.

She took a deep, shuddering breath and tipped the contents down her throat.

And promptly collapsed in a pile of lavender silk on the floor.

26

Elora

lora's head hurt, and the bouncing didn't help at all.

Wait, the bouncing?

Elora struggled to open her eyes, but could only make out the arms of someone wrapped around her by starlight. She was on a horse that was steadily trotting through the thick forest. The moon was high in the sky and the sea of stars would have made an incredible sight had she not felt nauseous to her core. She opened her mouth to ask who the hell was taking her God knows where but promptly threw up instead. She clutched at the stranger's arms for balance and retched off the side of the saddle, until she was left dry heaving with an empty stomach.

"Would you like some water?"

"Yes," Elora's voice cracked, the only word she was able to say before falling into a fit of dry coughing.

"It's in the pouch on the right side of the saddle."

Elora fumbled until she felt her hand latch onto a cool water skin. She gratefully tipped her head back and let the water refresh her. Nothing had ever tasted as good. The entire water skin was soon empty and she found another one in the same pouch and promptly drained that one as well. This time, the water didn't taste sweet.

"Who are you?"

"It's me, Aerin."

"Aerin? I-"

Realization crashed down on Elora. She remembered. She remembered everything.

A scream rose in her throat.

"Aerin, what the *fuck?*"

"Tarhael, if you would be so kind as to set a fake trail, now would be an excellent time. No need for the both of us to be screamed at..."

A tall figure on a massive warhorse a little ways ahead of them veered off sharply to the right at Aerin's command. Tarhael was soon swallowed up by shadows.

"You find all of this funny, do you?" Elora didn't bother to keep the bite out of her voice.

"Quite the contrary actually. I'm risking a lot by trying to help you out here."

Elora balked. She thought she might collapse under the pressure of the realization.

"Thanks for being so *early*, Prince Aerin. You really took your sweet time, didn't you?"

There was nothing more Elora wanted to do than peel off his arms from her waist, but due to her lack of experience horseback riding and current impending breakdown, she was forced to admit that she needed him for balance. When Aerin didn't offer any protest, she sat and stewed in an awkward silence.

"Still, thank you. For saving me. I still don't really understand what Elladan did, or how any of this happened, but being Fleur felt like a living nightmare..." she trailed off, unable to stop the tremors racking her body. Elladan had twisted her sense of self so badly that she had no idea she was anyone other than a pretty fae girl who'd caught his eye. She didn't want to remember, to think about it, but images of the days as someone else flashed through her brain, turning her stomach. As much as Elora tried to keep the tears from flowing, they did anyway. In some way, it was a release of all the confusion, fear and hurt she had accumulated while being Fleur, and some other part of it was her body and mind shutting down, retreating into survival mode. She wasn't sure how long she had been trapped in Fior Domhan, but it had to have at least been over a week, if not more. Elora couldn't bare to think about how freaked out everyone must be back home.

Aerin didn't say anything but tightened his arms around Elora as her body was racked with sobs and eased the horse a little bit, from a fast trot to a more leisurely walk. They continued in silence for the better part of an hour, until Elora collected herself enough to ask where they were going now.

"Just please be honest with me. Everyone has been keeping things from me for far too long, and -"

"I'm taking you home, Elora."

"What?"

"I've finally found a way to get you home."

Aerin didn't offer any other explanation but Elora could pick up on the hints. While she still didn't know why he hadn't interfered earlier, she understood risky this was for him. But he, and Tarhael, were the only ones sticking their necks out for her in this strange realm, and for that, Elora was grateful.

"Thank you."

Elora didn't mean to doze off again, but she must have at some point because the morning sun was beginning to peer through the treetops, shyly making its way towards the heavens. The horse was still moving at a steady rate and Aerin's powerful grip hadn't relented a single bit. She leaned back, trying to undo some of the pain that had gathered in her lower neck and spine from being slumped over in the saddle for hours, and felt the back of her head bump against Aerin's chest. He was solid behind her and warm and she thought for the briefest moment that his chest seemed like a nice place for her head to be. He cleared his throat and Elora jolted forward a little, grateful Aerin couldn't see the red tinging her cheeks.

"We're here."

"Huh?" All Elora could see was treetops and mountain ridges, bathed in the usual colors of autumn. She realized with a start that they were on top of a mountain peak.

"As hard as I tried, I couldn't figure out how you activated the portal you came through, but this might be a location I can use." Seeing the puzzled look on Elora's face, he continued. "You're half fae, remember? Far as I can tell, you can probably do all sorts of things I don't know about, portal magic included. Portals have been banned for centuries and studying them has been outlawed long before I was born, but I've read all we have on them. Lucky for you." His voice was low and dead pan, but she had the sense that if she turned around, there'd be a smirk on his lips.

"So you've been researching how to open portals again?" Elora rubbed her aching thigh muscles, rolling her neck as she spoke. She felt like she was running on fumes and hope, refusing to think about what Elladan had done to her.

"In essence, yes. I can explain all the other details when we get to your side of things."

"Wait," Elora interjected, halting her movements. "What do you mean we?"

"I'm coming with you."

"What? No you're not. I've had *enough* of fae men fucking up my life." She forced herself to take a deep breath when she felt him tense behind her. Perhaps that was a *bit* harsh. "You've never been to the human world. Why would you even want to come? How would you explain yourself?" Elora didn't know how to tell him that she never wanted anything to do with the fae realm ever again, including him. She just wanted to go home and have this all be a forgotten memory, a nightmare to be locked inside the vaults of her mind, never to be revisited.

"Either I come with you, or you're not going home at all."

Rage balled up inside of Elora, hot and fierce, until she felt a pair of cool hands on her own. Aerin's. He sighed and when she peeked over her shoulder she found him staring into the distance, jaw tight.

"Look - Elladan and a few other people from my father's court have been sneaking into the human realm and making contact. For years. I have no idea how he does it, and I can't ever seem to catch my brother or anyone else in the act. It's the only possible explanation I can think of. I know for a fact they don't have access to some secret runecasting that I don't have, and I can't find anything in the royal library. The Dohari Gates I know of have all been sealed up with magic, some for centuries."

"Dohari Gates?"

"The things you've been calling portals."

"And you're telling me you found a way to reactivate them again?"

"No, more like creating new ones. If I tried to use an old one, it would alert my father and give our position away. I've been working on a method to create portable portals over the last few years. Essentially, they're temporary gateways, with only enough magic to anchor them momentarily before they vanish. Traditional Dohari Gates are anchored to important places where fae and human cultures intersect, namely monuments and libraries where there are still minions of fae. Each portal connects a distinct place in the human realm and the fae realm, and because of the importance and deep bonds between these places, the portals tend to be permanent. Mine? Not so much." He reeled off the information fast, with a bored shrug, as though it was perfectly obvious.

All Elora could do was stare. "I, um, think I understand you?"

"The point is, we're going to make a temporary portal so we can get away quickly and not leave a trace."

The thought of more magic made Elora feel a little sick.

"Close your eyes and think of your home." Aerin instructed, letting go of her and dismounting with ease.

"Oh, we're like, going *home*? You can do that?" Her apartment. It felt so distant now. Her heart picked up pace.

"I can't, but you can." Aerin smirked and Elora glared at him. "I've been working on this runecast for ages, I'm excited to try it out." He sounded genuinely happy about it and it took Elora a minute to separate his words from his tone.

"Wait, you've never even tried this before?"

"Not exactly."

"Not exactly?" Elora's voice was rising in pitch even as she tried to tell herself to *calm the hell down at least he's trying to get you out.*

"Look. Tarhael can't keep distracting Elladan or my father. It's only a matter of time before they begin to look for us in earnest, and Elladan has the best hunting eagles in the realm. It would only be a matter of time before we're found out."

"Okay, so what do we do?" The wind was stronger up here atop the mountain, and it bit into Elora's cheek, jolting her. Fior Domhan was beautiful, breathtakingly so, at least the areas she had seen. But she couldn't wait to go home.

"I'm going to write out the runecast, but you need to stand next to me and copy the runes that I write. Tarhael told me he gave you the basic rundown of how magic works here. You're half fae, so I know you have at least some latent magical capabilities that we don't know about yet. Even if you don't know how to perform magic yet, the fact that you have fae blood in you should be enough to activate the runecast. I hope."

Elora raised her eyebrows but Aerin had already turned away and started working on the runecast. The notepad he was using was much larger and thicker than the one he normally kept in his pocket, and had a worn leather cover. He handed her a multicolored pencil and small notepad and began writing in his own, slowly, so Elora could follow. The sun was beating down on them, as though mocking their efforts. She gritted her teeth and squinted her eyes at Aerin's notepad, wishing he would write just a little bigger. Not wanting to make a mistake, she copied Aerin's Eolas script at a snail's pace. After the better part of the hour, Aerin stood up and stretched, back cracking as he raised his arms above his head.

"All done." He gazed over Elora's runes, eyes rapidly moving back and forth as he scanned her handiwork. "This is good. Now put your pencil down and imagine your home. Picture as many small details as you possibly can."

She took a deep breath, filling her lungs with the cool, clean mountain air. She opened her mouth to ask Aerin what they would do if this failed, but thought the better of it and clamped her jaw shut again.

"Don't forget to envision your home *clearly* or Áine only knows where we'll end up," Aerin said grinning.

"The prince decides to show his sense of humor now," Elora muttered, rolling her eyes. *Here goes nothing.*

Elora put the pencil down and shut her eyes tightly. A door appeared in her mind, it's white paint chipping and worn, a stark contrast to the vibrant home that lay beyond it. Elora saw the door open and waves of longing washed over her as she envisioned her little slice of the universe. Plants of all shapes, colors and sizes adorned the walls, painting the apartment with strong greens, bright reds and oranges. There were splashes of purples and blues, the faint scent of earth and vanilla in the air. She could see her dining table set up for two, her couch and bean bag chair facing the small television and all the paintings she had accumulated over the years finding spaces to hang nestled amongst all the plants. Her guitar was resting against the wall nearest to her couch, and for a moment, Elora felt like she was home again.

When Elora opened her eyes, the very air before her trembled and ripped apart, a rainbow dancing across nothing. The tear in the air looked very similar to the hole she had fallen through, and a sense of deja vu and apprehension washed over her.

"Jump, Elora!"

"Are you crazy? We'll die if we jump from this height!"

Aerin was running at her. As he got close, his hand latched onto her wrist, dragging her with him. Her screams were lost to the wind as he jumped, taking the two of them soaring through the air towards the growing tear.

The last thing Elora saw was flashes of light, and then darkness.

27

Elora

Elora opened her eyes. The thumping of her heart was so loud it wouldn't surprise her if the damn birds perched on the power line outside could hear it. A small bubble of laughter pushed past her lips at the sight of them. Pigeons. Real, honest to God pigeons. Relief flooded her veins as she stared at them through the dirty hallway window. The stupid, fat gray birds didn't exist in Fior Domhan.

It'd worked.

The portal had *worked*.

She turned on shaking legs towards her door and nearly sobbed at the sight of it. She started towards it, reaching for the silver metal handle before stopping short, realizing with a sinking feeling that she didn't have her keys.

Aerin shifted behind her, dragging his gaze from the pigeons, his eyes wide and lips parted slightly as though in shock. He blinked a few times before reaching into his pocket, retrieving a set of keys, complete with the little dolphin key chain her father had brought her back from a business trip when she was a child.

He held the keys out to her. "Raewyn got them from the clothes

ELORA

you wore when you arrived."

Elora nodded mutely and took them from his palm. She hesitated for a few moments before sticking them in the keyhole, slowly turning it with bated breath. There was a soft click, and then the door was creaking open.

She nearly fell to her knees at the side of her home. Plants adorned every free inch of her apartment that didn't have paintings hanging from it. All in all, it looked like the cozy workspace of a crazy artist. The way she liked it.

And in the middle of it all, ransacking her apartment, were her parents.

"Mom? Dad?" The words came out much shakier than she had anticipated, but it was the best she could do without bursting into tears. The two people frantically tearing her place apart froze and turned around ever so slowly.

"*Elora*? Is that you honey?"

"Yeah, hi mom."

"Elora!" Both her parents shrieked together and rushed her, nearly tackling her in their excitement.

"I missed you guys too," Elora said against their chests, no longer able to keep in the tears. "I've missed you guys so much." She let the tears fall freely and sobbed for what seemed the hundredth time in days.

"Elora Han. WHERE ON EARTH HAVE YOU BEEN FOR THE PAST TWO WEEKS?" Her mom pulled back from their embrace and scolded her. She stepped back a few paces, putting her hands on her hips and squaring herself towards her daughter. "You haven't shown up to work in two weeks, Helen called me a few days ago. Alice said you weren't returning her calls and-" she abruptly cut off, noticing Aerin. "And who might you be?"

"Hello, Ms. Han. My name is Aerin Auretaeas. Nice to meet you."

Elora blinked rapidly at Aerin, unused to this sudden pleasant attitude.

"What business do you have with my daugh-"

She was cut off by Aerin gently blow across his notepad. Elora's parents cut off whatever it was they were about to say, their eyes wide and lips parted in protest. A few heartbeats and slightly confused look later, Mr. and Mrs. Han were all smiles.

"Aerin, great to see you!" Elora's father said, eyes kind and smile wide.

Mrs. Han beamed and walked over, arms open to embrace him.

"A word please," Elora hissed, wrapping her fingers around his wrist in a grip of steel and dragged him down the small hallway. "What the hell did you just do to my parents?"

This was why she hadn't wanted him here. Why she wanted to leave anything to do with the fae back in Fior Domhan. She was barely restraining the urge to drop to the damn floor and scream - two weeks of rage and confusion building inside her. He'd just cast magic on her *parents*. It was too much. Everything was too much.

"A little too early in our relationship to be in your bedroom already isn't it?" Aerin glanced around Elora's room, and she wondered what it looked like from his eyes. Compared to his home, she imagined hers was underwhelming. Her bed was big, nearly taking up half the space in the rather tiny bedroom. Heaps of clothes were scattered haphazardly across the closet and floor, and her desk was cluttered with dozens of printed pages and notebooks, stacked atop her laptop. Her prized possession - the typewriter she'd bought with her first paycheck as a teenager - sat at the corner of her desk near the window. The rest of her room was an echo of the living space, covered in plants and paintings.

"Eyes right here elf-man," she chastised. Aerin's eyes shot back to her. "And no, that wasn't funny." Elora's voice was brittle and sharp as she glared at him.

"Sorry, sorry. I didn't do anything to hurt your parents. I merely removed any instances of being stressed out about your disappearance. I've prepared more versions of the runecast for anyone else who might have been distressed by your unexpected trip." He must have seen the skeptical look on her face because he hurriedly added, "The brain is truly remarkable in how fast it reconstructs artificial memories and to unify the differences or lapses in memory. Right now, your parents will have come to the conclusion that they're here for a brief visit. I've put in memories of me being one of your friends from college that you didn't talk about too much. You did go to college, right? I really don't know how anything works around here."

"Am I just supposed to trust you? You say you only removed memories of freaking out over my disappearance, but how can I trust that's all you've done? How can I be sure their minds can handle what you've just done? You say their brains are going to be fine, and they'll figure out ways to make things connect, but how will I know that it won't hurt them? *How can I trust you?* After everything your brother did? You could be just like him! You held me at knife point for fuck's sake Aerin!" Elora was unraveling, an ache the size of a fist blooming in her chest, throat tight.

"Just like Elladan?" The silence between the two of them was agonizing and heavy, and Elora swore neither of them were breathing. "Right." He turned and walked out of her room, apologized to her parents for leaving so abruptly, and left.

"Aerin seems like a lovely man, honey," her father was saying around his mouthful.

"He is," Elora replied, pushing her green beans around her plate, ignoring the way her heart clenched at the mention of him. While she loved her mom's home cooked meals, everything fell flat in comparison to the flavors and scents of Fior Domhan. She regretted what she'd said to Aerin, but that didn't mean it wasn't true. God knows what would have happened if she'd stayed with Elladan - trapped as Fleur - but if Aerin had genuinely cared, why didn't he get her out sooner? She couldn't help the seed of suspicion that sprouted in her stomach. *He risked his life to help you, Elora.* Shame wormed its way through her belly, choking off the rest of her appetite. She thanked her mom for the wonderful meal and went to wash up.

Her parents were a little surprised when she hugged them hard and told them to visit often, but they both promised her that they would come visit her again before the week was up after her dad's business conference. Then they left and Elora was alone. There was an ache in her bones that she didn't want to name.

She paced her kitchen, running her hand along the cool counter top, clearing down after dinner. What now?

Something glinted at her from the corner of the counter under the shelves that held her coffee cups. Her phone. Her very dead phone, but her phone nonetheless. Had Aerin put it there? She'd forgotten all about it in Fior Domhan, but presumably it had been stashed with her keys while she was there. She dug the charger out of the 'everything drawer' and watched the little battery icon change from red to green. Somehow, it still worked after everything it had been through and the second she switched it on, dozens of missed call notifications and texts lit up the screen. She cringed. The most recent notifications were from the bookstore manager, Helen, her parents, and Alice. *Ah, shit. Alice.*

Alice's frequent messages had dwindled down to nearly nothing during the two or so weeks Elora had been gone, and she bit her lip against the wave of guilt. Alice was one of the only people in recent memory that Elora remembered truly connecting with, dating app or not. They weren't serious - more like friends with casual benefits considering neither of them had wanted a relationship - but still. She scrolled through the many messages of Alice asking her how she was, or where she was, or if she was busy. She sighed and flopped onto her couch, phone still clutched in hand.

"Would starting with a pickup line be worse, or just a straight up booty call?" she wondered aloud to herself, trying to shake the melancholy that had settled over her like dust. She could call Alice, beg for her job back from her manager in the morning and get on with life like usual. She could. She would.

"Both would be pretty bad, if I'm being quite honest."

"Holy shit, what the fuck Aerin?" Elora leapt from her seat and stared up at the dark haired boy looking down at her, a half smirk lurking on his face.

"Both of those options make me think you're not going to get laid tonight."

"Oh, and you're such an expert at that, are you?"

"I can give you a few pointers if that's the best you can do." His half smirk grew, complete with a singular raised eyebrow and twinkle in his eye. His black hair hung like a swath of pure night around his shoulders, and the shadows made his eyes look a deep forest green.

Dammit, he's actually kinda cute with that smirk. The thought slipped out unbidden and she wrestled with control of her emotions and the ridiculous notions of his hotness from her head. *What the hell is wrong with you Elora? Get a grip on yourself. Focus.*

Scowling, Elora went to sit at the kitchen table, as far as she could possibly get from Aerin in her tiny apartment. She paused, the weight of his arrival crushing her. Her tone turned serious as she gazed at Aerin for a few seconds.

"Nothing is ever going to be the same again, is it?"

She watched Aerin open his mouth once, close it, and try again.

"If you're asking if you're going to be stuck with me for the time being, yes. Unfortunately, this isn't all some fever dream, but now that we're here we can figure things out. Step by step. Day by day." His voice was unusually soft. He felt *sorry* for her. It hurt more than his normal broodiness.

"Where did you go earlier when you stormed out?" Elora knew she hadn't offered a formal apology but by Aerin's relaxed posture, she guessed he wasn't holding a grudge.

"I went to go check on the rest of your friends and people who might have missed you."

"How did you know who they were?" Elora went statue still, eyes boring into Aerin's. "Or where they were?"

"Magic."

She threw her phone at him, anger running hot through her veins. He caught it easily and placed it down on the arm of the sofa. The calm, easy fluidity of his movements only fueled her irritation. When he didn't offer up any further explanation, she worked her mouth, trying to find the words.

"You can't just do that!" she fumed, shaking. "What is wrong with you?"

Aerin's jaw tensed. "A thank you would suffice."

Elora balked. He didn't care how massive a violation that was. He didn't care about much, apparently.

"I'm going to bed." She turned her back before he could see the tears threatening to fall. She was really fucking sick of crying. Sick of this helplessness.

"Goodnight."

She ignored him and slammed her bedroom door behind her.

28

Aerin

Aerin watched Elora's breath slow down until it reached an even rise and fall. He looked around the apartment once more and did a double take in surprise. The plants that had looked withered and in desperate need of water were suddenly healthy and vibrant. Aerin was smart enough to know that a single watering couldn't have done this. They looked as though they'd been tended to religiously - flowers with bright petals, leaves a lush green, stalks strong and stable where, just hours ago, they'd been drooping. He turned back to Elora, sighing slightly. He'd originally come to check on her - despite the hurt that lingered beneath his skin from the accusations she'd spewed his way earlier - knocking on the door to no avail. Except, for some inexplicable reason, he'd stayed after cracking the door to make sure she hadn't run away or been kidnapped by his deranged brother. Of course, he told himself as he ran a hand over his face, of course she was just sleeping. A reasonable explanation. Obviously. She looked completely at peace, tucked into a little ball underneath a bright green duvet and Aerin found himself wishing that things would stay for her this way. It would be much more convenient if he didn't care at all. He'd never quite mastered the icy carelessness his brother and father possessed, no matter how convincing his mask was at times. He turned away, closing her door again with a soft *click*.

The mortal realm was louder than he expected. Even now, he could hear the distant *thump* of upbeat music, the steady engines of cars rushing past outside, a permanent hum of electricity. It was unsettling but fascinating. He'd always craved information, experiences. Hungry for anything that could get him out of Autumn. Now, he was finally out and it didn't seem real. He'd put it off for so long - always finding a reason to stay. Tarhael. The pixies. Sure he'd missed some piece of vital information in the cracks of the stone in the library. He was tied to a kingdom he didn't want and no matter how much research he did, he couldn't find a way to extract himself from it.

And then, there was her.

He couldn't sit back and watch Dioltas, watch his brother, infect her with its rot.

All things considered, he should hate her considering the threat she posed. He'd tried. But she wasn't some demon intent on causing chaos. She was just a girl - confused and hurt and, fuck it, strong as hell. Ever since she'd spat in his brother's face during their scouting-turned-rescue-mission, something in her had called to him. He'd fought against it at first, especially once he began suspecting her identity. He'd been rude, cold, callus towards her but he couldn't quite bring himself to apologize for it. It felt too much like admitting he needed to see that spark in her eyes light up again. He hoped his brother hadn't extinguished it completely.

Spying a guitar lying in the corner near the couch, Aerin picked it up and softly strummed a few chords, the music lingering in the air like the notes Blueberry sang. The instrument was nearly identical to the one he'd played growing up, a familiar weight in his arms. His heart clenched a little at the thought of the bird. It had been the right choice, leaving him in Fior Domhan but that didn't make his absence feel any less like a wound.

He'd expected to feel out of place in her home. Perhaps he was just used to feeling out of place in homes. His, though huge and grand, had always felt hollow and empty, no matter how many bodies filled it. Hers, though small and cluttered, was bursting with life and character. He liked it. He liked *her*. That hadn't been part of the plan.

It was dangerous for her there. If anyone else had discovered her… well, they'd make Elladan look angelic. As it was, Aerin was still unsure of Elladan's end game with her.

Closing his eyes, the music that flowed from his fingers was rich and pleasing and he played long into the night, hoping the music would take his confusion and fear too.

29

Aerin

It was funny, Aerin thought, how quickly he became comfortable in this realm. He was grateful he kept his hair long, pinning it with little metal clips he stole from Elora's bathroom so it hid the tips of his ears, negating the need for a full time glamour. He doubted he'd ever get used to the vehicles though - noisy, fast, metal cages that made the air stink. He refused to get in one, but the little screen Elora called a phone, and the bigger screen with keys she told him was a laptop, he was curious about. Though, of all the modern inventions he'd seen so far, the shower was his favorite. The first night he'd washed in her bathroom, he'd spent an hour under the spray until Elora knocked loudly on the door and yelled at him to get out before he put her bills through the roof.

He sauntered into the lounge as quietly as he could, feet light on the worn gray carpet. It had only been two days, and while he was perhaps more relaxed than he'd even been in his twenty five years at the castle, he had no idea how she was holding up. She was sitting in the same spot he'd found her in yesterday morning, knees tucked into her chest on the couch, some show about people trying on elaborate white dresses on the screen she called a television. He'd asked what she was watching and she'd muttered *daytime shit* so he'd left her alone, content to sit in the tiny guest bedroom-slash-storage-space and examine everything he could see.

Now, though, he was worried.

She didn't look up when he entered, blinking blearily at the people dancing around on TV, a blanket tucked close to her body like armor. He wondered if she'd moved at all.

"Elora?" he said softly, his voice startling a little jump from her. She didn't answer him though, merely turning her head a little to stare at him with wide, deep brown eyes. The determined spark he'd seen in her the first time they met had dulled, the way it had when Elladan had convinced her she was Fleur. "Are you okay?"

It was a stupid question, really, but he didn't know what else to say. *Sorry my insane brother manipulated your mind and assaulted you? Sorry you've just found out your whole life's a lie and you're not human? Sorry I took so long to get you out?*

Maybe just *sorry.*

She ran a hand through her tangled hair, knots catching on her knuckles, and furrowed her brow at him.

"I don't…" Her voice was quiet and cracking. "Uh…I don't…"

Guilt, icy and slick, ran through Aerin's veins.

He had the sudden, ridiculous urge to reach out and touch her, to put his hand on her shoulder, push her hair back from her face, smooth the worry line between her eyebrows out. He didn't. He stood, back straight, mouth dry, and watched Elora try to gather herself together.

What use was he to help? He barely remembered the last time he voluntarily got close to anyone other than Tarhael. He usually holed up in his chambers or the library, surrounded by hard facts and concrete knowledge. The intricacies of magic were fascinating - pulling apart the history to find the right runecast for the portal had been difficult, yes, but that was what he liked. A challenge. He could deal with numbers and letters and ink. There was always an answer hidden in them.

People, however, were different.

And he had no idea how to solve the puzzle that was Elora Han.

"Um...do you want a tea?"

Tea? He winced as it came out his mouth, but there was no taking it back now. He doubted he even knew how to make tea. He'd seen Raewyn do it, of course, but that was with little crushed herbs and flowers and everything was different here.

"Oh." Elora bit her lip, looking surprised. "Yeah, actually. Thank you." Her voice was still small, still fragile, but the words at least made sense now.

Aerin nodded silently and moved to the tiny little kitchen, finding a mug with a faded pink, purple and blue rainbow on one side.

"Are rainbows different colors here?" he asked before he could stop himself, ransacking her cupboards for tea.

Over the counter, he saw Elora's brows draw together, confusion spreading over her face. It was a nice change from the blank slate she'd been earlier, though. When she saw the cup in Aerin's hands, a choked laugh escaped her mouth and Aerin smiled. He didn't care that it was at his expense.

"No," she clarified, smiling in earnest now. "It's a pride thing."

"Pride?"

"Yeah." She pushed off the couch, her blanket armor falling off and revealing the loose black sweat suit she wore. "Like LGBTQ plus."

"Are those letters supposed to mean something?" Aerin found a half empty bottle of milk in the fridge that Elora's parents had dropped off and set it on the counter.

Elora chuckled, leaning against the counter as she watched him boil the kettle.

"You can't tell me everyone's straight in the fae realm," she joked, rolling her eyes.

"Straight?" Aerin's eyes widened as he suddenly realized what she meant. "*Oh!*"

She laughed properly then, the sound light and bubbly and intoxicating. "Pink, purple and blue are the colors of the bisexual flag. It means that I'm attracted to more than one gender. I like who I like." She shrugged a little, still smiling.

Aerin forced himself to stop staring at her mouth. He studied the cup. In Fior Domhan, there weren't flags or colors to represent any of these identities, but he liked the idea.

"Maybe I'll get one, too," he mused as he poured a trickle of milk in her tea. He'd learned by watching her that that was how she took it. She accepted it gratefully, wrapping her hands around the mug.

"Come on." She nodded towards the couch and her pile of blankets. "I'll show you all the flags and we can order you a mug if you want."

Something warm and soft bloomed in Aerin's chest at the sentiment.

In the end, they ordered Aerin a matching cup.

"I have to go back to work tomorrow," she was telling him, setting her box of pizza down on the table. Pizza, Aerin thought, might be his favorite human food yet.

He nodded at her. He hadn't thought this far ahead, but he supposed it was a good thing she was getting back to her old life. Even better, the animosity that had built between them had deflated. In its place was a sort of soft awkwardness, a quiet distrust, sure, but he could navigate that.

He didn't want to think about what he was going to do next.

"You can come with me if you want," she said around a swig of water. "You like books, right?"

He blinked dumbly at her. What kind of question was that? "Of course."

"And I thought maybe you would want to look at the book...the portal...that brought me to the um..." she trailed off, as if unable or unwilling to relive her time in the fae realm. He didn't blame her.

"Yes," was all he said.

Elora was right. They walked together to the bookstore, Aerin trying his best not to gawk at everything around them. It was overwhelming. The buildings were closely packed and sky high, grey monoliths that cast long shadows over the roads. And the *roads*. It took all his energy not to jump or bristle whenever a vehicle drove past, his heart pounding so hard it hurt. There was none of the nature he had grown up with here. No ancient, wizened trees, no lush grass or thick forest. Just concrete and glass and metal. The clothes Elora had bought him yesterday felt wrong against his skin - new fabrics that didn't hang quite right on his frame, denim jeans scratching his legs.

It was a relief when they arrived at Elora's work. They'd walked all of ten minutes, but Aerin's nerves were frayed and his skin prickled. The familiar, comforting scent of books calmed his frantic heart a little, though.

He spent the first day poring over the pages of the ancient text Elora had pointed out - one page now dotted with specks of dried blood. It made no sense, how little blood she'd spilled. Portals like that normally required a tremendous sacrifice of blood - so much so that it often left the fae opening them unconscious until they recovered. This - a half fae girl with a paper cut - was unheard of.

Elora seemed more at home in the bookshop than anywhere else he'd seen her and he was glad the owner had allowed her to return to her job after she'd grovelled over the phone. She grinned, the worry lines on her face less deep, her eyes crinkling at the sides as she ran her fingers over the spines, as if they were welcoming her home. He figured out how to order coffee from the cafe down the street after vigorous instructions from Elora, and vowed to work his way through the menu, savoring the new tastes and smells.

A shadow darkened the page he was reading, and he looked up to see Elora, hair high in a ponytail, running a hand over her forehead as though she had a headache. He frowned.

"What's wrong?"

She shook her head and sighed. "Nothing...it's just..." She tapped her fingers against the denim of her jeans, never taking her eyes off the book Aerin held. "It's stupid. I shouldn't miss any of it, not after everything that happened to me there. But...everything seemed more...vibrant there. Utterly fucking terrifying but utterly fucking beautiful and I -" Something between a dry laugh and a sob broke up her sentence. "I miss Raewyn and the pixies. They took care of me, you know? They *cared*. And nothing will ever be the same and I'm just supposed to go about my day like I don't know there's a whole other world out there? Another world that I'm part of?"

She was shaking, Aerin realized with a start. Her voice was cracking, but no tears spilled over her lashes. He couldn't tell if she was sad or angry or both.

"Sit," he encouraged, urging her down onto the little plastic folding chair he'd been sitting on. She did so, staring at her hands as they trembled. He wanted to tell her he understood the feeling, the disjointed nothing-is-quite-right-anymore-and-I-don't-think-I'm okay feeling. But he didn't.

She shook her head, and he watched her pull all her fault lines back together again. It was impressive. It broke his damn heart.

"Tell me about it," she said softly, gaze lingering on the little blood stains on the open page. Aerin leaned over and closed the book gently.

"What do you want to know?" He didn't know why he asked. He never offered up information, especially about his family or Dioltas - namely because sometimes talking about them felt a little like being set on fire. But she softened him around the edges, even after only a few days. He hated it. But he could never hate *her* for it. A muscle in his jaw ticked. This was going to be a problem.

She shrugged. "Anything. Everything. You know more about me than I do and I know nothing about you except that your brother is a dickhead and your dad's a jerk."

He stifled a laugh behind his hand. Her head snapped up, deep brown eyes meeting his, filled with questions.

"When are you going back?"

That question was simple enough, but Aerin felt it like a punch to the gut. He clutched his cardboard coffee cup in hand, the dregs now cold.

"Never."

30

Elora

"What?" Elora started, nearly falling out of her chair as her lips parted in shock.

Aerin sucked in a deep breath, and despite herself, she watched the rise and fall of his chest, the way the movement made his tattoos poke out of the collar of his t-shirt. "I don't want to go back."

"Why? That's your home, your family-"

"I have no family there," he replied, words so cold Elora shivered. "My half brother is a mockery of the kingdom. My father is just an older version of him. Full of festering self righteousness and greed."

Elora watched anger shape his face - jaw clenching, eyes hardening.

"Oh." What else was she supposed to say? She knew they weren't good people but the pure hatred in Aerin's words threatened to scorch her.

"You don't want to hear about all that, Elora." His tone was softer, almost apologetic. She reached out and put a hand on his arm. He shook her off.

"I do. But not if you don't want to tell me." She took a deep breath, rubbing at her temples. "I just…I want to understand. Everything feels like it's falling apart right now and nobody knows but me. But us."

Aerin was silent for so long she thought he'd decided not to tell her. But then-

"Her face is getting blurry now," he said, so quietly she had to strain to hear him. "I have a good memory. Her face has been clear in my head since the day she passed but now...now it's all fuzzy around the edges. I'm only twenty five. I have centuries ahead of me -" Elora refused to let her mind process that piece of information - "and one of those days, I won't remember the color of her hair, or the tune she hummed under her breath to distract me from my father's yelling." He paused, shrugging as if to shift the weight of it all. "My mother was the only real family I had. She wasn't married to my father. I was never supposed to be born at all. When she died, leaving me with my father and stepmother, the queen, I was alone. Elladan...it's not even really his fault. He is the man my father raised him to be. He was raised to be the next king but -" he cut himself off. "Never mind. Anyway, I was the outcast. The beating block. The kid Elladan used to show off how much his fighting skills had improved. I trained and I can fight well, but he was always bigger, stronger. So I kept to myself, lived in the library, taught myself about every corner of our history. The resident loremaster used to teach me, before my father found out and had him executed for treason. I had the flying fae, though." He caught Elora's slight frown and clarified. "The pixies, and a few other creatures you won't be familiar with. Animals, too." His frown deepened and a twisted look of pain shot across his face. "Tarhael was assigned as my guard, but we were always more than that. We were friends...well, more than that too. He named Blueberry." He chuckled a little. "Insisted that it suited him. I wish there was a way to talk to him." He ran his hand through his hair, messing it up just a little. Elora pretended not to stare and failed spectacularly. "Anyway, I still trained and fought and all the other physical shit I was required to do but...Eolas was always more interesting. I went so far back in the archives once that my father fired the book keeper and forbid me from ever looking again. He didn't like what I found."

"What did you find?"

"History he'd rather keep hidden." Aerin's eyes were bright when he looked at her. "About why our realms separated in the first place." Her eyes widened and he continued. "There never used to be this... divide. It was an extraordinary feat of magic put in place by multiple fae years ago. You see, we might have magic and enhanced reflexes, but humans began developing guns. Plans for tanks. Bombs..."

Elora swallowed heavily. "We suddenly matched your strength."

He nodded. "It was dangerous. If we fought, nobody would survive, not with the chaos it would ensue. And fae...well they like to be the ones in control. Even the Seelie courts, with their fair laws and kindness, hated the idea of being overpowered. Hence, the portals were sealed and travel to and from the mortal realm was banned. Only specific, verified fae were allowed to travel through, and it's not done often."

"Until me," Elora guessed shakily.

"Until you."

"Well, fuck." Elora sat back and blew out a harsh breath.

Aerin laughed, a low, husky sound that Elora wanted to bottle up. *Shit*, she thought, mentally chastising herself, *wasn't the first fae guy enough warning for you?* Even as she thought it, she knew she was wrong. They might share blood, but Elladan and Aerin could not have been more different.

"Elora?" His voice snapped her from her thoughts.

"Yeah?"

"I'm sorry. For what Elladan did to you. Not that I know exactly what else he did or if he hurt you other than drugging your water and making you believe you were Fleur-"

"Wait, what?" Elora's stomach flipped. "He *drugged me?*"

Aerin looked alarmed. "Yes. To suppress your worry, your natural anxiety about your unusual circumstances, your desire to leave. Didn't you notice the water tasting different?"

Elora dug her nails into her palm, focusing on the fine pricks of pain. She was sure she was about to be sick. "The water…" She shook her head, swallowing thickly. "It was sweet. I thought it was just different in the fae realm."

Aerin's fists were clenched at his side. "I tried to stop him. But he… well, it became obvious that brute force wouldn't work. I'm sorry it took me so long. For what it's worth, the pixies were looking out for you. They didn't tell me details, didn't want to disrespect your privacy but…I'm sorry. I'm so sorry. I had no idea that was what he was going to do."

"What do you mean?"

"I gave him the runecast." When she still said nothing, he sighed and continued. "To help calm you down while we tried to get you home. The pixies said that you were panicked. It was written only to temporarily ease your mind in case you were panicking and Elladan was instructed repeatedly to only use it once a day."

Elora frowned, heart hammering in her chest. She wasn't sure how to feel about that and, regardless, it didn't make sense. "I thought Autumn powers were associated with air though? Why was it in my water?"

Aerin ran his hand through his hair, shoulder slumped. His voice was quiet when he spoke. "Elladan has a secret. One that my father threatened to kill me over if I ever told anyone. He can't access any power through his runecarvings. He can hardly runecast. This kind of thing almost never happens, but it's not unheard of. My father ensured nobody ever found out, and the story they spun was that Elladan simply preferred straight combat over rune assisted fighting.

He has few friends in Autumn, but many friends - associates really - in Winter. I still don't know what exactly happened, but he courted a fae named Sarissa for several years. I saw her in the castle a few weeks ago and thought that they had started seeing each other again. I didn't think anything else of it, until Raewyn reported to me that she thought the water Elladan was giving you was laced with something-" His voice broke, and he stared at her, eyes glassy. "I tried to stop him. I really did. I should've got you out sooner. I am so sorry."

Elora shook her head, staring at him. She took a few deep breaths, trying to process everything he'd just told her. She assumed that Elladan must have runecast on his own but learning that Aerin had been responsible, no matter how good his intentions, unsettled her. But when she looked at him, how devastated and broken he looked, she knew she couldn't blame him. The fight she'd heard, while half conscious and feeling as though she was dying, it must have been them. The bruises -

"Did he do that to you?" she blurted, sitting forward in her chair and staring at Aerin's chest as though she could still see the injuries, even through his clothes. "The bruises."

Aerin refused to meet her eyes.

"I can't believe I ever liked him."

Aerin snorted. "He was nice to you. That's the problem. He was nice until he wasn't. He was always like that. But he has half the damn court convinced he's an angel walking, and the other half are too scared to say anything."

Elora shuddered at the memories that assaulted her. Too much. This was all too much.

She stood, checking the time and realizing she was supposed to close the shop half an hour ago.

She grabbed her keys, turned to Aerin and sighed.

"I need a drink."

He smiled and her heart did a stupid little flip that felt all to similar to how it had once reacted to Elladan. Her stomach twisted at the unwanted comparison.

"Elora?"

She wondered briefly if she'd ever get used to the way her name sounded on his tongue. Like a song lyric he knew by heart.

"Yeah?"

"Can I stay?"

She frowned.

"Just for a little bit," he clarified, a faint blush staining his cheeks. "I don't really know how anything works here, but I'm a fast learner. I just um...can I stay with you until I figure it out?"

And, really, there was nothing else for her to say except, "Of course."

31

Elora

Elora's life somehow impossibly returned to a semblance of normal. Her weekly visits with Helen resumed, despite the fact that she couldn't bring herself to write anything, even though her visit to Fior Domhan should have been a wellspring of inspiration. It was strangely unsettling how normal everyone was and how nonchalantly they treated her. She planned movie and mall hangouts, and saw her parents and sister again for dinner that week. But she spent every day feeling like she was standing at the edge of it all, half out of her body, unable to talk about the things that had turned her life upside down and shaken her so badly she didn't know how to find herself again.

Except when she was with Aerin.

"So," Aerin said while chewing what had to be his thirtieth slice of pizza this past week. She'd come home to find him with a stack of pizza boxes and a grin on his face. When questioned how he'd paid for them, he'd casually informed her that *humans like faerie gold*. She'd objected to his trickery, both upset and oddly impressed with his ingenuity in glamouring spare change to look like larger notes, but he'd already started eating and there was no point insisting he returned it. "You weren't lying when you said the computer really does revolutionize one's learning rate."

"Remind me what you've covered so far?" Elora smiled, happy for the distraction from her own thoughts.

"You know how I told you the fae still interacted with humanity up until a couple hundred years ago, but the human-fae interactions decreased dramatically after what humans would call one thousand CE. I was reading about the specific technological innovations that enabled humanity to go from worshiping the fae to matching them."

Elora's brows drew together as she absorbed his words, taking a sip from her glass. "Since the fae were so much more advanced and advantaged from the beginning, how come you aren't much further along technologically?"

"Therein lies the main difference between humanity and the rest of all sentient life on this planet." Aerin's eyes had the professorial glint that appeared whenever he was preparing to give a lecture about something he was passionate about. Elora refused to admit it was attractive.

She grabbed another slice, trying to avoid thinking about how it'd been paid for, sipped some more soda and settled in her chair for the incoming lecture. She'd learned how to get him talking - to draw out the enthusiastic, excited Aerin from the quiet, reserved one. After his confession about his family the other day, he'd clammed up at the mention of home or his brother, but he would tell her about his research without so much as taking a breath. It wasn't so much the information that interested her, as the man who was talking.

"Humans, as far as I know, are the only organic and sentient beings on this planet that don't possess any forms of magic. Like none whatsoever. But the advantage that humans have over all other life is their creativity and ability to innovate. If you have the chance to read about not just the fae, but any and every other sentient life forms, whether it's dragons, changelings, Inknaymabas - giant eels that control the weather - we all sense and see progress at very different rates. Humans tend to live less than a hundred years, whereas fae and other creatures tend to live for several centuries. Humans are blessed with incredible creativity, and the rest of us tend to not innovate in a technological sense. You can blame magic for that."

Aerin had a wry smile now, the kind Elora had learned that meant he was starting to fall into introspection. She topped his glass and heaped another slice of pizza on his plate to remind him to keep eating. He took an absent minded bite and sip before continuing.

"When you have magic, there is almost no incentive to innovate, and while the understanding of magic grows to incredible depths, fae haven't technologically innovated the way humans have in centuries, especially after the two worlds were split apart. We used to try to be more innovation minded when the fae and human worlds intertwined, but after the Gates were sealed and travel banned, all forms of advancement crawled to a near standstill for a while. From what I can tell, there was a lot of internal warring and disagreement among us all. Humans have a different perspective on life due to the difference in our life spans. Creativity is humanity's forte."

Aerin sounded almost jealous, if Elora wasn't mistaken. *But since I'm half fae...* "Hey, Aerin?"

"Mmm?" He responded, his head still stuck in the clouds.

"You've said that I'm half fae...does that mean I do magic like you and Tarhael did? *Real* magic, not just barely enough to go through a portal."

"You've already shown signs of magic, Elora. Incredibly powerful and potent magic."

Elora visibly recoiled.

"Um, what? You're just going to drop that on me?"

"I mean, you never really asked about it and it's not something you just casually bring up in conversation."

"I mean, yes, but -" Elora sputtered off into noises of frustration as words failed her. "Okay, this is big though!" She stood and began pacing, needing to move so she wouldn't scream at Aerin for not telling her this sooner. The idea that she, Elora Han, might be able to perform actual, intentional magic was both incredibly exhilarating and utterly terrifying at the same time. "Elaborate please."

"You know how you've asked me to water your plants when you're out on errands or grabbing dinner or whatever it is that you do."

"Mhmm."

"I haven't watered them once."

"What?" Elora glanced around her, and saw every single one of her colorful plants looking healthy. Especially so.

"My theory is that there's some sort of innate Eolas radiating off you that is revitalizing and giving life to your plants without you knowing it. It would make sense if you had noble or royal parentage, as you would need your carvings. But I can't be sure. Anyway, look." He pointed to the jade and aloe vera plants. "Not only are these two plants here incredibly green, they are both larger than they were when we arrived. And they haven't been watered in weeks."

Elora struggled to find the words. She stared at her plants unblinkingly as though they'd tell her the answers. "So...what kind of magic can I practice?"

"That's the million dollar question, isn't it?" Aerin replied, the fingers on his right hand tapping the table the way he did whenever he was thinking about something. "The only way to know for sure is if you start practicing."

Elora sharply sucked in a breath. How could Aerin just casually ask her if she wanted to learn magic? Did he realize how insane that was? She steadied herself and exhaled before answering.

"You know, I've started and written so many stories about magical characters and worlds," she broke off, shaking her head. "Are you serious?"

"What reason would I have to lie?" Aerin replied dryly.

Elora swallowed and shrugged.

"Do you want to start tomorrow?"

"*Tomorrow?*" Elora could barely keep the excitement off her face, a giddy bubble of anticipation rising inside her.

"Sure, why not?"

Turned out, Eolas really was a whole new language.

Aerin had Elora start with learning all the generic runes that were used in many runecasts, regardless of the type of magic a fae possessed.

"Remember, depending on the Court your fae parent was from, you won't be able to use some of these runes I'm teaching you, but I'm teaching you just to be safe until I can figure out for sure what seasonal parentage you have."

Elora learned about the different types of powers that were associated with the various Seasons, mind constantly swimming through the depths of all the information. Aerin explained everything Tarhael had, but in more depth.

"If you know the Eolas alphabet, and the syntax and grammar structures of how to build runecasts, everything else will come easily to you."

He had her memorizing and translating runecasts every evening when Elora came home from work, and over the next week, Elora would study the runes while Aerin borrowed her laptop to learn as much about the human world as he possibly could.

"Aerin?"

"Yes?"

"Have there been any half-fae before me? If humans and fae lived together, then there had to have been, right?"

Aerin sighed and ran his hands through his long hair, tangling his locks. Elora knew this was his semi frustrated look when he didn't have information being asked for.

"The thing is, human and fae relations was one of the really well destroyed and hidden sections of knowledge after the portals were sealed and while I know that there were several notable half humans and fae in history, there haven't been any born in since..." he trailed off, doing the calculations in his head. Aerin's eyes widened as he said, "Elora, you're the first half-fae to be born in at least a thousand years."

A brief silence ensued as Elora took the information in.

"But won't the others still be...?" She paused, suddenly feeling foolish. Aerin raised a brow at her. "I mean, fae lifespans are longer than humans, right? So won't any of the others still be um...alive?

Aerin blew out a short breath and lent forward so his elbows rested on his knees. "Fae live longer, sure, but not *that* long. We mature at the same rate as humans until we hit around our early twenties then our aging slows dramatically. But at most we live for four centuries."

Elora blinked. *Four centuries.* Her heart stuttered in her chest at the thought of potentially having that much time ahead of her. It was daunting.

"So, how long do half fae live then?"

"About the same I think, if the old textbooks are reliable."

Elora thought she might be sick. Goosebumps rose along her skin, and her breath shortened. She stared down at her hands, shaky in her lap. She couldn't think about this. Not now. It was incomprehensible.

She rose her head, forcing the information out of her mind. Aerin offered a brief smile and she smiled back a little halfheartedly. Their gazes met and locked. Aerin's eyes were big and dark, the brilliant green all too easy to fall into. Heat zipped across her skin, chasing away the gooseflesh, a flush creeping up her neck.

Aerin blinked, and the moment was over.

Elora scolded herself for reading into it. It was just a look. That's all. She hoped her heart would actually listen to reason for once.

"Elladan said that the reason why the fae and humans split apart is because of the humans, and it's why the fae hate humans today."

"Not quite. I mean, based off what I've read, humans do seem terrible at times. But the fae weren't much better. If anything, the fae were responsible for the initial rift between them and humans."

"What do you mean?"

"It's a really long story but if you want, I can properly talk about it after you get a little better with Eolas. But humans aren't the only ones at fault. The blame is even in my opinion."

They sat in silence for a few more minutes until Aerin lifted his head towards the window.

"It's been two weeks since we left," Aerin said, staring beyond Elora at the crescent moon dangling in the sky.

Elora's breath shuddered as she nodded. It felt like years since she felt the crisp breeze sting her cheeks, since Raewyn had chastised her for not sitting still while her hair was being done, since she'd tasted fae wine and laughed and -

Since Elladan had taken her and molded her into Fleur. Into a perfect little fae girl. Her stomach rolled, the sudden urge to shower in scalding hot water sparking across her skin. Every time she thought of him, she wanted to scratch her skin off until she couldn't feel the ghost of his hands anymore. And though she thought she might feel a little better if a new, softer touch replaced the memory of his, when Alice had suggested Elora stay the night after their dinner a few days ago, she'd spun straight into a panic attack. She'd called off the benefits to their friendship. Alice understood, but it didn't make Elora feel better. Her medication eased the anxiety, but she'd yet to find something that eased the memories. The fear that woke her at night, the what ifs that haunted her dreams. So, as much as she wanted his touch replaced, erased, she wasn't sure she was ready to try. Not yet.

But she glanced over at Aerin, thinking *maybe soon*. She expelled the thought from her mind, knowing fine well that wasn't how this worked, and feeling slightly guilty for it even crossing her mind.

The hours slipped by as Elora and Aerin fell back into studying, but Elora knew the familiar somersaults her heart was starting to do. Worse, she was sure he felt nothing towards her. They had mutually shared motives, that's all. If she tried, maybe she could convince herself that the knowledge didn't hurt. Having Aerin near her wasn't helping, and she decided that going to bed would probably be the best course of action. She glanced at the couch Aerin slept on in her tiny spare room and promised herself that she would find something more comfortable for him soon. He'd adjusted remarkably well to the lack of luxury but the old, sharp springs on that thing would ruin his back.

Not that she cared.

"Hey, I think I'm going to go to bed early tonight."

"Hm? Oh yeah, okay. Night."

Elora gave him a pathetic wave and headed towards her room. Stopping by the edge of the living room, she looked back at Aerin, who was already lost in endless Wikipedia pages. His black hair was pulled back in a ponytail with one of her scrunchies (blue with little yellow flowers) and he was blowing at the strands that had escaped. He was wearing a loose shirt and gray joggers that she'd grabbed for him, and seeing him in such mundane clothing was short circuiting her brain. His brows were furrowed in concentration, and she let her eyes linger for a few heartbeats before closing the door to her room, taking her medication (having finally picked it up the day after they got back on her run to get Aerin more clothes) and falling into bed.

32

Elora

The crashing woke Elora.

It sounded like her entire wall was being caved in. She scrambled out of bed, fear curdling the confusion in her stomach. Frantic shouts bounced off the walls and she tore out of her room, breath leaving her in a rush when she took in the remains of her apartments. Chunks of alabaster and wood lay littered all around the space and she could make out the shapes of dark creatures pouring in. Her hand flew to her mouth to stifle her shriek as she watched the shadowy creatures, back lit by the moonlight - winged beasts, claws the length of her kitchen knives, inhuman screams pouring from their open jaws. They looked like nothing she'd ever seen, or even read about - a horrible mix of multiple creatures, giant bat-like wings, snouts similar to wolves, tails that whipped through the air. The winged creatures held other beasts in their claws, and they let go as they closed in. Elora looked up to see entire sections of her ceiling missing. The cloying scent of ash coated her apartment, and she pressed her hand over her mouth as though that would stop the sour taste stinging her throat.

Aerin. Where is Aerin? Where is Aerin? Where is- She searched frantically for him among the chaos, finally spotting him fighting an enormous tiger looking monster, a winged demon bearing down on him from above. She screamed.

The sound echoed around her as a bright green light flared, washing the entire apartment in its glow. Elora's body felt like she'd been struck by thousands of needles, her skin burning like it was being ripped apart. Nearly blacking out from the pain, she staggered and gripped the door frame for support, squeezing her eyes shut and bracing for the impact of one of the invaders.

But none came. She wrenched her eyelids open, blinking rapidly as the bright light faded and the scene before her became clearer.

Her plants had grown ten times their size out of nowhere, and her entire apartment looked like an overrun jungle, thick stems and leaves the same height as her enveloping her living space. Her breath halted. The plants were *moving,* twisting and reaching as though they were alive. They were grabbing this way and that, entangling the monsters and stopping their destruction, tightening their grip the more they thrashed.

A hand grabbed Elora's wrist, tugging her back towards her room. "Come on!"

A bloody gash ran down the left side of Aerin's face, dripping deep red onto this shirt. He pulled her into his room, slamming the door behind them.

"Aerin, the plants, your face, I-"

His arms wrapped around her, silencing her, and a bright gray blue light began spilling from Aerin's skin. Elora watched, equally horrified and fascinated as wings sprouted from his back. Distantly, she thought that they reminded her of an angel's wings, plush gray feathers that glowed faintly blue that spanned nearly the width of the whole room.

"Hold tight," was all the warning Elora got before Aerin leapt through the window, shattering glass and leaving the howling monsters behind.

"Aerin!" Elora screamed as they tore through the cold night air, wind whipping her hair into knots and leaving her skin stinging. It was *freezing* up this high, and she curled closer to Aerin's warmth, shivering. "Where the hell are we going? What the fuck just happened?"

She was spiraling and she knew it but she didn't know how to stop. Terror and confusion, a combination she was used to by now, wreaked havoc on her mind. She was too shocked to cry.

"I don't know! Fuck, Elora, I don't know."

He so rarely swore, or spoke with anything other than a calm tone, and that, more than anything else, worried her.

"We can't stay here," he said, his words nearly whisked away by the wind, the beating of his wings loud against the quiet evening sky.

"Obviously!" Elora fought the urge to look over his shoulder at her ruined apartment.

"No, I mean we can't stay *here*," Aerin clarified. "In this realm. We can't put other humans in danger."

Elora's stomach sank. Horror set her nerves on edge, a riot of emotions buzzing in her brain.

"No. No no no. Aerin I can't go back, I *can't* -"

"I know, I know." His grip tightened on her, as though trying to hold her together. "But we don't have a choice. If we stay, they'll come for us again, especially now they have both our scents and possessions to track us with. I don't want to go back either, but I can't keep us safe here."

"Can't we just go away from New York? A different country-"

"I don't have the resources here to guarantee your safety. There's somewhere in Fior Domhan-" he cut himself off with a curse. "I was hoping not to have to return. At least not soon. But we stand a better chance there, where no one else will get caught in the crossfire."

She knew he was right. Nobody else deserved to get caught up in their game of cat and mouse. The thought of anyone else getting hurt, or being collateral damage, made her sick. As much as the idea made her want to scream herself hoarse with dread, the fae realm, logically, was the best choice.

Unfortunately, her anxiety didn't respond well to logic.

"So, do we go to the bookshop? I can get a paper cut again." The joke fell flat, a pathetic attempt to distract herself from the incoming panic attack she could feel building in her bones, but Aerin just shook his head.

"They'll be expecting that. We can't use that portal again - it will take us right back to the hill near Dioltas Castle. That's the last place we need to be."

Despair coiled around Elora's ribs, and her breathing came in short gasps. "Then what?"

"We find another one." Aerin's eyes grew distant and then he picked up speed, flying them so fast Elora had to squeeze her eyes shut.

She expected the flight to scare her. Logically, being this high off the ground with a man - no a *fae* man - holding her so close to his chest she could hear the pounding of his heart, should have scared her. And yet the warmth of his body against hers, the solid press of his fingertips into her thigh where he held her were grounding her, stopping her from floating away entirely into her own panic.

They were well away from the apartment now, and nothing seemed to have followed them. The plants, miraculously, must have held.

She couldn't process what had happened. None of it made sense. How had they been found? *Why* had anyone come looking for them? Who had sent those shadow creatures, and how the fuck had all her plants come alive?

Her head hurt and the sight of blood drying on Aerin's cheek only increased the pressure behind her eyes.

"Don't scream."

That was all the warning she got before they were plummeting to the earth, Aerin's wings tucked close to his body, the ground rising steadily to meet them. She bit the inside of her mouth to avoid shrieking, bile stinging her throat, the taste of blood and terror lingering on her tongue.

Seconds before they would have hit the ground, Aerin's wings snapped back out and lowered them softly, Elora's entire body shaking with adrenaline as he set her down. She stumbled, head spinning and he quickly picked her back up again.

"I'll be fine," she mumbled, though the world felt like it was dancing. "Put me down."

"Not the time to be a hero, Elora," he chastised, carrying her swiftly towards what looked like a door -

"Wait." She blinked to focus her eyes, suddenly realizing where they were. "What are we doing here? We can't get in -"

The Statue of Liberty loomed above them and Elora tipped her head back to get a glimpse at the top of it. She'd lived here so long and never once bothered to visit it. Certainly never thought she'd be sneaking around it in the middle of the night, running away from horrifying shadow demons.

"God, I need a holiday," she muttered against Aerin's chest, his low laugh rumbling through her.

"Blood," Aerin said abruptly, setting her back on her feet. She was still dizzy, but she didn't fall this time. They were tucked close to the base of the statue, and Elora couldn't see any reason why he'd brought them here.

"Uh...what?"

"We need blood," he repeated, crouching down and running his hand over the building. In the darkness, she could barely make out the little raised letters on the stone. Aerin, apparently, had no problem finding them.

"Do you want me to like…cut myself?" she asked warily, watching him wipe off the grime from the words.

"As much as I hate the thought of you being hurt," he said in a low voice. "Given the fact you managed to travel with a few drops last time, it would probably be best if we use your blood. I'm afraid I'll need all the strength I can get when we enter Fior Domhan. I don't exactly know where this Gate will take us."

Well. Elora swallowed, understanding his reasoning, though the thought of intentionally returning to Fior Domhan made her skin crawl. Deeper, beneath the dread and fear and bone deep confusion, there was the tiniest spark of longing. Something far too close to excitement for Elora's comfort.

"Yeah," she heard herself saying, shivering in the thin cotton pajamas she still had on. "Yeah, I can do that. Makes sense."

"Here." Aerin handed her a dagger she recognized all too well.

"This fucking thing," she mumbled, examining the bone handle, remembering the pressure of the blade against her neck.

"Just cut the tip of your finger and spread it on the rune," Aerin explained, guiding her hand so she could feel the raised symbols. She refused to think about how she could feel the calluses on his fingertips from guitar strings. Refused to acknowledge the fact her heart tripped when his thumb rubbed over the back of her hand.

Instead, she sliced a shallow cut into the top of her finger and spread the warm blood over the stone.

At first, nothing happened. Aerin sucked in a sharp breath and murmured something that sounded like profanity in a language she didn't know.

And then -

"Go!"

She was falling, colors swirling around her as she fought to keep her grip on Aerin's hand. He'd tugged her through the second it opened and despite the fact this was her third time traveling this way, she was nowhere near used to it.

The cold shocked her first. More so than the rough landing that sent shock waves up her spine, or the way Aerin was holding her hand so tight his knuckles were white.

Her teeth chattered almost immediately, and she jumped to her feet to avoid the cold seeping through the back of her pajamas. The thin soled shoes she'd slipped on before they got whisked away did barely anything to stop the icy ground assaulting her though, and she wrapped her arms around her waist reflexively, tucking her hands under her arms.

"Well," Aerin said, standing and running a hand through his wind swept hair. "At least it isn't Autumn."

33

Elora

Elora had lost track of how long they'd walked for. Aerin had created a little bubble of warmth around them, stopping Elora's fingers turning blue and halting the chattering of her teeth entirely. While the magic still unsettled her a little, she was grateful.

"North of here," Aerin was saying as he walked beside her, the frozen grass crunching beneath his boots. "There's a plant that I can use in a runecast that will keep us hidden. Properly hidden, this time. I can only assume that my father, or my brother, was responsible for the attack in New York." He winced.

She shrugged, refusing to think about the loss of her home. The loss of her safety. Now wasn't the time for tears.

"Can you do it again?"

"Do what?"

"Make plants grow," Aerin said, as if it was obvious.

"That wasn't you?"

He laughed, the sound encased in their little bubble. Elora stared at him.

"No." He raised his brows at her. "I have Autumn magic. That means air and mind. I can't grow things, or manipulate life. Autumn is the *in between*. The area between life and death."

Elora shivered at the description.

"I have no idea how I did it," she said quietly, unable to digest the fact that she'd done it at all. A seed of excitement had taken root in her when Aerin had first brought up the chance that she'd have magic but she never expected to be faced with it quite so abruptly. It terrified her.

"Try while we walk."

So she did. They walked and Aerin explained the intricacies of innate magic - *focus, envision what you want to happen, connect with the soil, feed life into the dead earth* - over and over again until Elora thought her brain would melt out her ears. Frustration set her nerves on edge and she stamped the dead grass beneath her useless shoes.

"I can't, Aerin!" she snapped. "I have no idea how to do any of this. I wasn't brought up here! I'm not like you."

He wasn't looking at her though. His gaze was rooted to the ground beside her foot. She frowned.

"No, Elora. You're not." His voice was breathless and quiet, laced with awe. "You're something much, much stronger."

She followed his eyes and pressed her hand over her mouth to stifle the shocked gasp. There, beside her shoe, was a twisted, thorny vine, the once dead grass, white with snow and ice, had thawed and turned green, little daisies unfurling around her.

"Typical," Aerin joked, grinning so wide his eyes sparkled. He poked at the vine with the toe of his boot. "Couldn't have grown me a nice rose?"

She gaped at him, fighting the smile that threatened to break through her shock.

Elora bent down and traced the strong stalk of the vine with careful fingers, then plucked one of the daisies from the ground.

ELORA

"Here," she said sarcastically, reaching out and resting it behind his ear, the tiny white petals poking through his dark hair. "Happy?"

He blinked at her, his green eyes wide and filled with an emotion Elora was too nervous to place. Her pulse sped up.

He touched the flower softly, smiling. "Very."

Shit, Elora thought, immediately returning to the vine. *Focus.*

"Don't hate me for this." Aerin looked genuinely sorry as he led her away from her little patch of greenery and sighed. "We can't leave a trail."

Seconds later, an icy wind swept over the scene, freezing her flowers and leaving nothing but dead grass in their wake.

The lump in her throat was thick and unexpected.

"It's okay," she said, but her voice was too wobbly to make it convincing. The guilt on his face only made it worse. "Come on. We need to keep moving."

She made it about twenty minutes before curiosity burned its way through her teeth.

"Why do they want me so much?"

Aerin sighed. "I don't know. But you are...special." She winced and he chuckled. "It's not just your smell..." He elbowed her good naturedly when she scowled at him. "Though that's still masked, of course. It's the fact your magic is so potent you can open portals with a few drops of your blood, perform incredible feats like the stunt you pulled at your apartment without so much as practicing. It's the fact that we have no idea who your parents are, or how you even lived so long undetected. It's the fact that you're...well.." he trailed off, looking sheepish.

"I'm what?" she pushed, but he just shook his head, eyes narrowing as he indicated for her to be quiet. A chill ran down her spine, but she obeyed.

Faster than she could track, Aerin spun her so she was behind him, dagger out and held to the throat of a thin, vaguely humanoid creature that had something gold and shiny clutched in its spindly fingers.

"What business do you have with us?" Aerin said, far too calmly, his voice low.

The thing tilted its head and grinned, revealing dull yellow teeth. Its skin was dirty and pale, scaly in patches and Elora noticed with horror that its fingers had one too many joints as it opened its palm to reveal her ring. It was a cheap piece that she'd had for ages, thrown on yesterday because it complimented her outfit. She'd forgotten to take it off before bed.

"What the fuck?" she sneered before she could help herself, rubbing the spot on her finger where it had been and wondering how the hell the thing had removed it from her without her knowing.

Aerin looked at her and rolled his eyes.

Oh, right, silent. Oops.

"Give it back before I spill your blood all over this frozen shit hole," Aerin pressed the blade against its gray skin for effect and Elora fought the urge to check her own neck for blood.

"Or," the creature spoke, its voice oddly melodic. "I could trade you. I'll tell you a secret and take this gift as payment." It held up the ring for emphasis.

"No," Aerin near growled. "I know your type. Trickster fae. You'll get nothing from us."

Elora wasn't listening. She pushed past him and stared the creature down.

She'd read the legends about making deals with fae. But the ones about the food and dancing had proved to be lies, and she was sick of being the frail wisp of a girl who needed protecting. She wanted answers and nobody would give her them. This *thing*, whatever it was, could prove useful.

Besides, curiosity had always been her downfall.

ELORA

"Okay."

"Elora, no -"

"What are you, pretty thing?" the creature cooed, wide gray eyes scouring her. She refused to back down, despite the sudden urge to bathe in scalding water.

"Elora," she said simply, raising her chin. "From New York."

The thing laughed, the sound tinny and jarring. "Oh, sweets," it said, examining the ring with a long nail. It was valueless, but she wasn't about to tell it so. "You really have no idea, do you?" It reached out, dragging a cold finger along her cheek, despite Aerin's dagger still pressed to its neck.

"Watch your mouth." Anger flared through Elora as she spoke. She was sick of being the butt of the joke, the last one to know anything. Fuck that. "Or I'll rip out your throat."

Aerin nearly lost his grip on the dagger she was eyeing as he turned to her, eyes wide and heated.

But the thing just grinned, worn, yellow teeth showing. "Good to know you've got the spark it'll take to tear them all apart."

She blinked and it was gone.

Aerin's dagger pressed against nothing but air, the vague scent of rotting meat the only trace that it had ever been there in the first place.

"What-" Elora breathed, spinning wildly to try to catch sight of it. "What the hell! You lied! You owe me a truth!" She was screaming, but she didn't care.

Aerin holstered his dagger in his belt again and slammed up a wall of air, blocking her voice. His face had paled, the heat she'd glimpsed briefly in his eyes when he threatened the creature thoroughly doused.

"Aerin?"

He didn't answer, merely shaking his head and clenching his jaw before taking off again, footsteps quiet.

Elora blinked, the creature's words replaying in her mind and followed him through the desolate, frigid land.

34

Elora

Neither of them spoke for an hour - Elora turning the thing's words over and over in her mind until they dissolved like popping candy. Nothing made sense. Her skin itched, her heart not quite settled into its usual rhythm.

Aerin hadn't so much as looked at her since the trickster fae had spoken. He had erected a wall of adamant around whatever he was feeling, and his face had returned to the same cold mask he wore when she first met him. She hated it.

Finally, Aerin looked back at her, making sure she wasn't drowning in the snow, before forging on.

"Where are we?" Her voice was brittle and sharp.

"I don't fucking know," he snapped at her, expression tight. "Does it look like I have a map?"

Elora scowled at him, fists clenching around the thin material of her shirt. "Fine. Keep sulking. I'm sure that will help things."

The questions she had earlier were forgotten as she braced herself against the sudden cold. She was used to New York winters, and the snow there was no joke, but this was absolutely ridiculous. Snow kept falling, so thick she could hardly see ten feet in front of her. And it was cold. *So* damn cold. The winter air here bit into her skin unlike any weather she had ever been in. Everything in Fior Domhan was more vibrant but more violent and visceral, too.

"Aerin, what the *fuck?*"

He glanced over his shoulder at her before re-erecting the dome of air, warming her bones again. "Oops."

She barely resisted the urge to hit him.

"The forest here seems to be thinning a little, so maybe we're getting closer to a major road?" Elora forced her voice into calm complacency, a verbal handshake. He took the bait, shoulders dropping a little as the defensive stance he'd taken relaxed.

"Yeah, let's focus on getting out of the forest and see where the road takes us."

They continued their trudge through the woods, until trees gave way to snow dusted roads. Elora squinted against the white haze, trying to focus on a yellow light flickering up ahead.

"Aerin, do you-"

"Yes."

They took off running at the same time.

"This inn looks…cozy," Elora finished, doing her best not to be pessimistic.

"Cozy? It looks like it's about to fall over." Aerin ran a hand through his hair, stepping forward to hesitantly knock on the tilted wooden door, holding his breath like he half expected it to cave in at his touch. After a few moments of silence with nothing but the howling snow to fill it, the door creaked open a few inches and a pair of beady eyes stared out.

"How many?" an old lady's voice called out.

"Two," Aerin replied, gesturing to Elora next to him.

There was a little more hesitation before the door creaked open the rest of the way, revealing a tiny old fae lady with a wizened back. The rest of the inn matched the dilapidated exterior and the few patrons drinking at the bar looked up as they entered, but quickly went back to their tankards.

"You just missed dinner but breakfast is served in the morning."

Elora's stomach chose just that moment to growl and the innkeeper gave her an unsympathetic shrug as she went back around the counter and looked at Aerin expectantly.

"Well?"

"Oh, yes. Payment." Aerin coughed and made a show of patting down his pockets.

"Can you pay?" The woman's eyes stormed as she watched them, crossing her arms over her chest.

"I…"

"Hello. It seems my companion here forgot to bring money, but would we be able to earn our keep here? We would be more than willing to clean or do anything else necessary to earn our stay. It's only for one night." Elora made her voice sugar sweet, an enthusiastic smile on her lips like they hadn't just spent hours in the freezing cold. When the innkeeper hesitated, she pressed her advantage. "Please. You wouldn't make us go back out into the snowstorm, would you?"

The innkeeper considered them for a moment or two before answering. "I don't run a charity around here. If you two sweep and clean the inn then I can give you a room towards the back."

"Yes, we would love that. Thank you so much!"

"The brooms are near the kitchen entrance." With that, the innkeeper turned away and went to attend the other customers.

They obeyed, grabbing the box of cleaning supplies - a bucket and mop, brush and old rags. As they cleaned, Elora noticed Aerin studying her movements carefully and realized with a short burst of laughter that he'd never cleaned before. He glared at her, but dutifully memorized her movements and copied.

When they were finally finished, it was dark outside and the woman at the counter gave them brisk directions to their room. Elora's body ached from the travel and subsequent chores and the thought of a bed had her near crying with anticipation.

"So, where are we going tomorrow?"

"Spring," Aerin answered, putting the key the innkeeper had given them.

Aerin went quiet as the door at the end of the hallway swung open, revealing what could only be called a bedroom in the barest sense of the word.

"What the hell?" Elora couldn't keep the annoyance out of her voice. It had taken them nearly three hours to clean the place and they couldn't even get a decent room?

"There's no heating…" Aerin trailed off, eyes narrowing as he took in the room. Elora pushed past him to see for herself, stomach flipping a little.

"There's only one bed."

Besides the bed and the tiny vanity with a dirty mirror, there was hardly any other space in the cramped room. Looking around, Elora took in the cracked wooden floorboards, where God knows what could come crawling out of, and a tiny window that was boarded shut. The walls had suspicious stains on them and the bed looked old and rickety. Sighing, Elora moved towards it at the same time Aerin did.

"Sorry," she muttered. "You've done a lot of magic today. You can take the bed."

Aerin eyed her. "You take it."

"It's really not that big of a deal. I used to sleep on the floor in college a lot. It's a long story. Anyway, just toss me a blanket and I'll be fine."

Aerin paused for a moment and considered her. "Am I that bad?"

"Excuse me?"

"I mean, I can't be the ugliest person you've met. What's so bad about sharing the bed together?"

"I...well..it's that..." Elora couldn't really give him a valid reason, heat crawling along her cheeks.

"Does the idea of getting in the same bed as me excite you that much?" His voice had dropped, smooth and teasing.

Elora responded by jumping in the bed, pushing Aerin off the edge. He landed in the muffled heap, an impish grin on his face as he righted himself.

"May I?"

Elora snorted. "Please, be my guest." She didn't tell him how fast her heart was beating, how she couldn't help but hyper-focus on every inch of him as he climbed in bed with her, how she was suddenly, inexplicable sure that she wanted him to be the one to make her feel new again. Feeling the heat rising in her body, and hoping to obscure the blush blooming on her cheeks, she turned away from him, rolling as far to the edge of the bed as she could without falling off. Silence fell for a few heartbeats, Elora too nervous to so much as take a deep breath. Her nerves were interrupted by a foot poking into her leg and a hand jabbing into her shoulder blades.

"What the hell?"

"What?"

Not in the mood to play games, Elora turned her head to see Aerin in a starfish pose across the bed, limbs splayed out, taking up as much space as possible. Rolling her eyes and letting out a grumble of annoyance, Elora scooted even closer to the edge, but Aerin's limbs followed her. "For God's sake Aerin, I swear -"

She was abruptly cut off as Aerin pushed her off the bed. Landing in a tumbled mess, Elora shrieked and launched herself at him, wrestling with him for a better grip. What she was going to do when she had him, she hadn't the faintest clue. But he was bigger, stronger and undoubtedly better trained. The breath left her lungs as she ended up beneath him, her arms pinned. Her laughter choked out as she met his eyes. Every nerve in her body felt like it had been lit up, the air between them alive and buzzing, his grip on her wrists strong but not sore. Heat spread low in her stomach.

"I win-"

Elora's lips met Aerin's, cutting him off. Her eyes were already closed and she didn't see his widen in surprise before he leaned into the kiss, mouth pressing softly against hers. Aerin tasted like autumn spices and fresh air, cut with something Elora couldn't quite describe but worried was all too addictive. He melted into her, his hands releasing her arms to tangle in her hair, the other resting on her hip. She deepened the kiss, tracing her tongue over his bottom lip. His tongue met hers seconds later, the kiss turning frantic as he matched her intensity. Both his hands found her waist before she was spun, Aerin twisting them both so she was on top of him.

Elora straddled him as he lay on his back, her hands on his chest. She could feel the flex of his muscles as he tensed beneath her touch. She broke the kiss and stared at him, breathless, his eyes heavy lidded but steady as they met hers. His hair had escaped the elastic and splayed around his shoulders. When he looked at her, she swore she could see fire burning in his eyes. Aerin's hands slid up around the back of her head and he pulled her down to crush his lips against hers again. His mouth trailed down her neck, pressing open mouthed kisses over her fluttering pulse. A gasp flew from Elora's lips as she shifted against him, needing closer, needing the friction, needing *him*. There was no room in her mind for anything but *him*, drowning out every little anxiety that tried to plague her. She squirmed on top of him, warmth pooling between her thighs as she felt the evidence of how she was affecting him. His teeth grazed her neck and she shivered, whimpering slightly at the need pulsing in the air between them. She didn't mean to take it further - to start grinding her hips against his, but Aerin matched her rhythm and she promptly forgot why it was a bad idea at all. Their lips met again, the kiss harder, more urgent now. A soft moan escaped her lips as Aerin caught her bottom lip between his teeth, panting softly. He had one hand on her hip, holding her against him, and slid his free hand up her shirt. He paused, thumb tracing the edge of her bra, before he pushed it to the side and touched her torturously softly. Elora moaned against his lips. There were too many layers between them, even as she rode him through their clothes, the friction not nearly enough to ease the ache growing inside her. She had to stifle a scream when his thumb made contact with her nipple, the touch sending electricity through her body. Aerin groaned at her reaction, hand flexing at her hip.

Suddenly, he broke away, lifting Elora from his hips and placed her back down next to him. Dazed and slightly hurt, Elora scrambled up and away from the bed.

"Aerin, did I-"

"It's fine," he said, his voice low and gravelly. "I'm sorry. Are you okay?"

Elora frowned at him. Was she okay? She felt like a live wire, lit up and left wide open, horribly vulnerable under his stare. She shivered. She didn't know. Instead, she said, "I don't regret it."

Aerin's eyes flashed with heat, but cooled just as quickly. "We should sleep."

She tugged on the hem of her shirt, skin still tingling where he'd touched her moments ago. "Right. Yes."

They didn't speak as they climbed onto the bed, Elora perched on the edge, the space between them cold and vast.

35

Elora

Someone was yelling.

Elora screwed her eyes tighter shut, fighting to cling onto the last remnants of the dream. But the mattress dipped beneath her and the blanket was yanked off her shoulders. Icy air wrapped around her skin, urging her awake fully. She sat up, eyes bleary, stomach in knots.

Aerin lay beside her, face contorted in anger or pain, she couldn't tell. He was still asleep, but his fists were clenched and his breaths were coming in rapid gasps. He yelled out and Elora jumped.

A nightmare.

Aerin was dreaming, and whatever it was that he was seeing was terrifying him.

Elora reached out tentatively, resting her hand on his shoulder and shaking a little.

"Aerin, wake up, it's just a dream-"

"Get off!" He twisted violently, voice foggy with sleep, a muscle in his jaw ticking. Elora's heart picked up it's pace.

"Aerin, come on-" She tried again, nudging him harder this time, both hands on his shoulder, his skin sticky with cold sweat beneath her touch.

"Elora?"

She couldn't tell if he was awake or not, but the tension had seeped from his body, his face smoothing out. A sigh shuddered from her chest, her heart aching a little at the sight of him.

"Come here." He was definitely still asleep, she decided. There was no other explanation for him tugging her back down to the mattress and pulling her tight against his chest. She decided she must still be asleep too because her body burrowed closer to his, seeking warmth, his strong arms around her waist, the now calm beat of his heart beneath her head.

If she was awake, she wouldn't be this close to him. *Cuddling* when things were still so tense and awkward from the definite mistake she'd made by kissing him. But they were dreaming, tangled together beneath the blanket, and so she reasoned with herself that it was okay. She was just helping him calm down from whatever terrors he'd seen in his nightmare. That was all.

Just a friend helping another friend out.

She fell asleep halfway through convincing herself of it.

She woke the second he left the bed, eyes opening slowly as she grumbled about wanting to sleep more. Aerin snapped at her from where he stood at the door, which was near vibrating on its hinges with an obnoxiously loud banging.

"What the hell?" It occurred to Elora that she had been saying the particular phrase a lot recently, but then again, her entire life had been upended.

"Shh, it could be anyone behind that door."

Elora frowned, but the knocking that had the door shaking sounded again and she scrambled out of bed, barely registering the sudden temperature change that set goosebumps along her exposed skin. Aerin pulled his dagger out, creeping over to the door. He yanked the door open, simultaneously throwing the blade up to the neck of whoever lay beyond it.

But the second he did, Aerin found a knife at his neck too.

"C'mon, I taught you that trick. Isn't it a bit early for knife play?"

Elora watched Aerin's face light up in a grin, recognizing the voice.

"Tarhael!" Aerin threw the knife on the floor and hugged the guard tightly, who had to drop his dagger to avoid skewering his own prince. "How did you even find us? What happened after we left? What is going on?" Aerin's voice was tense as he released his friend and stepped back, his usual armor falling carefully back into place. Elora ignored her disappointment at the sight of it.

"One thing at a time Aerin." Tarhael had to stoop his head to enter the tiny inn room and chuckled at the sight of the singular bed. "You really moved on from me that quick?"

Aerin went tense and stammered out an excuse while Tarhael continued to laugh.

Knife play? Moving on? Realization dawned on Elora and she pushed down the unexpected twinge of jealousy that shot up from her stomach.

"I can't be that easy to replace," Tarhael said, lightly punching Aerin in the arm.

"Tarhael," Aerin warned, voice dark with protest.

"I see," Tarhael continued conspiratorially. "So, is this official yet or-"

"No!" Elora cut Tarhael off, then blushed, not having intended her denial come off so strongly. She didn't know how to articulate what she had with Aerin yet, and was too tired and confused to do it now. Besides, she didn't want to get in between Aerin and Tarhael, whatever it was that they had. She had to admit that they made a striking pair, both unfairly attractive, Aerin lean and radiating a calm sort of danger, Tarhael a head and a half taller with a giant grin on his face.

Perhaps sensing the awkwardness in the room, Tarhael cleared his throat and continued, his grin disappearing as he spoke. "I was able to find you with the tracking runecast you gave me before you left. Turns out, it does work even if you go through a portal. Anyway, I have bad news. Elladan is scarcely an hour behind me. We need to *move*."

Elora's jaw dropped.

"What? Why didn't you fucking *lead with that?*" Aerin's eyes narrowed as he hastily shoved his hair out of his face with the leather band Tarhael handed him. Somewhere along the way, he'd lost her scrunchie. It shouldn't bother her as much as it did. "How did Elladan find you?"

"I don't know." Tarhael sounded frustrated. "I only have my horse so we'll need to steal horses from the stable next door if we want to keep ahead of him."

As much as Elora adored animals and hated the thought of stealing them away from their owners, her self preservation kicked in and she admitted that they realistically had no other choice. Aerin stuffed the water skin Elora was sure they were supposed to return to the owner into Tarhael's satchel and the three of them made their way out of the inn and into the stables. Tarhael pulled what appeared to be a few sugar cubes out of his pocket and coaxed the fittest looking horse towards him while Aerin muttered to it and stroked it's mane.

Elora marveled at how the two worked in tandem, not needing to speak to each other, simply understanding what the other needed. They fitted the horse with its bridle, and the saddle soon thereafter. Elora couldn't help the pangs of jealousy that hit her stomach, and found herself getting very annoyed at her own heart. *Elladan could be here any moment, and you're going to be jealous of Aerin and his best friend?*

"Elora? We're ready."

Tarhael's voice broke into her thoughts and she realized that both fae were mounted and ready to go. She grabbed his outstretched hand and he swung her up easily, though she landed with all the grace of a newborn deer trying to find its feet. As she settled, shouts rang out in the distance and the mad galloping of hooves echoed in her ears.

"That would be Elladan. *Hiyah!*"

Tarhael dug his heels in and his horse took off, flying through the snow laden woods, Aerin close behind. Cold wind whipped Elora's hair against her face, and the sound of wing beats filled Elora's ears.

"*Fuck!*" Tarhael cursed behind her, urging their horse faster.

Elora risked a glance behind her and her heart lurched. Behind them, a familiar enormous eagle flew - deep brown feathers fluttering with the force of its wings beating, sharp talons long enough to make Elora wince. She still found it as beautiful and entrancing as the first time she'd seen it, but now fear replaced her wonder. Elladan rode atop the bird, black cloak billowing behind him. In the distance, other eagles were closing in, and Elora could make out the armor of Autumn soldiers astride the giant eagles. Tarhael and Aerin still had the advantage, but Elladan was getting uncomfortably close, his mount faster without the icy paths to contend with.They rode hard, extracting every ounce of energy from their animals. Nobody dared speak except for Aerin confirming that Elladan was still on their trail when Elora didn't want to look back again.

"That fucking eagle," Tarhael muttered to Elora over the sound of galloping hooves.

"Our horses are flagging, and Elladan's been steadily gaining on

ELORA

us the past few minutes. We have to get out of here," Aerin yelled, the wind from the eagle's wings threatening to whip his words away. His words terrified Elora. Panic gnawed at the edges of her throat whenever she thought of Elladan and what he had done to her. She hadn't told anyone about the way her skin scrawled and her stomach tightened whenever she saw someone who looked a little too much like him in a crowd or how sometimes she dreamed she was back in his bed again and woke with shaky hands and a damp pillow.

"There's no time!"

Fear closed off her throat and panic settled in, rooted deep in her heart. Her breaths became labored and she felt the edges of her vision start to fuzz. It was now or never. She needed to face Elladan and get this ordeal over with before she succumbed to a full blown panic attack. There were three of them, and only one of Elladan. Besides, Tarhael was even bigger than Elladan. And yet, she still wasn't sure of their odds. She knew what Elladan was capable of, how deep his cruelty ran. Aerin and Tarhael may take pause at the thought of killing him, but he wouldn't give them the same mercy. The thought of either of them getting hurt because of her was unacceptable.

So she did the only thing she knew would work.

Before Tarhael could react, Elora threw herself off the horse.

36

Elora

The ground was *hard.*

Elora wasn't sure what she'd expected, really. But *shit.* She cursed, the sound muffled by her body as she curled up, mentally chastising herself for her poorly thought out act of heroism.

She'd landed well, thankfully, and though her side ached from impact, she didn't think she'd broken anything. Her breath still came in little gasps though, her chest constricting.

"What in Áine's name, Elora?" Tarhael yelled at her from his horse, eyes wide as he yanked on the reins to stop the animal.

Aerin was shouting her name, cursing in a way she'd only heard once before, and guilt slammed through her harder than the fall.

But it was too late now. Elladan was nearly on her, the thundering beats of the eagle's wings echoing in her ears.

Go, she thought, pleading with them as though they'd somehow hear her. *Run, please, go.*

"Fuck!" Tarhael's eyes were wide as he snapped his gaze between Elora, Elladan and Aerin. "Fuck, Aerin, we have to go."

"No!" Aerin's teeth were bared in anger as he shoved his best friend's hand from his arm. Tarhael lent over in his saddle again, gripping

Aerin's arm tightly to force him to look at him.

"Aerin, we have to go *now*. Or we'll all be fucked!"

She watched the indecision play in Aerin's green eyes, her own filling with tears. There was only one real choice and she knew it. She watched him realize it, too.

She watched him turn, dig his heels into the horse's side and gallop away.

Relief eased some of the guilt inside her but both emotions were quickly swallowed whole by Elladan's voice.

"Well, gorgeous," he crooned, drawing out the compliment in a way that made Elora shudder. "What do we have here?"

"Help." Her voice sounded fractured, as close to breaking as she was.

"What's that, darling?"

"Help," she said again, forcing her voice louder. "Please, Elladan, help me." God, she hated the satisfaction that burned in his expression, the way it hardened the corners of his mouth and set the deep brown of his eyes alight.

"Stand up, beautiful."

She obeyed, even when her very bones objected.

"Whyever would you run from me?" he taunted, eyes narrowing as he looked her up and down. He still sat atop his bird, which landed with ease, huge talons digging into the rough path. He was every bit as intimidating as she remembered. She fought the urge to scream, run, throw up or a combination of all three.

"I…" she stumbled over the words, staring at the frozen ground beneath the shitty, worn down shoes Tarhael had stolen for her. "I was scared and I wanted to go home but I was wrong." Her lip trembled, and she hunched her shoulders inward. "I'm so sorry, Elladan, please help me. I never should have left you."

His head tilted to the side a little, like a predator deciding whether to drag out the kill.

"You left with my *brother*, Fleur."

Oh fuck, she thought, trying to hide her shock. In her panic, she'd forgotten entirely about the name he'd given her, about the fake person he'd created. It felt like a test, his use of that name and the half sob that came from her lips was only partly faked.

"He said you were tricking me," she babbled, hating the whine in her voice. Hating the lie. Hating the thought of hurting Aerin like this. "But he was wrong. I missed you so much."

"I warned you about him." Elladan's voice had softened a fraction. "Don't you trust me?"

Another test. It was funny how, now that she was so removed from her attraction to him, he was predictable. His ego was so big she swore she could see it wrestling his heart in his chest, trying to climb its way out his throat, blinding those eyes she'd once looked at with such wonder.

"I do," she answered, looking up at him through her lashes. She'd learned how much he liked feeling as though he had control. How he was willing to take it back at any cost. "I do. I made a mistake, Elladan, please. Please, take me home?" The words tasted sour on her tongue.

"Get up."

Elora scrambled to her feet, trying not to shake.

"Do you expect me to believe you, just like that?" Faster than she could track, Elladan reached out, grabbing her chin and tilting her head back to meet her eyes. Elora froze, hair raised on the back of her neck and her arms. He shook his head at her then sighed and released her chin. "I suppose I can't very well leave you here." He stepped back and held out his hand.

She blinked at him, staring at his outstretched hand, black gloves covering his skin. He looked ever the dark prince he was, dressed in all black atop his mount, smug pride in his eyes when she accepted his hand and let him swing her up into the saddle with him.

She sat in front of him, with his arms around her a little too tightly, his grip on the reins so strong she felt bad for the beast. She tried desperately to force air into her lungs and not focus on the awful sickness in her stomach.

"We can't go back home tonight, beautiful." His breath was warm on her neck as he spoke, lips skimming over her skin. She hid her revulsion behind a shiver.

"Why not?" Mock disappointment tinged her words. She'd really rather take her chances out here in the winter forests alone than return to that damn castle.

"It's too far for a day's journey," he explained, nudging the eagle into motion. "We'll camp tonight and set out again in the morning." He signaled to his men atop the other eagles, and motioned them to continue on their journey chasing Aerin and Tarhael.

She nodded, hoping he couldn't feel how fast her pulse was racing. Beneath her, the eagle opened its wings and began its ascent. This had been a terrible idea. His closeness was making her palms sweat, her stomach tie itself up in knots, the insistent urge to *run* pounding through her head.

Instead, she sat atop the eagle and simpered as Elladan chastised her. Spewed more lies in the shape of apologies. Told Elladan how much she despised his brother, all the while picturing his arms around her instead.

By the time they stopped for the night, Elladan's suspicion appeared to have blown away on the wind.

Her thighs ached from riding, but it was her heart that hurt the most.

The clearing wasn't big, but wide enough for their tent and the bird. The landscape had barely shifted all day. It was still shades of white and gray as far as Elora could see, spindly half dead trees dotting the ground, the occasional distant sound of some creature Elora prayed to every God she ever learned about in school she'd never have to meet.

She supposed she should have paid more attention to the route they'd taken, but it had all looked the same. Besides, she had no chance of surviving long enough on her own out here, even if she did manage to escape Elladan now. No, she'd made it this far. She could use Elladan's ego to her advantage. She had to.

Out of nowhere, torrential rain tore from the sky, so loud Elora jumped and nearly tripped on a patch of slick ice. Warm arms wrapped around her, steadying her.She wished he'd just let her fall.

"Protection," Elladan said, nodding to the rain. "Notice how we're not getting wet?"

Elora was used to magic by now. The rain poured hard and fast, but avoided the little dome Elladan had created, leaving them, the tent and the eagle utterly dry.

"You can control the weather?"

He laughed. It felt like sandpaper on her skin. "No, gorgeous. Just the rain."

The rain? Elora's brow furrowed. She didn't remember Aerin mentioning any powers relating to the weather, aside from the wind he was able to control. Aerin had said that Elladan was atrocious with runecasting, and controlling the rain seemed like it would be a complex runecast. She'd certainly never seen him or Tarhael control water before.

"Oh. Uh…why did you make it rain?"

Another laugh that made her want to risk the forest. "Nobody will bother looking for us, or you for that matter, in this rain. It's dangerous enough here without worrying about the wet or the ice."

Fuck fuck fuck. "That's good," she made herself say. "Thank you."

He smiled at her, pressing his lips to her cheek, the scratch of his stubble on her jaw making her tense.

"I'll finish setting up camp," he told her, his hand lingering on her waist. "How about you make some tea? There's supplies in the saddle bags."

She nodded dumbly, unpacking a little tea kettle and accepting the bundle of miraculously dry wood Elladan had salvaged from the rain. She didn't bother asking how or why. She didn't have the energy to care.

His back was to her, so trusting. So tempting. She bit the inside of her cheek, both pleased that he underestimated her and furious about it.

She set out both metal cups, dried floral tea crushed into the bottom of each one, and stared at the contents, an idea itching the back of her skull.

Fast. She had to be fast.

Imagine the roots beneath the earth. The texture of the leaves, the color of the bloom. A tingling crept down her neck and spread into her shoulders, inching down her back. It soon turned into a searing fire that traveled across her veins, as if everything she was imagining was begging to be let outside.

"Tea's ready!" she called after a few minutes, cold sweat dripping down her spine.

He turned from their tent - far too small for Elora's liking - and smiled at her. She forced a grin onto her lips, the Fleur facade sliding back into place.

He took the cup she extended, the one she'd made sure was in her right hand, and sipped. He didn't thank her.

She didn't know why that disappointed her. The simple lack of manners, the lack of…well…*humanity* in him. It chilled her. Where once it was alluring, fascinating, addictive, now it just unnerved her.

She drank her own tea in silence, letting the warmth defrost the chill that seeped into her bones as he talked about Aerin, tuning out his speech about *weakness* and *laziness*, savoring the slightly sweet floral taste. She hadn't missed him, but she had missed this tea.

The sun abandoned the sky slowly, casting the most vivid violet hues Elora had ever seen across the horizon, as though an artist had dipped a brush into every shade of purple they owned and set to work.

But it ended, so fast Elora's heart stumbled, and darkness swamped them.

"Come to bed, beautiful."

Elora would have rather jumped off a cliff, if she was being honest. But her legs moved, the tiny fire was kicked out and the tent held open for her.

So she entered, stared at the two bedrolls and thick blankets and swallowed the terror choking her.

The things in the woods were angels compared to the monster standing beside her. At least they were unapologetic in their evil, their intentions on display and clear. Elladan was dangerous in an entirely different way.

But so was she.

She lowered herself down beside him, turning to watch as his eyes drooped shut, his body going limp, breathing evening out.

The herb had worked. She'd never been more grateful for magic in the short time she'd known she possessed it.

Never been more grateful to Aerin for showing her how to coax life from the dead ground, or the book shop she worked in - *she was probably fired again* - for buying in that little book on plants and their medicinal properties.

Never been more grateful for Elladan being so self obsessed that he didn't notice that she'd slipped it into his tea.

37

Elora

"Good morning, gorgeous."

If he called her *gorgeous* or *beautiful* one more time, Elora thought she might be sick.

"Good morning."

She'd been up for hours, watching the sun rise lazily above the horizon, perched at the edge of the tent, too scared to wander far, but not wanting to be close to Elladan for a second longer. She'd slept for a grand total of two hours, broken up into thirty minute stretches, because she had no idea how long the sleeping herb would last in Elladan's system.

She'd kept the eagle company, watched small birds flitter about in the rain outside their dome, feathers slick with water and shimmering like dew on grass in the pale sunlight.

"I had an idea." The words fell from her lips before she had the chance to think better. For a second, Elladan was silent, only the sound of the rain and the ruffle of the eagle's feathers breaking the air between them.

"What is it?" He sounded reluctant, but not suspicious. The weight on Elora's chest eased slightly.

"I hate Aerin nearly as much as you do-"

"Not possible." His voice was so low it was near a growl. She bit the inside of her cheek to keep her fear hidden.

"Okay, maybe not," she amended, pasting a smile onto her lips. "But you want to take him home right? So your father can finally brand him a traitor?"

He'd told her as much in his rants yesterday, and though she'd tuned a lot of it out while trying to figure out some semblance of a plan that wasn't likely to end up with her dead in a ditch or being eaten by some horrible unseelie fae creature, she'd heard enough.

"Isn't it better to go after him now? So he can't get away? Surely the rain you called last night will have slowed him down and it's obvious you're faster than him anyway so..." She cast her eyes downward, making herself smaller, so small she knew he'd never view her as a threat. "I'm sorry if I'm overstepping. I'm just trying to help. I want the best for you..."

A soft sigh, the sound of footsteps as he approached her, and then his arms around her waist. He pulled her into his chest and she fought the instinct to sense, trying to encourage her stiff muscles to relax into his hold, despite the fact his touch made her skin crawl.

"I never would have pegged you as the cunning type, Fleur."

Shit. She blinked at him innocently.

"Cunning?" she echoed, frowning. "I just had a lot of time to figure him out while I was gone, that's all. I know what he's like, Elladan. Let's be honest, there would be nothing stopping you waltzing into his camp and dragging him back with us if I wasn't in the way."

"I want to keep you safe," he said softly, and her stomach clenched painfully. "Eat something. We'll discuss this unsavory topic after. I've missed you."

There was a flash of something all too much like sincerity in his eyes. When he looked at her like that, it was easy for her to see how she'd been so manipulated by him once. Even before the literal mind games he'd played with her, she'd been intrigued by him.

And, now, in the middle of a frozen wasteland, planning the capture of the man she was falling for, she couldn't help but wonder who Elladan could have been had he been raised by a less callus man.

So, she ate. Apple strips Elladan sliced with his dagger and slightly stale bread. It all sat like a stone in her stomach but she smiled the whole while, sipping water from the canteen and blushing appropriately when Elladan complimented her.

She tried to help him pack up the tent, the urge to move itching under her skin, but he insisted he could do it himself. She rolled her eyes when he turned his back, lip curling in a sneer, but smoothed her face into calm kindness the second he looked over his shoulder at her.

"Come on, then," he said when he was finished, helping her into the saddle with shockingly gentle hands. "Let's go catch a bastard."

Elora was glad she was facing away from him. She focused hard on the silky feel of the eagle's feathers, the flip of her stomach as they took off, ears ringing at Elladan's remark.

Elladan had called off the rain when they left camp but even so, the air was damp and the ground was muddy and the journey was bleak. Elora's whole body ached with the travel and bone deep exhaustion, her stomach and thigh muscles screaming with the effort of keeping herself upright in the saddle. She refused to lean back against Elladan, the thought of having to be any closer to him made her breakfast threaten to show again.

By the time darkness once again threatened to blanket her in despair, Elladan, too, was waning. She felt him tense behind her, a harsh sigh warming her neck.

"This was a ridiculous idea," he muttered, as though he didn't expect her to hear. She was beyond caring. Every step they took in the direction of Aerin was a step closer to never having to feel this man's touch again, never having to hear the name *Fleur* spoken like a compliment.

Still, she forced herself to bow her head and say, "I'm sorry."

The eagle was near exhausted when Elladan perked up, leaning closer to Elora so he could see over her shoulder.

"Ssh."

She obeyed, breath hitching in anticipation.

There, in the near distance, was the small glow of a fire. A figure sat beside it, stoking the flames, shoulder length hair the same color as the night around him. Elora's pulse began racing, as Elladan eased them both from the eagle and instructed it to remain hidden in the trees.

"Quiet, Fleur." Elladan whispered in her ear, eyes narrowed. "Remember, he's mine to kill."

Wait, Elora's mind began buzzing, *kill? He was just supposed to want to capture him.* Panic replaced the excitement but it was too late, Elladan was already ahead of her, near silent even in the quiet night.

She thought she knew fear.

She was wrong.

She took off after him, her terror for Aerin coursing through her veins, thick and hot. Just when Elladan was nearing the edge of the pool of light cast by the flames, she tripped. The figure by the fire looked up abruptly, green eyes wide, his hand immediately flying to the handle of his dagger. Relief soothed the pain of Elora's knees from where she'd landed hard on the cold ground, but the immediate anger on Aerin's face as he met her eyes made tears well in hers.

Not the goddamn time, she chastised herself, rising and running into the little camp where Aerin now stood, facing off with his brother.

Her half formed plan was beginning to unravel.

"Are you here to kill me, brother?" Aerin asked with remarkable calm, the word *brother* sounding more like an insult than an affectionate term. He refused to look at Elora again. Aerin ran a finger down the blade of his dagger, holding Elladan's hostile gaze. "Then again, that is the only way you'll ever be crowned heir, isn't it. What a shame…"

He didn't get to finish his sentence. Elladan was on him in an instant, hand around his throat, crushing the words from his tongue. Aerin swiped out with the dagger, catching Elladan's arm with a shallow gash before Elladan wrenched the weapon away and threw it into the muddy grass.

"I'll be kind," he hissed, a feral grin spreading across his face. Elora's feet felt glued to the spot, her mouth hanging open in a silent scream. "I'll let you choose. Drowning…" A stream of water flew through the air, the canteen by Aerin's bag beside the fire emptying as Elladan called on it. Shock shot through Aerin's features, his eyes widening as they locked onto the water. Confusion settled in Elora's chest at the sight of it, heavy and uncomfortable. "Or having your throat cut with your own blade," he hummed mockingly, delighting in Aerin's struggle to wrestle free. "Both humiliating. I wonder which is slower…"

Elora snapped. Her voice started back to life, a scream cross battle cry echoing through the air as she threw her arms up, wrenching life from the dead earth, thorny vines like the one she'd first conjured coiling up and around Elladan's ankles. He yelled in surprise, releasing Aerin and swaying on his feet, the water he'd been commanding splashing harmlessly to the ground.

Elora didn't stop until his arms were pinned, too, then gagged him for good measure. The pounding in her head had ceased slightly, clarity seeping in and sharpening the edges.

"Holy fuck." Aerin breathed.

Aerin.

She exhaled in a rush, barreling towards him and nearly knocking them both on their asses as she launched herself into his arms. He stiffened briefly but softened fast, returning her embrace and holding her tight to him. Tears threatened again but she pushed them back. Not in front of Elladan.

"What the fuck was that, Elora?" he asked into her hair. "Do I mean nothing to you? I risked everything for you and you just - why would you ever do that-"

"To save you, you fucking fool!" She had the absurd urge to laugh, but settled for burying her head against his chest and breathing in his calming scent. "I didn't want you getting hurt and he, well... apparently still has a soft spot for me."

She felt him tense and pulled back.

"You're mad at me."

He ground his teeth together and though it was abundantly clear in his eyes that he was relieved to see her, she could tell he was hurt. Guilt had its hand around her throat.

"Um...well, I brought you a present," she tried to joke, gesturing to Elladan, still wrapped up in her vines.

"Some present." Aerin smirked, the hurt dimming a little. "Next time you get me a gift, make it less murder-y."

Despite everything, she laughed. "Okay."

He sauntered over to his brother, angling his head to study the plants holding him still, ignoring Elladan's muffled shouts.

"This is good, Elora," Aerin looked back at her, awestruck. "Like, seriously powerful magic for a novice."

"Novice?" She was grinning, she couldn't help it. "I'm insulted," she joked, the pressure on her chest easing.

He turned his back on his brother, ignoring what had to be a painful set of bruises blooming on his neck and crossed to her, catching her chin gently with his forefinger and tipping her head so she was looking at him. The world could have ended right then, she thought, and she wouldn't have noticed.

"It's kind of hot," he admitted, eyes bright. Her own eyes widened in surprise. "All that power." His gaze dipped lower, to her mouth. He lent close, so his lips brushed her neck when he whispered, "maybe you should tie me up like that sometime."

Elora died. Well, at least, her heart skipped so many beats she was shocked she was still standing.

He moved away before she could find enough brain cells to respond, already turning and focusing on his brother again.

"As much as I hate to say this," he said to her over his shoulder. "I think we need to let him speak. I'm sure he has a lot of very interesting things to admit."

It pained her to do it, but she did. Or, she tried. But her emotions were scattered in a hundred different directions and whatever connection she'd had to the vines had dissipated. "Uh…I can't."

Instead of getting angry, Aerin just chuckled and plucked his bone handle dagger from the grass, wiping the mud away before reaching out and hacking through the vine on either side of Elladan's mouth, *accidentally* catching his cheek with the tip of the blade.

"-disappointment, you pathetic excuse for an heir-"

"Save me the dramatics." Aerin, it seemed, had found his feet the longer he was away from the castle. Elora watched, rapt, as Elladan's face contorted in shock. Satisfaction flooded her.

"And *you*-" Elladan ignored Aerin and turned to Elora, his face red in anger. Elora made herself hold his eyes, arms crossed over her chest. "You *bitch*." Aerin moved to hit him, but Elora held up her hand. She wanted to know what he had to say. "You really think I would let you back into my bed after everything you've done? Manipulative, human trash like you? You deserve each other. Shame neither of you will get long enough to live out this ridiculous little fantasy."

Elora's eyebrows furrowed. "You think I ever wanted back in your bed? I never wanted to be there in the first place! You had to *literally fuck with my brain* to get me anywhere near it!"

Elladan laughed, bitter and tinny. "You wanted me." She shook her head, clenching her fists at her side, but he continued. "You give yourself far too much credit, *Fleur*, for how clueless you really are."

Aerin's blade was at his throat before he could continue. "Be careful, brother," he warned. "That *clueless half human* currently has you restrained and at her mercy."

Elladan spat in his face. A bead of blood ran down his neck, spreading across the vibrant green plants around his chest, Aerin's face inches from his and he dug the blade in. Not enough to do permanent damage, just enough to make it hurt.

"Answers. Now."

"She doesn't know, does she?" Elladan's confidence hadn't wavered. Not once. Elora didn't know whether that made him brave or stupid. It was a thin line, the difference between them, and he toed it with precision. Aerin's lip curled in a sneer. "Oh, brother. That's not very nice of you, is it? Keeping secrets from your little pet?"

Elora felt like she was on fire.

"Elladan-"

"No, no, you wanted answers, and I'm here to give them to you." Elladan's eyes were on her now, nothing but hatred reflected in the deep brown. "You thought you could trust him, didn't you?" He delighted in her discomfort, the way she had to fight to keep from fidgeting. "Do you want to know why nobody knew who you were? How you managed to live undetected in the mortal realm for twenty two years? Why you could use the portal with such little sacrifice?"

And, damn him, she did.

"You never wondered why you were so in tune with plant life? Animals?" He was dragging this out and they all knew it. His smile never wavered. "I've been calling you the wrong name all this time."

"Yes," she shot back, finally finding her tongue. "My name has never been Fleur."

He *tsked*, mocking her. "I should've been calling you Princess. Or Queen now, I suppose."

Anger flooded her. "Enough of your games, Elladan."

Aerin's grip on the dagger had loosened, his focus shifted from his brother to her. Instead of anger, or denial, his face was twisted with guilt.

"Aerin?" Her voice came out hollow and quiet.

"Elora, I'm sorry-"

"What are you talking about, you fucking sociopath?" Elora stormed up to him, snatching Aerin's dagger from his grasp and pressing it against Elladan's throat until he made a pained gurgling noise. Good.

"The truth, gorgeous. Only the truth."

Tears blurred her vision. She was alive with anger and indignation, her skin buzzing with it. The vines around him began writhing like serpents, coiling tighter, thorns sprouting deadly sharp. Elladan's cry of pain only fueled her.

"*Aerin.*" His name came out like a plea, hopeless and cracking.

"It's true, Elora."

Her body went numb. Static overwhelmed her brain.

38

Aerin

Aerin stared. He didn't know what else to do. The vines were so tight now that Elladan was unconscious and he wasn't quite sure he was still breathing. He didn't move to help his brother. He didn't deserve it. Though he didn't relish the thought of murdering him, he couldn't deny that he wouldn't mourn a damn day for the man he'd become. The boy he once was, maybe, in his childhood years, when he was still soft around the edges and held Aerin's hands when he was learning to walk, or drew the rune for *wind* in the dirt and made Aerin trace it with his chubby finger until a little breeze picked up and fluttered their hair.

Yes, he'd mourn the boy.

But not the man.

He wasn't looking at Elora when she collapsed but the *thud* of her body hitting the damp ground spurred him into motion, Elladan forgotten. She was in his arms and then on his lap beside the sputtering fire, skin cold and damp with tears. He was still angry at her, hurt more than anything, but it didn't change the fact his heart felt like it was about to climb up his throat at the thought of her in danger.

She stirred against his chest as he ran a soothing hand up and down her back, eyes fluttering.

"Whoa!" a male voice shouted from the edge of the camp. Tarhael. Aerin had almost completely forgotten he'd gone out to forage for anything edible and collect whatever wood was dry enough to light. "I left you alone for *half an hour* and now there's a dead body and a traitor in our camp?"

"Dead body?" Aerin turned his head slightly to see Elladan, who, admittedly, did look pretty dead. Shit. "Oops."

"*Oops!*" Tarhael gawked at him, incredulous as he threw the fruits of his foraging onto a log beside the fire. "What in Áine's good name, Aerin?"

"Well, Elora came back," he explained, as she stirred again. "With Elladan. I don't think she's a traitor. She did what she thought was best."

"So, just like that you're all loved up again?"

Aerin resisted the urge to punch his friend in the face. "No," he said instead. "But she's hurt. Worn out. Áine only knows what he did to her, Tarhael. Not to mention the power she expended on well…that." He gestured vaguely to the vines.

"That was all her?"

"Well it sure as hell wasn't me," Aerin quipped, raising a brow.

"Shit." Tarhael blew out a breath. "How is she *that* powerful? She's half fae, and she's been training for like half a day."

"Uh…right well…"

"Apparently I'm a fucking princess," Elora mumbled, lifting her head to meet Tarhael's wide eyes. "Fuck my head hurts."

"Drink." Aerin held out his hand for Tarhael's canteen and he obliged grudgingly. Elora drank deeply, thanking them before returning it.

"You really thought I'd betray you?" she asked groggily..

"I don't know, Elora." Aerin looked away, age old hurt flashing in his eyes. Tarhael scowled at her, clearly protective of him.

Awkwardly, she picked herself off his lap and staggered to the giant log serving as a bench next to him. She landed ungracefully, but managed not to end up in the dirt. Aerin resisted the urge to pull her back against him, to hold her just a second longer until he was sure she was okay.

"How long have you known?"

He was silent for a minute, unsure of how much to admit, before he sighed and said, "Since you arrived. But I wasn't certain until the trickster fae mentioned the prophecy."

"*Prophecy?*" Elora balked. "You didn't think this was important information to share with, oh I don't know, the fucking subject of the damn thing?"

"I wasn't sure, and I didn't want to upset you." Aerin ran his hands through his hair, shaking his head. "I promise I'll explain it later, but right now, we have more pressing matters at hand."

"No shit," Tarhael agreed, cringing.

"What's more pressing than this?" Elora asked, indignant.

"Well, the dead prince, for one." *And the fact that he just commanded water when he wasn't supposed to be able to runecarve at all.* The sinking feeling in his stomach that had been there since Elora had jumped off the horse was worsening, and the more he thought about his brother's apparent power, the harder it became to breathe. It was too much to think about right now, he had to keep moving. He had to help Elora.

Elora's mouth snapped shut so fast she nearly bit her tongue. Her face drained of color, her hands shaking in her lap. Aerin's stomach sank at the sight. "Oh, God…"

"It's okay," Aerin reassured, desperate to make the nauseous look on her face go away and her shaking subside. "Someone was going to have to kill him sooner or later. But we can't leave him like that to be found."

Aerin pushed to his feet and grabbed the pack resting against the logs. He rummaged through it until he found what he was looking for, a little pouch that was probably intended as a coin purse. But it had worked in a pinch, just the right size for what he needed. He opened it, grabbing a pinch of the powder inside and gesturing to Elora.

"Open your hand."

She frowned at him, rubbing her hands along her arms as though she was trying to warm herself up. She'd bitten her bottom lip so hard she'd left a little indent with her teeth, and despite the situation, he had the near uncontrollable urge to trace it with his tongue. *Get it together*, he told himself. When she made no move to honor his request he rolled his eyes and added, "please."

Finally, she relented, extending a shaking hand towards him. He sprinkled the crushed herbs into the center of her palm. She looked down at them, confusion fluttering across her face.

Aerin suddenly wasn't sure this was a good idea. Too late now. He knelt down beside her, trying to hide his nervousness. "It's to help with…uh…" he didn't quite know what to say. What to call it. He'd seen the small, white pills she took back in the mortal realm, read the side of the bottle when she wasn't looking. "Anxiety."

Her gaze shot to him, eyes wide and glassy. His stomach dropped.

"It's just that I know, uh, that you have um…" *fuck this wasn't going well.* He cleared his throat and tried again. "I found a little patch of flowers that are supposed to help with nervousness. I used Eolas to enhance their properties, to make it as close to what you had back home." Elora still hadn't spoken. Aerin panicked. "You just take it with water. I know it's not as convenient as what you had before but I can keep working on it. It's a variation of the original runecast I wrote when you first arrived. But after studying the medication you took, I rewrote it and adapted it so it will mimic your pills, with none of the side effects. I apologize if it was presumptuous. You don't have to take it. Of course."

Her bottom lip wobbled a little and Aerin stared as her eyes became watery. Áine above, he thought he might implode if she kept looking at him like that.

"You did that for me?" Elora sniffed, visibly trying to stop herself crying. He wanted to bundle her in his arms and let her sob, but he knew she wouldn't accept his comfort right now. Instead, he waited, nodding. "Even though you thought I'd betrayed you?"

He shrugged. Truth was, he'd been out of his mind when she'd left with Elladan. They needed a plan and they didn't have one and Tarhael had insisted they break for a rest before attempting a rescue mission. He'd simply seen the little patch of flowers, growing between the twisted roots of a tree, and recognized their properties. It hadn't really occurred to him that he wouldn't see her again to give them to her. The idea was too unacceptable to bear. Making the medicine had distracted him from the awful, all consuming feeling of failure. At least, in doing this, he was helping in some small way.

Elora stared at him, lashed heavy with tears. She'd stopped crying now, though she was still shaking slightly. "Thank you," she said, so softly he had to strain to hear her. She tipped her head back and let the crushed petals fall onto her tongue, swallowing them with a mouthful of water. "Thank you, Aerin."

He smiled at her, cheeks heating. He cleared his throat. "Let me know how it works. It may need tweaked a little and I'm not sure how it will compare to the medicine in your home."

Elora wrapped her arms around her middle and smiled back.

Across the fire, Tarhael coughed loudly, breaking the tentative silence. Aerin chuckled.

"I have an idea-" Tarhael began.

"If it's as bad as every other suggestion you have ever made, I don't want to hear it."

"Hey! You liked the time I suggested we do that thing, remember-"

The sound of Aerin's boot hitting Tarhael's shin appeared to break Elora from her daze. It was worth the death glare his friend shot at him as a result.

"You can stay here." Aerin squared his shoulders and stood. "We'll sort this out."

Tarhael looked appalled by the suggestion. Aerin scowled at him until he grumbled and drew his blade to begin hacking away the vines.

"Fucking Elladan," he muttered under his breath, just loud enough to hear. "Even in death, he's a pain in my ass."

39

Elora

"First things first. A glamour." Aerin narrowed his brows and pulled out his multicolored pencil and notepad, writing runes with the confidence of someone who had written the same characters a thousand times. "Glamours are some of the first things we learn. Simple stuff really." He blew over the notepad and looked over at Tarhael and Elora through his lashes. "I don't have time to work out the fine details so, Tarhael, you have to remain your massive size and Elora, you're going to have to stay looking like a girl." A few moments later, Elora looked at Tarhael and did a double take.

"You're..." she trailed off, studying the man before her. His features were totally different, his hair longer, his eyes the wrong shade of brown. It was as though an artist had attempted to draw Tarhael from a really vague description. Elora wouldn't recognize him if she didn't know better. "You look wrong."

Tarhael laughed, a booming noise erupting from his chest, hearty and comforting. It was the first time Elora had felt any warmth in nearly a day. "You'd be surprised at what changing even a single facial feature can do for one's appearance."

ELORA

"Do you tell all your favorite people that?"

Elora frowned at him, reaching up to touch her own face. The bridge of her nose felt more prominent, her cheeks less full. She wasn't sure whether she was glad that she couldn't see the changes or not. The memory of Elladan making her *fae* rose like a sickness inside her. The herb medicine Aerin had given her earlier seemed to have worked, though, settling the buzz inside her brain. She was still thrown for a loop at the fact he'd made it for her. The thoughtfulness of it alone made her heart pick up pace, never mind the skill involved.

"It's not the best but it'll do." Aerin shrugged, bringing her attention back, frowning at the stares she and Tarhael were giving him. He had changed his own looks - his eyes now a pale blue, his dark hair nearly blond, lips thinner, jawline less pronounced.

"That's just creepy," Tarhael decided, making a face at his friend.

"I agree," Elora seconded.

"Just be grateful we don't all look like the wanted runaways we are anymore," Aerin reminded them. "Come on, let's plant this body as a decoy."

Elora winced when she saw Elladan's face had morphed into Aerin's and shuddered. She looked away quickly.

"Finding 'Aerin' should buy us some more time. But it won't be long until my father notices that Elladan hasn't been responding to any of his communications."

Neither Elora nor Tarhael knew what to say to that. The three of them heaved the coffin made of vines into the forest and tossed Elladan unceremoniously to the forest floor. They stood around in an awkward silence for a few minutes, Aerin's face unreadable. Elora pressed her hand over her mouth and squeezed her eyes closed, trying to stuff the rising tide of guilt and muddy emotion back down.

It was silent, except the awkward shuffling oh Tarhael's feet, until Aerin abruptly suggested that they continue traveling through the

243

forest to avoid detection.

Elora didn't know how to feel as they rode through the forest. She chose to sit in front of Aerin this time, but wondered if it was too soon, as the roiling emotions inside of her grew. She didn't know how to feel about Aerin keeping such pertinent information from her, didn't know how to feel about being on the run in a world she knew barely anything about, didn't know how to feel about Elladan's death. *I killed him.* He'd hurt Aerin for *years*, was certainly capable of hurting her too if given the chance but still…she never anticipated *killing someone.* She hadn't meant to of course, but it didn't matter. Elora Han was a killer. There were several arguments she could give, namely that Elladan had been on the verge of killing Aerin and that she wasn't exactly able to control her powers properly. But every excuse felt hollow. An emptiness gnawed at her, dull but insistent. Elora felt like she was floating, spacing out, reminding her of when she was Fleur. She wouldn't ever let herself feel that way again.

"How could you not tell me?" The afternoon was fading into dusk and they cast long shadows across the ground. "How could you keep that from me?"

"Elora I-"

"Didn't you think I had the right to know? Or did you know what was best for me, the way Elladan kept promising that he knew what was best for me and was going to keep me safe?" Aerin looked like she had just slapped him in the face and perhaps it was a little unfair after what he'd done for her, but she didn't care. "Tell me what the prophecy is. Right now." Aerin shifted behind her and she was surprised when he halted the horse and hopped off. Walking in front of her, he closed his eyes for a few moments and took a deep breath, holding it before he slowly exhaled.

"There's a prophecy. I can't recite it word for word - it was told in the old tongue - but it tells of a daughter of both fae and mortal blood. A girl born of both worlds. Her destiny is to shape and lead the fae..." Aerin paused, running his hand through his hair, refusing to meet her eyes. "Before destroying us. Wiping away tradition and custom. Reforging the entire world in the palm of her hand. She's supposed to be our savior and then our doom."

Elora's laugh surprised her just as much as it surprised everyone else.

"You think it's me? Just because I'm half fae? Please, I barely have a handle on my powers." A sort of wild panic sprouted inside her, a warm rush that spread throughout her limbs. Dazed, she noticed she was glowing green again.

Around them, flowers, vines, and sapling trees sprouted from the earth, covering the ground in a layer of new growth. It covered the area in a wide circle - her newly birthed nature the only greenery around that wasn't coated in snow.

"Case in point," Aerin said, gesturing all around him. "Scholars studied the prophecy for years. There's hidden metaphors about life and regrowth which can be attributed to the Seelie Courts. Most likely, Spring. Then you came along - a walking mystery, half human, half us - and your flat is fucking full of plants so it wasn't hard to connect the dots. But it was hard to tell you. What did you want me to say? *Hi Elora, you're wonderful and all, but I think you're going to destroy my people and the world? You're the harbinger of doom? The apocalypse personified?"*

Elora took in the information, stunned, unable to think of anything to say except, "But how did I end up in the mortal realm? Neither of my parents are fae."

Aerin sighed and closed his eyes once more, cringing a little. "This is where the story gets dark. I snuck into my father's chambers about a year ago, stole his secret records and histories and copied them before slipping them back into his chambers. As far as I can tell, he has no idea I did it. I can only assume I'd be dead if he did. The prophecy was issued around five hundred years ago when the fae were waging war with humanity for control. But after the prophecy, the fae collectively decided it would be better to cede control of most of the world to humans and retreat to Fior Domhan. Relationships between humans and fae were strictly outlawed, punishable by death. These rules were enforced-"

"How do prophecies even work though? How can you know you can trust them? Nobody takes fortune tellers seriously where I'm from."

"Prophecies are different. The gift of foresight or prophetic dreams, isn't something you can runecast. It's part of the specific and select types of magic that us fae can't perform. The Runecarvers are the only ones who have foresight - ancient magic. The Runecarvers are a whole other story but they're the four daughters of Áine, The Goddess Who Sleeps. One in each Season. There's been prophecies before that we've interpreted wrong. But they always come true - regardless of whether they've been misinterpreted."

"Does the prophecy specifically mention a girl from Spring that is half fae being responsible for the downfall of the fae?" Elora was frantic now, skin buzzing with desperation. "Could there be any other interpretations? Is there anything unclear about the wording?"

Aerin hesitated several moments before answering. "...No. There are several extremely ambiguous things about the full prophecy but it is very clear on two things. One, this person will have blood from both humans and fae, and two, they will be both from Spring and an outsider."

"Then what other possible explanation could there be? This entire damn prophecy is literally about me!" She was screaming but she couldn't stop. It would have hurt less if he'd slapped her, she thought.

"Elora. Listen to me. I care about you. I don't want you to get

ELORA

hurt, or to be in danger. Clearly, both have happened. But don't let anything or anyone, especially not this, tell you what you can and cannot do."

Droplets of rain interrupted Aerin, and Elora tilted her head back, letting the water cool her skin and her temper. The rain quickly thickened into a downpour and moments later, they were all drenched.

"Can we finish this conversation tomorrow?" Aerin asked, shouting over the rush of rain. His hair, shorter with his glamour, was plastered to his face, thick drops of water coating his eyelashes. She hated him, in that moment, for the way he made her want to kiss the rain from his skin.

"Sure." Elora's voice was half hearted and barely audible. She had nothing else to say, but Aerin was already moving towards Tarhael, pausing by his friend and studying their surroundings, brows furrowed and mouth pressed into a hard line as though he was concentrating.

Elora blinked the water from her lashes and frowned when the downpour suddenly ceased to soak them, bouncing off some invisible dome that had appeared around them. The sound reminded her of rain on a car roof - driving home in storms, watching the weather turn while cozied up under her father's jacket. She shook her head, turning back to Aerin.

"What did you do?"

"It's a simple shield of air that blocks out anything the size of raindrops and larger, but keeps the air molecules flowing so we can still breathe," he answered quickly, shrugging.

Tarhael grinned at Elora's shocked expression. "You'll get used to it," he promised with a wink.

They broke for camp, unable to see much through the dark rain shower. Not much was said as they pitched the tents Tarhael had brought and ate the rations from the massive pack on his back.

Sleep eluded Elora that night, the strange hollowness still haunting her. She'd been so overloaded with information that her mind had shut off completely, as though afraid that processing what she'd been told, what she'd *done*, would hurt her too immeasurably to recover from. It wasn't until the first rays of sun poked through the clouds that Elora finally drifted off, her dreams plagued with a dying Elladan pleading for her to save him.

40

Elora

It was well past noon when Elora blearily crawled out of her tent. The events of last night crashed down on her once more and she shoved them away, almost choking on the acrid taste they left in her mouth. She couldn't afford to think about Elladan now. She felt like she would shatter into a thousand pieces if anyone asked her how she felt. So she asked about her parents instead.

"Can you tell me who my parents were and how they were killed?" She needed to know. Needed to have some sort of connection to them. She'd never been *that* bothered about finding her birth parents before, but she'd always thought the chances of actually learning anything about them were infinitesimal. Now, she was ravenous for information. Anything to tether her.

"Um, I don't know if that's the first thing we should talk about in the morning…but sure," Aerin said warily, as Elora leveled him with a stare that brokered no dissent. "Your fae side is mostly likely Queen Endra, the ruler of the most powerful Spring kingdom. Spring's territories are supposed to be based in the same land mass near South Korea in the human realm, where she most likely met your father."

"My parents told me I was left on someone's front porch as a newborn. No note, no explanation, nothing. I was turned in to the authorities and my parents adopted me a month or so later." She breathed deeply, recalling her confusion, and later anger, at the lack of information her parents had. "Guess that makes sense now." Elora loved her parents dearly but it was satisfying, cathartic, learning the truth after all these years.

"Queen Endra used to sneak into the mortal realm. I don't know how she did it, but it was rumored that she was incredibly talented with Eolas so it stands to reason she could have figured something out like I did. Anyway, she fell for a mortal man there during her frequent visits and decided to marry him. She was the crown princess at the time, but when her mother, the Queen, grew old and retired, it was up to Endra to take the reins. She knew the backlash it would cause, so she did what we did and hid her husband's scent and put a glamour on him. I can't find his name anywhere in the historical records though. I only managed to find this information during a trip to the Seelie Courts years ago. Snuck into the library in the Summer palace and found records stuffed between the pages of an old book."

"So my birth mom fell for a mortal dude and decided to just bring him over?"

"Pretty much. You definitely take after her in terms of impulsiveness." He winked.

Elora felt a smile tug at the corner of her lip. "Okay, so Endra brought her mystery mortal man over to Fior Domhan. What then?"

"As you know, the Seelie Courts, who have traditionally been more accepting of humans, contain Summer and Spring. The Unseelie Courts - Autumn and Winter - kinda hate humans. Unfortunate that you dropped into an Autumn kingdom. But yes, Queen Endra brought her husband over and disguised him. At that time, the Seelie Courts were pushing for reintegration between the fae and humans, led by none other than Endra herself. The Unseelie Courts were obviously against this. They'd been arguing about this issue for centuries. Unfortunately, right around when Endra brought her husband over to Fior Domhan, another of the Runecarvers uttered a prophecy very similar to the first about a half fae girl."

"So two of these fortune telling fae things basically said that a girl that was half fae from Spring would be responsible for the destruction of the fae?"

"Um, essentially yes. It didn't help that Aureole was more specific. She claimed that it would be the next girl to be born half fae and human."

"Great. It's not everyday you have multiple magical beings spout prophecies about you." Elora slumped, head in hands, trying to focus. "Okay, so what happened next?" Judging by Aerin's stressed out visage, there was more to come.

"So after Aureole's prophecy, even Summer had to withdraw their support. The King of Summer pledged to Endra that Summer would support a peaceful but secret co-existence with humanity, while the Unseelie Courts called for war against the humans. My father led the war efforts, and Autumn and Winter wanted to destroy the humans once and for all before they could advance even more. From what I gathered from my father's records, even the lesser Spring nobles were pushing Endra to end reintegration talks and accept a peaceful coexistence. Having just brought her partner over to Fior Domhan, I suppose that Endra, too, was torn about what to do. Endra agreed, and with the help of the Summer King, they managed to placate Autumn and Winter against immediate retaliation. Endra pleaded for a unified council of fae to deal with the prophecy, like the fae council of the past that led the fae over to Fior Domhan and sealed the portals. She wanted all Seasons to come together, but before that could happen the solstice came and went and Endra discovered she was pregnant. Here's where the records differ. I'm not sure if someone found out Endra's husband was mortal, or if it was discovered during her pregnancy that her child wasn't fully fae but either way, Endra was betrayed. Information made its way to Autumn and Winter spies and assassins were sent at once. Queen Endra and her husband fled, but they were found by Autumn agents and killed. It was said that they killed the child as well, this half fae and half human babe, but you're living proof that something went awry in the assassination attempt."

"So... that means..."

"Yes. My father, King Harkan and Queen Valdaea of Winter conspired to have your parents killed."

41

Elora

Elora knew that Elladan and King Harkan were awful, immoral people but hearing it from Aerin felt different. Now, knowing the history behind who she really was, it felt odd staring at Aerin, standing beside him. His father had killed her biological parents. Had tried to kill *her*. Her mom had chosen to have her despite the danger and she wasn't sure if she should be grateful or horrified. In the back of her mind, a voice still whispered that she had killed Elladan, whether she had meant to or not. A killer judging another killer felt a little hypocritical. She was overwhelmed, over sensitized, over exposed.

What was this strange iciness spreading across her stomach and into her heart? The crushing, suffocating feelings were suddenly replaced by the same numbness she had felt earlier, only colder, shutting down the anxiety rising steadily like a wave threatening to drown her. It was becoming too familiar, this feeling.

"Hey, how are you taking all of this?" Aerin's voice was rough, jagged at the edges. It snapped her back into reality.

"I don't know." That was the truth. "If I keep thinking about all of this, I think I'm going to go crazy." Her breath was coming in little starts, like her lungs couldn't quite open up wide enough to let the oxygen in.

Aerin studied her, brows furrowed. He was unreadable with this new face. Elora hated it. Wanted to rip the glamour off him with her bare hands and beg him to tell her how to feel. To lie and promise it would be okay. She'd take hollow reassurance over none at all.

Tarhael hovered beside them, still atop his horse, expression open and sympathetic. It only made the ache inside Elora worse.

"I'm sorry, Elora," Tarhael said, voice thick. She shook a little.

"We need to get you to Spring. They'll know more about what to do with you from here. The Queen will have more information on your parents, the prophecy and your powers. It's a long journey there. Will you be okay to ride?"

Elora stilled, realization clicking into place. "There was never a plant to help us hide, was there?"

Aerin averted his gaze, chest rising and falling in a sigh. "No."

She should be angry, she thought distantly. Disappointed, at least. But she felt nothing but resignation.

"Aerin?"

"Hmm?"

She didn't have the energy to yell or fight. She needed a sense of normalcy in her now shattered world. The only thing she could think of that would give her some connection to her apparent roots. The one thing she could control.

"Will you still teach me how to runecast properly?"

Aerin paused halfway in the saddle, eyes wide and mouth parted slightly in shock.

"If that's what you want."

She didn't know what she wanted now. Normality? A hug from her mother, a kiss on the forehead from her father. Their voices, smooth and cooling, still accented from before they moved, telling her they loved her, that everything was okay.

But she couldn't have that. Couldn't return to them, not now, not with the danger trailing behind them. She refused to put anyone else at risk. She dreaded to think about the damage those shadow creatures could have done to innocent people if she hadn't managed to stop them.

Instead, she nodded and accepted Aerin's help into the saddle. Her thighs burned as she settled onto the horse and she latched onto the pain like a lifeline.

They continued through the icy forest, Elora half a breath away from drowning in the wellspring of emotions rioting inside her.

Hours later, Elora's hands ached from trying to copy the shapes Aerin showed her. She was still on horseback, peering through the animal's ears to see the characters Aerin was on carving into the soil with the tip of a dagger. Tarhael kept complaining that he would blunt the weapon like that, but Aerin insisted that they had more than enough daggers to go around. Her notebook was filled with the Eolas alphabet, characters she was desperately trying to process and memorize. It was a nightmare. Trying to learn a whole new language, a dangerous one at that, while her head was swimming with half formed emotions she refused to acknowledge, was exhausting.

"Uh, guys," Tarhael huffed from atop his horse. "Not that I want to break up your whole *royals doing cool magic* lesson, but does anyone want to maybe, I don't know, figure out where we're going?"

Elora blinked at him. She'd assumed he and Aerin had a plan. Apparently, she was even more naive than she realized.

"You could do with remembering some of these, too, Tarhael," Aerin quipped, erasing the lines on the ground with a swipe of his boot to cover their tracks.

"Aerin, I swear to Áine, I will jump off this horse and kick your ass if you don't answer my question."

Elora felt like she was watching a tennis match, gaze flicking between the two men as they spoke.

"Fine," Aerin relented, sighing as he helped Elora back onto their horse again. "We're nearing the Spring border. There's a little town half a day's travel away, so if we continue into the night, we can get rooms there."

Elora fought to control her breathing. "Spring?"

Tarhael's narrowed eyebrows softened slightly as he saw the expression on her face. "You'll like it there," he assured her. "It's insufferably bright and so are the people, but it seems like the kind of place you'd belong."

She chose to take that as a compliment. Fear and excitement warred inside of her at the thought of returning to the Season she supposedly hailed from. As much as she was trying to quell the anxiety she felt ever since Aerin mentioned the ridiculous prophecy, it was eating away at her sanity, even with the little doses of the crushed flower she'd been taking.

Aerin's arms slipped around her waist as he brought her close to him. She tilted her head back but squeezed her eyes shut when she met pale blue eyes instead of the bright green she'd grown to love. She focused on the feel of his body against hers, his fingers stroking soothing lines up and down her arms, the muscled chest she lay her head on. She was still upset with him for not telling her everything before, but the contact was steadying and she relished it.

"It'll be okay, love," he whispered to her, and her breath hitched for an entirely different reason.

Not the damn time, she scolded her body but God, the endearment shot heat through her.

She shook her head, forcing herself back into the present. "You're

ELORA

not the one whose entire life has been a lie," she said, perhaps more harshly than necessary.

"True," he allowed, kicking the horse up into a trot as Tarhael pulled ahead with a roll of his eyes. Elora caught the small smirk that betrayed his emotions, though. "But if it's the truth you want, what better place to find it than your home?"

Home. Tears stung the back of her eyes at the word. Home had once meant New York, or the smell of her mother's perfume, her father's singing. Home used to mean the bookstore, the boba place she'd been in when she got her college acceptance, the dozens of plants she had crowding her apartment.

Now?

She sat up straight, severing the contact with Aerin. She still had no idea how to feel about him, what had happened between them, all the things he'd kept from her. It hurt more than she wanted to admit.

"I think I've had enough runecasting for one day," she mumbled. Her head hurt with everything she'd learned, to say nothing of her heart.

"Okay," was all Aerin said, guiding them on through the land of ice and snow, the protective bubble still encasing them ensuring they were warm.

It was dark by the time they reached the border but Elora's heart still lurched as they approached.

The first sign was the trees - gradually, they grew leaves, first sparse and clinging to life, but full and green by the time Spring approached. The ground thawed too, ice fading seamlessly to grass. The scent of blossoms and lilac drifted towards them as Aerin lowered the dome of air and Elora filled her lungs with it.

Even in the dark, it was beautiful. No, beautiful didn't do it justice.

It was the stuff of Elora's dreams. They passed through the first copse of trees, so tall the tips faded into the sky, stars poking through the highest branches, and emerged into an open field full of wildflowers. A rabbit poked its head up through the grass, ears perked, and Elora met its wide gaze with her own. Before Aerin could stop her, she was dismounting, the rabbit disappearing into the field, and trailing her fingertips over the petals. She reveled in the warmth of the night air, head tilted back to take in stars she'd never seen before. She lowered herself to the ground, cheeks damp, a purple bloom clutched in her fist.

She stayed like that for as long as Tarhael would let her, until he insisted she stand before someone found them.

She did, reluctantly, tucking the flower into the pocket of the coat Aerin had slung over her shoulders, unable to form any words for the sense of peace that had enveloped her.

The soft glow of a town called to them, though Elora would have simply slept in the field of wildflowers if they'd let her.

"Let us do the talking, Elora," Tarhael said quietly, concern shining in his eyes. Elora was too stunned to speak so she just nodded, busy taking in every detail she could, suddenly starving for everything this place had to offer.

"What is this place?" she asked when she'd found her voice again, though the words came out breathy and soft.

"Anixi," Aerin answered, his smile evident in the lilt of the word. "It's the kingdom your mother was from, as far as I remember."

She said nothing else until they were at the outskirts of the village and Tarhael was instructing them to wait while he found an inn. She nodded dumbly and once he was out of sight, she turned to Aerin.

"It feels…different here." *Understatement of the damn century.* She never wanted to leave. The little village they stood outside of was sleepy and quiet, made up of a few rows cottages and what appeared to be an inn, flowers on every windowsill, lanterns hanging from the walls illuminating the pathway.

"Different how?"

"Like..." She sighed, unsure of how to explain the bone deep belonging that had overtaken her. "Like I know the land."

Aerin nodded. "It makes sense. You were born of this kingdom. It's literally in your blood. And, with your magic, you connect to the land and its animals. Eventually, you'll be able to reach out, like a tree with its roots, and feel the frequencies of them resonating through the world."

She stared at him, dumbfounded.

"AERIN!" Tarhael's voice broke her from her reverie, the thundering of hooves echoing through the air. Suddenly, lights flashed on in the houses, doors opened, the muffled sounds of fae shouting and talking to each other filling the air. The door to the inn was thrown wide and a few dreary customers spilled out, rubbing their eyes.

Aerin stiffened behind her and Elora's heartbeat kicked up a gear.

"Tarhael," Aerin greeted as his friend pulled up next to them. "What's going on?"

Fae had exited their houses in record time, sacks on their shoulders, children in their arms. They were mounting horses, some burying what looked like scraps of paper in their garden, until the earth glowed softly before fading. Runecasting, Elora realized.

"We have to leave, now."

"What? Why?"

"They're coming." Tarhael sounded out of breath, his usually cool facade cracking.

"*Who* is coming, Tarhael?" Urgency coated Aerin's words, his fingers flexing on the reins.

"Winter. Autumn."

A beat of silence hung heavy between them, Aerin's sharp intake of breath loud in Elora's ears.

"Spring is under attack."

42

Elora

The thing about fear, Elora thought, was that once it became your perpetual state of existence, you forgot how anything else felt. She was almost numb to it now, although she could feel Aerin's heart pounding as he lent over her, her own pulse was unfazed. Sure, the news had unnerved her and she was scared for the civilians, guilty, too, but she couldn't find it in herself to fear for her own life any longer.

It was exhausting.

They were galloping with the small crowd that had fled the village. Tarhael informed them before his breath became too short that a scout had rushed to the inn not a minute before they'd arrived, claiming to have seen army movement from Winter. It had long been known that there was tension Seelie and Unseelie Courts, and apparently Autumn's sudden announcement that the daughter of the former Spring Queen not only survived the assassination, but was now somewhere in Fior Domhan, had been the straw that broke the camel's back.

Neither of the three of them could work out why Autumn had decided to announce their discovery, nor how they discovered her in the first place. She assumed Elladan had something to do with the original attack in New York, but he was well on his way to rotting in a Winter woods now. Had he told the King about her after she and Aerin fled?

Elora had no room left inside her for these revelations and questions, for more fear, for anything, really. She remained hollow, save for a sharp pang of guilt shooting through her every now and then as the sound of hoof beats and cart wheels surrounded them.

The army was at least half a day away at their current pace, the scout had insisted. He had spotted them from miles away, thanks to his gift of sensing movement through the ground and had runecast speed in order to reach the village as fast as he could. Thankfully, Aerin estimated, the civilians would be far enough away to avoid harm by the time the Winter troops reached the village, especially with the endurance runecasts they'd hurriedly set before they left.

For now, at least.

They slowed their pace occasionally, allowing everyone in the little group to exchange food and water, or to comfort and change crying children. Elora was grateful for the glamour Aerin had cast on them, and the additional scent masking runecast he'd kept up since they returned. She moved between the people, trying to understand what the hell was happening.

"The attacks started about two weeks ago," a woman with a toddler asleep in her arms whispered when Elora asked. "I don't know how you didn't hear. A few Summer villages were ransacked, then a town farther down the border in Spring. We thought it was just the Unseelie pushing the boundaries again, fueling their need for chaos…" Elora saw Aerin flinch slightly at that. "But now…well…"

"They say it's that girl!" a man piped up through a mouthful of bread. "The prophesied one."

An elderly woman hit him over the back of the head with her palm.

"Nonsense, Oak. Rumors, that's all."

"No," someone else argued, "the King of Autumn himself announced it."

"Since when did we trust either Unseelie royals?" the woman countered, but Elora began to tune them out.

Her. It was her. Whatever destruction was coming, it was because she lived. Sickness roiled in her stomach and she bit down on her lip so hard she tasted blood.

"Move out!" Tarhael called. He'd immediately taken on a leadership role when they left the village, his natural charisma and cool confidence drawing the others to him. He was sitting atop a high hill at the green valley they'd stopped in, playing lookout. His standard coolness had returned, unflappable and reassuring. Apparently, he'd decided they'd rested long enough.

The sun was beginning to crest the horizon by the time the group stopped at another town, far enough away from the original village to be safe while they restocked, slept and then spread word. They'd been traveling for hours, moving north towards the capital. Elora's exhaustion was a living thing inside of her. Now that the numb shock had retreated, her legs burned, her thighs feeling like jelly when she dismounted and nearly fell face first into the dirt. She was so tired she'd long since stopped appreciating the beauty of the kingdom, her eyes barely managing to stay open. She was sure she smelt of stale sweat and desperately needed to bathe - her hair hung limp around her face and dirt was trapped under her fingernails. After she'd slept, she'd wash, she told herself. If she tried now she might drown.

Aerin was far better off than her. She wanted to punch him for how unruffled he looked. Sure, his brow was furrowed in worry and his hair had seen better days, but he still smelled like autumn, comforting and heart achingly familiar.

"Áine above, my ass is numb," Tarhael grumbled as he slid from his own horse, coming to grab the reins from Aerin and lead both beasts to the stable block the local inn owner had offered up. Between the taverns, inns and locals, there were enough rooms for their group to stay in. The generosity of the Spring fae only made the cruelty of Autumn clearer to Elora.

To be fair to him, Elora thought Tarhael had a point. She'd stopped feeling half of her body hours ago and the parts she *could* feel she wished she didn't.

"Go sleep," Tarhael told them. "I'll be there in like five minutes once I've found these guys a nice comfy stable." He gestured affectionately to the horses with the reins in each hand. "And for the love of Autumn, Aerin, please no knife play while I'm gone. I'm far too tired to deal with that shit." He winked as Elora spluttered.

Aerin glared after his friend before relenting and walking with Elora to their assigned room - a twin bed room in the inn. Elora collapsed within two seconds of seeing the bed, barely remembering to take her shoes off before her head hit the pillow. A padded out bed roll had been placed between the two single beds to accommodate the third guest at short notice and Aerin shed his own shoes and jacket before lying down on it, leaving the other bed for Tarhael.

Elora briefly heard Tarhael enter, then lock the door behind him. He and Aerin muttered something about a scent blocking runecast, but Elora was too tired for specifics and quickly succumbed to the pull of sleep.

"Time to move, sleepyheads," Tarhael's far too cheery voice roused Elora from sleep. She debated throwing something at him, but Aerin beat her to it. The pillow hit him in the face with a soft *thud*, eliciting a grunt from the man. "Oi!"

"How long do we have?" Aerin asked, sitting up and running a hand

ELORA

through his sleep mussed hair. Elora refused to look at him. Aerin in the morning, rumpled and heavy-lidded, was doing ridiculous things to her heart, even with the glamour still firmly in place.

"Enough time for you two to wash and shove some food down your throats. I'll get the horses ready and meet you outside. Be fast, we're leaving for the capital soon."

Elora cursed into her blanket and forced herself to stand, every muscle in her body screaming at her to lie back down. She pressed on, cringing when she looked down at her dirty, sweaty clothes.

They rushed to get ready and despite the bone deep ache in her body, Elora felt significantly more alive after a bath. Tarhael had gone to the trouble of sourcing her another outfit from one of the women in town, a simple set of riding leathers that, other than being slightly too tight on top, fit her surprisingly well. Much better than the thin, filthy, cotton pajamas she'd been in until now.

She wondered if Tarhael had slept at all, considering how organized he was. But, judging from the lack of dark circles and his bright, wide eyes, she assumed he just had a better tolerance for fear and travel than she did.

True to his word, he had tacked up the horses, both of which now looked much fresher than yesterday and was waiting atop his mount outside the inn. A crowd of people milled about in various states of readiness, clearly preparing to evacuate the town for the capital.

"What's the plan, Prince?" Tarhael whispered as Aerin and Elora approached. Aerin's hair was wet and messy, the short cut of the glamour making Elora do a double take. Beads of water still clung to his skin and Elora fought to remind her body that she was mad at him. It didn't care. The urge to step into his arms and kiss the side of his neck where a bead of water had slid down, disappearing into the top of his shirt, was overwhelming. She clenched her fists tightly at her side instead.

265

"Straight on to the capital," Aerin answered smoothly, grabbing his horse's reins. He extended a hand to Elora and all but lifted her into the saddle. She couldn't decide whether to love or hate him for it. She was supposed to be mad at him, furious, for keeping such huge secrets from her. And yet, the thought of carrying around the weight of that anger for a second longer made her want to burst into tears.

"What are we going to do?" she asked when he was seated behind her, radiating warmth that soothed the hurt in her heart.

"I don't know," he admitted as the crowd began to move out of the town, taking them with it. "But I don't think this will end with peace."

She swallowed thickly. "It's my fault."

She heard Tarhael snort from the horse next to them, and scowled in return. "Yes, Elora," he mocked, rolling his deep brown eyes. "It's entirely your fault that you were born. How dare you?"

A weight lifted off her chest at his words and she smiled. Still, her skin stung with the fact that her mere existence was putting so many fae at risk. It didn't matter that she had no idea who she was until a few days ago, or that she was helpless to change it. The feeling of peace that overwhelmed her upon entering Spring had long since faded, leaving a sourness in its wake.

Aerin murmured something she didn't hear, too consumed by her own guilt as it ate away at the softest parts of her. Then -

"Holy fucking shit."

Her head snapped to the right, staring wide eyed at Tarhael.

"Sorry," he said sheepishly, pointing ahead of them. "But look."

Suddenly, their horse was cantering and Elora gripped the horn of the saddle to stop from tipping sideways. Aerin swapped the reins to one hand expertly, slipping the other arm around her waist to steady her. The heat that bloomed under his touch was purely coincidental, she decided.

Then she saw it.

Or, rather, them.

At head height with the horses, flew a little group of winged fae. Red hair streamed behind the one in front, the skirt of her deep orange dress matching the hue.

"Raewyn!" Elora couldn't help it. She was shouting her friend's name before she could stop herself. Aerin squeezed tighter, no doubt to tell her to quieten down, but excitement bubbled up inside her, threatening to spill over.

The pixie turned and narrowed her eyes, slowing down so she could study Elora. Then her gaze traveled to Aerin behind her and her eyes went wide and panicked. Fuck. Elora had entirely forgotten that Aerin didn't look like Aerin at all.

"Who-" Raewyn began, but Elora cut her off.

"It's me," she said excitedly, gesturing to herself, then lowered her voice so nobody else would hear when she added, "Aerin had to change how we looked cause...you know..."

Raewyn blinked at her with stunned confusion. "Elora?"

Elora nodded and the pixies crowded her, hugging her, Aerin and Tarhael with enthusiasm. Elora laughed, accepting the welcome with open arms and a light heart.

"How did you get here?" she asked when they pulled away.

Lydia sighed, curly hair escaping it's fastening and a light sheen of sweat coating her brown skin. How long had they been flying for?

"We left when we heard what had happened with Elladan. How awful he'd been to you. We didn't know how bad it was..." she trailed off, looking apologetic. Elora's face softened. "We've been traveling ever since, trying to help everyone fleeing from the attacks. We've always been just ahead of them, like now."

The joy that Elora felt at seeing her friends again eased the guilt a little.

"Are you going to the capital, too?" Aerin asked, voice still low.

Raewyn nodded.

Elora breathed deeply, looking around them at the crowd of innocent civilians, wondering how much more their lives were going to change in the coming days. Her head pounded. How much more was she endangering them by being here with them?

"Aerin," she began, before she'd even thought it through.

"What is it, love?"

Her stomach clenched. "We should break away."

"What do you mean?" Raewyn piped up.

"Is there another route to the capital? It's just...I can't help but wonder if these people would be safer without me here. If someone finds out..."

"She has a point," Tarhael agreed with a sigh. He looked around him, gaze settling on a forest to the west. "We can cut through there. Not nearly as deadly as the Winter lands and it'll separate us from the rest of them. It'll only take an extra day considering we're a small party. There's no way a large group could travel through those trees easily."

Aerin considered behind her, before adjusting his grip so his hand rested on her thigh. Elora stopped breathing at the contact.

"Is that what you want?" he checked with her, thumb tracing small circles on her leg.

God, her body really needed to get a grip. It was all she could do to get enough breath into her lungs to say, "yes," and even then, it came out pathetically shallow.

She heard his smile when he said, "okay then."

They broke away as quietly as they could, the pixies joining them without question, and Elora felt lighter for it. She was still squashing the horror, the fear, the guilt as best she could. Soon, she worried, it would swallow her whole.

Instead, she focused on Aerin's even breathing, his hand on her leg, the contact grounding her as they entered the thick forest and left the path behind.

43

Elora

"Your rune for 'change' isn't correct," Aerin corrected her. "Here." He placed his hand on top of hers and helped her trace the twig in the dirt. The strong grip of his fingers on hers was comforting, the familiar weight of his body against her soothed Elora's nerves and helped her breathing even out. "Now, the rune for specification."

They'd been traveling for two days, riding through the day until their horses waned. At night, over the soft light of the campfire, Aerin taught her how to use runes - to craft magic in the dirt, to harness the power that fizzed beneath the surface of her skin. It was infuriating and tiring and she spent most of the time getting it wrong. But the irritation fueled her. She needed to be doing *something*. Anything that meant she wasn't sitting on her ass waiting for the world to collapse around her. If she mastered this, she could be useful.

Elora narrowed her eyes in concentration and drew out the remaining runes before looking expectantly at Aerin. She had been in charge of the group's glamour and she was getting better, slowly but surely.

"Wait-" She reached for the scrawls in the dirt before Aerin could speak, seeing her mistake. "The proportions aren't right yet. Let me try again." As she redrew and adjusted the runes, she reviewed what Aerin had taught her. *Clearly visualize the result you want to see. Be as specific as you can with the runes.* The rules and structure for runecasting reminded Elora of the few programming classes she had taken during college. She wasn't sure if that should terrify or encourage her. She'd been shit at programming, but noticed the similarities between the logical structures of the runecasts she was practicing. She rearranged some of the symbols for *old* and *gray* and scrawled the new runecast on the sheet of paper resting on the ground. She shoved the paper in the shallow hole Aerin had made with his boot, covering the top with loose soil. It glowed softly green as she stood, waiting for it to take effect.

"Tarhael, how do I look?" Aerin looked at his friend expectantly, mouth quirked in a lopsided smirk.

"You look like an elderly fae. The sort of grandpa that would give you nightmares."

"Is that an acceptable way to address your Prince?"

"As far as the kingdom knows, you're missing and presumably dead. I'll call you whatever I want, old man." Tarhael grinned and spurred his horse forward to go scouting. The pixies spread out among the trees, darting in different directions in pairs, checking for any sign of danger.

Aerin rolled his eyes after Tarhael and turned back to Elora. "Well done. You're getting better."

Elora blushed, then chastised her body for its reaction, mildly annoyed that she was always finding one reason or another to turn cherry red around Aerin. "Should I feel tired or anything? I haven't really felt anything physically as I've been practicing…magic." She paused before the word *magic* - it tasted like sherbet on her tongue, fizzy and sweet and no matter how much she said it, it still didn't sound real.

"Energy consumption and the trade-offs of magic," Aerin hummed his approval of her curiosity, his expression morphing into his professor face as he continued. "The thing about magic is, it's likely not at all what you've imagined it to be. I've read some of the mortal books in the library and at your bookstore and it's vastly different from what the fae can do. Runecasting takes practice and preparation, and it isn't the sort of thing you can do on the fly. It's not anything like magic you'll find written in your fantasy books or movies."

"But what about the magic you do without runecasting? Like when you flew us to safety, or created that dome thing to protect us from the rain?"

"Patience." Aerin laughed a little, the corners of his eyes crinkling with amusement. "All fae possess the ability to runecast but only royals and nobility have the ability to cast magic from within without the guidance of anything else, because we carry the blood of the first fae of each of our Seasons. We're the closest descendants of the children of the Runecarvers, and so our magic is more potent. Here. This should help." Aerin hopped off his steed, planted himself square in the grass and abruptly pulled off his shirt.

"Hey!" Elora protested, voice squeaking with shock though she wasn't at all displeased with the sight before her. "Give me a heads up before you do that!"

"Why? So you can control your blushing? It's fine, you're pretty when you blush."

Elora was too far away to punch him, so she settled for sticking her tongue out at a now half naked Aerin. His face was still changed with the glamour, but his body was the same. It was near impossible to look away from him. He wasn't massive or bulky the way Tarhael was, but his muscles carried the sense of effortless grace Aerin gave off when he moved. His arms and shoulders were toned and the

272

defined abs gave way to a built back covered in tattoos. They were the same tattoos she had seen once before, but now that they were much closer, she could see the intricate elegance to them. He had a pair of angel's wings on his back in dark blue and the detail was perfect, down to each feather. A pair of outstretched hands, a fraction of a gap between both of their fingers, spanned the side of his upper back and down into his lower hip and a simple band circled the top of his left arm. She saw Blueberry tattooed to his left shoulder and found herself missing the bird.

"Done staring yet?"

"Please," she replied, trying to sound unfazed and failing miserably. In an attempt to salvage the situation, she rolled her eyes again. "What do they mean?"

"You've already met Blueberry. I have royal blood, like you. It's a genetic thing, as far as I can tell, but fae who have royal blood in them have access to two more types of powers in addition to the two that they're given to runecast. And that's not counting the generic runes all fae can cast." Catching the blank look on Elora's face, Aerin hastily added, "Did Tarhael not tell you about it that time on the balcony?"

"Um, not really. He only explained the difference between runecasting and the tattoos royals get. I know most of the rune symbols and alphabet, but that's about it."

Aerin ran a hand through his hair and considered for a moment.

"Okay, well to keep it short, all fae have the ability to runecast excluding extreme cases. Each fae has two powers that they're born with, depending on what Season they're from. I'm Autumn fae, and the two powers I can express through runecasting are telekinesis and memory manipulation."

"That's...an interesting combination." Elora's chest constricted a little at the memory of *Fleur*. How her memories had been erased, twisted, pieced together all wrong until she didn't remember herself anymore.

She couldn't stop her face crumpling. She trapped her bottom lip between her teeth, desperate to keep it from wobbling.

"I-" Aerin's voice was tentative, rougher than she was used to, as though he wasn't sure what to say to make it okay. "I'm sorry, Elora. Really fucking sorry. Elladan told me that he wanted to look through your memories in order to see if you truly were the girl from the prophecy. I agreed, out of self interest, despite the fact I should have fucking well known not to trust him. But I needed to know if you were being truthful, to make sure you weren't sent from a Seelie kingdom to try to bring us down. I may hate my pathetic excuse for a family, but that doesn't mean the innocents in our kingdom, however little there are, deserve to suffer if a misguided fae decides to bring it all down. Ridiculous really. I should've known, shouldn't have taken his word, after everything -" Aerin cut himself off, steeling his expression before he soldiered on. "I had no idea that he was going to take the runecast I prepared for him and have someone else alter it so he could hurt you like that. I-"

The ground rose up much quicker than she thought it would and Elora hit the ground tumbling, the breath knocked out of her.

"Elora, what the hell? Are you okay?" Aerin's arms wrapped around her and held her in a sitting position.

"I'm fine, I'm fine," she coughed and tried to suck in a few deep breaths.

"What were you thinking?"

"You looked you were going to cry-"

"Did not."

"Did too."

"Did not."

"Okay fine. You looked *sad* and I'm halfway to crumbling just at the sight of all that guilt, so I tried to get off the horse to come give

ELORA

you a hug but I somehow ended up on the ground."

"You practically threw yourself off the horse." Aerin's voice was light and amused, though his grip on her was sure and strong.

"Hey, I didn't make fun of you the first time you hid behind me when the garbage truck came by."

"Fair enough." Aerin dipped his head in acquiescence, a little smile brushing against his lips once more.

Her expression grew serious again, though she wouldn't meet his eyes. "Aerin, I understand. And I don't hold it against you. I really don't." She took a deep breath, steadying herself. "I...I trust you. I shouldn't. I should be mad at you, want to make you hurt for everything that's happened. I've tried. But I can't, goddammit, Aerin I can't."

And then she kissed him. Their lips met - soft spring meeting new autumn, tentative and unhurried. He was gentle, kissing her like he was savoring every swipe of her lips against his, but his grip on her waist was strong. Unyielding. Rooted. She wrapped her arms around his neck as he pulled her into him, a hand tangling through her hair. She kissed him back harder until their lips opened and their tongues met. She lost herself in him. She was done holding back. She was done questioning her feelings. She was-

"I thought you were teaching her magic, Aerin. The runecasting kind. Also you're shirtless." Tarhael's deep, amused voice surprised Elora as she shoved Aerin away and tumbled back to the ground again.

"Yes thank you Tarhael. I had no idea I was shirtless." Sarcasm dripped from his words, but he didn't seem at all bothered about the turn of events. "You were awfully sneaky."

"I came back normally, making a normal amount of noise. You two were the ones too oblivious to notice."

Elora could feel the heat exploding through her cheeks, a strawberry stained sign of her embarrassment, and sighed. Her blush would be the end of her. "Is everything okay?"

"Yes," Tarhael said. "It's a little crowded up there, so we should camp here for the night. I'll scout another path tomorrow a little further away from the traffic." He turned back to his mount and began unpacking the tent and supplies from the saddle bags.

Aerin coughed and Elora smiled as she noticed the faintest tinges of pink leaving his cheek. He pulled his shirt back on and he gave her half shrug. "I don't and can't really keep anything from him so it was a matter of time anyway. Now, where was I?"

"Something about your powers. Memory manipulation and telekinesis?" Truth be told, the kiss had been extremely distracting.

"Right, yes." Aerin cleared his throat. "So when fae reach the age of thirteen or so, they conduct their very first runecast, which is a revealing runecast to figure out what their specific talents are. You runecast according to your Season, so for me, I write Eolas with multicolored lead, blow over it and wait for three heartbeats. When the Autumn fae first wrote with Eolas, they used several pencils of different color. Tedious," Aerin smiled. Moments later, the cloth glowed with the runes for memory and telekinesis. Here."

Aerin reached into his pouch and pulled out his little notepad and pencil, scribbling quickly. He leaned back with a satisfied expression on his face as the apple Tarhael had been eating flew into his outstretched hand.

"Hey! I thought we agreed you wouldn't do that anymore!" Tarhael shook his head, already reaching into his pack to grab another one.

Aerin took a bite out of the fruit and gestured with his free hand. "I don't know where this runecast came from. Honestly, it's infuriating how much information the fae lost when we cut ourselves off from the mortal realm and retreated into Fior Domhan. Long story short, each fae has two magical capabilities that they are born with, they are revealed when they are thirteen or so, and that's the gist of it. Oh of course, that's after the general runes."

"Like the glamour you have me practicing."

"Precisely!" Aerin was in full swing professor mode, and he clearly wasn't about to stop anytime soon. Elora could do nothing but sit back and watch, rapt. "In addition to the two capabilities, the foundation of fae magic rests on the general magic we're born with. Such abilities include glamour, glamour detection, temporarily enhanced physical traits such as speed, strength and endurance, being able to communicate in any language, and preventing yourself from almost any diseases. You can also figure out the date, time, and where you are as well." He frowned for a moment, and then started again. "It's kind of funny because you start taking these things for granted. But yes, these are the generic magical capabilities fae are born with, if you look at things from a macro perspective, the fae are quite limited in what sorts of magics we can perform. There are creatures and entities that can do far greater things than us."

"Hey, you're going off on a tangent again," Tarhael warned from the other side of the campfire, already inside his tent.

They laughed and Aerin continued. "Even though fae have two distinct magical capabilities, we still have the entirety of the rune alphabet to use. There's some pretty creative applications we've come up with. For example, telekinesis simply doesn't involve summoning things to me. I can write a complicated runecast to keep things suspended in the air which is why I can do this." Cracking his knuckles, Aerin wrote something new in his notebook and gently blew over it. Elora hadn't even noticed Aerin doing it earlier, but moments later, her eyes widened with wonder as the tent sprang up without rods and poles, just holding its shape in the air.

"What? How did you-" she spluttered.

Aerin laughed, a rich and comforting sound. "We could have done this, but I was saving it until I had a chance to show off how creative magic can be with runecasting, no matter the initial limitation of power fae might have. It also gets much easier with practice if you've already performed the runecast several times before. Most of my runecasts are muscle memory at this point. But it's always important to try to innovate, expand and make old runecasts more efficient. "

"Yeah, yeah, thank you professor Aerin. He's been saving that for days, and we've all been having to put up tents manually," Tarhael grumbled from inside his tent.

"Nothing like a lesson well taught. While runecasting doesn't take much out of the user, nothing really, you can't prepare runecasts in advance and you need to cast a fresh one each time. It also takes time to runecast, it isn't something you can do on the fly. Runecarving on the other hand, is how we flew here."

"Your tattoos?"

"Yes. The tattoos carved onto my back allow me to do the same things runecasting does, but with different abilities and without need to shape the runes. The runes are already carved into my back, allowing me to activate them at will. It's why I glow blue when I use them and you glowed green back when we escaped. There is a cost however. While I can do nearly anything with my two carved powers, air manipulation and air removal, it takes a heavy physical toll. You need to train it the way you do with running or weightlifting, and even then there are limits. Genetic potential is one of the explanations for discrepancies between royals with similar powers, but runecarving mostly comes down to training and physical limitations. Royal fae get their carvings anywhere from ages fifteen to eighteen, so I haven't been training with mine for very long either."

Aerin's lecture was cut short by noisy snoring from Tarhael and Aerin shook his head ruefully. "I've always had a knack for putting him to sleep," he said, chuckling, rubbing his hand over the back of his neck.

Elora smiled briefly before asking, "so how did you get your runes tattooed onto you?"

"Carved, but-"

"Is there really that much of a difference?"

"No, but saying carved makes it sound cooler."

Elora laughed, watching the way Aerin's eyes crinkled at the side when he joked.

He smirked at her before continuing. "Air manipulation means I can control the air around me, whether it's shaping the currents around me to fly, or forming the shields against the rain like you say a few days ago, or creating little tornadoes, or really anything I can imagine. Although it takes a ridiculous amount of practice. Air removal is also what it sounds like. It's the inverse of air manipulation in a way. It allows me to remove the air from a certain setting, being able to deprive a certain object or radius of air."

As the words sank in and Elora started to wrap her head around the implications, she couldn't help the small bud of fear that began to bloom at the extent of his power. But he continued speaking - earnestly, about the way he handled airflow and made his gardens bloom and helped children think they were flying during the last solstice celebration warmed Elora to her core. Only Aerin would take a power easily abused for evil and find such *good* uses for it.

"You have royal blood too, Elora. The way you summoned plants to your defense and the way you drugged Elladan proves it more than the prophecy. And the fact that I've seen you glow green. The problem is, you can't fully express, control, nor train your innate powers because you don't have your carvings yet."

"Let's do it right now then. I just need some sort of plant to drug me or numb the pain, and I'll be good to go." Elora knew it sounded absurd, but she didn't care. She had spent the majority of her life daydreaming and writing about magic people in fantastical settings, and she would be damned if she didn't do everything in her power to learn magic. Not when it actually existed. Not when, if she could get a grip on it, she could *help*.

Aerin shook his head and eyed her. "I love your enthusiasm. I really do. Except I, unfortunately, don't possess the power to help you find your powers, or do the carvings for you. You would have to visit the Lady of the Lake."

"Like...Nimue? From the Arthurian legends?"

"You've heard of her?"

"I mean, I do have a history degree from Columbia University." Elora pinned him with a look and he shrugged.

"No, I just think it's fascinating how different the stories are. Everything from the legends are mostly made up, except she is literally a lady from a lake. She's one of Áine's daughters. The Mother of Spring. There are four sisters - the Runecarvers - and they never leave their dwellings. I had Aureole give me my carvings but none of what I went through is going to help you. Each process is extremely different. But we need to get you to Nimue, in order to get your carvings done so you can access your powers. I have a feeling you're going to need them before this is all said and done."

Aerin's expression had gone tight and pained, as though was remembering something that he'd rather forget, but she decided not to push him on it. "So, is that where we're going to go then?"

"No, we're still heading to the capital. I only know where Aureole is because I'm a prince and I had to visit her, but each Season guards the location of their seers very jealously. They're essentially state secrets, if you will. Since I'm not privy to where Nimue is, we still need to head to Anixi, the capital kingdom of Spring, and hope Queen Briella allows us access to her libraries. Instead of beheading us on the spot as enemies."

On that somber note, they called it a night. Elora settled down under the slivers of night sky peeking through the little slits in the roof of the tent, the stars looking like a thousand little candles from her angle. Her head was buzzing with information, but she eventually found sleep, along with dreams of trees and flowers erupting from her hands.

44

Elora

"Aerin, I got it!" Elora's glamour took hold, changing Aerin and Tarhael to look like two of the pixies that flew with the group - Lydia and Fern. Raewyn laughed, elbowing Lydia as the other woman frowned at Tarhael.

"Good." He'd only said one word, but she could hear the genuine pride in his voice. Her heart swelled, the slight rush of blood from her head leaving her with an uncomfortable lump in her throat.

"Okay, now reverse it."

"You look quite good as a pixie," Tarhael drawled, and Aerin smacked him in the arm.

"She hasn't tried this yet. Let her concentrate."

Elora narrowed her brows in tight concentration and carefully drew out the runes required before burying the paper in the dirt. the runes required into the ground with a little twig she had found. Aerin and Tarhael returned to themselves once more.

"Alright, now write a runecast to enhance your endurance and strength. You're going to need it. We'll arrive at Anixi today," Aerin said, one brow raised.

It had been nearly a week of filtering in and out of various refugee camps, trying not to draw suspicion but Elora had stolen off with Aerin every morning and night to practice her runecasting. It had paid off, apparently, her magic progressing at rates even Aerin thought fast. *Natural, he called me,* Elora grinned, a rush of giddiness sweeping through her.

Magic was starting to feel less like a foreign body and more like reaching out to an old friend.

The first Elora noticed when they began to emerge from the forest was the thickening of traffic. There were traveling refugees as far as the eye could see and Elora gleaned the worsening condition of Spring and Summer as she overheard snippets of conversation.

"I heard the garrison at Alvarson surrendered!" an elderly voice called out.

"They say that Queen Briella's army was trapped retreating and lost another battle!" a young woman's voice said.

Elora found herself praying to Áine - she didn't even know who she exactly was but remembered Aerin invoked the deity quite frequently - that everything would be okay.

They had been forced to leave their mounts behind the night before, traffic thickening to a point where everyone was marching on foot and Elora did her best to ignore the slow burning in her calves. The runecasting she had done to boost her strength and endurance was working. Elora didn't think she could have walked the past seven miles or so without it. Tarhael led the way, using his massive bulk to clear a path for her and Aerin while the pixies took advantage of their small stature to skirt between bodies in the crowd.

"We're almost there," Tarhael announced, heaving his arms against the crowd.

They ascended the hill, trees thinning around them, signaling an end to the forest they'd called home for the previous two nights. Filtered sunlight coalesced into radiant sunbeams kissing Elora's face as the forest finally fell away to expose open plains and hills. The crowd surged forward as one, only to stop as abruptly as it started, a collective gasp rippling through them.

Elora shoved her way to a better vantage point, bumping shoulders with tired fae, the grumbled complaints and speculations a constant thrum in her ears. She couldn't stop the gasp from escaping her mouth. In the slight dip between two vibrant green hills sat a gorgeous walled castle sat - surrounded by a half constructed wooden fort and palisades. The castle looked like it was made of the clearest alabaster, its white walls nearly touching the clouds. It shone in the sunlight, flowering vines crawling up the sides of the turrets, hints of pink and red and yellow peeking out from behind the walls, teasing at what Elora could only assume was a grand garden. Several groups of soldiers blocked the refugees, armed to the teeth.

"What the hell is going on?" Elora demanded, turning to Aerin.

"I don't know. Briella is known for her kindness and generosity. This is highly unexpected of her. Although, to be fair, the last time I actually saw her was when I was nine."

Guards approached Elora's section of the crowd and began to address them, monotone and tired.

"A message from her majesty Queen Briella of Anixi, Queen of Spring, ambassador of the Seelie Court. She welcomes you all, but is gravely saddened the circumstances could not be happier. While she understands the plight of her people, and those fleeing here from other seasons, there is limited capacity and-"

"Bullshit!"

"Lies!"

"Are you going to leave us out here to die?"

The accusations, jeers, and boos rose up all around Elora like a living creature, overwhelming and insistent in its chorus. The guards forged on, determined, but the news didn't get any lighter.

"Anixi and the surrounding city within the walls are filled to the brim, more than two hundred percent over capacity. Her majesty's royal army is in the process of building forts and palisades to accommodate additional refugees and anyone else who needs a place to stay. Blankets and food will be provided. I ask you all to stay together and in your tents until we can finish the fort. I repeat, stay orderly and stay together. Queen Briella will do everything in her power to protect you all." With that, the leader of the little troop of guards began walking back to where the construction was happening, soldiers in tow.

The fae around them grumbled, but most were placated by the promises of food and blankets, seemingly mollified by the fact that protection was being built. The guards promised to have patrols all throughout the day and night around the outer borders of the refugee campsites to protect them.

"What are we going to do if we can't even get into the city?" Elora asked.

"I'll figure out something. C'mon, let's get settled for now," Aerin said, voice tense, as he shouldered his pack and searched for somewhere to set up camp.

"Are you crazy? No."

"Tarhael, you know this is the only way-"

"I said, are you out of your mind?"

"Tarhael-"

"I've been guarding you ever since we were kids. This is not happening. Do you even understand the danger? You're a Prince of Autumn, Aerin. A damn *Prince of Autumn*."

Elora watched the two argue back and forth, never having seen either of them this heated with the other before.

GIRL OF BONE AND IVY

She was on Tarhael's side, not that she planned on interrupting them to say so. Aerin had announced that he was going to fly over the walls when night fell, sneak into the library to collect the information they needed before flying back out. To which Tarhael had responded by bursting into laughter before realizing Aerin was dead serious.

Elora pulled her thin blanket around herself, though the night was warm, and watched the two argue. Darkness was different here than in the Unseelie Courts - gentle, welcoming, open. The moon hung high in the sky, a nail thin crescent, hiding among the bright sea of stars as if it too was worried about the Autumn and Winter forces bearing down on them.

"You've never even experienced reconnaissance training," Tarhael hissed.

"I've done plenty with you," Aerin retorted. "It'll be the same."

"No it won't. You won't have me there."

"Tarhael." Aerin grabbed him by the shoulders and looked him square in the eye, every muscle in his body tense, voice tight with barely restrained urgency. "You and I have been through everything together. Every success, every failure. You've been there every time I devised a new runecast and you were beaten alongside me every time I pissed my father off. But you can't be there this time. I am not strong enough to carry you over the wall and evade the sentries at the same time. Nor can you turn invisible. We're wasting time here. Elora needs to meet the Runecarver before my father's forces arrive. And we haven't the faintest idea of where the fuck to find her."

Tarhael stared at Aerin, teeth clenched so tight Elora was worried he'd crack one. He closed his eyes for a brief second, exhaled and then grabbed his friend in a hug so tight it looked painful.

"Stay safe. And be quick about the whole damn thing." Tarhael pulled back to grip Aerin's shoulders. He shook his head a little. "Is the glamour on your wings ready?"

286

ELORA

"When do I ever disappoint?"

Aerin stepped out of the embrace and turned to Elora. They hadn't spoken about the kiss earlier in the week, and Elora was suddenly unsure what to do with her hands. Now certainly wasn't the time to talk, but what was she supposed to do? Kiss him goodbye? Hug him? How did one say *hope you don't die risking your life for me* to a guy they'd kissed twice and then promptly pretended it never happened?

"There are a lot of guards." Elora immediately cursed herself. *Of course there are a lot of guards. There's a damn war going on. How is that the best you could come up with?*

"There are indeed. I'll be off then." Aerin raised a brow and smiled at her.

Elora watched Aerin sneak through the half constructed fort until he was pressed against the wall, a vague sinking feeling in her stomach. A faint blue light began to emanate from him and she stared, still awestruck, at the outlines of his gorgeous wings as he shot up the wall towards the sky.

Wait.

She could see him. Others could too as a murmur broke out among the camp, a few fae shouting and pointing towards the glowing blue figure streaking through the sky.

"Shit!" Tarhael was already up and running.

Elora scrambled after him, heart rattling the bars of its cage so violently her chest ached.

"Why the fuck isn't his glamour working?" she panted in Tarhael's direction as she desperately tried to keep up.

Tarhael didn't answer. He didn't *have* an answer. His gaze was fixed on Aerin's figure, nearing the top of the wall, too high, too far to hear their warnings.

The first dark streak that shot from the top of a turret missed. The second didn't.

Aerin stumbled mid flight, body dropping a few feet before he caught himself on a gust of wind again.

But the guards didn't falter. Another arrow flew true. Then another. And another.

Aerin's silhouette dipped again over the crest of the castle walls, wings beating frantically as he fought to keep himself airborne. Elora watched, helpless, as they failed and Aerin spiraled down, behind the walls and out of sight.

A scream tore itself from her lips, coating her throat in fire, her body shaking as she stared at the castle walls. She and Tarhael were close now, near touching distance, the rest of the crowd having been too frozen with shock to stop them rushing through. She was still screaming when her hands, no, her entire body began glowing a hazy green.

The ground disappeared from under her. Wait, no, that wasn't right. The ground was still there but she, inexplicably, was rising fast, higher and higher until her breath was snatched by the wind rushing past her. She was numb, shaking, throat raw from sobbing or screaming or shouting, she couldn't tell.

She looked down and immediately wished she hadn't. A huge tree stretched below her, her feet balanced on the highest branch, leaves unfurling around her, the trunk thick and sturdy as it grew closer to the castle walls.

Elora could see Tarhael through the leaves, clutching onto one of the thicker branches for dear life. She wanted to call to him, help him climb, but her mouth wouldn't work. Wouldn't move. Before Elora could get her bearings, she was somehow at the top of the walls.

The world stopped moving, the tree trunk groaning slightly before it settled. Elora's head felt like it was being split open and trying to think was like wading through thick tar.

The dizziness hit her next, a brick wall of exhaustion and nausea.

She fell to her knees, the rough bark scratching her skin as the corners of her vision began blurring and fading to black.

Strong arms wrapped around her as her vision washed away completely, the steady movement of being carried swaying her into unconsciousness.

45

Aerin

erin's shoulder *hurt*. No - it *burned* as though someone had plunged the left side of his body into white hot flames. Tears stung his eyes and warmed his cheeks, and what little breath he could force into his lungs made an ache bloom in his chest.

Fuck. The Queen must have had stronger wards than he'd anticipated. Stupid, really. Cocky arrogance left over from the influences of the Unseelie Court - thinking he could best the damn Queen of Spring. Ridiculous.

Aerin cursed low under his breath, but no sound came out. The ground, thankfully, had not come at all - a bed of soft moss rising up to meet his injured body instead. Small mercies and all.

Muffled voices surrounded him and through his blurry vision, he could make out the shiny tips of swords and arrows aimed at his chest and head. If this was Winter, he didn't doubt one of those weapons would already have become closely acquainted with his brain.

"Who is he?" A female voice, low and sweet like the syrup Elora insisted on drowning her pancakes in. *Elora.* Aerin hoped Tarhael would look after her. Not that he doubted his friend, but still -

"….of Autumn…"

Oh Áine above -

"And what is the son of the King of Autumn, an *Unseelie Court*, doing in my kingdom?" The woman spat the words like they were poison. Aerin didn't blame her.

"He-"

"And who in Áine's name are they?"

Who? Aerin blinked rapidly, willing his dizzy head to focus. He pushed to a sitting position on the mossy ground, head swimming and shoulder screaming in agony. One of the arrows had impaled itself deep in the fleshy part of his shoulder, the arrow head so deep it was no longer visible. He'd been grazed by others, but that pain barely registered.

"Queen." A familiar deep voice had Aerin turning his head, another horribly strong wave of pain shooting down his arm. "Please allow us to apologize -"

"No," the woman, Queen Briella, said smoothly. "I don't think I will. You will answer to me, first."

Aerin fought to focus his vision, Tarhael's bulky form coming into focus, and in his arms -

She was unconscious, dark hair flopping over her eyes, all their glamours destroyed by the wards around the castle.

"Elora!" His voice was thick and painful but he didn't care. Barely noticed the steel pressed to his throat, the sharp intake of breath from Tarhael.

"She's fine, Aerin," his friend said soothingly, then, because he apparently couldn't help himself, "and so am I, thanks for asking."

"Escort them to the throne room."

Tarhael's eyes went wide, but he dutifully followed the guards away. Aerin's head pounded so badly his vision blurred before he could focus on Briella, and darkness swarmed again.

46

Elora

Elora was warm. She burrowed closer to her pillow, fluttering in and out of consciousness. Why did her body ache so badly?

Her pillow was rising and falling, a slow but steady beat beneath her head. What the hell? She sat up abruptly, confusion overwhelming the need to sleep, and nearly landed on her ass. She wasn't in bed, she realized with horror, nor was she resting her head on a pillow.

No -

"You're not a pillow," she said, voice cracking. She smothered her mouth immediately, mortified that the words had ever made it past her lips.

Tarhael laughed, but it was strained. He still held her close, hand flexing on her waist.

"No, I'm not."

Elora frowned and followed his gaze. Where the hell were they? The last she remembered Aerin had been hit and -

Oh God. Visions of leaves and branches and dizzying height flickered behind her eyes, a sick feeling causing her stomach to flip. A goddamn tree, the height of the walls guarding the Queen's home.

ELORA

"Oh God," she whispered aloud this time, eyes wide.

The room was huge, but felt cozier than it should have due to the sheer amount of greenery. Climbing flowers covered one wall almost entirely, blooming pale pink and orange, violet and white. The ground beneath them was polished white marble and the high ceiling, like the other walls, was white with gold leaves painted intricately across it. A throne room, judging by the elegant throne made from woven branches, moss covering the seat where velvet would normally be, ivy leaves climbing the arms and back. Atop it sat one of the most beautiful women - *fae* - that Elora had ever seen. Her long dark hair was braided intricately, threaded with pink petals, and perfectly framed her face. Warm brown eyes bore into Elora, the woman's glossy pink lips falling open as if in shock. She stood, her long green dress sparkling in the sunlight that streamed through the giant windows, and tilted her head to examine Elora. She was tall, Elora realized with a start, with full curves that filled her dress perfectly, the sheer panels at the side a window to the soft curve of her hip, the rise of her stomach.

"It's rude to stare."

Elora blinked and brought her eyes up to meet the Queen's. The crown atop her head was golden and fashioned to look like twigs and flowers, inset diamonds near blinding when they caught the light. Elora's palms itched to hold it.

"I'm sorry," Elora stuttered in response, awe coating her words. She nudged Tarhael and he released her, lowering her feet to the floor but keeping an arm around her waist to steady her. She leaned into him gratefully, still exhausted.

"While I appreciate the new greenery you've taken upon yourself to add to my castle," Queen Briella smirked, "I would have preferred a more formal introduction. As it is, I will settle for a good explanation." She sat back on her throne, a relaxed smile on her face.

293

Elora blinked at her dumbly.

"You're not going to..." she trailed off, unsure of what to say. "Throw us in a dungeon or something?" She was sure King Harkan would have had her beheaded by now if this had happened in an Autumn kingdom.

But Briella only laughed, eyes sparkling with amusement. "Should I?"

"No, Queen," Tarhael cut in abruptly, bowing his head. "We are grateful for your kindness."

"I see no point in punishing you quite yet," Briella continued. "After all, I am curious as to why the Prince was flying into my home as though he owned it."

Elora bit her lip, suddenly very conscious of the disheveled state of herself. She tried to smooth her hair out of her face, tucking it behind her ears. They were once again rounded. Plain.

"We need your assistance." Elora fought for her eloquence, but the persistent headache behind her eyes refused to let her access half of her damn brain.

"So do a lot of fae."

Elora nodded. "I know, I'm sorry. It's...I'm..."

Before Elora could finish that statement, the doors behind them blew open and Aerin rushed in, shoulder bandaged and color drained from his skin. Elora nearly hit the floor with relief. He ran to her and Tarhael, yanking Elora from his friend's side to tuck her against his chest. She was sure the movement had to have hurt him, but he didn't seem to care. She wrapped her arms around his waist and breathed in the comforting scent of him, allowing him to calm her frayed nerves.

"Never do that again," she reprimanded him as she pulled away, scowling up at him. He smirked and shook his head, taking her hand in his and turning to face the Queen.

"Queen," he said, bowing his head like Tarhael had done.

ELORA

"Prince."

An uncomfortable tension coiled between the two royals and Elora panicked. The last thing any of them needed was more animosity right now.

"Aerin." He turned to her, brows furrowed, dark hair wild around his shoulders. Blood had dried into the front of his shirt, the bandage holding the wound closed already crimson with fresh stuff. Her heart damn near stopped at the sight of him. "Take off the cloaking runecast."

For a second, Elora thought he would object, but he only sighed heavily. He looked as tired as she felt.

The Queen eyed them from her throne, the guards on either side of her and at the door alert and ready. Tarhael reached over and put his hand on Elora's shoulder, squeezing once in silent support.

Aerin gritted his teeth and dropped the runecast cloaking Elora's scent. It was trickier than a glamour, more permanent, and the wards hadn't stripped it like they had their disguises.

Briella's eyes went wide.

"You."

Elora couldn't tell the difference. She smelled the same as she had before as far as she was concerned. But, clearly, the fae thought differently. She had no idea what to say.

"My name is Elora," she began, begging her voice not to waver as she looked at the Queen, atop the throne that called to her very blood despite how much she'd been trying to drown it out. The whole room felt like something out of her dreams. "And my parents were murdered twenty two years ago by the King and Queen of Autumn. I was supposed to be dead too. Except, well…" She gestured vaguely to herself.

"How is this possible?" The Queen's voice was shallow, her shoulders tense.

GIRL OF BONE AND IVY

"I grew up in the human world," Elora continued, gathering strength. "With human parents who adopted me as a newborn. I had no knowledge this world even existed until I got a damn paper cut -"

"Elora," Briella said slowly, tasting her name as though trying a new wine. "Your parents were my predecessors. They'd have liked that name." Tears shone in the Queen's eyes and Elora's heart stumbled. "They were wise and kind and dreamed of a better world. They did everything they could to protect you."

Elora's throat tightened with grief for the parents she'd never met. Was it even possible to grieve something you'd never had? She didn't know, only that there was no other explanation for the tender ache in her chest.

"I am glad it was not in vain." Briella's voice was soft and warm.

Elora didn't know what to say to that.

After a beat of soft silence, Briella continued. "Regardless of the questionable company you keep, this is your home. Your birthright. You will always be welcome here."

Elora wasn't fast enough to stop the tear that streaked down her cheek. Her parents had lived here, loved here, dreamed of a future here. Her bottom lip trembled.

"Why were you invading my home, Prince?" She turned to Aerin, pressing her full lips into a harsh line.

Aerin shifted uncomfortably. "To find records of the Lady of the Lake."

The Queen's brows furrowed, her voice lowering as she spoke. "Whyever would you need that?"

"So that Elora can receive her carvings."

Slowy, Briella sighed, full cheeks puffing out with the weight of it, as though she was resigning herself to some sort of decision.

"Do you wish to receive these carvings, Elora of Anixi?"

Elora shivered at the title, an unexpected warmth rushing through her veins. She nodded.

"So it shall be."

Aerin and Tarhael gaped at the Queen.

"Wait," Elora said, confusion swirling her thoughts. "You don't… resent me?"

Briella's face softened. "For what?"

"The crowds of fae looking for refuge for one," Elora began. "The Unseelie Court rallying their forces because of some sort of prophecy I didn't even know I was involved in." She swallowed thickly then added, "for surviving."

"I could never resent you for living," Briella responded, kindness coating her words. "King Harkan and Queen Valdaea would have attempted an invasion eventually anyway. They've been looking for an excuse for war for years. They have never truly been capable of peace." She shrugged, the capped sleeves of her gown bobbing with the movement. "Your presence simply accelerated the timeline a little. Besides, there are several other unfulfilled prophecies floating around out there and they never, *never*, mean what we think they do. Those who claim to be able to interpret them are simply filled with so much arrogance their brain has rotted."

Despite herself, a vision of King Harkan and Elladan flashed in Elora's head. She snorted.

"You do not deserve to be condemned for something you haven't done," Briella continued. "Your actions speak for your character enough. I have never witnessed raw magic so potent - to grow a tree that big that fast to save someone you care for?" She smiled. "I would be a monster to hate you for protecting those you love."

Aerin tensed. Elora chose to ignore her choice of words, and nodded her gratitude.

"Thank you."

"I assume you hold no allegiance to the Unseelie Courts."

"Uh..." Elora fought the urge to laugh, but Tarhael was not as lucky. Aerin bit his lip to stop smiling. "Certainly not. These two, and the pixies outside, were the only good things to come of my time in Autumn. I would die before I gave Harkan my loyalty."

Queen Briella nodded. "So, Prophecy," she grinned, addressing Elora by her reputation. "I suppose you're joining the fight."

Elora stood up straighter, Briella's cool confidence relaxing her.

"Yes," she said. "I suppose we are."

47

Elora

"Can we talk further? In private?" the Queen asked Elora, narrowing her eyes slightly at Aerin.

"Oh…" Elora's gaze darted between the men flanking her and Briella. She swallowed thickly, straightening her spine. "Of course."

She shook her head when Tarhael moved to accompany her and followed Briella out of the large room, down the hallway, away from listening ears or prying eyes. She nearly tripped a dozen times as they walked, her head craned back to marvel at the glass ceiling of the corridor, perfectly clear to provide a view of the brilliant blue sky above. Curtains of ivy draped over the walls, a dizzying array of flowers nestled between them. Birds of all shapes and colors flitted between the open windows and perched on the vines. Small trees were rooted at the base of the walls and castle, providing stability and a platform for the intertwining vines and branches.

"Do you like it?" Briella had paused, turning to look at Elora with a knowing smile on her face.

"Yes," Elora breathed. "It's beautiful."

"Each wing of Castle Anixi has different types of forestry, natural decorations and accents. It would be my pleasure to show you it all properly some time."

"That sounds amazing, Queen Briella."

"Call me Briella in private. You are royalty too, after all." Briella laughed as Elora gaped, a light and airy sound as if Spring permeated even her laughter. "I brought you here in the hopes of hearing your full story, without the influence of the others to taint it. How did you get here?"

So Elora told her story. They sat together on a plush green sofa, the sun smiling down on them as Elora told Briella everything. She had nothing to hide, and it wasn't as though, if Elora refused, Briella couldn't source the information herself. The Queen listened, head tilted slightly to the side as though she was rifling through it all in her mind. She made Elora pause and repeat sections, particularly asking for details on how Aerin had managed to open the Gate that took her back home.

When Elora finally finished her tale, they sat in a heavy silence for minutes, Briella absentmindedly rubbing at the nape of her neck with her right hand. "You said that these creatures appeared at your place in New York during the middle of the night, yes?"

"They crashed right through the walls and windows."

"Did you see any fae among them?"

Elora frowned. "I don't think so. Why?"

"It seems our enemies are far more powerful than I thought. And have access to powers I didn't know they had."

Elora's stomach sank at the news, though the Queen appeared to take it in her stride, no outward sign of distress showing on her face.

"When Aerin spoke of research on the Dohari Gates, did he mention any other people? Any associates?"

"No," Elora answered honestly, confusion tainting her tone. "Oh, wait. Aerin was working alone but he did say that he discovered that his father, Elladan, and a few people in the inner royal council had been using the portals, but he hadn't been able to figure out how they were doing it."

Multiple emotions from surprise to rage flitted across Briella's face before she recomposed her mask of queenly calm. "I see. Thank you for being so open with me." Briella sighed, but the ever present soft smile on her lips stayed in place, no longer faltering. "When Aerin dropped the runecast masking your scent, I didn't believe it at first, assuming trickery. But your scent is unique, undeniably *other*."

Elora was used to comments about her apparent scent by now, but still found herself fighting a laugh. "Why did you believe us so readily? What if we were faking it?" She probably shouldn't have asked but she couldn't deny that she was curious as to why the Queen had taken so little security measures against her.

"Queen Endra wrote a runecast long ago that would alert her when a human stepped into Anixi. It was her way of knowing when her lover, your father, Junhan, was here. She must have given him a way to access Dohari Gates without her runecasting, allowing him to come and go as he pleased, though I've never been able to figure out how. Years ago, when I took over, I found the particular runecast still active and never bothered to remove it. When you stepped inside Anixi's borders, you can only imagine my surprise at seeing the runecast activate and alert me. I didn't believe it until you came barreling towards the castle on a giant moving tree." Briella sat back in her chair with an amused grin.

"Sometimes, it all still feels like a fever dream," Elora admitted. "But it's only going to get worse from here on out, isn't it? Though I suppose it can't get worse than being drugged by a Prince."

Briella's smile vanished, sympathy appearing in its place. There was a pause before she said, "After Queen Endra died, my sister Kandrix was to be Queen. But she drank poisoned wine and was killed. I still haven't found her murderer to this day."

Elora stared at her, at the guilt and grief shining in her dark eyes, and opened her mouth to offer her condolences. A knock at the door interrupted their conversation, the sound firm but insistent.

"Come in," Briella called, her calm smile falling back into place.

A cadre of heavily armored fae marched in, armor glinting in the sunlight.

"My queen," the fae at the front greeted, dipping her head.

"Commander Loranelle. Did you find out what happened in the western outskirts?"

Elora shifted in her seat, uncomfortable and slightly intimidated.

Briella's generals and officers turned to face Elora properly for the first time. Loranell's eyes widened at Elora's human features and her nose twitched as she registered Elora's scent for the first time.

"Well?" Briella cut in, forestalling any questions or reactions.

"Yes, my Queen," Loranelle coughed and turned back to face Briella, regaining her composure. "The western outpost is completely overrun and we were sighted. Autumn sent out raiding parties to tail us nearly the whole trip back here. They've repurposed the forts, shoring up defenses inwardly and setting traps. My conclusion is that they are preparing for an extended campaign."

Briella swore, letting out a litany of new curses that Elora made sure to add to her vocabulary. "Was there no sign of Dathanielle or Voramier?"

"No. None at all. Their entire force was wiped out. Our scouts have also reported that Autumn is a weeks march away at best."

"They will be here sooner, I can promise that." Briella's eyes turned feral, a grim determination hardening her features. "Start the evacuations and call back every single soldier you can reach. Tell them to congregate here, at the capital. We fight."

48

Elora

Like Aerin had insinuated, the directions to the Lady of the Lake were, quite literally, under lock and key.

Briella led them through corridors of the same shining marble and gold accents, constantly interspersed with ivy, vines and blooms in every color under the sun. Elora couldn't stop staring at everything - reaching out to run her hand over every leaf wondering if, twenty years ago, her birth mother had done the same. Her mood was still tense from Commander Loranelle's revelations, and as they wound down underneath the castle, Elora lost count of how many different sets of stairs they had taken, distracted by the stone in her gut, weighted by fear and apprehension.

They passed dozens of strong wooden doors before they came to the one Briella indicated. The slight scent of mildew and moss hung in the air, giving the sense that the room had not been disturbed in quite some time. A gold symbol in the shape of what Elora could only describe as a woman made of water adorned the front of the wood. She reached out to touch it, running her fingers over the shining hair and jumped straight back into Tarhael when the thing started glowing. He caught her with an *oof* and helped her right herself without ever taking his eyes off the door.

"What-" Elora began, alternating looking between her hands and the door. Briella stood beside her, smiling a little sadly.

"Only Spring royalty can open Nimue's door," she said softly, reaching out to touch Elora's shoulder with warm fingers. "If there was any doubt before, there is none now. She enchanted her symbol centuries ago, so that only those who belonged to Spring and meant no harm could enter and learn her location."

Elora blinked, a lump in her throat. The door swung open soundlessly, a rush of cool air blowing out.

"If you two are going to enter, I need to know you're true," Briella challenged Tarhael and Aerin. The former rolled his eyes, the latter simply nodded, staring at Elora with something suspiciously like hunger in his eyes.

"What, do you want a damn blood oath or some archaic shit?" Tarhael half joked, one eyebrow raised.

Briella considered him with pursed lips. "I was going to suggest something less intrusive, but now that you mention it…" She produced a glittering dagger from nowhere, the hilt iridescent silver, the point deadly. A green gem was set in the hilt, glowing softly.

"Arms." She held out her hand expectantly, and Aerin and Tarhael begrudgingly offered their forearms. Briella grinned. "Do you swear on your life you will not talk of the secrets you are about to learn to anybody outside the four of us present here?"

Aerin and Tarhael responded at the same time, "I swear."

Quickly, Briella pressed the blade down onto each of their arms, letting a few deep red drops fall. She caught them in her palm and clenched her fist. The dagger disappeared into the folds of her skirt and Aerin pressed a hand over the shallow cut. When he removed it, there was no sign there had ever been a wound there at all. Tarhael followed suit, grumbling while he did so.

ELORA

Elora watched in awe and horror as Briella opened her palm. Where there should have been blood, instead there was a tiny ruby.

"Good." She tucked it into the same pocket as the dagger. "Now if you lied, I can invoke a blood curse." She winked and Elora gaped.

"A *what?*"

Aerin rolled his eyes. "Archaic."

"Resourceful," Briella countered.

"What the hell just happened?"

"She can use our blood to cast an old rune," Tarhael explained as they entered the dimly lit room, the door closing behind them as silently as it had opened. "That will probably maim us. I knew a guy once who castrated the man sleeping with his wife."

Elora was speechless.

"It's old magic," Aerin continued. "Barely anyone uses it now. There's better ways of revenge."

Briella only smiled and shrugged. "But this is much more entertaining, no?"

Elora shivered and turned away, staring at the room around them. It was dark, lit only by suspended balls of light that cast a faint green glow across the stone walls. Where the castle had been bright and colorful, this room was calm and quiet. She swore she could hear the rushing of water, though she couldn't find the source.

"I will give you the same instructions everyone else is given," Briella said quietly, pressing a hand to the stone wall as though greeting an old friend. She rattled off a series of directions that Elora attempted to commit to memory. Aerin inclined his head, listening intently. "From here," she gestured to the room around them, "you will be transported outside of the castle, to the furthest region of Anixi. If you want to be fast, Aerin will need to fly you both the rest of the way." Elora nodded. "I hope you know how important it is that you complete this, Elora."

305

Elora breathed deeply, fighting the urge to shake with anticipation and nerves.

"I want to do this," she said. "I want to help."

Briella reached out and cupped Elora's cheek in her palm. "The Unseelie Courts are ruthless. Brutal. They take no prisoners and leave no survivors. While we are strong, they may well overpower us. But you..." she trailed off, looking wistful. "You, Elora, could change that. Become something they fear, not because of some stupid prophecy, but because of your power."

Elora was wide eyed and scattered. Did she want that? Did she have a choice?

"I'll try," was all she could promise.

"I know you will, daughter of Spring." She released Elora and straightened her skirts, sliding back into the regal facade like a second skin. "Tarhael, you will remain here and help rally our forces and protect those searching for safety. The pixies," she winked at Elora and Aerin, "can tell us the information they gathered in their travels."

Elora didn't ask how she knew that. The damn plants probably told her.

"Ready?" Briella opened her arms wide and urged them back against the farthest wall.

Elora sucked in a harsh breath. Aerin grabbed her hand and squeezed.

"Yes."

Briella placed her hand on Elora's shoulder, her other on Aerin's and *pushed*.

And then they were falling.

49

Elora

The colors were of Spring this time, bright pinks, the pale gold of newborn sunshine, a hundred shades of green: the dark, earthy undertones of forestry, the sun dappled green of tree top canopies, the bright vivid shade of new leaves.

It was over as abruptly as it started, causing her to lose balance and fall over, soft grass breaking her fall. She fought the urge to laugh as she spied Aerin in the same predicament, barely managing to steady himself before he ended up on his ass.

"That was different." Her voice was slightly breathy, her heart still pounding hard against her ribs.

"That's an understatement," Aerin huffed, holding his injured shoulder and grimacing. She looked away quickly.

"So this is the edge of Anixi." Elora spun in a slow circle, inhaling the rose scented air deeply. It was as beautiful as the rest of the kingdom, but quieter. Untouched. Still slightly wild. Something simmered in her blood at the sight of it, a longing she didn't fully understand.

"It is, as far as the maps go." Aerin watched Elora closely. "Best way to keep a secret is to not document it at all."

"Is it *that* important to keep the Runecarvers hidden?"

"Of course. They are the only path to a royal fae attaining their full potential and they play a big factor in helping to balance power among the four Seasons and between the Seelie and Unseelie Courts. They're the daughters of the Goddess Who Sleeps."

"Áine?"

Aerin nodded.

Questions jostled for attention in her head, but she shoved them back. There was no time for a history lesson, not now. Elora strode to a babbling stream, the water clear and clean. She stooped, cupping it into her palms and drinking. God, even the water tasted better in Spring. The liquid washed down her throat in a torrent and Elora felt like she had just downed an energy drink, the way she was starting to buzz. Aerin noticed the shift and gave her a knowing smile.

"Seems like your body is finally starting to react the way it should. If my experience was anything like yours is about to be, you're going to need to keep your energy up. How are you feeling?"

Elora blinked at him, the question surprising her. "I'm fine. Just a tad nervous."

A lie. Total lie, if she was being honest. But *freaking the fuck out and overloaded with information* didn't feel like an appropriate thing to say when she was meant to be saving a whole Season. How the hell had it come to this?

Aerin's hands flexed at his side like he was tempted to reach for her. "You're going to be just fine. You're one of the most badass people I know."

"Where did you learn that phrase?" Elora laughed, chest a little lighter. "Let's get a move on, I have tattoos to get."

"Carvings, Elora. Carvings," Aerin corrected her with mock severity.

Then she was in his arms again, tucked close to his chest as the soft blue glow embraced them. Aerin winced as he rolled his, grunting slightly. Elora inspected his shoulder as rested against his chest, the blood from earlier now dark and dry. The bandages had unraveled slightly and she peeled them back to see the wound.

There was none.

Just a tender bruise, skin stained red, and a raw patch of new skin slightly pinker than the rest.

"You're healed." She had to shout over the wind rush, tipping her head back to watch his face.

"They're Seelie fae, love," Aerin chuckled a little and smirked. "They weren't going to leave a friend of Spring royalty maimed."

Elora shook her head. "But in Autumn-"

"They wouldn't have bothered with a healer in Autumn," Aerin's smirk faded as he spoke of his home, eyes losing their amused spark. Elora regretted bringing it up at all. "They'd have left me to dig the arrow out myself as punishment for getting hit at all." He shrugged, but it was awkward and lopsided.

Elora snapped her mouth shut for the rest of the journey. Aerin flew fast and by the time the first leg of the trip was done, he was coated in a sheen of sweat. The sun hung low in the late afternoon sky, casting a heavy glow tinged with red and pink to the ground. He landed gently on the grass and Elora turned to see him wipe some of the sweat off his forehead with the back of his hand. As much as she wanted to savor how he felt underneath her fingers, she knew now was not the time. She extracted herself from his grip fully and stepped back to examine their surroundings.

"So this is Deuchan Firin huh?"

"I guess so. In English, it roughly translates to *The Forest of Truth and Trial.*"

"Kind of corny, don't you think?"

"Careful. Don't want Nimue overhearing us," Aerin replied, stretching his sore shoulder. "Alright, Briella said to just follow the forest path until we reach the bridge. So to the bridge we go."

They walked in a companionable silence, Elora trying and failing not to think about how her fingers occasionally brushed Aerin's, the cool dusk breeze leaving their cheeks tingling as they made their way through the winding forest. Night was falling now and just as it seemed the path would never end, a bridge appeared at the edge of Elora's sight. It was unlike any she'd ever seen - arched, with wooden planks wrapped in vines and overgrown branches. A river raged beneath it, the water wild and winding further into the forest. Flowers of all shapes and colors dotted the railings, petals full and sturdy despite the breeze blowing off the water.

Elora stopped. And stared.

"The bridge looks...wild," she whispered.

"Agreed. A wild bridge." Aerin's tone was joking, but he too had lowered his voice to barely above a whisper.

"Aye, and a wild mountain troll at that too."

Elora jumped and covered her scream with her hand. She felt Aerin's hand tighten around her free one, nearly crushing it in his grip. They both stiffened and turned while the deep gravelly voice laughed, the sound echoing around the forest and sending flocks of birds into the air. Aerin was the first to speak.

"Briella didn't tell us that you would be here."

"She most likely already told you a little more than she should have," the creature rumbled.

"And how would you know?" Elora challenged, mustering up her courage and praying her voice wouldn't crack.

"Little birdies tell me what I need to know and I know you're on the brink of receiving a sound spanking from Autumn. Winter, too, but the bulk of the army coming for Spring is Autumn fae."

As if on cue, a sparrow flitted up to the troll's shoulder and chittered excitedly in its ear.

ELORA

Elora desperately tried to calm her nerves and take the massive creature in. They stood well over ten feet tall, their bald head level with high tree branches. Their skin was light gray but Elora swore that when it caught the moonlight, it looked pale blue. They were wearing nothing but a loincloth and their physique made Elora take a step back. Their muscles had muscles. Studs of rock stuck out of their back and shoulders and there was a battle ax the size of a small tree strapped to their back. Their deep purple gaze was on Elora and there was a certain honed keenness to the mountain troll's appearance that belied their jovial tone.

"Well?" they asked, looking down at Elora and Aerin expectantly.

"Who are you?" Elora wasn't quite sure of the formalities now, but surely a basic *get to know you* couldn't hurt.

"I'm Jojin, the resident mountain troll of Deuchan Firin. And who might you be?"

"I'm Elora of Anixi and this Prince Aerin of Dioltas." Elora's voice didn't crack or break, despite the strangeness of her title on her tongue, and she was grateful.

"The prophesied daughter of destruction and an enemy prince. A most unlikely pairing, but this will make for a fascinating story," Jojin mused. When neither Elora or Aerin said anything in return, instead standing gaping at them like they were trying to catch flies, they shrugged and continued. "As Queen Briella may have mentioned, there will be three stages of this journey for you, young Elora. But your leg of the journey ends here, Prince Aerin. There's actually lodging for you." Jojin gestured to their right to a small cabin nestled in between two pine trees.

Aerin looked like he was going to protest, but thought better and nodded, jaw tense. "Of course. This is Elora's journey, and Elora's alone." The words were forced, but it was apparently enough to appease Jojin.

311

GIRL OF BONE AND IVY

"Good. If you would be so kind, Prince Aerin, bid your farewells to Elora and proceed to the cabin. There will be vegetable stew and some freshly baked bread waiting inside." Having finished their speech, Jojin resumed listening to whatever it was the birds were chattering in their ear, giving Aerin and Elora the illusion of privacy.

"Elora I-"

Elora cut him off, surprising both of them by throwing her arms around his waist and holding tight. "Thank you. For everything."

"There's nothing to thank me for," Aerin replied, voice gruff. He stepped out of her embrace and studied her for a second. It was too dark for her to read the emotion in his eyes, and she suddenly resented the sun for setting. He pasted a smirk onto his face, but it didn't crinkle the edges of his eyes like usual.

He turned away, starting in the direction of the cabin, pausing only to call over his shoulder, "don't die!"

Elora took a deep breath and walked up to Jojin, who turned their attention from the little bird back to her. "Let's do this."

"As you wish. Follow me." Jojin turned around and headed to the bridge, the rushing of water growing louder as Elora followed. "Are you sure about this Elora?"

"Yes."

"I will ask you one more time. Are you sure?"

Elora forced a breath into her lungs. For better or for worse, she couldn't ever go back to normal. She had powers, and with power came responsibility. Her presence tilted the delicate balance of things here, and it was clear that no matter how far she tried to run, she couldn't escape the destruction that seemed to follow her. There was no running now. Innocent fae were under attack. Her home - as strange as it was to call it that - was under attack. She could act now and think later.

"Yes. I'm sure."

ELORA

"Good. Follow me."

The bridge was sturdier than Elora expected, though she had to watch her feet to make sure she didn't trip. She traced her hands along the greenery adorning it, and had paused to admire a soft pink rose when Jojin turned around and looked down on Elora once more, their immense build and height casting a shadow over her. They studied her in silence until Elora couldn't take the scrutiny anymore.

"How long have you been doing this?"

"Guarding the bridge to Deuchan Firin? Oh, I'd say the past seven hundred years or so." They grinned, registering the shock on Elora's face. "This is kind of a lifelong job," they chuckled. "I've seen a Spring royal or two in my day, and there have been a few strange cases, but a half fae who grew up in the human world? That's a new one. I know you have no idea what to expect, but just follow my lead and you'll be fine. Hopefully. Now close your eyes."

Hopefully? Elora cast that bit of slightly concerning information aside, and did as instructed, shutting her eyes.

"Good. Now breathe. In and out. Listen to the gentle roar of the water surging past. Smell the fresh forest air and let it fill you. Let everything else fall away. Open yourself up, Elora."

Elora tried to listen to the water and smell the air. She breathed as deeply in as she could and exhaled. The familiar feeling of falling overtook her, sending her pulse rocketing. She flailed her limbs and opened her eyes, panic pounding through her chest. All was black.

The ground was smooth beneath her, the twisted wood of the bridge nowhere to be found. Elora opened and closed her eyes to no avail. It was pitch black, so much so she couldn't see her own hand in front of her face.

"Jojin?" Her voice cracked, but she was beyond caring. *What the hell was going on?* "Jojin, where are you? What's going on?"

There was no answer.

313

50

Elora

Blinding light flared into existence and Elora stumbled back, covering her face with shaking hands. Her eyelids flashed red when she squeezed them shut, and she waited tentatively until the light had faded to pry her eyes back open. She squinted, blinking rapidly to try to adjust her vision and stumbled back a few steps when her surroundings finally came into view.

Hundreds of animated replicas of herself were suspended in the air around her, each enacting a specific memory from her childhood. There she was on her first day of kindergarten, falling and skinning her knee. She saw the first time she shared toys with her friends and the first time she volunteered at the homeless shelter. She saw seven year old Elora lying to her parents about breaking the sliding glass door, choosing instead to blame their dog. She saw herself grow from elementary to middle school. The sensitive girl, easy to pick on. The people pleaser. The girl who couldn't say *no*. High school Elora was quiet, withdrawn, walked with her head down. She had lost her confidence somewhere between the cracks of the pavement she walked every day to school. Those who knew her called her a lovely and kind friend - the girl who was always at the end of the phone, no matter how late. The girl who baked cookies for birthdays but always, inevitably, burned them. The girl who gave house plants as gifts because *everyone needs a little life in their room.* She recognized the selfless, caring parts of her, but she also saw the fear. She saw herself too proud to call for help at age five, stuck too high in the tree in their backyard, the resulting scrape on her leg that had left a faint white scar. She saw herself lie to the first girl she'd kissed insisting *it meant nothing, I only like boys,* when they both knew it was a lie. Saw herself cringing when her parents mispronounced an English word, or being embarrassed by their accent at parent's night. She saw herself screaming at her last boyfriend when, during their breakup, he'd had the audacity to suggest that she was *floundering, Elora. What now? I don't even know who you are. I don't even think you know who you are.*

Shame slid through her, icy and oily, as she watched the faces of those she hurt, chased quickly by a slick sort of guilt as she watched her younger face crumple into tears. She knew herself to be loving, gentle, and kind. She had fought tooth and nail to love herself, the soft folds of her stomach, the deep brown of her eyes, the heritage her parents passed along so proudly to her even when the world told her to be ashamed of it all. Wore a fake smile for so long that it eventually became real, her confidence unfurling like a rose. But she was also timid and quiet at times, unable to speak up when it mattered most, often saying the wrong things when she *did* try. She knew she shied away from forming relationships with challenging people, knew she valued time with herself in a way others weren't willing to accommodate.

The pictures dancing all around her shifted and now, Elora couldn't recognize the girl she was shown. It was her, but it... *wasn't.* There was a girl dressed in green and blue dancing in the wind, atop a bed of flowers, spinning raw nature from her fingertips like a weaver at the loom. Trees sprang up around her and fields of flowers spread far and wide in her wake. Her smile was wild and unrestrained as vines of ivy whipped around her. A crown woven from thorns and flower petals adorned her hair, and the very air around her shimmered with life. Joy, hope, life and desire sparked into existence, as if they were physical forces threatening to bowl Elora over.

This woman in front of her was a queen, a force to be reckoned with. There was a righteous fury burning in her eyes, and Elora knew in her heart of hearts that this was the figure she had dreamed of being her entire life. The images of this new Elora danced everywhere she looked, helping farmers grow their crops, healing the sick and dying, always surrounded by animals. The images grew bigger and bigger, swirled around her faster and faster until it was almost too much to take.

Wait, who is that?

Elora whipped her head to the left, where she thought she had seen a glimpse of someone who looked a lot like her, but taller, with shorter hair and ears that pointed at the tips. There it was again. She turned right this time, but it was gone.

The images dissolved as quickly as they'd appeared. Darkness descended once more.

Disorientated, Elora stumbled a few steps before righting herself. Her palms were sweaty, her legs shaky, her pulse far too high to be healthy, she was sure. She stood there for what felt like hours, until she had no choice but to sit down, slumped in the dark, head on her knees as she tucked them close to her chest. *That was my whole life,* Elora thought, swallowing the painful lump in her throat. *The good and the bad, the beautiful and the ugly.*

The vision of the powerful woman carving landscapes with her palms burst to the forefront of her mind. She wanted to reach out and grab it, to latch on to the potential she so desperately craved.

Could I ever be that girl? The girl Elora witnessed towards the end had been confident. Sure of herself. Perhaps most importantly of all, that girl had been willing to fight for what she believed in and what was right. That girl had been unafraid to lead, to do what was necessary.

"Can you do that Elora? Can you become that girl?"

The voice was lilting and female, all around her and nowhere at once. Elora scrambled to her feet in surprise.

"Who are you, Elora?"

"Who are *you*?" she countered, but the voice ignored the question.

"I will ask you only one more time. Who are you?"

Elora swallowed thickly before she answered. "My name is Elora Han. My birth mother was Endra, Queen of Spring before she was unjustly murdered." Elora realized she didn't even know her fae surname, but continued anyway. "I grew up in the human realm, and accidentally found myself in the Dioltas kingdom of Autumn, where I was betrayed by Prince Elladan. I was saved by his younger brother Aerin and we fled back to the mortal world. I'm here now, having escaped monsters who sought to kill or kidnap me, trying to do my part to save Spring from imminent invasion by Autumn forces." Elora realized she was sweating, panting from the passion in her voice.

"And who are you to think that you can be of any value?"

"I-" Elora faltered, unsure, wiping her palms on her trousers as she fought for words. "I've been told that I am the subject of a prophecy. That I will unite and then destroy the fae. It stands to reason that any being capable of such acts would hold power. Aerin and Queen Briella assure me I have power running through my veins, ready to be unleashed once I receive my carvings." She paused, steeling herself before continuing. "I never asked for these powers or for any of this to happen to me. But for once, I want to do something. So let me help. Let me help my friends drive our enemies back and prove that the prophecy doesn't apply to me. Please." Her voice came out as a whisper towards the end.

The unbodied voice considered her for a moment and Elora didn't know if she had answered correctly. If there even *was* a correct answer.

"Hello?" She ventured once more.

Nothing.

Silence.

Until Elora heard scratching. Then snarling. The hair on her arms and the nape of her neck prickled and a pair of eyes flashed in the darkness, bright yellow. More pairs of eyes blinked into view and Elora slowly turned in a circle, finding herself surrounded. The growling and snarling grew louder and Elora's terror rose with the noise. She dropped to her knees, to at least try carving runes with her fingers - though she didn't even know what to runecast - but the floor was smooth and solid, like cool marble. The sounds grew nearer still, the bodies of the beasts slowly becoming visible. In her mind's eye, she pictured the savage demons that had come for her in the dead of night, in her own bed, and she locked up, joints seizing. Her mouth opened but no sound came out. The monsters came closer still. Amidst the peak of her nightmare, Elora realized distantly that the monsters were not monstrous at all. Nor were they demons.

They were animals.

Almost sobbing with relief, Elora dropped to her knees and extended her hand flat towards the nearest creature, fingers shaking slightly as she offered a bridge between them.

Her hands found smooth fur, a warm body, strong muscles rippling under her grip. A wolf. The antlers of a deer pressed into her back, and several weasels scampered over her knees, squeaking slightly. Elora finally found her voice, laughter spilling from her lips.

Near hysterical with relief, she tipped her head back and laughed until tears spilled from her eyes and she found herself hugging a grizzly bear with one arm, a white tiger with the other. She played with foxes and chipmunks, stroked the velvet soft feathers of bird, squealed as she was suspended mid air by the strong trunk of an elephant. As the darkness lifted, more animals arrived. There was an endless amount of sniffing, prodding noses, claws and paws, until sunlight was shining through the last of the shadows and Elora could see the animals around her clearly.

One by one, the creatures nuzzled her and then left, turning and padding off into the distance until only one remained.

The wolf.

He was huge, his fur thick and silver, streaked with flecks of creamy white and deep black. Eyes the color of the sky on a cloudless day met Elora's steadily and the wolf perked his ears when she smiled a little at him. He took her in for a second more, before padding over to her, nuzzling her, affection apparent. His playful demeanor reminded her of Oberon, her old Australian shepherd. Her heart squeezed painfully at the memory as she sank her fingers into the wolf's coarse fur, scratching him between the ears.

"Such a pretty boy," she hummed at him, calm seeping into her bones. "What's your name?"

The wolf looked up at Elora, pausing his affection, his piercing blue eyes expectant.

"Jaspar? Mmm, no, that's too human. How about Relvar? No? Not into the fantasy vibes?" Elora stared at the magnificent wolf and tried out several more names, all of which the wolf promptly rejected. She rolled her eyes at him."You're not making this any easier you know," she scolded, but the tone of her voice was all love. She sighed at the creature sitting at her feet, cocking her head at him as her mind rummaged for a suitable name. She was half tempted to call him *Muffin*, just to see the objection in his eyes. Food names were always a hit with dogs - surely a wolf couldn't be *that* different.

She grinned as her mind cleared dust off a word. It was perfect.

"Boba," Elora announced, watching the animal for his reaction. He huffed, but curled up, apparently content with his new title. Boba - the treat her father always bought her after soccer practice as a child, even when she lost. A synonym for love in her dictionary. A sliver of home in this realm - a reminder of her family as she found another.

"A delightful name indeed." A voice that sounded like music and swelled like the ocean waves echoed from behind Elora.

The breath promptly left her lungs as she whirled and locked eyes with the most ethereal creature she'd ever seen.

51

Elora

Elora thought she ought to be used to *ethereal* by now. The fae were plenty mysterious and beautiful, with their pointed ears and abounding athleticism and magic. But the woman in front of her was in a league of her own. Her eyes were big and dark, like the deepest blue of the ocean Elora had always been too scared to dive into and her hair was long and straight, a wet, glossy black. She had pale blue, near iridescent, skin and wore a sheer blue gown that floated behind her, shimmering like light reflecting on water.

"Nice to meet you, Elora. I'm Nimue."

"Uhh…hi." Elora was too busy staring, open mouthed, to form a coherent sentence in response.

"Is that all? I imagine you have a million questions." Nimue's voice was light and amused, a smile curling the corners of her full lips.

"I do." A strange sort of calm washed over her. That worried her more than if she'd been freaking out. Why was she so calm? Surely she should be panicking right now - with a goddamn *wolf* at her feet and a living legend, apparent *daughter of a goddess,* in front of her. And yet, all she felt was peace.

"Walk with me, Elora." Nimue turned around and walked - no, floated - away. Elora could think of nothing else to do but obey, hurriedly following her over the soft grass. Boba huffed as he stood and trotted behind her.

Nimue looked over her shoulder and smiled as she snapped her fingers. Suddenly, Elora found herself in a tree house, smooth wood beneath her feet instead of silky grass. She stumbled over her own feet as she took in her new surroundings, heart pounding.

"Welcome." Nimue extended her arms in a sweeping motion. "Come, I'll show you the view." Nimue floated up a ladder to the upper level of the tree house.

Gaping, Elora followed suit, her breath catching in her throat as she scrambled to the top.

Nimue lived on an island. The huge tree the house was built in sat in the center, surrounded by a jungle - thick vines, lush vegetation and so many plants, it would take Elora years to identify them all. The sea sparkled before her, a brilliant clear blue, beyond the white sand beaches and palm trees. Elora turned in a circle, taking in the lush green mountain range, the peaks secluded in the clouds. The echoing squawks of parrots and toucans colored the warm air, followed by the screeching calls of monkeys as they swung from the branches beneath where they stood. The house itself was more like a wooden mansion nestled in the thick branches, built from smooth, light wood. The scent of fresh rain and perfumed flowers coated the air as she inhaled deeply, her skin buzzing with awareness of the boundless *life* around her.

"Do you like it?"

"It's...it's what I imagine paradise to be," Elora breathed, voice ragged. "It's perfect."

"To you, I suppose it is," Nimue answered, a smile tugging at the corners of her lips. "Any other fae from a different season would disagree most strongly with you. But it's perfect for me, too. I built it."

"Built?"

"Shaped, if you want to be precise. My domain shifts and changes according to my will and desire, so the geography changes nearly everyday. Deuchan Firin is my home, and this island on the lake is the center of it all."

"Wow." Elora wasn't sure what else to say, mind working overtime to take it all in. She could see Nimue up close now, could examine the angular lines of her face, the leaves etched into the skin on her forehead like a crown, what looked like a vine trailing down the side of her face and neck, disappearing into the folds of her gown. The markings glowed a soft green, staining the air around Nimue with an otherworldly haze. Nimue caught her looking, raising a deep blue brow.

"Yes, Elora?"

"Who exactly are you?"

"I'm Nimue," she answered. As if that explained everything.

"Aerin said you have three sisters. Are you fae?"

"I do have three sisters. They are the Runecarvers for the rest of the seasons. But we are not fae, child. We are something far older. An ancestor to the fae you could say. There are no others of my race, save for my sisters. We have been here long before the humans and the fae, and we will be here long after."

"Um, okay." Elora didn't press the issue any further, slightly unsettled by the description. She should demand they get a move on, to go through whatever tests Nimue had planned so she could be awarded her carvings and return to Briella to help.

But Nimue simply said, "are you hungry?"

"Yes, " Elora found herself saying. Given the chance to think about it, Elora realized she was ravenous.

"Go wash up first. I'll have dinner ready by the time you're done. Go back down the ladder and keep going down until you reach the first floor. You'll find Boba waiting for you, and he'll show you to your chambers." With that, Nimue disappeared and left Elora still looking around in awe at the island.

Nimue had said they were surrounded by a lake but it certainly looked like the ocean to her, with no discernible land mass in sight beyond the waters. Shaking her head incredulously, Elora started the descent back down the tree house. Or tree castle. Whatever it was. She marveled at it all - the paintings and tapestries depicting what she assumed were the forests and jungles of Fior Domhan, the statues and sculptures depicting every animal imaginable adorned the home, some of creatures she had only ever seen illustrated in fantasy story books. Natural light filtered through the thousands of tiny holes in the roof made of tightly woven vines and excitement colored the peace flooding Elora's veins. It was a strange feeling. Her mind was experiencing sensory overload and great wonder while her body hummed to the tune of this island, limbs relaxing, her heartbeat slowing.

Boba waited patiently by the final set of ladder rungs, and she jumped the last few steps. Boba pounced, tackling her and knocking her to the ground, his huge form looming over her. Laughing, she nuzzled him while he licked her face, joy filling the air around them. She shoved him off and stood, Boba rubbing his head against her stomach, urging her to follow him down the closest hallway. Occasionally, the wolf paused, looking at her expectantly as though trying to tell her something, but Elora had no idea what. The huge, carved door that they stopped before broke her out of her musings and she saw Boba looking at her with that same expectant face. She ruffled the fur on his head, turning the polished wooden handle with her other hand.

ELORA

The room was simple. There was a bed grown from more of the same vines and ivy that decorated the house and a small desk nestled in the corner. Entering the room revealed a small closet next to the bed where there hung three identical outfits. Each outfit was the same green hue of the tree castle and woven from an unidentifiable fabric that felt silky but offered surprising stretch and resistance. Elora wasn't sure why she would need a room to herself. Perhaps to sleep after receiving her tattoos? The thought of staying longer had longing sparking through her blood, followed closely by the familiar cold wash of guilt. There was no time to play house. She had to get back, fast. She washed up quickly in the little sink under the window.

"C'mon Boba, let's go find Nimue," she said absently to the wolf, closing the door as she exited the room and setting off in search of the Runecarver.

Elora didn't need to go far. She reached the ground level of the tree, stepping out into the jungle, the thick, mossy floor soft beneath her feet. The gaps between the trees and vegetation offered a peek at the beach beyond, where she could just make out the pale figure sitting serenely on the sand.

Elora joined her, the warm sand sifting through her toes as she removed her shoes from her aching feet. The sun had begun to set, sparking panic in her gut.

"How much time has passed?" she asked desperately, heart in her throat.

Nimue looked down at her, eyes kind. "Time is different here, daughter. Do not fret." She gestured to the array of food in front of them, served on wide, flat leaves. Boba was already gnawing on a huge hunk of meat, ignoring Elora's confusion.

"Some of my sisters acquired a taste for meat, but I've never could bring myself to," Nimue said, watching the wolf.

Their meal was an assortment of salads, soups, breads and cheeses, and Elora tucked in hungrily. She listened while Nimue told her about Duechan Firin and how the island changed depending on her moods after she grew restless of the original design.

Elora worked up the courage to ask about Spring magic, out of both curiosity of her own potential and a desperate need to feel connected to this land and the power it possessed.

"There are many ways Spring magic can present, but the most common are: the ability to summon and talk to animals, growing and nurturing plants and living things with ease, building and crafting anything your mind can conjure from the earth, animating such things, being able to sense any living thing through the ground, healing, the ability to teleport around anywhere there is nature, provided you've seen it before. Of course, magic isn't as cut and dry at that, and occasionally, I am surprised." Nimue looked delighted at the possibility of something unknown. Taking in Elora's expression she added, "I know that's a lot, but you'll have four abilities you'll be able to use after your carvings. No fae can harness them all, lest they grow greedy. Greed breeds violence."

Something suspiciously like pain flashed in Nimue's large eyes, but it was gone before Elora could think to ask about it. Then again, asking anything personal of a damn near goddess seemed ill advised, so maybe it was for the best. Nimue was beautiful and kind, yes, but also intimidating and poised. Elora had to fight not to cower in her presence.

Elora swallowed her mouthful and tried to keep up with everything Nimue was explaining. "Aerin told me there was a way to reveal what type of runecasting I'd be able to do."

"Has he told you about the general runecasts you are capable of performing?"

"Yes, boosting my physical abilities, glamour, all of that. But what happens if I try to runecast something from a different Season?"

"Try."

Elora set her plate and utensils down and began carving in the dirt. She wrote out the runes for 'bread', 'nearest', 'air' and 'me', adding all the proper linking verbs and conjugations. She waited, but nothing happened. She double checked her runes, triple checked them even, but nothing happened.

Nimue gave her a knowing smile before continuing.

"Every country, nation, culture has a language. Why not the earth? My sisters and I received magic from our mother and we in turn imparted these runes to our children - the fae. These runes are the language of the world, a so-called key to unlocking the fifth element, if you may. Spring's magic is derived from Earth and nature, Summer's is derived from fire, light, and physical strength, Autumn's magic is derived from air and mind, and Winter's magic is derived from water and death. But there is a fifth element. Some call the fifth element *God*, others call it magic. We call it Eolas, the 'creation language'. The fifth element simply *is*. It provides the underlying current of life to all things physical and spiritual, and these runes are the language to unlocking them in this realm. But not everyone can unlock all parts of the fifth element and that is why there are certain powers you can and cannot access."

"That's why we each have two runecasting abilities?"

"That, I suppose, is genetic. A fail safe to ensure no fae has too much power."

"What about the royals?"

"Most fae are born with two specific abilities they can wield, depending on what Season they are from. Royal fae however, have access to two additional sets of powers that they inherit in order to rule and keep peace within their kingdoms. These powers are expressed through carvings on your skin and while they can be shaped and called upon more frequently than traditional runecasting, they will exert a physical toll on your body as a price the way runecasting does not. Runecasting doesn't require anything from you, but you must write it out and activate the Eolas. Runecarving on the other hand, is something more innate, something more akin to a physical characteristic or a muscle you can train."

"Why only noble fae?"

"That's a very astute question, something I'd like to see you discuss with young Prince Aerin."

"It doesn't really seem right. Is it genetic?"

"To a certain extent, yes. There is a genetic component to who can inherit royal blood."

"Is that why the fae have still kept the monarchy? As a means of control and power?" Elora grew angrier as she spoke. "That's so incredibly backwards. Are all the royal fae complicit in only marrying other royals to keep power over everyone else?" Disdain and disgust slithered under her skin.

"It's a question that I think you should discuss with your friend Aerin. From what I know, he's very familiar with the topic." Nimue's voice was strict, but calm, reminding Elora of her place.

Elora blinked, fighting to calm herself. Nimue was right. Elora didn't understand the full gravitas of the situation and she was here to unlock her powers so that she could help people, not condemn them. She inhaled deeply.

"So, when do I get my carvings then?"

"Right now, if you wish."

"Oh." Elora hadn't expected it to be so quick but better now than later, she supposed. Especially when every second counted.

"Have you eaten enough?"

"Yes, thank you."

Nimue waved her hand and the picnic cleaned itself while she walked over to Boba and murmured something in his ear. Boba glanced at Elora several times before padding over and nuzzling her, eagerly licking her face.

"I love you too," Elora laughed as she returned the affection, stroking her hand down his back. Satisfied, Boba bounded away, tail wagging like a puppy.

"He likes you," Nimue said. "You know the last person to find a familiar was your mother, Endra."

"A...familiar?"

"A creature linked to your soul. A companion. Your birth mother was the last royal under me to find a familiar when she received her carvings. Her's was a white tiger, a marvelous creature. Finding a familiar is rare. You should consider yourself blessed to have found Boba. A creative name as well. I know it's a mortal drink, but I've never tried it."

Rare? Endra had a familiar? A tiger? Elora's head swam with the revelations, and she felt a strange sense of pride that she was following in her birth mother's footsteps. "I think Aerin also has one, a little bluebird. It's even tattooed on his shoulder."

"Ah, that's the equivalent of a beloved pet, not a familiar. A familiar can only be found in the Runecarving process. What your friend has done is a very convincing imitation. A tattoo, you say?"

"Yes, he has the bird tattooed onto his shoulder next to his runecarvings. Its name is Blueberry. He can summon the bird and talk to it."

"Can he speak to it telepathically?"

Elora hesitated. "No, I don't think so."

Nimue crossed her arms and pursed her lips. "He must have been paying close attention during the process. How insightful." She looked at Elora, an analytical expression written across her face. "Keep him close to you. He seems extremely resourceful and unusually talented. What Aerin did is an imitation of what happens here during the runecarving process. He doesn't have the power nor the ancient magic required to runecarve himself but I assume he tattooed a rune onto his shoulder to permanently speed up the summoning process for his pet bird. It's an extraordinary runecast, now that I've considered it, but it's essentially a shortcut. He most likely only has to renew the runecast every solstice, instead of casting it every single time. Remarkable really. I'm pleased that you'll be in good hands after you receive your carvings. Are you ready?"

Elora didn't particularly feel ready, but it was now or never. She cleared her throat, straightened out her shoulders and answered, "I'm ready."

"Then let us begin. Have you done your revealing runecast yet?"

"No, Aerin has only told me about it."

"Very well. Copy my runes very carefully." Nimue began tracing runes in the dirt with her finger and Elora followed suit, being extremely careful and meticulous as to not mess anything up.

A few moments later, Elora saw the runes for 'perception' and 'travel' floating in the air before her, glowing a brilliant green.

"There you go," Nimue said, sounding pleased. "The two abilities you will be able to runecast are teleportation and sensing things through the earth. For example, if you want to travel instantaneously, you can runecast from one body of water to another. You won't know which one you're transporting to, so unless you have a map, you'll find yourself in a completely random place unless you specify exactly where you intend to go. If you wanted to visit a kingdom neighboring Anixi and you had been there already, you could go to the royal gardens and teleport from an oak tree there to an oak tree from the neighboring kingdom. But you need to have been there in order to go specifically to the places you desire. Understand?"

Sort of. Elora nodded.

"The second ability you have is being able to sense all living things through the earth. You'll be able to extend your senses through the ground and separate the various vibrations and frequencies to search for any living thing nearby."

Elora soaked all the information in, processing. The fact that she was capable of everything Nimue had just described seemed so insane, her knees wobbled beneath her. "Will I be able to do all this in the human world as well?"

"Of course. The human and fae worlds are the same, just separated by magic. Are you ready to move on and see what your carvings will be?"

"I am."

"Good. Follow me." Nimue began walking towards the sandy shoreline, leaving no footprints in her wake. Elora followed dutifully.

"I was able to summon nature." It seemed important to mention when standing on the brink of something as life changing as this.

"Were you now? Tell me about it."

"I once grew flowers to drug a captor of mine and then to entrap him in a web of vines. I also summoned a tree to scale the walls of Anixi to save Aerin when he was shot. I …uh… glowed every time it happened." It sounded ridiculous now that she was saying it out loud.

Nimue considered Elora's words for a minute. Then two. Then three. Finally, she exhaled a long breath and looked directly at Elora.

"Your powers will often respond to your emotions, especially in times of great emotional distress, even when you haven't received the carvings yet. It's good you found me when you did. Your power needs guidance, direction. It needs control. Only you can master and give it those things, with the help of your carvings. Left unattended, your own magic would rip you apart." She said it so matter-of-factly, it took Elora a moment to process the words.

Elora shivered, body going tense as she tried not to think about blowing up into a million little pieces.

Nimue hadn't shifted her gaze from Elora, head tilted to one side as a curious gleam shone in her eyes. "If everything you've described is true…you may be the most powerful royal fae I have seen in centuries. Stronger than your mother even." Nimue paused, a soft smile tugging at the corner of her lips as she looked Elora up and down. "The prophecies will say what they say. The future will play out how it will. But you get to make your own choices, Elora. Your power is beyond anything the world has seen in at least a thousand years. Are you sure you want to unleash its full potential?"

Elora's heart thundered as she considered Nimue's question. They stood, barefoot in the sand, the wind threading their hair into the night sky. The stars twinkled above them, flecks of bright hope reminding Elora that every second mattered. Like it or not, she was stuck with this power. It was up to her to do good with it.

Fuck the prophecy, she *would* do good with it.

"We can only play the cards we're dealt to the best of our abilities," she replied with more calm than she felt. "I want to control this power. I'm ready."

"Very well. Turn around Elora. Undress and close your eyes."

Elora did as she was told, turning and undressing, the cool breeze caressing her bare skin. She inhaled and closed her eyes, unsure what to expect, body on high alert. Then she heard the singing.

A soft, beautiful melody echoed through the night, it's lilting tune reverberating through her soul. The music brought tears to Elora's eyes, and she felt the passion in her bones. The music grew louder, swelling in conjunction with the crashing waves on the shoreline. Nimue's entrancing voice was everywhere, enveloping Elora in its rhythm. The ancient melody continued in a language Elora didn't know and she began to feel drowsy. A strange heaviness settled in behind her eyelids, and Nimue's instruction to keep her eyes closed

ELORA

was not helping the urge to sleep in the slightest. Elora's breathing fell into rhythm with Nimue's song until a scream broke the trance followed by a flare of pain blooming across her back.

Elora toppled over. She knew she was still screaming, but she couldn't hear herself anymore. Her ears were ringing, drowning out everything else. She tried to open her eyes, but all she could see was bright, blinding white.

Her body went limp against the damp sand.

52

Elora

The pain was like nothing she had ever felt before. Searing agony wrapped around her, holding her in a tight grip, a torturous burning that throbbed in rhythm with her heartbeat. The pain mocked her, its ghastly smile reminding her that no matter how hard she struggled against it, she couldn't get free.

She didn't know what day it was or how long she'd been in bed. Ribbons of sunlight danced across the bandages on her stomach, the pain barely an echo of the agony it had been before. Clarity and cognition returned to Elora in one fell swoop, and she nearly fell out of bed, in an attempt to scramble to her feet. Fighting back the panic crawling up into her throat, she lurched towards the door.

"Elora. It's okay. You're safe."

A deep, gravelly voice bounced in her skull. Elora whirled around, but nobody was there. Except for Boba, who had been napping by the foot of her bed and had now lifted his head, ears perked up with that familiar expectant look on his face.

"Boba?"

He growled softly in understanding. *"It's me. Now that you have your carvings, we can speak."*

While the sounds made from his throat were growls and barks of various pitches, Elora could feel the strong bass of his voice in her head, clear as day.

"I can hear you!" Shock hit her hard and she rubbed her hand over her chest, though the ache was deeper.

"I can feel your emotions, too. We're soul linked." Boba tilted his head to one side, standing and stretching. *"Before you ask anything else, give Nimue a chance to explain. She's better at it than me."*

"Okay," Elora exhaled a long, slow breath to keep the impatience at bay. "Show me where she is."

Boba padded towards the door but stopped and looked at her for a perfunctory head rub. When she hesitated, he said, *"just because we can talk to each other now doesn't mean you should treat me any different."*

"The Big Bad Wolf, worried about missing out on head scratches," she teased, but ran her hand over his fur, finding comfort in the solid steadiness of his body next to hers. "Let's go. I need some answers."

"Elora."

Nimue was facing away from them, leaning on her balcony, watching the languid waves lap the shore.

"Nimue," Elora responded, voice cracking slightly. "What's going on? All I remember is you singing, then the pain, and then-"

"There isn't much to be said," Nimue interrupted calmly, watching Elora begin to spiral. "The ritual went perfectly. I successfully saw the runes that belonged to you and carved them onto your skin. That is all. If you haven't looked, I suggest you do so now." Nimue waved her hand and the loose tunic Elora had been wearing simply disappeared.

"Hey!" Elora protested, crossing her arms in front of her chest before realizing it was only her, Nimue and Boba in the vicinity. Shyly uncrossing her arms, Elora gazed into the mirror Nimue had propped beside her.

Intricate deep green vines intertwined on her arms, running all the way up to her shoulders. The tips of the leaves started at her wrists, before stretching up her biceps, trailing off as they curved around her shoulders. She turned slightly to inspect them, mouth agape. A highly realistic wolf's head was etched in gray onto her right shoulder blade, it's eyes a bright blue. Her gaze darted from her carving to Boba and back again, a disbelieving laugh bubbling in her throat. The likeness was uncanny.

"Are these...vines of ivy?" Elora asked, tracing the green details on her forearms.

"Indeed they are. Do you like them?"

Elora nodded, unable to stop looking at the art adorning her.

"If you look carefully, you'll find the rune for *life* embedded in the ivy leaves and the rune for *animal* embedded in the wolf's muzzle. Your ivy vines represent your power to call *life*. First, you will be able to summon all manners of plants and nature. In essence, you can summon living things. Eventually, your power will extend to restoring life or healing those around you. Mind you, you can't bring back the dead, or cure a disease or condition someone was born with, but you should be able to mend most other wounds. But learning to call and restore life in the manner of healing will take a lot of training. Your second rune is *animal*. This enables you to summon and talk to animals. Not just Boba. He is your familiar - soul bound to you - but you'll be able to summon other living creatures in the vicinity and talk to them as well. Any questions?"

Elora had about a thousand.

ELORA

"How do I train? And who will teach me?"

"I will."

Elora's mouth dropped open. She'd thought this would be simpler - a matter of receiving her carvings, opening up her power more, and then returning to Spring. But staying, training, with Nimue would take time. She didn't have *time.* So she shook her head, grabbing the tunic from the floor and dressing quickly. "I need to get back. Aerin, Briella, *Spring* needs my help. I can't just leave them to train-"

"In this, my dear child, you do not have a choice."

53

Elora

"Again."

Elora gritted her teeth and tried again. She braced herself, and plunged her open palm onto the soft soil, envisioning a forest of vines erupting forth. The ivy on her arm glowed green and a few dozen measly vines shot - well, okay feebly poked out - from the ground. A surge of energy left her body and she sat down hard, exhausted.

"Better. Go drink some water and try again."

It had been nearly two weeks since her training at Deuchan Firin began and Elora was growing more and more frustrated with her progress, or lack thereof.

"How much time has passed back home again?"

"Not even a few hours. Stop worrying, you have months of training time," Nimue laughed as she sipped her herbal tea. "Next time you try, put more intent into what you're imagining. The vines should be impatient to grow by the time your hand touches the ground."

Elora nodded her understanding as she gulped water from the big gourd nearby. An entire day on Nimue's island, Elora had learned, was the equivalent of only a few minutes outside. So while Elora spent days training, Aerin was probably sipping tea and relaxing in the cabin. Elora tossed Boba a new bone and went back to try again.

The next few weeks were filled with the same routine: waking up, practicing her runecarving abilities, eating, practicing her runecasting abilities, then ending the day with a short lesson in combat skills. The training was honing her mind, her skills and also her body. She was stronger, faster, more alert. Outwardly, she didn't look much different - she still had soft edges, curves that she had no intention of flattening, but she felt like a force to be reckoned with. At night, Elora studied the mountain of old books Nimue had provided and learned more about the history of fae, Spring and the intricacies of Eolas, and all about the natural flora and fauna found in Fíor Domhan, their properties and which could be used for healing or harming. Nimue was demanding, consistently pushing Elora to her limits and yet, Elora could think of no better teacher, even when she was cursing her and her mother into the damp sand.

She learned to summon animals of all kinds to her using different signals and how to communicate best with the various animal species. She learned how to sprout different plants and eventually even how to heal flesh wounds. She wasn't powerful or knowledgeable enough to heal internal organ wounds, but Nimue assured her that it would come with time and practice. Elora practiced teleporting all across Nimue's island and learned to listen and find any living creature in the vicinity, hand pressed to the ground to sense the vibrations through the earth. She practiced her general runecasting abilities, and Nimue made sure that there was no stone left unturned in her magical training.

They were nearing three months of training when she finally broached the topic of returning to the outside world.

"We've covered the basics of all your abilities and I've done my best to give a broad education of all the topics you're going to need to keep studying. I'll conduct a final assessment tomorrow and, should you pass, you're free to leave."

"How much time has passed back home?" It felt strange calling Fior Domhan home, but Elora supposed that her little apartment back in New York could never be home again. She wasn't sure whether the thought upset her or not. She never *belonged* there. Not like she did here. Here, she had a purpose, direction, goals. It was intoxicating. She was no longer wandering, feeling lost and inadequate. She was someone. Perhaps she always had been. Maybe Fior Domhan had just opened her eyes.

"Almost exactly a day. Time grows short for your allies back in Spring, but you've learned more than enough to be of use in a battle if it comes to it. Even though you've only just begun to breach the potential of your power, you should be able to continue your learning and training without me, especially with Aerin's help."

"Can one person really make that much of a difference? There will be armies fighting, and fae warriors who have much more experience than I do - in combat and with...Eolas," Elora caught herself before calling it *magic*.

"Do you want to know one of the reasons why the fae split the world in two and hid their portion of it all those centuries ago?"

"Aerin told me it was something along the lines of constant warring between the two groups and humans rapidly advancing in technology and conquest."

"Partly." Nimue floated a closer to Elora until they were mere inches apart, reaching her hand out to cup her cheek. "Children born of a fae parent and a human parent were some of the most powerful figures in history. Both in human and fae lore, almost all of the miraculous deeds you hear about were from offspring of both mortals and fae. You don't have the training and experience of the opponents you will face, that is true. But the offspring of both Nox and Áine are gifted with nearly limitless power and potential. You can change the course of any battle or war you fight in, Elora. Regardless of the prophecy, you can change the course of history itself."

Elora wasn't sure what to say, nor was she sure how to process what Nimue had just said, so she merely nodded and forced her confusion down. There would be time to rummage through her feelings later, to analyze herself through all the new lenses that kept being thrust into her hands. But not now. Now, all she could think was - "I'm going to miss you," she blurted, cheeks immediately flaming.

"I will too. Teaching you has been the most fun I've had in ages." Nimue blew her a little kiss before floating away to do whatever it was that ancient spirit goddess ladies did during their downtime.

"Do you feel ready to go back?"

Elora rolled the question across her tongue, debating how to answer. She decided to go with the truth.

"Honestly, I don't know. I am proud of all the progress I've made and everything I've learned, but I don't know if I'm ready. I don't know if I can do what is expected of me." *I don't know if I can face the war coming.*

"Will that stop you from trying?"

"No." Elora's answer came out a lot more confidently than she had intended, surprising her. "Innocent fae are in danger, largely because of my existence, and I know what I need to do. I know that this whole thing is supposed to be about me, but it's also so much bigger than me. This *power* it's…a double edged sword. Half the time, I love it, am grateful for it, consider it a gift. But the other half…it feels like a curse." Elora inhaled deeply, clenching her fists at her side, trying to force some calm into her bones. She unfurled her fists slowly, relaxing her shoulders. Petals, soft and new and pink, fell from her palms, landing on the sand at her feet. She stared at them. "I don't want to be a curse." She looked up at Nimue, eyes blurry but stance strong. "I'm not sure anything could stop me from trying."

"Well done, daughter." Nimue floated over to Elora and kissed her on the forehead, her lips careful and quiet. She smelled of hyacinths and fresh rain. Her presence left a pleasant aftertaste, a sort of earthy goodness that was impossible to forget. "You've passed the test."

"Huh?"

"I've observed your progress over these past few months. I already know the extent of your abilities and how much further you can go with that mighty potential of yours. I merely wanted to see if you had grown emotionally and spiritually along with your physical powers."

"Oh." This felt like goodbye. "Will I ever see you again?"

A hint of a smile graced Nimue's mouth. "Will you ever see me again in this context? As the Lady of the Lake? As the Runecarver? No, no you will not. But I don't think it is ever wise to say *never*."

"So is this goodbye then?"

"It is."

Boba bounded to Elora's side as if sensing the imminent farewells and nuzzled against Nimue. She reached down and rubbed his belly, murmuring in his ear. Boba perked up, at attention. He huffed his ascent to Nimue - something Elora still found fascinating - and padded over to Elora's side. She couldn't help the tears that sprang into her eyes, and tried to force them down unsuccessfully.

"Oh, don't cry," Nimue chided. "All I've done is make life difficult for you these past few months. You should be happy to see the back of me." She wrapped Elora in a tight hug and pressed her thumb onto Elora's forehead. "I'm so proud of you child."

Everything went black.

54

Aerin

Aerin paced until his feet ached. It had been nearly a full day since Elora had left with the troll, and he was in half a mind to throw open the cabin door and hunt them down, to demand they show him where they'd taken Elora. But he knew, deep in his heart, that such actions would only hurt her.

Receiving one's carvings was a journey you had to take alone. He wouldn't rob her of the experience, no matter how much he itched to hold her again, to reassure himself that she was okay. He wasn't quite sure when their tentative allyship had grown into something that resembled...well...*caring* like this.

He'd scared her, he knew, back in Anixi. He'd been rash, desperate, and though his shoulder had almost fully healed now, he could only hope the trust between them hadn't broken with his fall. He should've been more careful, taken more time to scout...Áine only knew what could've happened to them all if Briella had been less compassionate. It always shocked him, the Seelie kindness. Often, as a child, he'd squeezed his eyes shut in bed late at night and prayed to the Goddess Who Sleeps that he would wake up in a Seelie kingdom instead. In a house that felt like a home, with a father who didn't hurt him, a mother that still lived.

He shook his head, cursing himself for such morbid thoughts. He wasn't a child hiding under the covers anymore, but he did briefly consider invoking the goddess' name to ensure Elora's safe return. The runecarving process was brutal. It exposed the rawest parts of oneself, forced them to see the best and worst of their souls. It broke people apart and then put them back together. Mostly, for the best. Sometimes for the worst.

Elladan had been different before his carving.

He'd gone into Aureole's home as a boy, and returned a mock king. Aerin didn't know what he'd seen, but Elladan's eyes had darkened, become haunted. He'd been cruel ever since, cunning and manipulative in a way he wasn't in childhood. Aerin didn't doubt that it was his father's doing, but there was more to it. Of course, his brother had never allowed him to figure out *what*, exactly. No, whenever Aerin tried to ask, Elladan had lashed out, cutting him down both literally and emotionally.

So Aerin had stopped asking. Mourned the loss of his brother the way he'd mourned the loss of his mother. He was good at mourning.

When he'd met Tarhael during the guard trials, Aerin had refused to talk to him. He'd decided, weeks prior, that he wouldn't befriend any of the applicants. He didn't want to grieve again. He'd only been nine, Tarhael eleven, but both boys had long since ceased being children. Tarhael was big even then, towering over the other noble son's sent to compete for the honor of serving the prince. Aerin was drawn to him even then. Tarhael had always excluded a calm warmth that Aerin craved.

So, despite his vow to hate every one of the damn applicants, he'd found a piece of his soul in Tarhael. They'd been friends ever since. More than friends, once they reached adulthood. Though it had never been more than sex and companionship. Tarhael, Aerin had

344

discovered, didn't want nor need romantic attraction, preferring sexual chemistry and friendship. And Aerin had decided it was probably a bad idea to be romantically involved with anyone anyway, considering his tentative standing in the court. His father was forever attempting to find suitors for him and Elladan, even though both men rejected the attempts. Aerin hadn't even met his latest suitor. He didn't know why his father still bothered.

Elora needed to return soon, Aerin decided, or else he was going to go insane reliving the painful past while he stared out the window in search of her.

His heart tripped over itself as a shadow passed in front of the window. For a brief second, he thought it was her, and the rush of overwhelming relief and joy nearly knocked him off his feet. But it was only a forest creature, not fae at all.

If he'd been confused over his emotions before, he wasn't now. No, it was abundantly clear to him what his heart was telling him.

Really, he'd been stupid to deny it before.

They'd talk, he vowed, when she returned. He'd tell her. Just in case something happened in battle. She deserved to know.

And, maybe, secretly, he had begun to believe that he deserved to know, too.

55

Elora

Elora could feel everything.

The twitch of a mouse's tail in a patch of long grass, the fluttering of feathers before a bright blue bird took flight, the way the petals of the flowers swayed in the breeze. It was overwhelming, the sweet scent of nectar, the buzz of bees in their hive, the soft thud of the wolf's paws beside her.

And yet, she wasn't scared. Didn't panic. She'd never felt more grounded in her life. It was like her skin finally fit perfectly, the sense of self she'd always searched for wrapping around her like a warm coat.

She knew there was bloodshed in the future. Knew there were things she had to do with this newfound power. Knew, in a few days, her world would be once again tipped on its head.

But, right now, all she could think about was him.

She knew what she had to do. If she was being honest with herself, she'd known for a while. She just wasn't scared anymore.

The little cabin came into view, the soft glow of firelight separating it from the forest surrounding it. Elora rested her hand atop her companion's furry head and silently told him to guard the door as

346

she ascended the few steps and reached out to turn the handle.

She never made contact. The door swung open before her fingers even grazed the wood.

There, in front of her, was Aerin, his face lined with worry, frantically taking her in and checking her for any signs of damage with wide, bright green eyes.

Fuck, he was beautiful.

The whole world seemed to still when his eyes finally met hers. She expected to be nervous, to have to try to calm her galloping heart, but instead it just felt *right*. She felt like she was coming home.

"Elora-" he began, lips parted slightly in awe as he glanced between her and the giant wolf. "You..." He shook his head, a small smile curving his lips. "I'm not even surprised. If anyone was going to come out of the challenge looking like a myth with a damn familiar at their side, it would be you."

Her heart stuttered slightly, warmth flooding her.

Aerin stepped back to let them in, reaching out to run a hand over the wolf's coarse fur.

"So, what happened?" he asked, closing and locking the door behind them. Boba nuzzled Elora's legs.

Elora just smiled and shook her head.

"Oh," Aerin said, misunderstanding. "You don't have to tell me-"

"It's not that," Elora interrupted, unable to stop staring at him. "I'll tell you later."

"Oh, right, you must be tired-"

She shook her head again, stepping closer and placing a hand on his chest. She could feel his heart beneath her palm, the strong muscles beneath his shirt. She bunched the fabric in her fist and looked up at him.

"I don't want to talk," she continued, voice low. "And I don't want to sleep."

His eyes darkened as he looked down at her, but his hands remained by his side.

"Elora-"

"Aerin." She tilted her head back and brushed her lips against his, pressing herself against him. He sucked in a sharp breath and she felt him tense. She pressed a kiss to his jaw, then his neck, sure to take it slow, to give him the opportunity to push her away, to tell her she'd got it all wrong.

Instead, she found her back against the wall, Aerin's arms caging her in, his eyes locked on her with dark intent.

Heat bloomed low in her stomach and she bit her lip.

"Do you have any idea how long I've wanted you for, love?" he asked, and Elora shivered. "You need to make sure you want this. Because my self control is thin as fuck right now and I don't know if you understand what that means for you."

Elora tore her gaze away from his mouth to blink at him. She had no idea what he was talking about but God did she want to find out.

So instead of answering him, she pulled her shirt over her head and let it drop to the floor.

Aerin went still. He still had her trapped between him and the wall, the air between them thick and hot with tension. Elora thought she might go mad with it. Might go mad if he didn't kiss her, touch her.

Fuck his self control. She wanted to snap it between her teeth.

Finally, Aerin met her eyes again. His gaze was near predatory.

"Safe word."

She blinked. Bit her lip to stop her mouth falling open. She wanted to ask what he wanted to do to her that would require a safe word, but decided it really didn't matter. She'd let him do whatever the hell he wanted as long as it meant he'd touch her. Her skin was on fire under his eyes and she could see the muscles in his arms bunch as though he was fighting the urge to touch her. Good.

She'd used safe words before, with Alice and other partners, and appreciated him asking.

So she licked her lips and said, "strawberry."

He laughed, a short sound that sent shivers all over her skin. "Strawberry it is."

She paused, blinking as she tried to force her brain to work. "What about birth control?"

"I take a weekly tonic," he answered easily and Elora was instantly grateful for the wonders of fae remedies.

She didn't have time to catch her breath before he was kissing her. Her spine dug into the wall as he pressed against her, mouth teasing hers, teeth nipping her bottom lip until she opened for him.

She was drunk on him, burning for him, pliant beneath him as he threaded a hand through her hair to angle her head for him. He deepened the kiss, tongue sweeping across hers, swallowing her desperate whimper as he tightened his grip on her hair.

She'd kissed him before but this felt different. Like a confession. His intent was clear in the way he owned her, hand near painful in her hair, all tongue and teeth and the promise of more. Heat pooled between her legs as his other hand trailed down her hip, the barest of touches coaxing so much response from her body. He chuckled against her skin as she shuddered, dipping his head to kiss the fluttering pulse on her neck.

She was a live wire, so sensitive every touch was torture. She was half dressed, a thin slip barely covering her chest, her leather training trousers still on. He pressed torturous kisses across her collarbone she pulled at his shirt, desperate to feel his skin against hers.

"Patience, love."

"I have none," she shot back, but it came out breathless and needy. He seemed to recognize the desire in her voice and pulled back, letting her strip the shirt away from him and throw it away. She ran her hands over his sculpted chest, trailing her fingers down his stomach and across the waistband of his trousers. He tensed under her touch, jaw clenched as he watched her stare at him.

She began to slip her hand beneath his waistband but he grabbed her wrist and pinned her against the wall, silencing her protest with another kiss.

"My turn first."

She was over his shoulder before she could register what had just happened.

"What the hell, Aerin?" She clawed at his back, refusing to acknowledge the fact that she didn't entirely hate this. She felt him laugh beneath her.

"As much as I love the idea of fucking you against the wall," Aerin said roughly, opening the door to the bedroom, "I want you on the bed the first time."

Elora shut up her protests quickly as Aerin kicked the door shut behind them. The room was dark, but there was just enough light to see. He set her down on the bed on her back, bracing himself over her. Elora had long since lost control of her breathing, and the need for him only grew the longer he looked at her like he wanted to devour her whole.

"I've imagined this so many times," he told her as he traced his hand over her waist. The thin fabric of her slip did nothing to lessen the feeling of his hand against her skin and she gasped when he thumbed her breast through the material. His gaze was fixated on her, the way she reacted to him, the part of her lips and heady lust she knew must be shining in her eyes.

"So have I," she admitted as he kissed her neck. The words seemed to undo him.

"Hands above your head, Elora," he demanded, gripping her hip so tight it hurt. She obeyed. Maybe she'd have fought the control more

ELORA

if she hadn't been so damn out of her mind with the need to feel him. "Keep them there." He lowered himself down her body, undoing the front of her trousers. "Lift your ass for me."

She did, and he undressed her quickly, until she was naked under him, breath ragged, thighs damp with need. He stared at her for a long moment and she resented the fact that he was still partially clothed.

"Fuck, Elora," he said, words low and rough. He cupped her ass and yanked her towards him, placing teasing kisses along her stomach and hip bones. She nearly died at the sight of him kneeling between her legs, mouth so dangerously close to where she needed him. "You're the most beautiful fucking thing I've ever seen."

She wanted to see him, touch him, taste him more than she wanted her next breath.

She reached for him. Her wrists were in his grip in an instant, pressed into the pillow above her head.

Fuck. Her face flushed, eyes widening. She tried to hide the effect it had on her, but she could see the approval in Aerin's eyes.

"I need to touch you," she told him, heart giddy when he groaned in answer.

Instead of answering he kissed her, roughly and deeply, and slid his free hand down her body. She arched into him, panting slightly in anticipation.

He ran his fingers over the sensitive skin on her inner thigh, and she fought the urge to grab his hand and put it where she needed.

"Aerin, please," she begged, writhing beneath his touch.

He traced circles at the top of her thigh with his index finger. "You sound so good when you beg."

Without warning, he dragged a finger through the center of her and circled her clit. Elora gasped, pleasure sparking through her blood. She turned molten beneath him.

GIRL OF BONE AND IVY

"Fuck," he swore again as Elora moaned, his touch driving her out of her mind. "So wet for me."

He bent his head to kiss her with an urgency that betrayed his own need. He adjusted his position to watch her face as he slid a finger inside her. Elora bit his bottom lip in an attempt to hide her moan, but *God* she was already so close. She didn't know if it was the heightened senses or simply just *him*, but every breath she took only increased her ache for him.

He added another finger and curled them inside her, hitting just the right spot to make her gasp for air. Slowly at first, then faster as she whimpered under his touch, he thrust in and out of her, until she was sure there was no damn oxygen left in the room.

"Aerin," she managed to say, though his name was more of a moan than a coherent word.

"Elora," he answered, eyes dark and heavy lidded as he stared at her. "Come for me, love."

It was too much. Him, his damn fingers, the way he looked at her like he'd never seen anything he wanted more.

She shattered, screaming his name into his mouth as he kissed her, the heel of his palm pressing against her clit.

When she'd come down from the high, albeit still shuddering a little with aftershocks, it was to find Aerin staring at her with outright adoration mixed with lust so strong she thought she might get drunk on it.

"You'll fucking ruin me," he told her, letting go of her wrist and moving his hand back up to her waist. She took advantage of the freedom and grabbed his hair, pulling him down to kiss her. She kissed him like she was starved, like the only way he could understand what was going through her mind was if he tasted it on her tongue.

"Let me," she said to him, breaking away just enough to whisper. "Let me show you how good it would be to let yourself fall."

352

ELORA

This time when she reached for his remaining clothes, he let her. He eased himself off the bed to help her and she watched, wide eyed and open mouthed as he undressed fully.

"Jesus Christ, Aerin," she said when his clothes hit the floor. She hadn't meant it to come out her mouth, but somewhere between the first kiss and the orgasm, the filter between her brain and her tongue had disintegrated. She didn't think she'd ever wanted anything the way she wanted him right now. Couldn't think past the all consuming need to have him inside her.

So she said the one thing she knew would indeed ruin him.

"Please."

Her back hit the mattress, his hand around her throat, not enough to cut off her air, just enough to make it clear who was in charge. Clear who she belonged to. It was a side to Aerin she doubted few had seen. And though she adored the reserved, collected side he presented to the world, there was no denying the way her body reacted to him like this. She was so turned on she could barely breathe.

"Open your legs."

She did, watching the way his body reacted to the act, to her submission. She wanted to memorize the way he looked at her, the things that made him lose control, wanted to spend hours mapping out his body with her tongue until she knew him by heart.

But she didn't have any patience left. Later, she told herself as she hooked her heels around his back and urged him closer. His hand left her throat and braced his weight on the mattress beside her head.

He held her gaze as he entered her, the half formed gasp that flew from Elora's mouth at the movement capturing his attention. She closed her eyes, tightening her legs around his waist, needing him unrestrained.

"Look at me," he insisted, grabbing her chin until she opened his eyes. "Are you okay?"

She didn't know how to tell him that she'd perhaps never been more okay in her life. Already the pressure was building inside her again, the feel of him too much to bear. She needed him to move, to fuck her the way she knew he wanted to. She needed him to stop holding back.

"Fuck me, Aerin," she pleaded, moving beneath him, urging him further inside her. "I want you. All of you. Stop holding back."

He closed his eyes for the barest of seconds before he thrust inside her fully, the shock of it taking all the air from her lungs. Her head hit the headboard, but she didn't care. She moved with him, mindless except for the feeling of him, of them, the heat coiling between her legs.

He grabbed her thigh, adjusting the angle so he hit her clit with every thrust, releasing her to tangle his hand in her hair, splayed out across the pillow beneath her. He tilted her head back to expose her throat and lent down, kissing her neck, scraping his teeth across her pulse in the way he'd learned made her moan.

"Aerin," she gasped, knowing by the way he picked up pace that the sound of his name on her tongue, the way she made it sound like a prayer, the tell tale clenching of the blankets in her fists was driving him insane. He released his grip on her hair to slide his hand between their bodies.

"You feel so fucking good, Elora," he told her, sliding his thumb lightly over her swollen clit. She gasped, arching into his touch, trembling beneath him.

She said his name again, hands clawing at his back, nails scraping at his inked skin. She swore, but it was breathless and near indecipherable.

This time, when she tipped over the edge, he went with her, his mouth against her throat, her name on his lips.

After a few minutes, they caught their breath and she unwrapped

ELORA

her legs, but kept her hands splayed possessively across his back. He eased off of her but took her with him when he lay down, pulling her close against his chest and kissing her softly, trailing his hand in soothing motions up and down her spine. She cuddled close to him, though they were both far too warm now, listening to his heart return to its normal steady thump beneath her head.

"Your carvings," he said abruptly, apparently suddenly realizing he hadn't taken the time to look at them yet.

She grinned against his chest, pushing up on her elbows to smile at him.

"You want to see?"

He laughed. "That's a stupid question. The answer to whether I want to look at you will never be no."

She ached when she stood, her legs trembling a little, but it was a good sort of pain. She turned her back to him, suddenly self conscious despite how intimate they'd been minutes before. This was a different sort of intimacy. Tender.

She didn't hear him move but suddenly his hands were on her back, tracing the lines of the ivy curling around the top of her shoulder and down her arms, then giving the image of the wolf the same treatment.

"They're perfect," he mumbled, entranced. She shivered beneath his touch, body lighting up for him like a damn neon sign despite the fact she'd had him minutes before. She wondered if she'd ever get enough. She doubted it.

"You think so?"

He grabbed her around the waist and pulled her back onto the bed, pressing her back to his front and kissing her shoulder.

"*You're* perfect," he said against her skin.

She twisted in his arms to study him in the dim light. She'd seen him shirtless before, studied the carvings on his body, but still she found herself drawn to the plain black band around his left bicep.

355

"What's this for?" As far as she could see, there were no runes hidden in the marking. He tensed a little beneath her grip.

"It's a mark some royals have."

She frowned at him, pressing a soft kiss to his chest. "What for?" She knew she was pushing it, pushing *him*, but dammit she wanted him to let her in. She watched the hesitancy play across his face before he sighed.

"It marks the next in line to the throne."

She was sure she hadn't heard him right. "What?"

"It's how we choose between the children of the royals. Once the heir reaches maturity, *this* appears." His voice was strained but he pressed on. "Elladan didn't get one. And when I did, my father was furious. The bastard son. The failure. The beating block. Heir." He laughed, but it was humorless. His arms tightened around Elora. Her heart ached for him as she snuggled closer.

"You don't sound happy."

"I don't want the throne, Elora," he said softly. "I want nothing to do with a crown of cruelty."

She supposed she couldn't fault that. And yet...

"Is there no way to like...get rid of it? To name someone else heir if you don't want it?"

His gaze was set on the window on the opposite wall, a faraway look in his eyes. "Sometimes it's not about what we want, love. It's about what the world needs." He blinked, shaking his head as if to clear his thoughts and looked down at her. "Now, sleep. You won't be getting much of it tonight."

She hoped to God he kept that promise.

56

Aerin

Aerin woke with Elora caged in his arms and the duvet tangled around their legs. She shifted closer to him, her naked body pressed close against his, and he trailed his hand down the dip of her waist, still drunk on sleep and satisfaction.

"Good morning, love," he whispered, his arm tightening around her waist, allowing himself five more minutes of bliss before they were forced to face the day. He'd meant to *talk* last night, but he'd be lying if he said he wasn't bloody ecstatic at the turn of events. She sighed contentedly.

"Can we just stay here forever?" she mumbled into the pillow.

"I wish," he answered, moving her hair so he could kiss her neck. She shivered under his touch and he stifled a laugh. How she could be so responsive already after such little sleep was beyond him. The idea that she wanted him as much as he wanted her was beyond him. He'd be lying if he said his body wasn't responding to having her so close, though, despite the fact they both should've been thoroughly worn out. She was addictive.

"We have to go back, don't we?" Elora shoved her face into the pillow to muffle her words, clearly loathing the idea of leaving the bed as much as he was. She took a deep breath, Aerin forcing himself not to stare at her chest as she stretched her arms above her head, and rose from the warmth of the ruined sheets. There was a trio of light bruises along her hip bone where Aerin had gripped her and she traced them with her own finger, grinning.

"Oops," he said, tugging her back to him as he sat up. "I would say sorry but -"

"You're not." Elora laughed, leaning back into him. He savored the contact.

"It'll be okay," he murmured into her hair, pressing a kiss to her temple. A little frown line had appeared between her brows, and he knew it meant she was thinking of what was to come. The urge to care for her was burning through his veins. He was under no illusions that she needed him to protect her, not after her training, but that didn't stop him hating the idea of her being in harm's way. The idea of her hurt made him want to burn the world down. Even last night, after he'd taken her roughly, he'd cleaned her up, forced her to drink water, tied her damn hair up out of her face.

She shook her head against his chest, sighing, and shifted slightly, parting her legs in invitation. Aerin smiled against her skin.

"Fucking insatiable," he joked, but his hands were already wandering, sketching slow lines over her bare stomach. If she needed a distraction, he'd be happy to oblige.

Her breath stuttered a little before she spoke.. "We have to go," she said. He was sure she'd meant it to come out as a demand but instead it was a half hearted statement that only made him laugh.

"It would be wrong of me to leave you like this all day," Aerin said softly, swiping a finger through the slick dampness on her thigh. Elora gasped, then cursed herself.

"So much for my morals," she joked, but he heard the slight tinge of guilt in her words.

"The world won't end just because you stayed in bed an extra few minutes," he soothed. When she said nothing in answer, he lowered his voice, switching his tone. "Tell me to stop, Elora," he told her, raising his finger to his lips and licking it clean. He hummed appreciatively and she whimpered. He could get drunk off the taste of her.

He supposed he should be encouraging them both out of bed, rushing back to Spring. But his body didn't give a shit about duty and war when he had her naked and needy before him. Áine above, she was beautiful.

"Tell me to stop," Aerin repeated, cupping her breast with his other hand and running his thumb over her peaked nipple. He watched, rapt, as she bit her bottom lip, spine arching slightly at his touch. He loved how easily she reacted to his touch, loved watching her come apart for him. She was soaked and he'd barely started.

When she said nothing, he grinned. "Thought so."

He slipped two fingers inside her and she cried out. He didn't move, just held her, nipping her earlobe between his teeth.

"One day," he told her, lazily curling his fingers inside of her in a way that made her whole body light up for him. "I'm going to have you tied up at my mercy. I'm going to make you scream, beg me to fuck you. I'll make you so desperate to come that you'll cry." He'd been thinking about it longer than he wanted to admit.

"You can do what you want to me," she answered, bucking her hips in an attempt to get him to move. "I'm yours."

He let her ride his hand, cursing slightly when he noticed her reaction to his statement. "Good girl."

For a second there was nothing but her heavy breathing, the silky softness of her, the length of him pressed against her back. He made no move to do anything but touch her.

"When we go back," he said, withdrawing his fingers to slide them up to her clit. "And it gets too much or you feel like you're not in control, you come to me, Elora. I'll make sure you think about nothing else but us." She gasped as his fingers entered her again, his thumb circling her clit.

"Yes."

"Such a good girl this morning," he said teasingly, urging her head back so he could kiss her.

"I felt like being nice," she answered breathlessly, tightening around his fingers. "Don't get used to it."

"I always get what I want in the end, love," he reminded her, moving his hand faster until she was grinding against him, desperate. "See? Look how bad you need me. You'd do anything." She nodded, gasping. "Whatever you want, Elora. That's what I'll give you."

He meant it. He would go to the ends of the earth for this woman. He wasn't sure he was ready to acknowledge what that meant.

"I want," she moaned, fighting to form the words through the haze of lust between them, "to come. Please Aerin."

"I won't always be this nice," he said, grabbing her bottom lip between his teeth. "But how could I say no when you ask so nicely?" It was impossible to do anything but what she asked when she begged like that. He pressed down on her clit roughly, the bite of pleasure and pain sending her over the edge like he knew it would. She screamed his name as she came apart on his hand, back bowed.

Aerin grit his teeth at her reaction, so turned on it hurt. But this wasn't about him. She needed grounding, reassuring. That's what mattered. But *fuck* it was hard not to pretend the rest of the world didn't exist and take her again the way he wanted to.

When she'd relaxed and he'd finally calmed his own body down, he withdrew his hand and pressed a soft kiss to her lips. "Come on, love."

He helped her up and into the bath, soaping them both down before making her breakfast in the little, apparently fully stocked, kitchen as she braided her hair.

"We'll fly out of the forest and runecast back to Anixi," Aerin told her around a bite of toast.

She nodded, slipping a piece of bacon to Boba. He'd cooked it specially for the wolf, who he had to admit he already adored. He missed Blueberry like a limb but he didn't want to call on him until it was safe. He'd call for him when they returned to Anixi, he decided. The bird could wait out the battle in the castle if it came to it. He didn't like the uncertainty of having him out of his sight for long. He watched Elora wrap her arms around the giant beast's neck and bury her face in his fur, his heart clenching. The wolf licked her face and Aerin could've sworn he looked like he was smiling.

Pride warmed him as he watched them. She was so strong, so much stronger than even she knew. He wondered if Nimue had told her how rare true familiars were. He'd faked the process with Blueberry, but the last fae he'd heard of to come out of their runecarving with a familiar was Endra.

He wondered if it was a coincidence that her daughter had one, too. It seemed too neat, too tidy, to be chance. He frowned, considering.

"What about Boba?" Elora's voice brought him from his musings.

"He's fast as fuck," Aerin laughed. "He'll be out of the forest before us."

She nodded, clearly satisfied and began clearing their plates. They tidied quickly and stood at the door, the world waiting. She hesitated at the threshold. Aerin reached over and wrapped her hand in his.

"You can do this." No part of him doubted it, or her. He hoped his confidence rubbed off on her, squeezing her hand in his.

They left the calm safety of the cabin in favor of war.

57

Elora

Their trip back was fast and uneventful, Elora resting comfortably in Aerin's arms as he flew. His closeness calmed her, and she focused on breathing deeply to quell the storm inside her mind.

Tarhael was waiting for them when they landed. He nearly knocked Aerin over with his hug, before pulling away and gaping at Elora. Blueberry had arrived and perched happily on Aerin's shoulder, tweeting in his ear.

Aerin grinned. Elora's heart clenched.

"Áine above, Elora," Tarhael breathed, brown eyes wide. "Power suits you. Maybe I should've snatched you up before the Prince here got a chance."

Aerin's hand was in the air faster than Elora could blink. He clenched it into a fist, and Tarhael glared at him, gasping like a fish on dry land as Aerin pulled the air from his lungs.

"Nobody lays a hand on her."

Elora's heart all but stopped. She was horrified, despite the demented grin Tarhael still sported. And yet, under that, she was feverish with need for him. Ideas of what he could do to her with all

ELORA

that power flickered through her mind.

Aerin finally opened his palm and Tarhael inhaled a lungful before bursting into laughter.

"Oh you're so fucked," he said to his friend, clutching his stomach. When he'd found his composure, he turned to Elora again. "I'm surprised you can walk this morning. He must've taken it easy on you." He winked and dodged Aerin's punch with another laugh.

Despite herself, Elora smiled. She knew he had and she appreciated it, but she craved the things she knew he wanted to do to her. Wanted all of them.

They were interrupted by a familiar warm voice. "Elora! So glad you've returned. You're positively glowing." Queen Briella swept into view in a knee length sage green dress that suited her deep brown skin perfectly, bright eyes crinkled with her smile.

"Thank you."

"And who is this?" Briella smiled at the wolf, holding her hand out for him to sniff. Boba stayed firmly rooted to Elora's side.

"Oh, this is Boba," Elora said, running a hand through his fur. "My …uh…familiar."

A strange emotion clouded Briella's eyes but it was gone as fast as it came. "I am so happy for you. I'm afraid, though, that we must convene with the council to discuss less happy matters."

Elora hesitated. Briella noticed.

"It's okay." She bowed her head close to Elora's and whispered conspiratorially. "It's time to take a stand and prove your worth. Let them see that they were right. They should fear you."

Elora shivered but straightened her spine. She could do this. She knew she could. Or, at least, she could keep repeating it until she believed it.

The council chambers consisted of a large room, filled nearly entirely by a long wooden table, five seats on each side and a throne at the head. The seats were all taken except the throne, clearly reserved for Briella, and the chair to the right hand side. The Queen sank gracefully into her seat, waving a hand to Elora to urge her to sit beside her.

Elora hesitated. Her blood would only carry her so far, here. Sitting to the Queen's right would send a message that she only hoped she could back up with her actions. She obeyed, Aerin and Tarhael taking up their spots behind her like guards, faces stony and shoulders squared.

"Spring Council," Briella began, folding her hands in her lap, "meet our newest member. Princess Elora of Anixi, heir to the throne."

Elora's stomach dropped and she began to rise out of her seat, panic fueling her. Tarhael's hand on her shoulder stopped her, and she settled for gripping the arms of the chair until her knuckles were white

"Ah, yes," a fae man who looked middle aged - Elora had no idea how old he *actually* was though - sat forward, head tilted. "Endra's child. An honor to meet you. Your mother was a wonderful leader. I trust, in time, that you will follow closely in her footsteps."

Elora stared at him, mouth dry and pulse racing.

"I'm sure she appreciates the thought, Reed," Briella smiled, filling the beat of silence Elora had left.

Another voice rose, female this time.

"*Heir?*" She sounded dubious, her voice wary. "Briella, you know nothing of this girl except her blood. Don't be so hasty-"

"How did she survive? We can't trust her-" another voice joined in, angrier than the previous one.

The Queen held up her hand, mouth set into a firm line. "It is her blood right. But if you're worried about her proving herself, you won't have long to wait. There will be plenty opportunities for her to prove to you all just how strong she is. For now, I am still your Queen and I will not hear any argument on this. If you still have an issue with Elora after the battle is over, you will come to me in private and discuss your concerns. Is that clear?" Silence smothered the council, and Briella nodded calmly. Elora gaped at her, in awe of how easily she diffused the situation. "Now, time is running short and we must deal with the matters at hand." The others around the table shifted in their seats, and Reed nodded at Elora. "The Unseelie Courts are on the move. They will be here by dawn. I doubt they've come to talk."

Elora thought she might faint. She was wrong, so wrong. She wasn't ready for this. Tarhael kept his hand steady on her shoulder, squeezing for support, settling her nerves slightly.

"Our armies are rallied," another woman spoke up from the end of the table, "and the outlying towns have been evacuated."

Briella nodded, but she straightened in her throne, her shoulders tense. "Yes. You have all done well in preparing your kingdoms. But it will not be enough." A collective breath was held as the Queen paused, turning to Elora. "Elora may have been the catalyst for this, but she might also be the cure."

Elora swallowed.

"Our armies are strong, our people powerful, but we are not built for cruelty like the Unseelie Courts are. It is a fact we take pride in, but nonetheless, leaves us at a disadvantage." She reached out carefully and took Elora's hand in hers, pushing up her sleeves and exposing the ivy carvings. "I'm sure by now you all have seen what Elora managed with raw magic. Imagine what more she could do now Nimue has adorned her. Elora levels the playing field. With her, we stand a chance."

"Not to be rude," a new voice piped up, "but how do we know this girl can perform such feats under pressure? She is half mortal, and untried at that-"

Elora bristled. As much as she was nervous as hell about what

GIRL OF BONE AND IVY

was to come, she hated being underestimated by strangers. She'd been judged constantly in her life - for her appearance, or gender or sexuality. She was sick of it. "I'll show you."

Briella grinned, opening her arms in a sweeping gesture of *go ahead*.

Elora closed her eyes and breathed deeply, calling to the well of power inside her. She demonstrated small bursts of her power - growing roses from her palms, calling Boba in from where he stood outside the chamber doors, summoning a brightly colored bird and instructing it to fetch her berries from the gardens outside. When she grew vines around a member's legs to restrain him, Aerin's eyes grew dark and he shifted on his feet.

Appeased, the council members talked long into the night, debating strategy and politics until Elora's head hurt. Her role had been decided long ago and the longer she sat there listening to the intricacies of war, the more she began to doubt that she could ever step into the shoes of someone like the Queen. Not that she was considering it as an option. It didn't matter that she had royal blood, that her mother had been Queen before her, that Briella had dropped the whole *heir* bombshell.

Finally, Briella dolled out the verdict. Exhausted, but cautiously hopeful now that there was at least some form of a plan, Elora retreated in search of her rooms. Briella herself showed her the way down the dimly lit corridors of gold and white, ivy that matched Elora's carvings trailing across the walls.

Her rooms were enormous, filled with plants and a beautiful combination of green and gold. She vowed to explore them more closely in the morning, but the four poster bed was calling her like a siren song despite the anxiety churning in her stomach. Boba settled down at the foot of the bed, urging her to sleep through their bond.

Aerin had his own room, but she forced herself not to go to him. Didn't want to bother him. For all that she didn't regret anything

ELORA

they'd done, not in the slightest, she wanted to give him space in case he didn't feel the same way.

It didn't matter, though.

She woke up in his arms. She didn't know when he'd entered, but she didn't care. All that mattered was that in the face of everything else, he felt like home.

58

Elora

Heavy, hurried footsteps woke Elora. She could hear distant shouts, cursing and the clang of metal on metal. Aerin was awake, standing at the end of the bed strapping on his armor. Her familiar was nowhere to be seen. She frowned at the space where he'd slept.

"Didn't want to wake you until the last minute. Your armor should be here any minute now."

Elora slid out of bed and sipped the water waiting for her on the nightstand, trying desperately to steady her shaky hands. Just as she was about to review the plan with Aerin, the double doors to her chambers opened and Briella strode in, flanked by guards holding armor, her advisors...and Raewyn and Lydia, atop the back of Boba.

"There's been a slight change in plans. Fresh forces from Autumn are still flowing in, and it seems they've been preparing for this fight for even longer than we thought. The archers and runecasters on the walls are already on the verge of being overwhelmed and we're running low on food." Briella took a deep breath, as though trying to contain her emotions. "Aerin. Can you take command of the runecasters on the northern wall and drive them back until Elora

368

arrives?"

Aerin nodded curtly and finished strapping on his breastplate. He tucked his helmet under his arm and came over and kissed Elora softly. "Remember, keep safe and follow the plan."

"I'll be fine. I have Boba and powers now," Elora tried to keep her tone lighthearted, but fear had begun to dig a pit in her stomach. "Go give your father the ass kicking he deserves."

Aerin pressed a kiss to Elora's forehead, bowed to Briella, and marched outside, two of Briella's guards peeling off to escort him.

"You and the Prince make a good match," Briella mused. She waved her entourage outside and walked over to Elora, motioning the pixies to come closer. "Help Elora put on her armor and then meet me outside by the conference hall." Elora saw worry shine in Briella's eyes and reached out before she could think better of it, placing a hand on the Queen's arm. Briella sighed. "I don't know how much longer we can hold out, to be honest. Harkan is hitting us hard. I lost most of my main army in between the Raxishi Mountains. All I have left are the city guard, my personal guard, and a few militias."

"It didn't seem this bad during last night's meeting."

"That was before I knew Harkan was going to ambush my troops. He's the King of Autumn and an incredibly potent runecaster and warrior. Not to mention he's a brilliant tactician and general. I hate him but even I have to admit he has talent. Spring's never had to fight like this. We're healers. Summer has always done the bulk of the fighting, but they were caught by surprise as well. War has always been a distant concept. Naive of us." She chuckled a little self-deprecatingly.

"Briella..." Elora looked for words she couldn't find. "What do you want me to do?"

"I'll be joining you in battle. My carvings are mostly for healing and tracking, but I can Runecast and animate some creatures made from nature to fight for us. I know the initial plan was to have you hidden and provide support from the towers, but..." she trailed off tucking a strand of hair back into her tight braid.

Elora knew what Briella wanted.

Knew in the depths of her heart that hiding had never really been in the cards for her anyway.

"If the walls are scaled and taken, it'll be too late," Briella continued, oblivious to the acceptance rushing through Elora's veins. Dangerous, yes. Necessary? Also, yes. She'd meant it when she promised Nimue she'd try. She reached out to Boba through the bond, his approval nearly knocking her off her feet before she could so much as finish the question.

"I hate the thought of you getting hurt," Elora told her familiar, grateful when he padded over and lent against her side.

"Elora." Boba's voice sounded in her head, steady and sure. *"I can feel the very ground crying out, drenched in blood. I can help. Let me."*

"I know," she answered. *"I know."*

Elora turned to Briella. "You know that if the prophecy is true," she began, voice calm and quiet, "I could save you today and doom you tomorrow?" She didn't want to, hated the thought of it, but she needed Briella to know. Needed her to understand what she was asking if she wanted Elora to take on more than planned.

"I know," the Queen smiled, somehow still warm even donned in armor. "But you won't."

Warmth bloomed in Elora's chest as Briella took her hand, a serene sort of determination flooding through her at the touch.

"Then let's go make Autumn wish they'd never stepped foot out their miserable little Season," Elora replied as Raewyn and Lydia flew over and began dressing her, arranging the armor just so. It was lighter than it looked - thick leather trousers, a shining golden chest plate that they fastened around her with corset-like ties. Boba

ELORA

watched with keen eyes, as though ensuring they were doing it right.

"You've grown and changed so much since we've last seen each other," Raewyn murmured while helping Briella fit the breastplate over Elora as Lydia secured the fastenings. "You stay alive now, okay? Or we'll kill you."

Elora did her best to reassure Raewyn while going over everything she learned with Nimue in her mind, from the combat lessons to the most useful runecasts she could think of that would help Combat hadn't been her strongest area of training, but she was competent enough, she hoped, to hold her own.

"All done," Briella's voice broke Elora's train of thought as she glanced down at herself. Tall, flexible leather boots rose to her knees, the thick fighting leathers flexible but formidable. The chest plate accommodated her movements with ease when she tried it out, the long leather sleeves underneath supple and comfortable. Her hair was tied back in the same tight braid as Briella's, and then a helmet was slid over her head - smooth, the same gold as the chest plate, with nose and cheek guards that reminded her of the images of Spartans she'd studied in college.

The thought made her laugh, breaking the somber mood of the room.

Boba growled his approval, tail wagging, causing everyone in the room except Elora to jump.

"I guess that's a sign that Boba is ready," Elora said, satisfied at how her armor fit and clinked when she moved, refusing to acknowledge the tangled web of emotions inside her chest. "I'm ready, too."

"Shall we?" Briella asked, gesturing to the door as if she were about to lead her to a grand ball.

Elora followed Briella down the halls, flanked by Boba to her right and the pixies to her left. They walked in silence to the armory, Elora's shoulders heavy with the weight of the future.

59

Elora

The first thing Elora noticed about battle was the smell. The stench of blood was thick in the air, coating everything with a sticky sheen that made Elora's nose scrunch. The screams of the wounded were interspersed with the clangs of metal clashing against metal and the roars of battle cries. Vines and trees grew in bursts across the battlefield Spring soldiers lying dead on the ground at their roots, faces purple and tongues swollen and lolling out the side of their blue lips. *Choked to death.* The haze of battle muddied her thoughts, the sword she'd been handed a familiar heavy weight in her hand. Boba was right behind her, making sure no enemies could approach without her knowing.

She was still close to the castle walls, away from the bulk of the fighting, trying to take in as much of it as she could before she jumped into the fray.

"The walls, Elora. We need to get to the walls," Boba's voice sounded urgently in her head.

"Aerin should be on the northern wall. That's what we need to find."

Elora spun around as Boba growled his excitement.

"I've got his scent." He pointed in the right direction with his nose,

lip curled back to expose long canines.

Elora allowed herself another deep breath before leaving the relative safety of the castle walls. They ran together, spinning to avoid the slashes of swords, nearly slipping in the mess of mud and blood coating the once vibrant grassy ground. A tall man in deep red armor blocked her path, swinging a sword through the air, aiming for her head. She ducked, pulse loud in her ears, lashing out at his knees with her blade, catching him off balance. He stumbled back, avoiding the brunt of her strike. It was all she needed though, his focus momentarily gone. She reached deep into the bloody earth, wincing at the sheer number of people and creatures she could feel through it, pulling roots forward towards the surface. The man screamed as she tangled them round his ankles, felling him. The roots enveloped him, cutting off the noise, then his breath as they took the body underground with them.

For a second, she was frozen, staring at the upturned earth with horror, ears ringing. But Boba nudged her side, urging her on, and she swallowed the sickness. This was war. She knew she would have to kill in order to save. It didn't make it any easier, though.

She took off running again, Boba close beside her. Another Autumn soldier filled the gap of the last and Boba had his jaws around their throat faster than Elora could track, blood spraying across his fur and her armor. They went down, but another approached, yelling battle cries and curses. And another. And another. Elora's arm ached with the swinging of her sword, and she thanked whoever had designed her armor that it hid the glow of her carvings when she called on her power over and over, thorns piercing flesh, vines wrapping around limbs, screams cut off by red blossoms blooming in their throats.

Slowly, they made their way across the battlefield. With every soldier she killed, her heart grew heavier, her conscious not accustomed to the reality of battle. The closer they got to the northern wall, the less chaotic the fighting became. Elora finally found herself among Spring reinforcements, and nearly cried with relief when she spied Aerin, fit and fighting, atop the wall. He was flying above the massive siege towers that bore the Dioltas crest and arms. The fragments of several siege towers were already lying shattered, pierced by vines and trees, some simply disassembled.

He was glowing a powerful blue, his wings working overtime. She watched as, again and again, Aerin sent gusts of wind and tornadoes spinning across the siege towers and down on the other side of the walls where Autumn's forces were attempting to scale the wall. Whenever Autumn soldiers came too close Aerin he would make a fist and clench, and the enemy would fall by the dozens clutching and clawing at their throats. She knew how much that must cost him, wondered with a flicker of worry how much longer he could keep it up.

Beneath him, Spring fae held strong, the archers raining down a hail of arrows from the castle's parapets. Lines of spearmen held formation on the walls themselves, with ranks of runecasters furiously scribbling on the ground between the castle and the walls. Each runecaster had a soldier with a shield protecting them, and Elora witnessed firsthand how devastating their magic was. Several golems made from mossy stones rose up from the ground, clambering away to find enemy fae. Other runecasters summoned animated trees and vines to entrap and snare the enemy and built prisons from the living ground to capture soldiers by the dozens. More were rebuilding and reinforcing the defenses around Anixi's castle and Elora found herself cheering them on internally.

"Elora!" Aerin's voice cut through the noise and she turned to find him flying towards her.

She ran to him just as he was touching down, Boba circling them, snapping the neck of a wayward Autumn soldier who came too close.

"What happened to the plan? Why aren't you up in the parapets?"

"There are more Autumn troops than anticipated and Briella's forces were ambushed in the mountains. The northern wall is holding thanks to you, but the other walls are in complete chaos. We're going to be overrun unless I do something."

Instead of arguing with her, Aerin drew her in tightly, arms wrapping around her and smearing more blood on her helmet as he pulled back again.

"Start with the eastern wall and make your way down. Make them pay, Elora," he told her firmly, jaw tense. "Show Autumn exactly who you are." Aerin gaze bore into hers from behind his helmet, and though he was clearly tired from the fight, she recognized the sheer determination in his eyes.

"I will. I think your father deserves to see who stole his heir away from him." She winked and bounded away before Aerin could say anything else, Boba hot on her heels as Aerin took to the sky again.

Elora heeded Aerin's advice and started at the eastern wall. Spring soldiers fought tooth and nail but Autumn's forces were cunning and fierce, spattered in blood, teeth bared in wild grins as they slashed through Elora's allies. Anger became a living beast inside her, consuming the previous thread of guilt at the thought of killing, coiling around her ribs, urging the magic in her veins to *go*.

Living vines burst through the wet ground, thick stemmed and sturdy, tendrils wrapping around her, lifting her high into the air out of reach of the foot soldiers. She stood above the battlefield, wrapped in her power and screamed. Fury and grief poured from her as she unleashed herself on the Unseelie fae, vines extending from her tower in vicious whips. They tangled around enemy soldiers, choking them, slamming them into each other, felling them and tightening as they struggled until they finally stilled, limp. Elora poured her energy into her magic, summoning huge trees and animating them so they would fight for her. The animated forces crashed into the Autumn soldiers, driving them back up the wall and out into the forests beyond, where the trees chased them. She fashioned prisons made from hardened clay and mud that sprung from the ground and trapped enemy soldiers inside. Once she was sure the eastern wall was in good hands, the enemy forces severely thinned and the remaining Spring fae rallied and motivated once more, she moved onto the southern wall, ignoring the steady pounding of the headache behind her eyes.

Boba practically flew behind her, ripping into Autumn fae with reckless abandon, muzzle stained red. Every spear or sword strike seemed to miss him and though she swore she saw an arrow hit him dead in the flank, it bounced off harmlessly, tip blunted. She and Boba fought in tandem, and everywhere she went, the enemy fled. Her heartbeat pounded in her ears, but all she felt was an icy sort of focus, fueled by her earlier white hot rage.

Slowly, victory began to sound less like a foreign concept and more like a viable option.

Elora's monstrous vines were setting her back down near the northern wall where Aerin was when she saw a familiar blue shape spiral from the sky. Commanding her vines to climb back into the air, Elora watched helplessly as King Harkan entered the battle.

He was on the back of a giant flying eagle, flanked by several other fae soldiers clad in all black armor on surrounding birds. King Harkan held a bow as tall as he was, with arrow shafts that looked more like spears than arrows. His eagle swooped down faster than Elora could track, snatching Aerin midair in its razor sharp talons. *Her Aerin.* A spear stuck straight out of his back and his body was limp, dangling from the eagle's claws as it flew.

Elora screamed as Autumn forces cheered and surged once more, revitalized by the emergence of their King. She threw her arms

ELORA

forward and sent thousands of vines, adorned with thorns larger than swords, snaking towards King Harkan. He sensed them at the last moment and his eagle dived, maneuvering quickly out of the way. He slashed his hands forward and blades of hardened air sliced through her vines as though he was simply tearing apart a blade of grass.

Again and again, he slashed through them, a knife through butter, as Elora's throat became raw with anguish. She tried to make them thicker, stronger, but there were limits to her strength and exhaustion had begun to make a home in her bones. Elora tried to suppress her mounting panic as King Harkan started cutting her vines quicker than she could make them but before she knew it, she was tumbling out of the air, her tower slashed into pieces beneath her. Swallowing her panic, she summoned a thick, mossy branch from the nearest tree to catch her. The fall still knocked the breath out of her and by the time she got back up, King Harkan was bearing down on her. She tried to summon an earthen shield, but knew it was too late. Her limbs felt leaden, her head pounding, everything slow and sluggish as she took in the sight of the man she hated heading straight for her, a familiar wicked smile on his face.

"Elora!" Boba screamed in her head. She could feel his worry as keenly as her own, and also sensed the frustration on his end as he couldn't do anything. *"Call to me! NOW -"* Boba cut off as Elora squeezed her eyes shut and threw everything she had into summoning him the way she had her vines, her body crying out at the effort.

An ear splitting roar broke the air around her and opened her eyes to see a giant wolf. Giant was an understatement. Boba's head loomed over the walls, standing nearly as tall as the highest tower of Anixi castle. His shadow cast itself over nearly the entire wall as he tipped his head back and howled, shaking the very ground he stood on.

Holy shit, Elora's jaw dropped as she held fast to their connection, drawing on Boba's strength, in awe of him.

In a single leap, he intercepted King Harkan and his eagle, jaws closing around the bird's wing as he ripped it from the sky. The bird screeched, releasing its grip on Aerin as it thrashed in Boba's jaws. Her familiar ripped apart King Harkan's soldiers with his teeth, continuing despite the attacks Harkan hurled his way, though she could feel his pain through their bond.

She watched in shock, heart in her throat, searching the ground desperately for any sign of Aerin.

The tide of battle was turning before her eyes. It was now or never. One final push. She stood on shaking legs, spat blood from her mouth and called once more on her vines, hoisting herself into the air. Hastily, she knelt and scrawled a series of runes into the side of a thick vine with her nail, waiting until they glowed a faint green before she stood again. She sucked in a deep breath and hoped her voice wasn't as shaky as she felt.

"Harkan." His name tasted sour in her mouth but her voice soared through the air, volume magnified by the runecast. Around her, soldiers looked up, momentarily stunned. "You failed to kill me once. Want to try again?" Her voice was sickly sweet, condescending and laced with fake pity. She spread her arms wide, taunting him. Below her, the remnants of the Spring forces rallied themselves with a cry, hoisting standards and flags, charging forward one last time. Elora screamed with them. She screamed in defiance of the odds, she screamed in defiance of evil, and above all, Elora screamed for victory.

Harkan didn't come.

She wasn't sure whether that was a good or bad sign but there wasn't time to care. She watched the soldiers clash below, saw the way they fought despite their injuries and exhaustion. A half formed idea solidified in her mind. Reckless, really, with such little research

ELORA

but Gods above, they were *so close* to victory she could nearly taste it.

She couldn't kill the remaining Autumn forces, as aching and exhausted as she was. But there was something else she could do to help.

Nimue had told her that the ability to grow things would eventually evolve into the ability to heal more than scrapes and aches. Elora didn't have time for *eventually*.

No, all she had was desperate, searing hope.

She took a deep breath. Quite possibly her last. She couldn't be sure how much energy this would take from her, but she was fairly sure it could kill her. She had no idea if it would work at all. But she'd promised to try. This was her trying.

She clasped her hands together and *willed*. Elora willed every single fae fighting against the Autumn fae to heal. *To be.* Again. Again. Until they stopped taking damage, their wounds sealing as soon as they were made. Something warm and wet dripped from her nose, the taste of copper coating her tongue. She was pretty sure she was screaming, agony threatening to tear her apart. Still, she continued, vaguely registering the feeling of something shattering inside her. Her heartbeat pounded through her head, nausea and dizziness crashing over her. She blinked rapidly, gritted her teeth, and summoned more.

The Spring forces soon realized that they couldn't take damage and were, at least for these few moments, untouchable The roar that echoed out from the army was one of vengeance and victory. Elora watched through blurry eyes as they swept back what was left of Autumn, until a brisk wind whipped her hair against her face and she froze. Slowly, agonizingly, she turned, barely managing to stay upright. Harkan, atop a new mount, studied her with dark eyes, blood coating one side of his face, armor torn down the middle.

"To the death," his voice sounded in her head. *"Till next time little Queen."*

"To the death," Elora agreed.

He saluted her mockingly then turned, fleeing with the rest of his forces.

The Autumn army had fully splintered, and another thunderous cheer went up as her army realized their victory. Elora smiled, her thoughts turning to Aerin. She couldn't see him, but then she couldn't see much anymore. She could heal him, she knew she could if she could just *find* him.

Except, well, something was fractured deep inside her. Broken. It *hurt.* More than that, it beckoned, a shadowy hand promising sweet sleep if she just took it. God, she was tired. Bone achingly exhausted. Strength fled her body like the retreating army fled the field, the black splotches across her vision growing larger every time she blinked.

The air is getting thinner, she thought blearily. It was either that or it was getting harder to breathe. The dizziness that had been creeping up in her head wouldn't go away and now threatened to suffocate her. She tried to think, but it was hard to form thoughts when they kept slipping through her fingers like she was trying to grab water.

The darkness grew nearer, so sweet in its siren song. She was helpless to resist as she placed her hand in its, and let herself be led away into nothingness.

60

Elora

Elora was pretty sure she was dead.

Either that, or she wished she was. It felt like her body had been taken apart and put back together again.

She gasped at the all consuming ache, struggling to force her eyes open against the onslaught of pain. But underneath the ache, there was warmth. Distantly, she registered the soft pressure of a pair of arms around her waist. She took stock of her body - it had been brutalized, that was for sure, but it seemed to be in one piece, despite her earlier suspicions. And someone was holding it, holding *her*, so tightly she was sure there was no space to fall apart.

Aerin. Of course it was Aerin. Really, it was always going to be Aerin.

She rolled to face him, ignoring the way her body screamed in protest, reaching up to cup his face, assess his steady breathing, run a hand over his chest to check for the arrow wound that felt like it ripped her heart out. Intact. His bare chest rose and fell steadily and his lips were parted slightly as he slept. Like this, eyes closed, face soft and open, she could almost believe that nothing had happened. That they were just two people, in bed, together. That nothing but them existed.

Except, there had been a battle. There would be a war. And yet, somehow, Elora was also sure that there would be *them*. There would be roses among the thorns. No matter how many times she cut her fingers searching for them.

Maybe, for now, that could be enough. Maybe, in this bed, with a body that was more pain than person, that could be what mattered. Just for now. Just for a little bit.

She wanted to know what had happened after she passed out. She knew Harkan had retreated, and undoubtedly the final Unseelie warriors had followed suit. It was funny, she thought, how cowardly he was in the face of real danger. So used to his throne, his crown, his posturing, and yet when it came down to it, the second he was unsure of his victory, he ran with his tail between his legs.

It didn't add up.

It seemed too easy.

Something uneasy curled in her gut, turning her blood to ice, the unshakable feeling that something was *wrong* tightening her heart strings.

"Love," a sleep softened voice, a word spoken like a lifeline, so easy for her to grab hold of. She didn't hesitate.

"I'm here," she whispered back, nuzzling closer to him. He was wearing nothing but underwear, she realized, and wondered who the hell had cleaned him up. She, too, was in a silky nightdress, no sign of blood or dirt on her skin. She suspected it had been Raewyn. The thought made her heart ache. She owed that girl ... something. What gift said *thanks for wiping my enemies blood from me?* Chocolate?

"What's going through that pretty head?" Aerin asked, voice thick and eyes half lidded. God, she could stare at him for decades and never get bored. She traced a thumb over his jawline, the sight of him alive and healthy and *hers* the balm she needed.

ELORA

"I'm so glad you're okay," she told him, eyes stinging with sudden tears. Not now. She would think about it later, allow herself to feel fully, but now, she wanted to soak him in. She blinked them back furiously.

"Are you?" Aerin roused himself from the sheets, running his hands over her, eyes narrowed and serious as he inspected her skin.

Elora fought the urge to shudder under his touch. It was natural, at this point, her reaction to him. Instinctive. Her body lit up the second he touched her, looked at her. *She* lit up. The pain became secondary, distant, unimportant when he looked at her like that.

Her attempt to hide the flames that licked at her skin in the wake of his touch was pathetic. He noticed. She saw the second he realized, the way his eyes darkened, his touch grew more purposeful, his brows furrowed slightly in question.

She hurt, she knew he must too, but she didn't care. They needed this. This connection, the reassurance that they were okay, that they weren't leaving. Neither of them knew how to put it into words. But they didn't need to, not when they could show it like this.

61

Aerin

She smelled like freshly cut grass and weeping rain mixed with the barest hint of lavender. Aerin didn't know that rain could have a smell but with his nose near her bare skin now, he didn't have any other words to describe the way her scent wrapped around him. He wondered how she'd taste. He saw the same hunger kindle into flames in her eyes, the way her gaze changed from languid to alert. He was already starting to harden, and felt Elora tremble slightly at his touch. Grazing his hand down her body, Aerin shifted so he was looking down at her. Elora was already closing her eyes and leaning upwards for the kiss, but he stopped her with a finger on her lips.

"Strawberry, right?"

Elora opened her eyes, cheeks blooming crimson. "Yes," she whispered breathlessly.

"Mmm..." Aerin trailed off, one hand propped up on the bed to keep himself above the girl he so desperately needed and the other hand trailing lower, finding a home between her thighs. "You want me, love?" he asked, as if he couldn't feel the evidence of her want on his fingers. His voice was unused in the morning and deeper than normal. Rougher. He playfully stroked her thighs between the sheets and Elora squirmed, trying to clamp down on his hand.

"Yes, Aerin. I need you."

"You're going to have to earn it."

He was already tilting his lips closer to hers, his own body tingling with anticipation. Her lips met his fervently and he molded his body around her, drawing her in. She opened her mouth and he deepened the kiss in response, their tongues meeting as their limbs tangled. She pressed into him, urgent and demanding. Legs encircled and interlocked behind his back and he moved his lips down her body.

Elora's neck was soft and delicate, and Aerin's tongue savored the way she responded to his lips on the sensitive skin there. Her hands found the back of his neck, then his hair. Elora grabbed fistfuls of his long locks as he started to nip at her neck, sucking gently. He cupped Elora's head and gently pulled her hair to allow himself better access. Elora's soft, breathless gasps were now low throated moans and she panted against him as he left a trail of kisses down her neck. Aerin was so turned on it hurt, and pressed his length between Elora's legs slowly, invitingly. She moaned louder and tried to buck against him, but he used his hips to hold her down and control the pace.

"Good girl," he whispered in between kisses, as she fought to stay still beneath him.

"Aerin, please, I-"

Elora cut off as Aerin's hand slid under her thin night dress and found her peaked nipple. Cupping her breast, he rolled her nipple between his thumb and index finger. He teased her again and again, pressing hard, then softer, drunk on Elora's moans. There was only so much he could take before he couldn't hold back.

"Fuck," he swore as Elora's hand found him underneath the blanket, gripping him. Aerin remembered how he had almost been taken from the girl he desperately loved - *fuck he loved her* - and being here with her now, hearing the way his heart pounded for her, how his body begged for her, Aerin decided he needed to have her. Now.

"I don't care what the plans are, you're never doing anything like that again, you hear me? No running into battle unless I'm by your side. You're mine. I won't lose you," Aerin said softly, rocking against her, causing a moan to flutter past her lips. The realization that he'd come so close to losing her made his heart clench.

Elora's eyes widened at Aerin as he spoke and she gripped his cock harder, stroking him. "I'm yours," she agreed. "Let me prove it." She moved up to kneel and Aerin stifled a groan as he took in the sight of her on her knees, reaching to pull his underwear off fully.

"Not so fast, love." Aerin stood up from the bed. "You want to know how I taste?"

Elora's response was to reach for him again. She was stopped by an invisible wall of air. "Aerin?"

"You have to earn it," he repeated as he stepped forward and grabbed the blankets, tossing them to the floor. Cupping Elora's face in his hand, he leaned down to meet her eyes. "I want that pretty mouth wrapped around me as much as I want my next breath, but first you have to come on my tongue."

He kissed her one more time, before he ripped the night dress off her, leaving her naked before him. A warm current of air swept under her, carrying her towards him, suspended slightly in front of him as he took her in. He made her wait, the silence echoing between them as Aerin ravaged her with his eyes. Finally, he met her gaze. She stared back at him with an intensity that made his self control boil over, evaporating completely.

Aerin shaped the air into an extension of his hands and gently traced them over Elora's body. She gave a small start of surprise that quickly morphed into a moan of pleasure as he cupped her breast, the other hand trailing up her body to wrap around her throat, gently at first, as he gauged her reactions. She was so wet he could barely think straight at the sight of her. He squeezed a little harder and she whimpered a little, eyes fluttering shut as she tilted her head back, subconsciously allowing him better access. He watched Elora floating in front of him, trembling and moaning, eyes rolling back a little as he choked her and teased her nipples without ever touching her properly. The sight nearly undid him completely. The next time she opened her eyes, Aerin was waiting, kneeling in front of her. Elora must have enjoyed the sight because Aerin felt her hands reaching for him.

"Remember how I said I wanted to you fuck you against the wall?"

"Fuck, Aerin-"

She cut off as Aerin kissed his way up her thighs, pressing his lips against her softly, savoring the taste. She bucked at the contact and Aerin licked her clit once, before standing back up. Elora was whimpering now and he smiled as he walked towards the wall opposite from the bed. Summoning another current of air to keep her elevated against the wall Aerin hooked Elora's legs over his shoulders and resumed his place between her thighs.

Aerin tightened his grip on her as she sat on top of his shoulders and bit the inside of her thigh, chuckling against her skin when she jumped and then immediately moaned as he soothed the sting with his tongue. He continued his torture, kissing her thighs and lower stomach, mouth everywhere except where she wanted him most. He could hear her whispering his name, begging him over and over.

"Who do you belong to?"

"You. I belong to you." Elora's voice was no more than a hoarse whisper, and her legs were trembling where he held them. "Oh fuck, yes, right-" Elora broke into incoherence as Aerin's tongue found her clit. He didn't tease her any further, instead licking her with reckless abandon. He dragged his tongue over her swollen clit, settling into a rhythm as he alternated between licking and sucking softly. He smiled against her as her legs tensed, driving her to the edge until she screamed his name as she clamped his head between her thighs. He felt her toes curl inward and her hands tug at his hair and he dismissed the air that held her in place.

Elora's full weight settled on Aerin's shoulders, and he stroked the flat of his tongue over her lazily, easing her through the aftershocks. She was panting, her eyes lidded, and she draped her arms around his neck.

"You taste so fucking good." Aerin grinned as Elora swore at him and he slid her down from his shoulders until he was holding her in his arms. He held her for a few moments more, until her roaming hands found his hard cock.

"All this for me?" she teased, still breathless. "My turn now."

"Your turn," he echoed, eyes glued to her as she smiled and slid to her knees.

She wrapped her hand around him, eyes wide and dark as she drank in the sight of him. She licked her lips.

"You have no idea how much I've wanted to do this since our night in the cabin." Elora licked the precum from the sensitive head of his cock, teasing him, smirking as his jaw clenched and a harsh breath hissed between his teeth. She stroked slowly up and down his shaft as she teased him with her tongue.

"Elora..." Aerin sighed her name, a rush of need coursing through him. Desire burned through his blood and the sight of Elora's mouth wrapping around him made him throb and stiffen even more. She looked up at him, her gaze unwavering as she increased her pace, stroking him faster while sucking on the tip. She did something with her tongue that made him see stars, eliciting an involuntary groan from him. "Fuck, love," he panted. "You're a goddess." Aerin closed his eyes and leaned back a little, groaning a little louder when she repeated the movement.

AERIN

"Mine," Elora said, now stroking him with both her hands as she took him deeper.

Aerin responded by placing his hand over the back of her head, encouraging her to speed up. To his surprise, Elora let go of him with her hands and took him completely with her mouth, taking as much of him as she could, swallowing when he hit the back of her throat.

"Elora…" He looked down at her, her eyes half lidded with lust as she looked up at him through her lashes. The sight only made Aerin clench his abs more, waves of slow pleasure rolling through his body. "You're so good at this. Keep going, love. Don't stop." He brushed some of her hair from her face, and Elora slipped a hair tie from her wrist and deftly tied her hair, not missing a beat.

She sped up, reaching around to grab Aerin's hand, placing it on the back of her head again. He moved his hips at her demand, fucking Elora's mouth.

"So good for me," his ground out, voice low and quiet. He thrust his hips harder and pushed Elora's head down onto him. She took him eagerly, and Aerin felt the last vestiges of his control evaporate. She felt like heaven, and the ocean of pleasure inside of him deepened, a mounting pressure building steadily. She gagged and he tried to pull back, but she refused, smirking around him as his eyes widened at her.

Aerin gave himself completely to her and knew the bliss on his face was obvious. He didn't bother trying to hide the effect she had on him. Each time they made eye contact, Aerin felt himself getting a little closer to the edge. He couldn't hold out for much longer.

He reached down and tugged her off him, immediately missing her mouth. "Up."

He bent to help her to her feet, summoning ropes of air as he lifted her, effectively chaining her to the wall. Her breath came in short pants, face flushed and hair messy from his fist, lips swollen.

She was fucking perfect.

"You want me to fuck you?"

She didn't hesitate. "Yes."

Aerin heard a sharp gasp that gave way to a deep throated moan as he thrust inside her, bracing his hand on the wall beside her head, the other cupping her ass to hold her against him.

"Always so wet for me," Aerin murmured as he fought for his composure. Her response was to arch her back and rake her nails down his as she groaned Aerin's name once more. "You're mine."

Aerin thrust into her again, harder. He kept one hand on Elora's ass and thumbed her clit with the other. Elora's moans were indecipherable now and he alternated between teasing her clit and gripping her ass hard enough to leave marks. Elora wrapped her legs around his waist, the brief flecks of pain from her nails driving him further to the edge.

He thrust hard, keeping the pressure on her clit as he bent his neck to tease her nipple between his teeth. She tightened around him and he cursed against her skin.

"Aerin, *oh fuck!*" Elora panted. "I'm going to come, I-" She shattered around him, head tipped back, lips parted, legs shaking slightly. The sight of her climax sent him over the edge and Aerin thrust deep as he came, her name and taste on his tongue.

They stayed like that for several minutes until Elora climbed out of Aerins embrace and tottered over to the bed, where she promptly collapsed. She laughed, the sound ringing clear and bright.

"You're magic. Literally." She was still breathless when Aerin flung himself on the bed right next to her.

"You're fucking ethereal, Elora. And delicious. You're just so fucking *good*." He shook his head at her, unable to tear his gaze away from her.

Elora rolled her eyes, leaning over to give him a quick peck on the lips. "You already made me finish twice. No need for the sweet talk."

"What can I say? It's the Unseelie in me. We're full of manners in Autumn," he said drily, one eyebrow raised.

She laughed again, mattress shaking slightly beneath them as she covered her face with her hands, happiness rolling off her in waves.

Aerin looked at the girl who had blazed her way into his life only a few short months ago. This girl, who had upended everything he thought he had known about the world. This girl, who was powerful beyond imagination. This girl, the apparent end of his people, naked in his bed, her smile so wide he swore she could outshine the damn sun.

This girl, who had chosen him.

Why him? He still had no idea. But he knew that he loved Elora as surely as the sun rose each morning, as permanent and as real as the runes etched into his very skin. He didn't know what the future held, but he knew in his heart of hearts that Elora was his.

62

Elora

The door swung open so hard it smacked off the wall, the sound echoing in the sudden silence of the room. Elora snatched the sheets to cover herself, cheeks pink, hair wild. The visitors didn't care. Their faces were drawn, Tarhael's eyes sad, Briella's shoulders slumped.

Elora's heart picked up pace, fear replacing the warm glow in her body.

Something was wrong.

She knew. Before they said anything, she knew.

"It's not over," she said, more a statement than a question. Tarhael shook his head, meeting Aerin's gaze as Briella held hers.

"How bad?" Aerin demanded, recovering remarkably quickly.

"Elora, I'm sorry-" Briella started, shaking her head. Her hands were shaking, Elora noticed dimly. Her stomach opened into a pit, her heart fumbling its rhythm. "We've just received information about King Harkan and Queen Valdaea..."

"Just tell me!" Elora begged, feeling as though she was standing at

ELORA

the edge of a precipice, breath held, waiting for someone to shove her off.

It was Briella that did it.

Elora's scream shook the palace.

She didn't know how long she'd been running for, only that her legs were wobbling and her lungs were on fire. Boba loped steadily beside her the whole time, but his breathing was becoming strained, too, tongue hanging out his mouth as he panted.

When her legs finally gave out, she stopped and tilted her head back, noticing the still silence of the woods. Tear tracks stained her cheeks, her lips still salty with the residue. She'd hoped to outrun the terror and shock, but it seemed the emotions had no trouble keeping pace with her. Here, not even the bushes rustles, nor did the birds sing. Odd, she thought, for Spring.

She collapsed onto a broken log, trying to force herself to take deep breaths. She was shaking but she couldn't tell if that was the panic or the run. The others, she assumed, were still back at the palace, unable to stop her as she tore away. Her throat was dry and scratchy and she desperately needed water. But she wasn't ready to go back. Not yet.

Boba lay at her feet, silent but understanding. Through their bond, she felt waves of love and warmth, but they only made her want to cry more. She knew he felt her pain, wanted to comfort her, but she wasn't sure anyone could reach her now. She slipped off the log, falling onto her knees and burying her face in Boba's thick fur, holding him like a lifeline. They stayed like that until she couldn't ignore her thirst any longer.

"I'm going to find water. You can go. I'm okay now," she told him

GIRL OF BONE AND IVY

through the bond, sitting up.

"I want to stay as long as you need me."

"The connection goes both ways," Elora chastised him, *"I know you're starving. Go. Go hunt. After, if I'm not back, let everyone know I'm okay and I'll be back soon. I just need a few more minutes."*

She couldn't stay there with them. She needed space. They wouldn't understand the crushing grief and fear weighing down on her. They'd been upset, sure, pitying and worried but not the way she was.

Boba shook himself and got to his feet, nuzzling Elora as he did so. After a few licks and a reassuring head pat from Elora, he bounded away in hunt of food.

Elora knelt and placed her hand against the dirt, reaching through the earth in search of water. Sensing rushing water nearby, she stood and began to walk on aching legs in the direction of the source, quickly finding a babbling stream.

Here, the forest was a little more lively and less unnerving. The shrill trilling of birds was present once more and when Elora paused, she could hear the rustling of the undergrowth. Eagerly cupping her hands together, Elora brought the water to her lips and gulped it down. It was sweet and refreshing, tingling slightly on her tongue. She drank again, the water soothing her throat, the taste reminding her of something, a memory she couldn't quite bring to the forefront of her mind.

Then she was reeling backwards, retching and trying to throw it back up. She stumbled, falling on her back and felt the air leave her body, her mouth open in a silent scream. The forest had gone dead, and an uneasy, eerie feeling crept up her neck. The very air was still and panic gripped her, scrambling to her hands and knees and trying to throw up the wretched water again.

It was too late.

The drugged water was already coursing through her body. Her

ELORA

limbs were heavy and her mind was starting to fog up, making it hard to think. But her heart was still pounding, and it echoed loudly in her ears.

"Miss me?" The voice made Elora freeze, rooting her to the ground where she was keeling over, retching. The voice slid over her, disbelief and oily terror spreading from the pit of her stomach. "That's not how you used to greet me. But then again, you were lying last time."

He stepped forward from the shadows, now standing clear in the sunlight on the opposite side of the creek. He grinned, an ugly smile, one Elora didn't miss in the slightest.

He was shirtless, his upper chest etched with carvings of waves in alternating black and blue. There were other figures with him, but they were too blurry to make out through Elora's rapidly fading vision. He turned to someone behind him, and she could faintly make out a full skeleton imprinted on his back. Water from the stream rose around him, dancing around in twisted ropes, as he knelt down, gently cradling her in his arms.

"I'm here to help you, Elora. To help you fulfill your destiny. I'm here to take you home."

Epilogue

"I assume you've finished your preparations as discussed."

The room was low lit, the wine dark red and bitter, the air thick with the threat of violence. It was always like this in the Unseelie Courts, and Harkan and Valdaea thrived off it. The Queen grinned, all pointed canines and wine stained teeth.

"When have I ever let you down?" she replied smoothly, voice sickly sweet to cover the poison Harkan knew to expect in it. He returned a tight lipped smile and motioned for the servant to refill their glasses. The boy did so, head bowed, fingers shaking. Harkan snatched the glass back as soon as it was replenished, just to see the boy tremble.

"Soon, King," Valdaea assured him. Their titles were mere formality - as rulers, they rarely addressed each other using them. But Valdaea had a way of making his sound like an insult. His gaze hardened.

"It has been long enough," he continued, reclining in the velvet lined chair.

"Indeed." Valdaea crossed her ankles under her ice blue dress, the fabric rustling with the movement. Harkan eyed it hungrily. Talking violence with her always had his blood rushing. She was married, of course, but that was no matter. Her wife was at home, tucked up in her Winter castle. She never had to know.

It had gone against his every instinct to flee from that half fae bitch in battle. It grated on him even now, the look she'd had in her eyes when she thought she'd bested him. Little Seelie Court fae were always like that, though. So eager to see the light that they forgot to

EPILOGUE

check the shadows.

But he, he knew better. He *was* better. And no matter how much it chafed to turn his back on them, the only reason he'd done so was because he wasn't worried about being stabbed in it. Their honor was easy to exploit.

And now, the fun began.

"I wonder if the mortals will play," Valdaea mused, popping a fruit cake in her mouth, ensuring she didn't smudge her lipstick in the process.

"I'm sure they will," Harkan said, boredom lacing his words. "Though they are so fragile. So breakable. Any word from Morgana yet?"

The Queen just shrugged. "No yet, but I suppose we'll find out soon enough. That son of yours has proven himself useful. Has he accomplished that fun little mission of his yet?"

Harkan shook his head, saying nothing, merely pursing his lips slightly. Occasionally, his children were more than a thorn in his side. Often, though, they were more trouble than they were worth. Neither one was the heir he deserved, their mothers incapable of providing him even that. Disappointments, the lot of them. He sighed, smoothing his face into cool indifference.

The plan ahead of them would take a careful hand. His son couldn't provide that. He was still a child and it was time for the adults to play. Pushing aside the negative thoughts, Harkan focused on what was to come instead. The thought of entering the mortal realm after all these years brought a gleam to his eye, and his mouth twitched upward in semblance of a smile. Harkan raised his glass in salute.

"To bringing them to their knees."

Valdaea returned the gesture.

"To finally reuniting with the mortals."

They drank.

Acknowledgements

This started off as a joke between two friends about writing faerie porn during the pandemic, but now it's so much more. (We're still not entirely sure how it happened but we are so glad it did!) We cannot express how grateful we are to everybody who has followed this book from its conception, or who found us through that one viral video, or if you've only just heard of us. We love you all.

A massive thank you goes out to our beta readers - for your feedback and the hilarity of your comments. To the ARC readers, we appreciate you so much. Thank you for having faith in this series.

We'd also like to thank all the indie authors who supported us throughout this journey when we had no idea what we were doing! From formatting to marketing to just being there when we were frustrated, please know we wouldn't be here without you!

And to everyone reading this: you're making our dream a reality. We've wanted to be authors for as long as we can remember and it still feels so surreal that you're here, reading this.

We sincerely hope you loved this book. If you did, please consider leaving us a review! Reviews and feedback are so important for authors, especially indie authors like us!

ACKNOWLEDGEMENTS

Preorders for book two of the Runebreaker Trilogy are available now! "Boy of Air and Ash" releases on the 25th of March 2022. To preorder, search the title or the authors' names on Amazon.

Want to talk about all things Girl of Bone and Ivy with other readers? Join our reader Facebook page "Runebreaker Readers."

We are so grateful for your support. Our social media handles are listed below if you'd like to stay updated with our work or get in touch!

Instagram: @kingandkalanbooks
TikTok: @scarletkingauthor and @words_of_kang
Email: scarletkingauthor@gmail.com

About the Authors

Scarlet King is a bisexual twenty one year old university student. She lives in Scotland with her partner and toddler. She loves coffee, bookstores and ignoring her responsibilities in favor of writing. She has a bad habit of falling in love with fictional characters and hopes someone out there will fall for the ones she writes, too.

Damien Kalan is a twenty one year old university student from California and is currently weaning off coffee in favor of tea. He loves playing instruments and writing poetry in his free time, and is currently stressed out about post graduation plans. He picked up cooking during the pandemic and is now trying to land a book deal. Please wish him luck!

Also by Damien Kalan and Scarlet King

The Runebreaker Trilogy
  Girl of Bone and Ivy
  Boy of Air and Ash (coming 25th March 2022)

Printed in Great Britain
by Amazon